Slow Comes the Dark
Volume 1
Creeping Darkness

Vic Broquard

Slow Comes the Dark Volume 1 Creeping Darkness
First Edition
ISBN: 978-1-941415-65-8
Copyright ©2013, 2014 by Vic Broquard

http://www.Broquard-ebooks.com
Broquard eBooks
103 Timberlane
East Peoria, IL 61611
author@Broquard-eBooks.com

Artwork by Crooked Willow Studios.

For Morgan and L. Ron Hubbard

Table of Contents

Chapter 1—A Cold Beginning

Jason Mott, Engineer First Class, Rank Lieutenant, ID 41339. Duty assignment: Space Station Gamma-629, Abelard Sector. The twenty-one year old stared at his assignment papers, his first, took a deep breath, and left the shuttle bay of the deep space transport, which had brought him here to this giant station on the rim of the galaxy. The smell of metal, plastics, and oil assaulted his nostrils, while the litter on the docking bay floor caught his attention, reminding him yet again that his first assignment was in the dredges of the universe, hardly what the recruitment posters had promised. No indeed. Still, he was officially now able to do what he enjoyed most: blowing things up.

As a child, Jason had been intrigued with explosions. When he was ten, his first experiment had blown up his parent's chicken coup on their farm. Marvelous, exciting, amazing, spectacular—these and more flooded the ten year old's mind, followed by his first whipping, which only convinced him that explosions were worth the trouble. By the time his parents gave up and sent him to Zeta Military School, Jason was a master of blowing things up, large and small. It was there that he'd seen the many recruitment posters for the Federation Military Forces, the FMF as it was commonly known. He'd endured four years at the school before they too got rid of him by giving him his FMF commission. He'd broken all school records that had anything remotely to do with explosions, a record that pleased him, but hardly those who ran the school. Now he was free to "officially" blow things up.

However, assigned to this dismal outpost on the rim of the galaxy, Jason wondered just what he was doing here. What could he explode? Perhaps the station, he mused as he stepped around the litter and walked up to the security guard, his papers in hand. "Lieutenant Mott reporting for duty, sir," he saluted.

The tall, burly guard greatly in need of a shave, bath, and clean clothes, took his papers, stared at them, as though he could burn a hole in them with his icy stare, grumbled something unintelligible, and flipped on the intercom. "Captain Fontana, report to the docking bay." Turning to Jason, he added, "Your boss is Captain Fontana. She'll be here directly and take charge. Your duffle bags are being unloaded now. Go get them. Welcome to the HH, that's Hell Hole for you new recruits—Space Station Gamma-629. Get used to the stink. No one gives a damn how things look out here."

Jason nodded and glanced over his shoulder. "Hey, careful with that bag, unless you want to blow yourself to kingdom come!" he barked at the man who was tossing out the bags onto the metal deck. The grimy looking man pulled up short, a startled expression replacing his bored look. Gingerly, he sat the remaining bags down, muttering a curse beneath his breath. Jason, on the other hand, smiled. Oh how he loved to see other's reactions to explosions or even threats of such. He fought hard against calling out, "Boom!" just to see the man's reaction. In truth, that game seemed childish to Jason now, but he'd certainly done just that countless times in the past. No, he'd learned one thing: it was a rare person who loved explosions as much as he did. Maybe, he thought, he was here to help blow this space station up. Now that would be a challenge, considering how enormous the station actually was. He'd gotten a good look at it when the shuttle docked.

"Attention!" an alto voice barked. Mechanically, Jason turned around and stiffened as ordered. A tall woman wearing the officer's blues had joined the slovenly guard. She had shoulder length black hair, pulled back in a ponytail. Her uniform bore the dual yellow bands of a captain. His own blue uniform sported only a single yellow band, that of a lieutenant. Jason briskly saluted the officer, mechanically though. He never actually meant his salutes—not ever. He'd yet to meet an officer whom he truly respected. She was average looking but with deep blue eyes, penetrating eyes, eyes that didn't miss a thing, as they surveyed him from his polished boots up to his close cropped brown hair. At last, her eyes met his green eyes. "Lieutenant Mott, I presume?" she inquired formally.

"Yes sir. Reporting as ordered," Jason felt obligated to add as fitting a new recruit. He wanted to ask when he could blow something up, but wisely didn't.

"At ease, Lieutenant Mott. Bring your bags. Follow me," she barked. Jason got the instant impression his new boss was one of the no nonsense types, and he sighed as he picked up his three bags, stumbling along after her, trying to avoid stepping in the piles of litter. Perhaps this whole military thing was a mistake, unless he was here to blow up the station. From what he'd seen so far, that could well be a possibility.

Once they'd turned a corner and were now out of earshot from the guard, she relaxed, slowed her pace, and then halted. "Look, we only need to be formal around the station guards and the top brass, but those are seldom around. Captain Bess Fontana. You can call me Bess when we're alone. I don't much like the FMF formalities either. Another thing, it seems the 519th Infantry Division is bunking here temporarily. They're taking up all our extra cabin space, excepting for all the civies that is, so you're bunking with me. Hell Jason, it's good to have another engineer with me. It's been little old me for close to a year now. Come on; it's this way. Ignore the civies."

"Yes boss," Jason teased, making a play on her first name.

"Glad you recognize it," she retorted, playfully. "We have to pass through CA1 to get to our section." Seeing his baffled look, she added, "That's Civies Area Number One, officially. They barter trade goods there. Riffraff if you ask me, but then no one does or perhaps no one cares, not out here this far from civilization. You know you've been assigned to the shit-hole of the universe, right?"

"Kind of got that impression back in the docking bay. So when do we get to blow it up?" Jason replied, asking the only thing that was important to him.

Bess laughed. "Read your file. You seem to have a penchant for explosions."

"Yes boss, love them. Can't seem ever to get enough of them. Why, there's nothing prettier in this darn universe than a brilliant, huge explosion, not really," Jason admitted. Best get off on the right foot with her, he decided.

"Constructions. That's what I'm more interested in, so I'll leave you to the demolitions, if you don't mind," Captain Bess Fontana responded slightly more formally. "But I expect you to lend me a hand on construction details though. I promise to leave the demolitions to you. Christ, you can get killed doing that. Lost my number two engineer eleven months ago. Blew himself up. Accident, mind you. Did find enough bits of him for a positive DNA match. No, I hate the demolition side of this job. Give me the construction stuff any day. So yes, Jason, I'm rather glad that you're here."

"Okay, this has potential then. I blow things up and you build them," Jason concluded, a wry smile on his face.

At this point, they entered the civies area. All manner of crude stalls lined both side walls of the giant hub area, some fifty feet square. They had to walk through it to get to the hatches opposite them. Jason saw a kaleidoscope of fashion among the throng either manning the stalls or hovering over them. Bess pointed out, "Yah, we got folks from Scorpi-C, Gemma-D, Taurus-C, Bellatrix-B, Zeno-C—hell, we've even got some corporate honchos from Galactic Electronics out here, though I surely don't know why those big-wigs are out here. GE built this station, you know."

"Shit! I'd hoped to have left those kind far behind," Jason cursed. Three of the largest corporations—Galactic Electronics, Galactic Dynamics, and General Robotics—ruled the entire Federation. Long ago, the corporations took over all governing aspects of the many planets. Jason's meager but mandatory studies of history had convinced him that he wanted nothing to do with the corporations. Centuries ago, they'd poured huge amounts of money into the campaign coffers of the governing politicians. Some claimed they'd bought the elections. It was probably true, since those they backed won and then passed legislation greatly desirable for the corporations. However, that era was ancient history. Long ago, the corporations simply banded together, dispensed with the puppet political leaders, and took over all governmental control on all planets. That was particularly easy, since some of the laws their financially backed politicians passed literally bankrupted the ruling governments. Thus, the filthy rich corporations stepped in and took control, bailing out the worlds. Crossing a corporate representative was tantamount to a death sentence on most worlds.

Well, perhaps they weren't killed, but sent out here to Space Station Gamma-629, at the edge of the entire galaxy, Jason began to believe, as his eyes took in the poorly clothed men, women, and children hovering around the stalls, looking for bargains, if such could be had. Their clothing, while vastly different from world to world, was rather ragged, perhaps filthy too. Something else added to the odor filtering into his nose, as he passed by a group of fifty, none of whom took any notice of the pair in clean, blue uniforms.

"There's a dozen of these civies areas. We're entering the officer's sector of the station. Ah, here we go, first door on your right," she pointed out needlessly, since a placard on the door at eye height read: Engineer Quarters. Bess opened the door for Jason, whose hands were full with his three bags. Inside, Jason saw a small living room with attached kitchenette, about ten feet square. Three doors lay opposite the entrance. "My room is on the right. You take the one on the left. The bathroom is behind the center door. Dump your bags, and we'll go on a tour of the station. Oh yeh, there's a map on the couch. I picked it up for you yesterday. Figure you'll need it to find your way around."

Jason did as asked, picking up the map as he came out of his tiny cabin, having deposited his bags on his bunk. Time enough later to unpack. Jason quickly noted Bess had carefully marked their quarters on it, having refolded it with their sector of the station on top.

She continued her explanation, "So we're in the station's officer's quarters. If we meet anyone, be formal. Out beyond this sector, you only have to be formal if you see any of the brass nearby. Come on; there's a lot to see. Don't worry, after a few weeks, you'll know where everything is. First stop is the armory. We need to get you some weapons."

"Christ! We need to carry weapons around here?" Jason asked, growing worried. Perhaps there was more going on here than he first saw.

"We officers carry them. Helps keep the civies in line and the respect of the enlisted men, particularly what with the entire 519th here. Been around here for a month. No idea why, though," Bess admitted. "Everyone's really tightlipped about that."

At the far end of the officer's sector, they entered the armory, a huge room with racks and racks of weapons and munitions. Jason produced his ID card, and the orderly issued him a blaster and a stun gun. Meanwhile, Jason's envious eyes took in the mountain of explosives stacked neatly at the very back of the room. "Don't go blowing a hole in the hull," the orderly jested Jason, as he handed him the sidearms.

"No, I rather fancy those explosives you got back there," Jason replied. "Don't suppose you can issue me some of them, eh? Nothing like a good, bright explosion, is there?"

The orderly chuckled and jested, "Damned engineers."

After strapping them around his waist, he noticed that Bess also wore a pair around her waist as well. He'd not noticed this detail before. He took some comfort in the fact that he was now actually armed, though he would have preferred to have a backpack of explosives on him. The pair headed out on their recon mission, for that's what it seemed to be to Jason.

She pointed out the commissar's office. "You can pick up some light food stuffs for our kitchenette here between 08:00 and 18:00. Just need your ID card. Come on; we're off."

"The Galactic Electronics Corporation built this station, so some of the civies here do the maintenance work. There are a hundred security guards posted, but what with all the 519th here too, the commander has pulled us in to help keep order too. We go on duty at 18:00 for four hours," she explained. "So yes, it's crap duty for us as well."

For two hours, the pair wandered around the spacious station, though Jason became confused almost at once and merely followed her around like a puppy dog, taking in the varied sights. Promptly at 12:00, they arrived outside the

Operations Room door, located in the heart and center of the station. "Okay, time to meet the commander and get your official orders, lieutenant. This way," Captain Bess said formally. The two entered the room.

Here, Jason saw walls of monitors and men sitting in front of them. It looked like the standard war rooms that he'd seen during training. Commander Bill West, a fifty-year-old man with a goatee, looked up, rose, and returned their salutes. "Ah, you must be Lieutenant Jason Mott."

"Yes sir. Reporting for duty sir," Jason replied formally, hating this part.

"At ease, son. Has Captain Fontana given you a tour of this dump?"

"Yes sir," Jason replied, noticing from the commander's choice of words what his opinion of the space station was.

"Good. We have an over-crowded situation here, what with the whole damned 519th stationed here for a time. So you are on security patrol with Captain Fontana from 18:00 until 22:00 each night. Meantime, I understand you're an explosives expert."

"Aye, sir. Love explosions."

"Good, good. I've a job for you. If you hadn't noticed, this place is full of litter and crap, especially the docking bays. So I want you to clean the place up. I have six derelict transports. Put the crap in them, tow them away from here, and blow them up," Commander West ordered. "Think you can handle that?"

A big smile creased Jason's lips. "You bet, sir!"

"Good. Ordinance will supply you with what you need. Just make sure the debris is minuscule in size. Can't have chunks of stuff breeching transport hulls. Okay, dismissed. See you at mess." Both saluted, and the pair left.

"See, you get to blow things up," Bess teased him, once they were alone in the metal walled hallway.

"Hell, I'll sweep this place spotless if I get to make some really big explosions," Jason jested. "So, you lending me a hand with the cleaning?"

Bess laughed, "Hardly, lieutenant. That's your job. I have construction duties in the engine room. Civies need some help overhauling the plasma drives. That's one reason why the garbage has been piling up. Has been for three months, ever since the drives began acting up. Only got in the replacement parts two days ago, along with the corporate bigwigs. So happy cleaning," she teased him back.

Jason pushed a cleaning cart filled with heavy plastic bags into the docking bay. "That's the bucket over there," the security guard pointed out the derelict transport ship, scheduled to be destroyed. "Bout time someone cleaned up this mess," he added, returning to his post by the doors that led into the station from the bay.

While shoveling up the debris, Jason's mind focused on the future explosion, calculating the precise locations for his charges and their amount, something he had a knack for doing and something that came as easily to him as a breath did to others. It didn't matter he was playing janitor. No, the anticipation of the brilliant explosion was all that mattered. He envisioned some additives. A bit of cobalt or perhaps some carbon or perhaps—colorful. This first explosion, Jason decided, would be spectacular, announcing his arrival here at the rim of the galaxy. Minutes passed as the bags filled up before he decided on a rich, blue color additive to the fiery explosion. Then, he calculated the amount to be added to the explosive mixture to produce his desired effect. So occupied, Jason failed to see the two men who barged into the docking bay.

Two men wearing hoodies rushed into the bay, overpowering the security guard, who stood bored to death. One swift blow to the back of his head took him out. "Over there. We'll take that one," the other man whispered, pointing to the deep space shuttle that had brought Jason here only hours earlier today. Both men carried small pouches in their left hands, but drew their blasters when they spotted Jason scooping up trash some distance from them. Since he seemed self-absorbed, both men ignored him, moving quietly to the shuttle, before darting up its ramp. A moment later, the bay doors began closing, the noise of which caught Jason's attention. He stopped and gazed at the shuttle.

Just then, ten security men along with Commander West rushed into the room. Jason turned to them, surprised. "Stop them. Don't let them," the commander ordered, but it was too late; the shuttle lifted off. Commander West barked into his handheld comm, "Raise the docking bay's force field now! Don't let that ship depart!"

A voice came back audible to everyone, who, including Jason, were staring up at the large ship that was moving slowly to the exit portal, where a simple field kept the atmosphere from shooting out into space while allowing ships to pass through it. "Sorry, commander, there's not enough time."

"Well, shoot them down! Activate all firing stations! Don't let them get away!" Commander West yelled into his device, though he need not have. Jason watched the action, wondering what was going on. He felt a bit of excitement stirring within him. Perhaps this new posting wasn't going to be as boring as he had thought upon arrival.

The shuttle cleared the portal and shot off into the utter blackness of space. Here on the rim, looking away from the galaxy yielded the most intense blackness imaginable, while looking down towards it was spectacular, like looking at glowing diamonds encased in a milky, filamentary shroud, as though touched by God himself, if there was such a being. Jason wasn't religious and didn't believe in Supreme Beings. Never had, never would.

His ears picked up the dull thud-thud sounds of the outer cannons firing their blasts, but even he knew the shuttle wasn't going to be hit by automatically guided defense guns. He'd studied them at military school and chalked them up to futility attempts, though those who had them felt more confident in their defenses even though they were darn near useless, unless their targets were using computer controlled guidance systems. Any real pilot at the controls of a ship could easily outmaneuver such cannon. Hence, Jason wasn't surprised to hear a voice later reporting to the commander, "Sorry sir. The guns missed the ship. They're out of range now. Should we launch a fighter interception squad?"

"Hell yes. They have to be stopped!" the commander yelled and turned to head back into the station.

"Excuse me, sir," Jason spoke up. "You want that transport blown up?"

Until now, Commander West hadn't been aware of Jason's presence. He turned and saw the newest recruit. "Well, yes. Two spies have stolen valuable Intel. They have to be stopped."

"Sir, I can do it from your command center. I can create a wonderful explosion," Jason volunteered. He saw an excellent opportunity for yet another brilliant flash and took it.

"Son, if you can blow that ship to pieces, then let's get on it now! No telling if they are relaying what they stole as we speak," Commander West barked and ordered Jason to follow the group back to his command center.

Already, ten crews were scrambling to their two-man fighters, but the commander knew it could be hours before they actually intercepted the ship, if at all. Once they dropped into hyperspace, they'd probably make a clean getaway. "What do you need, son?" he asked, when they entered the command center, now bustling with men shouting orders right and left, a drastic change since Jason was here earlier.

"A computer with transmission capabilities," Jason replied. The commanded nodded, and Jason took a seat hastily vacated by another junior officer. Commander West watched over Jason's shoulders as he began typing. "I need the transponder code for that deep space transport, someone? Now," he called out.

"12493675," someone yelled back, and he typed in the numbers. Jason began working his magic.

"Too bad we won't be able to see this explosion," Jason mused. "Boom," he added. "They have just blown up. I so hate it when I can't see my beautiful explosion."

"What? It's really destroyed?" Commander West asked in disbelief.

"Yep. Crossed the fuel flow line with the hyperspace activator, rerouting it into the ship's combustion chamber, taking advantage of the badly programmed directional controls system found on all these corporate transport ships," Jason explained. "Boom," he added. "Well, a really big boom actually."

"Sir we have their last known coordinates," an aide called out.

"Send them to the flight crews. Have them visually verify the shuttle was destroyed," the commander ordered. Turning to Jason, he added, "Well done, son. Glad to have a demolitions expert onboard. You can return to your duties. We'll talk more at supper. Thanks for your timely aid." He saluted Jason, who hastily did the same and left. His feet, amazingly light; his face, alight with a smile. In the hallway, he whispered another "boom" to himself. *Ah, life is worth living when you can make things go boom.*

When he reported to the officer's mess at 06:00, he had filled one rusting shuttle with garbage and was ready to prepare his detonation charges in the morning. "Hi ya," Bess said, as he walked into the room, buzzing with chat. "Over here, once you get through the buffet line." Jason nodded, grateful for the offer. He rather hated entering a room full of total strangers. Always had. After helping himself in the line, he headed over to join his boss, though he did notice that other officers were pointing him out in whispered voices.

"Well, heard you shook them all up a bit this afternoon," Captain Fontana teased him, as he sat down across from her.

"Yeh, well no one could actually see the boom. Not so tomorrow. This one will be quite visible. Got one rust bucket loaded with the trash. So what was that all about? I mean with those two men and all," he asked, adding quickly, "or is it none of my business?"

"Dunno." Bess leaned over and whispered, "Spies. That's what's going around." She sat back and added, "Some of us thought perhaps it was sabotage, but hell, everything on this station is falling apart. You don't need sabotage to wreck this place; it's doing it by itself quite nicely. Corporate bigwigs should be able to see the results of their crappy work—that's assuming they even have eyes," she added argumentatively.

"Take it you don't like the corporate men," Jason commented.

"Scum of the galaxy," she replied, lowering her voice. "Best keep such notions to yourself around here, at least until the bigwigs leave. So how were you able to blow up that shuttle anyway? I've been asking myself that one all afternoon. There wasn't supposed to be any explosives on the transport. Did you sneak some onboard?"

"Nah. Back at the FMF academy, I pointed out the corporation's design flaw in that model of their deep space transports. You know about it?" he answered. Bess shook her head no, so he explained a bit more. "Given its transponder code, anyone can send signals that bypass all levels of security on the computer-controlled ship, and I crossed the fuel flow line with the hyperspace activator, rerouting it into the ship's combustion chamber. You take advantage of the badly programmed directional controls system. Then, boom! Hell, I even wrote the corporation about their design flaw, but naturally they didn't do anything about it."

"Damn, Jason, you're good. I didn't know that one, but I do now. Must have been a fiery explosion too," Bess replied. "Well, you sure got the commander's attention. Wonder if he'll tell us what's going on around here?"

"Maybe we're about to find out," Jason whispered. "He's heading this way. Who's that with him?"

"General Franco, head of the 519th," Bess replied, as both stood up at attention.

"At ease. As you were," Commander West said, pulling up a nearby chair, as did the tall, but pudgy general. "Excellent work today, Lieutenant Mott. You've a good head on your shoulders. Think fast in a crisis. This is General Franco, commander of the 519th Infantry Division. We've been going over your record, Lieutenant Mott. Set all kinds of records for blowing up things," he said a bit mysteriously.

Jason cleared his throat, "Aye sir. Now the johns, well that was just a prank sir."

Smiling, Commander West replied, "Of course. I won't tell you what mischief I got into back in my FMF academy days. As Captain Fontana has probably told you, you two are the only military engineers assigned to the space station. Got a lot of civies' engineers around, but only you two are official." He paused to let the significance of that idea sink into the man's head. He nodded to the general, who took over.

12

"With Commander West's permission, I may soon have a special assignment for the both of you. My Combat Engineers will be tied up on another mission. I'll see you're fully briefed when the time comes. Until then, secrecy is our best weapon, though that was likely compromised today," the general admitted.

"But I blew them up," Jason protested a little.

Commander West spoke up, "True, but my techies believe they were able to get off a short comm burst before the detonation. We don't know what was sent."

"Who were they? Or should I not ask," Jason gave in to his mounting curiosity and asked.

"Gamon spies, we think." Commander West added hastily, "This is a neutral space station. We have folks from over a dozen worlds here, from diplomats down to vagabonds, including some from Gamon-C. Some of the general's plans were stolen this morning. Surveillance cameras caught the pair, but they got away before we could corner them and arrest them. That's all I dare tell you at this time. Just stay alert. Keep the peace." With that, both men rose and left the pair to finish their supper.

"Come on," Bess finally said. "We're on patrol duty for the next four hours. Always go in pairs in case we have to stop fights." Jason rose and followed his boss out of the mess hall, grumbling about being demoted to a security guard.

"It's not that bad, Jason," Bess countered. "We get to walk around and look important. I've only had to bust up one fight in six months. Mostly our presence keeps things on an even keel. Besides, there are a couple of civies I'd like you to meet. Hey, you play Poker? We've a game going just as soon as we're off duty."

"A little. Not too good at it," Jason admitted. Card games seemed trivial to him, always had.

"Hey, keep your eyes open. This way, you will get familiar with the station as we patrol," Bess pointed out. The two set off, heading through the infantry quarters first. At once, Jason noted the distinct signs of military personnel. Doors were open, and he overheard men and women talking about their coming battle and the clanking of gun parts being assembled, sprinkled with profanities of all types.

Before long, the pair stopped before a short but very well-muscled woman, perhaps their own age, but at least six inches shorter than Jason and Bess. She wore the brown uniform of the infantry with sergeant's stripes on her shoulder. The giant MK42 assault gun in her hands caught Jason's full attention. *Hell,* he thought, *the gun is bigger than she is!* "Hi ya, Martha," Bess introduced them. "This is my new engineer, Lieutenant Jason Mott. This is a good friend of mine, Gunnery Sergeant Martha Spelling."

"Hi ya back at ya. Heard you like to blow things up. Word gets around fast 'round here. Good to have ya here. Just don't blow everything up; leave some for me and Gertrude here." She patted her enormous gun lovingly, adding, "We aim to kick some butt!"

Someone inside the nearest cabin yelled out, "Yeh, she needs a big gun to make up for her lack of a small gun!" Several other men chortled at the joke.

"Ya, some 'o you fellows can't even man your small guns. So someone's got to watch your backs, though I surely don't know why," Martha yelled her own insult back at them, raising more laughter.

Bess cracked a smile. "She dishes it out damned good." Even Jason grinned, taking an instant liking to this petite gunnery sergeant.

"I promise to leave some for you to blast, Martha," he stated, bringing another smile to her face.

"I'm on patrol duty too. No one tries anything when I'm around with Gertrude here," Martha explained. Bess and Jason chuckled and continued on their way.

Bess added, "She'll be at the Poker game later on."

As they entered the general population sectors, Jason noticed a total change in the demeanor of the inhabitants of the space station. Cowled, hooded faces predominated, as though attempting to hide their faces from the pair, as they walked along the halls and through the large meeting squares. "Secretive," Bess commented in a low voice. "See all kinds lurking around. Those in the yellow garb, they are from

Scorpi-C. Those wearing dark brown are from Gemma-D, usually. Those in the drab greys are likely from Taurus-C. The flashy ones in red are probably from Bellatrix-B. Those wearing mostly green clothes are from Zeno-C, probably anyway. Like I said, we have all kinds mixed in here."

She went on, "Don't need to tell you those wearing the black suits are the corporate bigwigs. Now if you see someone wearing fancy, expensive clothing, those are likely the ambassadors and their staff. Not all the ambassadors are total jerks, and not all of those working for the corporations are ass holes. You'll meet a couple cool ones at the poker game later on."

"K, but what's with those guys over there who look like they are hiding something from us," Jason replied, noticing a group of brown hooded men cowering from them while standing beside a market stall.

"Hell, who knows?" Bess replied. "None of our business, unless they cause trouble, which they aren't likely to do, since we're well armed. Keep on moving. We don't want to create a stink if we don't have to. Paperwork is a bitch." They moved on, leaving the whispering men alone.

Finally 22:00 came. Cleverly, Bess arrived at a cabin in the middle of the station just as their patrol shift ended. "Here we are. Poker time. Come on in. Everyone should be here by now," she explained. "Got some interesting people for you to meet." The two stepped inside. Jason was surprised to see a well-lighted game room. Actually, it was a refurbished cabin now outfitted with a gaming table taking up most of the living room-kitchenette area. Four others were already present when the two entered.

Jason saw a rather attractive young woman with long, wavy black hair, wearing a gorgeous yellow gown and tall heels, a shorter woman with brown hair, shoulder length, wearing a black corporate dress with matching pumps, a black haired young man also wearing a black suit, but without a tie, and the really short Martha—all sitting around the gaming table. Martha motioned to the two empty chairs.

Bess did the introductions, though the three new people already knew of Jason. Word had traveled swiftly. "Lieutenant

Jason Mott, this is the Scorpi-C Ambassador Drina Celestina, civies engineer Feliks Drugi from Gemma-D, and Doctor Gisa Wolfgang from Bellatrix-B. Those two work for the corporation, but you can trust them." Bess sat down opposite Dr. Gisa, leaving Jason to sit across from Ambassador Drina. He saw the piercing eyes of Drina scanning his and smiled. Here was a flashy woman who wasn't afraid to hide her femininity. Yet she radiated supreme confidence.

"Well, we meet at last, Jason," Drina spoke first. "Word travels fast. Excellent work stopping those spies today. All the ambassadors have definitely taken note of your arrival on Space Station Gamma-629."

"Yeh, well he's promised to leave some for me to blast," Martha broke in, causing several to smile.

"I'm trying to get the station's plasma drives back online. Real mess. Haven't been properly serviced in more than a decade," Feliks volunteered.

"Don't go getting yourself blown up like Bess's last assistant," Dr. Gisa cautioned in her soft voice. "I'm a doctor, not a magician. I can't glue bits of a body back together." Feliks chuckled at her jest. The ambassador didn't.

"Hey cards time. I'm the house dealer tonight," Martha spoke up. "Aces are wild. Someone dole out the chips. I aim to get even tonight."

While she shuffled and dealt, Jason decided to ask about the spies. "So what were those spies trying to get and why and for whom?" He directed his question at the ambassador, figuring she just might know.

"We aren't sure what's going on," she replied honestly. "It is highly unusual for an entire FMF infantry division to be on this station."

"Hell, it's never happened before, not that I know of," Feliks pointed out. Looking at Jason, he added, "Been here four years now."

"What I don't get is why I am here? Of course, I've been saying that for over a year now," Gisa added. Jason looked at her, and she explained further, "I'm more of a research doctor, genetics actually, not a patch 'em up doctor, though I can do that if I must. The div's got their own doctors as does the station, so why am I here? Hell, I surely don't know."

"There is something going on out here on the rim," Ambassador Drina spoke up, more for Jason's benefit than the others, who had heard this before. "We ambassadors don't know just what, or if some do, they aren't openly saying, but it spells trouble, real trouble. I'm certain that's why the FMF sent a full division out here. What they're actually going to do remains a secret. Even Martha doesn't know."

"Are we playing or talking?" Martha barked. "I'm in for twenty."

While the game progressed, Jason estimated each of the five was about the same age as himself, probably in their early twenties. From what he gathered, none were married. Certainly, both Gisa and Feliks were not the usual corporate employees he'd seen before on other worlds and stations. In fact, he rather liked both of them in spite of their employer.

Mid-game, Ambassador Drina commented, "What has many of us baffled is just why would the FMF send out a demolitions engineer here? Bess has her hands full of construction work, aiding the civies engineers. From the overall neglect of this station, it's obvious to many that more construction engineers should be assigned here and provided with necessary parts to repair this heap. So why send an engineer who specialized in demolitions?"

"Well, I can do construction work," Jason hastily justified, but added sheepishly, "but I do love to blow things up. Always have. Tomorrow, watch for the big explosion. I'm getting rid of a shipload of trash along with that rust bucket. Should be a really nice boom, colorful too."

Bess chuckled, "At least I don't have to clean up that mess in the docking bay!" All chuckled, and Jason figured they all knew the dismal state of the bay.

"Hey, I don't mind, if I get to blow it all up when I'm done," he added, bringing more chuckles. Around midnight, the game ended, though no one was a big winner or loser for that matter.

Once back at their cabin, Bess declared, "I get the shower first. Cya in the morning." Jason entered his room, tossed his three bags onto the floor, and hit the sack, asleep long before Bess had finished her shower. It had been a long first day on Space Station Gamma-629, but tomorrow promised a magnificent explosion.

Chapter 2—Plots Within Plots

Promptly at 09:00, Jason's big explosion detonated in a magnificent, brilliantly blue explosion, reducing the garbage and transport to fragmented bits, but at a safe distance from the huge space station and off the usual shipping lanes. Many observed the fiery display, thanks to Jason's warning. He expected to hear numerous comments about why was its color so incredibly blue, and that night, he wasn't disappointed. Jason then spent the rest of the day on cleaning duty in the docking bay, filling up another rusting transport, all the while working out the color to use in his next explosion.

***

At a kiosk in one of the busy civies areas, a hooded man spoke to another, "Well, your men failed. I've heard the data didn't get transmitted."

"Shit!" the other replied in a hushed tone, full of hostility. "You got any better ideas?" He threw it back in the other's basket.

"Yeh, Corporal Peterson is the weak link. Get to his family, and you can force him to get you another copy of the plans. See to it today. Use Abelard to transport it off the station."

"K. Peterson, eh? Know the fellow. Measly man. Shouldn't be hard. We'll get those plans today," the man whispered back and glanced about. Seeing no one watching him, he moved off, joining the throng of civilians hunting for bargains amid the kiosks.

Well he's a fool. He's my distraction. Good thing I made an electronic copy yesterday, the first man thought. *Now to find Kyle.* An hour later, he met with the hooded Kyle. "Here are a thousand credits. Take this to HQ on Gonda-C today. There's a shuttle leaving in an hour. Fail, and you're a dead man."

"Ask no questions; can't reveal anything. That's my motto. You got it. Easy grand," the pimple-faced man whispered back, accepting the tiny drive and the wallet of credits, stowing them beneath his hoodie. He turned and ambled away, blending seamlessly into the throng in the square.

Comm Officer Second Class Helmet Peterson's cell vibrated. While on-duty in the station's comm center, he kept it in vibrate mode. Deftly, he retrieved his phone from his shirt pocket. The id indicated it was from his wife. He pressed Accept and saw the short video. Two men were holding blasters to his wife's head. The text read: copy the division's plans onto a thumb drive, bring it to your quarters, and your wife lives. Fail, and she's dead.

Helmet swallowed hard. He stowed his phone back into his pocket nervously. What to do? If he were caught, he'd be tried for treason and probably shot. If he didn't, his wife was as good as dead. Everyone knew something big was about to happen, just not what. *Hell,* he thought, *no one knows what's going on.* He did recognize one of the thugs pointing a blaster at his wife, a very ruthless man, brutal even. *Even if I bring it to them, there's no guarantee they won't just kill us both. Shit!* Helmet pondered his dilemma for some time, barely able to perform his normal duties.

At last, he decided to save his own skin. Surely, both would be murdered as soon as he delivered the drive. He took a calculated risk and forwarded the message from his cell to that of Commander West's. Once he hit Send, he sighed. For good or ill, it was done, out of his hands. Either his loving wife would be murdered or not, but at least he wouldn't be shot for treason.

"Oh hell! Not again!" Commander West growled. The forwarded message was quite explicit. He knew he dare not take this to General Franco. Station security was his responsibility, not the general's. Besides, this was a station security matter, though it involved the general's plans. After thinking for a minute, he headed off to round up a dozen security men and Captain Fontana.

He replayed the short video for the small group. "Okay. We have to get into Peterson's quarters and take those two out before they can harm Mrs. Peterson. Ideas?" Commander West asked, looking at Bess for a bright way to do this.

Bess knew she was on the spot. "Well, we could evacuate the cabin's air, but that would take some time before it knocked them out, and they'd probably shoot her before they tried to leave. How about shock grenades and rush them?"

"Okay. Shock grenades it is. I'll have Peterson go there with a blank SIMM card. As soon as he enters, Bess, you toss in the grenades. Two of you will charge in. Kill those bastards. Since there is a good chance they can overpower two and because of the confined space, one or both might be able to flee. So we'll set up choke points. The rest of you, take up choke positions here, here, and here. Block all exit points to that hallway. If they show themselves, shoot to kill. Bess, go to the armory and get your grenades. I'll text Peterson. Be ready to roll in twenty," Commander West ordered, running his hands through his short hair, frustrated with the entire mess. Having this damnable infantry division on his space station was causing no end of security problems.

Thirty minutes later, a very nervous Peterson glanced at Bess and the two well-armed guards, as they stood on either side of his cabin door. Bess nodded encouragingly at him, and he knocked on the door, something he'd never ordinarily do. With two well-armed men inside, he took no chances and waited for them to open the door.

One opened it a crack. "Peterson? Got it?"

Peterson's voice cracked nervously. "Yes. On the SIMM card. I want to see my wife."

The man opened the door fully to allow him to enter. As he did so, Bess tossed in a pair of stun grenades. Boom. Boom. Both flashed brilliantly. The concussion was deafening, but the two security men charged in, knocking the stunned Peterson to the floor. Bess raced down the hallway, taking cover around a bend and behind two more security guards. She did hear the sound of blasters going off, not a good thing to hear on a space station! If one of the shots ruptured the outer hull, all hell would result!

The stunned rebel took two blaster shots to his chest, while his shot took out a chunk of the ceiling. In the nearby bedroom, the stun effects were nowhere near as severe. The thug decided to save his own skin. He headed to the bedroom door, but was able to see one of the security guards through the dense, grey smoke and fired, taking him out with a blaster shot. The other security man dove for cover, giving him the chance he needed. He raced through the smoke filled room and out the open front door, dashing down the long, narrow hallway.

Hearing footsteps coming toward them, the two security guards in front of Bess, stepped out to confront the oncoming man. Both men fired their blasters, while the fleeing thug did likewise. Bess drew her own blaster, fearing the worst. If the thug came around the corner, she would fire first, at least she hoped so. She watched as one of the security guards left arm disconnected itself from his left shoulder, dropping to the metal deck, followed shortly after that with the rest of the man's body. Then, she heard the words she most wanted to hear, "Got him!" She poked her head around the corner and saw the headless thug's body lying on the floor, blood pooling around where it's head ought to have been.

"Medic!" Bess barked into her wrist comm device and headed down the hall to see what the situation was inside the cabin. The acrid smoke rolled out of the cabin flooding the hallway, though many doors opened and faces peered out to see what was going on. "Get back inside!" Bess barked. "Air filters to max power now!" She heard an acknowledgment over her comm set, but she couldn't enter the cabin just yet. The smoke was too dense.

A security guard wearing a facemask moved up beside her and entered the room, his blaster drawn. Shortly, she heard his muffled, "Clear," and relaxed, though still wondering whether Peterson and his wife were alive, wounded, or not. Presently, the masked man carried Peterson out into the hallway, just as three teams of medics came running down the hallway. One set moved on past her to attend to the wounded guard, while the others halted beside the door, coughing from the smoke. They put Peterson on a stretcher and carried him off to the medical center.

Next, the masked man carried Mrs. Peterson out as well, while the uninjured guard managed to crawl out, coughing, barely able to breathe. Yes, it had been very dicey to fire off two stun grenades in such a confined space, but Bess now knew it had saved the couple's lives, though one security guard died and another lost his left arm. Once more, Bess thanked the stars that she'd gone into the construction engineer branch of the FMF!

At this point, the giant fans in the ceiling activated, spinning at top speed, sucking the smoke-filled air up and out of the hallway and the confined cabin. That's that, Bess thought and waited for Commander West to arrive so she could get back to her construction work on the plasma generators down below. "Well done, Captain Fontana. That will be all for now. I'll handle the paperwork on this one," he said, much to her relief. She hated filling out the massive after-action papers, which would probably just be filed in some darn box never to see the light of day anyway. She saluted and left.

***

"Well, I confirmed it. There was another attempt to steal the division's plans. Those were concussion grenades going off, just as we thought," Ambassador Drina explained to the other four ambassadors who had assembled in her private quarters for this special meeting. Mr. Ancel le Foquat of Gemma-D, Mr. Adler Schmidt of Bellatrix-B, Mrs. Anka Polonia of Taurus-C, and Miss Alis Anrhod of Zeno-C had accepted her summons, but all had heard the explosions going off. Each had sent their own aides off to find out what was going on, but Drina had beaten them. "Damn, this infantry division is making our work here darn near impossible," Ambassador Drina grumbled.

"It isn't safe to move around the station any longer, not without an armed escort!" Ambassador Alis complained bitterly.

"It's all that division's fault! What in the name of the galaxy are they doing here anyway? Why all this secrecy?" Ambassador Ancel argued, his voice, quite hostile.

"Well, something's going on, and we're out in the cold on this one. Has to be the corporation's move," Ambassador Adler pointed out the obvious. "So anyone got any good contacts with the corporations? Probably GE in this instance, since this is their station. Commander West answers to them.

Has anyone spotted more than normal numbers of corp personnel running around the station?"

"Not really, but then there's always the question of why they've brought Dr. Gisa Wolfgang here. She's a genetic researcher, that much I do know," Ambassador Drina replied.

"So have you gotten anything useful from her or that corp engineer fellow, what's his name?" Ambassador Alis asked.

"Feliks Drugi," Ambassador Drina answered dryly. "No. Neither of them has the slightest idea why they're here, particularly so with Dr. Gisa. She's quite upset she's out here instead of back home on Bellatrix-B and her research station there. They have no clue either. I'm certain of that."

"Well, I used my contacts inside the Command Center," Ambassador Ancel spoke up, "and I think it is safe to say none of the station personnel know what's going on either. If Commander West knows, he's not informed anyone on his staff, so perhaps even he is in the dark about the 519th's purpose here. Any word from home?"

"No, nada," Ambassador Anka answered. The others shook their heads in agreement. "Funny. The corporations gave us these ambassador posts to help bring peace between our worlds, and yet they're sending out the 519th to the rim without telling us why. How are we supposed to do our jobs anyway? These corporations have entirely too much power. They can do any damned thing they desire to anyone at any time."

"Careful what you say, Anka," Ambassador Drina cautioned her counterpart. The corporate bigwigs could easily consider her diatribe treasonous.

Ambassador Anka flushed. "It's times like this I rather wish we had one of those freaks, those mutants with telepathic skills here. They could find out what the devil is going on in short order." Several grimaced at her mentioning that, however.

Ambassador Drina spoke calmly. "Settle down, everyone. I called you here today to try another approach to this problem. Let us share all the Intel we have from our home worlds. Surely between us all, we can get some idea of just what this threat might be that has caused the corporations to send an entire FMF infantry division out here to the rim.

"Well, there's been some uprisings at the psi-crystal refinery on Bellox-D," Ambassador Ancel pointed out, adding, "but surely they don't need an entire infantry division to bring order there."

"No, there is only one purpose for a FMF infantry division," Ambassador Adler stated dryly, "and that is to conduct a large scale ground invasion. So what world out here in the middle of nowhere warrants a land invasion? That's the question we ought to be asking."

"I agree with Adler," Ambassador Ancel spoke up. "His point is valid. An infantry division has no other purpose than a land invasion, though hardly assaulting an entire planet. That would take many, many divisions. So it must be less than a planet-wide assault, but still a rather large one."

"I don't know if this helps any," Ambassador Alis began, "but I've heard word from home that a number of reconnaissance photo missions were recently done over Rho-C."

"Ah, now we're getting somewhere," Ambassador Anka declared. "So what do we know about this Rho-C anyway? I've not heard of it."

Ambassador Drina fired up her galactic 3-d projection and focused it onto Rho-C. "Ah there it is, about equidistant from Zeno-C and Bellatrix-B. This station is here," she pointed out it's location in the projection, "relatively close to Rho-C, closer than any of our worlds. What do we know about this world?"

Ambassador Adler consulted his handheld computer, reading aloud, "Ah, it has a yellow main sequence sun and a small population. Founded by the Galactic Electronics Corporation two hundred years ago. Research and development. That's all it says."

"What kind of R and D?" Ambassador Alis asked.

"Good question. Perhaps if we knew that, we might have some real clue what this is all about," Ambassador Drina pointed out the obvious. "Okay, let's all use our home world's computer databases and try to find out everything we can about this Rho-C world. Personnel who were sent there might give us clues as well. Let's meet here tomorrow, same time, okay?" The others agreed, and they departed, leaving Drina to her own thoughts.

Hours later, she rubbed her eyes and then put some drops in them. She'd been staring at computer screens for the whole afternoon. However, one small detail had caught her interest, and she decided to ask Dr. Gisa about it at the poker game tonight.

Back in her own quarters, Alis did much the same, though her database search was vastly more comprehensive, as hers was a very secret one. Then, she fired off a scrambled, electronic burst of information, knowing that she'd not get an answer for several days at best, so far was she from her "associates." Still, she knew she was on the front lines out here on the rim and in a key position at that. Her only real consideration at this time was whether to request the presence of a telepath on the station. She knew that would be a very last resort, fraught with danger. Still, if they didn't get some answers soon, she knew she would have to risk such a power move.

***

Each day, some fifty deep space transports arrived at the station. Many were corporate ships bring supplies and personnel, as they had done with Jason. This far out, a good half were independent contractors, plying their trade where they could. At least one would be a diplomatic transport on missions for their ambassadors, and one might be military or FMF in nature. Today was no exception. An independent transport landed around noon, unloading its cargo, while Jason continued his lengthy cleanup work in the docking bay area.

Jason took no notice of the men who unloaded the ship nor did he particularly notice that three, short-bearded men carried a stainless steel briefcase in each hand, as they walked past the security guard on duty. Once beyond hearing distance, one man said, "Okay. Make for CA1. Artemus is expecting us. Look for the red kiosk with a banner saying Ores."

Another man sat his cases down and activated his

26

wristband navigation device, punching in CA1. "Got it. Down this hall," he whispered, picking his cases back up and leading the way. His navigation aid allowed him to walk straight through the maze of the station to the large civic area, now crowded with people. After pausing to observe, they spotted the kiosk and headed there.

"Artemus is expecting us," the leader of the three whispered.

Without a word, the man motioned for them to duck behind the curtain back wall the kiosk, which the three hastily did, though making sure they were not being followed or observed.

"Ah, you've arrived at last. No problems I take it?" the tall, thin man said as the three strangers joined him.

"Artemus?" one asked. He nodded. "These are for you. You know what to do with them?"

"Of course. It shall be done," Artemus replied dryly, no emotion in his voice.

"The Master wants to know the details," the leader countered respectfully.

"The station engineers are all working on the overhaul of the plasma generators. It will be very easy for us to install these in the air filtration system. Not a problem. Besides, if some engineers get too nosey, I will arrange another systems breakdown to occupy them. Tell the Master all will be setup within two days. I will send him confirmation when the job is done. Okay?" Artemus asked, knowing they would have to take his word in this matter. These men had no idea how the space station operated, but he did. In fact, the plasma generator overhaul was partly his work. A little damage here and there had caused the units finally to fail and the overhaul begun. Until they were back online, the station could not move one inch from its current location. However, in reality, the station had no reason to move anyway.

After the trio departed the kiosk, Artemus summoned three of his own men, who carried the cases, while he held onto his fake work order. He wore an official civies engineer overalls, pretending to be one of them. His orders stated he was to make some minor adjustments to the station's air filtration system, which filtered the air throughout the entire space station. Only once did he have to flash his papers before the eyes of a very bored security guard, before they climbed down into the bowels of the station where the recycling machinery was located, handling refuse, air, and water systems.

An hour later, the six cases were empty. Each had held three cylinders, connected together and with a single activation device. Once in place inside the air intake lines, Artemus flipped a switch, verifying the red active light came on. Now armed, when the Master sent the right signal, all six devices would activate, and a green light would so indicate. True, Artemus had only a vague notion of the effects of this plot, but then he didn't expect to know more than he needed to know to get the installation job done. Promptly at 18:00, he sent off a secure signal that meant the system was armed and ready to go. He ate a hearty meal that evening, pleased with his accomplishment.

***

Proudly the black-bearded man with a matching goatee looked up from his tiny handheld computer. He'd just finished reviewing the invasion plans General Franco and his staff had drawn up, plans based upon faulty Intel that his men had cleverly supplied in bits and pieces on several nearby worlds. His was a carefully planned event, drawing the hated corporations and their FMF infantry division into a deadly conflict, but one in which he was certain of the outcome.

Yes, the Galactic Electronics Corporation had settled this desolate, remote rim world of Rho-C over two centuries ago, but had never truly populated it. No, it was their bioengineering research station. Here, corporation top scientists worked in total isolation and secrecy, developing special weapons, weapons of mass destruction, though not in the usual meaning of that turn of phrase. While they had developed some highly toxic chemicals, whose vapors killed within minutes of inhalation, that wasn't their main line of research.

Rather the focus of research had been on biological engineering: the modification of existing species and the

28

creation of completely new species, and yes, one of these species was homo sapiens. It had begun almost a hundred fifty years ago when they brought the eminent genetics engineer, Dr. Hans Von Grubbe, to Rho-C. Back then, corporation men had uncovered a vast stash of ancient genetic engineering research notes, complete with samples. The chance discovery of these records and samples were given to the doctor for evaluation. When he presented his report to top corp personnel, they immediately saw the immense value in such work, and ordered him and his team of scientists to this remote, new world.

Since those early days, research facilities expanded rapidly. Today, Rho-C boasted fifty such complexes, all devoted to bio and genetic engineering research. Originally, the corporations sent security men to protect the facilities, but those were lifetime assignments. Once sent to Rho-C, one was never allowed to return to his or her home world. Further, outside communications were kept to the absolute minimum and under extremely tight control. Even an unauthorized phone call carried a death sentence, though that sentence was more likely altered to that of becoming another "test subject," which the research constantly needed.

The researchers demand for more and more test subjects was filled by the corporations and rather easily. Once a month, a person would simply disappear from one of the hundreds of worlds under the vice-grip of the corporations, appearing later on here on Rho-C as a new test subject. Many had been of a criminal bent, as far as the corporations were concerned, particularly those who spoke out against their iron grip control of the worlds.

Thus, many of these "rebels" found themselves on this desolate world. In time, some of them escaped their cells and banded together, forming an underground counter-society. Some twenty years ago, a man known only as the Master rose to ultimate power. Under his guidance, the rebels eliminated the security guards, donating them to the researchers, who cared little whom their test subjects were, as long as the researchers were well fed, well supplied, and allowed to continue their work. The Master was clever, and the corporations took nearly twenty years to finally realize they no longer controlled their research world. Hence, the arrival of the 519th Infantry Division.

For the Master, this coming confrontation had been planned for a decade. Given that much time to prepare, the odds were stacked in his favor from the onset, though the corporations had yet to realize this detail. As the Master looked over the general's plans for his invasion of Rho-C, he saw the corporations still believed their original site was the main base of operations, when in fact the Master had moved everything away from this location, replacing much with interesting surprises for the incoming troops.

Since the obtaining of test subjects had always been the biggest hurdle that the biogenetic engineers faced down through the centuries, part of the Master's plan was to solve that problem by using these invading troops. Now that he knew where they would strike, he laughed snidely. It couldn't have been a more perfect choice. It was at this point in time that his tiny computer received a faint signal from Artemus, the single word Active. Now, the Master roared with laughter.

***

Poker time finally came. When Jason entered the cabin along with Bess, he could not help but ask, "Well, did you all see that beautiful, blue explosion this morning?" He took immense pride in his work.

Ambassador Drina smiled, "Why yes. How did you get it so blue? I've never seen such an impressive explosion before." Jason dominated the conversation for the next few minutes, explaining about adding the Cobalt to the explosive mixture. Martha merely dealt out the cards and won the first hand while everyone else was distracted by Jason, something which pleased her.

A little later, Ambassador Drina steered the conversation to what she wanted to know. "I say, Dr. Gisa, have you ever heard of a bio-engineer of the name Dr. Hans Von Grubbe? I think he must have lived a century and a half ago."

"Two cards please," the doctor said and added, "Why yes. Back then, he was an eminent bio-engineer. I believe he gave up his corporate research position to conduct some classified work, but he vanished without a trace right after he resigned his esteemed post. I'm surprised you've even heard of him."

"I see. Would you be surprised to learn he was sent to Rho-C?" Ambassador Drina probed a bit. "Two cards please. I will see you and raise you one credit."

"I suppose so, because I've never heard of that world. Where is Rho-C anyway?" she replied, giving the ambassador a most curious look.

"Not too far from here, if the galactic 3-d display is at all accurate," the ambassador answered, but saw no glint of recognition or suspicion in the doctor's eyes. Ambassador Drina then settled down to enjoy the game, confident Dr. Gisa knew nothing more about the situation that was evolving here on the station.

***

Meanwhile, General Franco held a private meeting with Commander West. "Okay, I'm now authorized to divulge a bit more about my orders. We're going to launch an assault on a renegade band. However, considering what we're going up against, I would like to request the temporary assignment of your two engineers to my division, Captain Fontana and Lieutenant Mott."

"But those are my only engineers," the commander protested.

"Bill, I know that. I give you my word I'll not put them in any real danger. I need their explosives training. You see, I need all my engineers in their combat roles, not standard demolitions. I'll see that a crack squad protects them at all times. I need them for a day at most, though I may well ask for them later on as well, if my engineers run into something they can't handle. This lieutenant of yours is one of the best demolitions experts I've ever come across."

"Thanks for that much. I don't suppose I have any choice in the matter," Bill replied.

"No, I could call the corps in on this, but I'd rather keep this between us," the general replied frankly. Both men ultimately reported to the corporations. Thus, if they were behind the general's plan, they would certainly ignore Bill's protests, and he knew that.

"I'll hold you to your word to keep my precious engineers safe, general. As you know, this station is being kept together only by the constant efforts of my engineers and the few civies the corporations deign to send here," Bill declared, making one last attempt to convince the general just how valuable Bess and Jason were to the station's operations. "Half of the systems here are broken down. The pulse generators are still not operational so we can't even move the station a lightyear, let alone a foot." The general grimaced, knowing what this meant. The station was pinned down, a most dangerous situation for any combat unit.

After a pause, Commander West asked, "So when do you need them? I hate being in the dark."

"Tomorrow. Have them report for a briefing at 09:00. The assault begins at 10:00. Good night, commander."

"Night general. Good luck," he added, figuring the general might just well need it, especially if he so desperately needed his two engineers!

Just as Jason was raking in his first pot of the night, his arm comm device vibrated and a message scrolled by, likewise with Bess. "Report to General Franco for a briefing at 09:00 tomorrow. Room 2012. B.W." Bess looked at Jason who looked back at her. "Well, that's weird. We're supposed to meet this general fellow tomorrow. Maybe we'll learn something useful."

"Hardly!" Martha teased the two. "The general seldom tells us anything at all that is useful, so don't be surprised if you end up with a zillion more questions after talking to him." She punctuated her declaration with a snicker. Ambassador Drina noted this turn of events carefully and began making plans of her own. Perhaps something was about to happen tomorrow. The card game ended a bit earlier than usual.

Chapter 3—Assault on Rho-C

Jason and Bess didn't need any notification the 519th was on the move, that this was their big day. As soon as they opened their cabin door, they saw the infantry troops marching through the hallway from their sector to get to the docking bay. Indeed, had they been able to glance into the bay, they would have seen the bay was filled with deep space transport ships, moved from temporary storage into the bay, each filling up with their assigned troops and supplies, before taking off to make room for the next transport to dock and load. Fully four hundred transport runs were required to get all ten thousand troops of the 519th down to the surface of Rho-C. Many shuttles made eight such trips that morning.

"Captain Fontana and Lieutenant Mott reporting as ordered sir," Bess barked upon entering the designated room, both stiffly at attention.

"At ease," the soothing voice of the general called out. Today, he too wore his sidearm, a new blaster. Both were surprised to see Sergeant Martha Spelling present, along with her monstrous MK42 assault gun, which she called Gertrude, standing off to one side. She nodded slightly to her two friends.

"You both are hereby temporarily assigned to the 519th division. I've a demolitions job for you to carry out. Come here and look at this 3-d map—you too, Sergeant Spelling. Her squad is assigned to provide constant protection for you two while you are with us. Now then, here is the situation. Rho-C was a top-secret, corporation bioengineering research facility. However, in recent years, some rebels have taken control of the main base, which we are seeing here on the layout board. It's located in the valley of an ancient meteor crash site. The valley is about twenty miles across. Now right here at this edge is the backdoor entrance to the underground facilities. It has a Class G blast door. This is where you two come in. The division doesn't have anyone skilled enough who can force those doors open, so we need your demolition skills. Your job is to crack those doors for us. My own engineering battalion is going to be fully engaged in their combat roles and can't be spared for this simple demolitions action. Sergeant Spelling will back you up and guard your backs while you get that blast door eliminated."

"Since this is a secret back entrance, we don't believe it will even be guarded. Once you have it opened, Sergeant Spelling, you'll lead your squad inside to search for rebels. If you discover any that you can't handle, you are to pull out and request re-enforcement. Probably, the safest move will be to take the two engineers in there with you. So you two, make hast to your armory and get yourselves equipped. I've all the explosives you can possibly need being loaded onto your transport. It will be leaving at 10:00 sharp, so don't be late. By the time you arrive at the site on Rho-C, the enemy will already be fully engaged, so you shouldn't encounter any resistance at all, hopefully that is. That is all. Godspeed and good luck." He saluted them, and the trio made a hasty exit.

"Way cool! Don't worry. Gertrude here has your back, though I had hoped my squad would be kicking some rebel butt. Ah well, this is important too. We have your back. Besides, I'll get a front row seat on the explosion. Never heard a blast door of Class G could even be forced open," Martha chatted excitedly, as they made their way to the station's armory.

"Anything can be blasted open; it just takes the right charges in the right places," Jason explained once he had a chance to say something.

Right on time, the trio marched up the bay ramp into the waiting deep space transport. Bess and Jason were now well armed with an assault rifle, two blasters, and a bag of recharge units for the three weapons. Plus they had an assortment of knives and other gear in the small packs on their backs.

"There you are," one of her men called out as Sergeant Spelling marched up the ramp. "We were thinking you were going to be left behind this time," he teased her.

"Hardly boys. We got ourselves a cushy assignment. I'll explain while they check their explosives," she replied with a wry smile on her face.

Jason quickly headed to the rear to check on the explosives. Bess followed behind him, more than willing to let him take the lead on this assignment. Blasting impossible to destroy doors was out of her league. She'd never been trained to get through Class G doors. "Well?" she asked, having given Jason some time to look over the manifest.

"Yep. Most of this stuff will be useless, but we got what we're going to need—thermite. Take about five minutes to cut through the doors, but unfortunately no boom or explosion. Bummer really. We should take along many of these other explosives and blow other things up as well. Hey, this is going to be the best chance I'll ever get to set off as many charges as I desire!"

Bess shook her head. Jason was in Seventh Heaven, but she hated every minute of this assignment. Besides, there was always the chance they could be shot or even killed. This was a battle, after all. Still, she did smile at his infectious enthusiasm.

"Well, got what you need?" Martha asked, when the pair rejoined them and took their seats.

"Yep. No boom though, so I will take along a bunch of explosives and set some off anyway. Can't let all this stuff go unused, can we?" Jason teased. Several of her men cheered him and one added, "Right on!" The shuttle lifted off while they were celebrating.

A half hour into the hour long flight, field reports began being fed over the ship's intercom system, particularly for the sergeant's benefit, since she was leading this group. The outer perimeter had been secured. That was what she most needed to hear, for that meant her mission was right on target and on time, since these blast doors were located there close to the rim of the crater. After that news, the reports were rather alarming.

***

First Regiment surveyed the valley and above ground complex from the rim of the ancient crater, the center of which lay around a hundred feet lower, though some ten miles distant. Thus far, they'd met no resistance at all, except a few

35

FLAK guns firing wildly from the center installation, hardly anything to worry about. Now, the three battalions fanned out and began their cautious descent into the crater. Simultaneously, the other two regiments entered the crater from two other side locations, about equidistant from each other. The idea was to hit the rebels from three sides at once in a crushing pincer movement the general had worked out. This way, no matter the layout of the rebel's defenses, they'd be caught in deadly crossfires, minimizing casualties to the 519th forces.

On the assault, the general divided his engineers among the battalions, and they carried flame throwers. He arranged his artillery around the rim to provide covering fire. Thus, as the three regiments or nine battalions moved down the rim on their ten mile hike to the center, the artillery bombardment began in earnest, a most noisy affair.

Three miles into their long hike, things began to change for the worst. Live video feeds were directed from platoon leaders on up the line, eventually reaching the general at his command post on the rim. "What the hell was that?" one grunt screamed. Some weird creature had suddenly shot up out of the ground, swallowed his buddy next to him, and then sank back into the ground. All around, the soldiers began blasting away at the ground, hoping to stop whatever these things were.

From his own observation post fifty miles distant, the Master watched his own streaming video from strategically placed cameras. He also knew that the shelling would soon wipe many of them out, but until then, he and his aides watched rather amused. "Our worms are doing their job rather well," an aide commented.

"Indeed. I do believe they are enjoying their feast," the Master exclaimed, very much impressed with the efficiency of the worms, one of the diabolical bioengineered species the researchers had developed and his men were putting to a good field test.

While some of the wild shots destroyed some worms, those that fed retired back to their underground caverns to sleep. By the time the last of the worms had either eaten or been destroyed, over half of each regiment's men were gone. At this point, the artillery had to cease firing for fear of shells landing on their own men. Emboldened by the total cessation of the worm attacks, the remaining men focused on reaching their objective, the large set of centrally located buildings.

"Good god! What the hell are those things?" Jason yelled. Many other curses surrounded him, as they moved into position close to the giant blast doors. They'd witnessed the carnage a good distance from their location.

"Some kind of vicious worms," Martha declared. "Thank God we're not down there, boys. Come on; we need to fulfill our mission. You and you, take up a position there and there." Hastily, she set up a wide flanking perimeter around the doors, while Jason and Beth began ferrying loads of explosives from the transport to the doors.

Beth then began creating "explosive bricks," leaving the doors in Jason's hands. Besides, she had never had much experience with thermite anyway. Rather, those worms had scared the crap out of her, and she wanted some good defense against them, figuring to set up a perimeter of charges, which she could set off at the first signs of a worm attack here on the rim.

Meanwhile, Jason began affixing the thermite to the thick blast doors, placing the precise amount at the key fracture points. A half hour later, he was ready to detonate them. "Okay, everyone get back and don't stare at the intense light. It'll burn out your retinas," Jason cautioned. Once Martha gave him the go-ahead signal, Jason pressed the fire button. A small explosion ignited the thermite, which then burst into an intensely brilliant and incredibly hot fire. Liquid metal flowed down the sides of the doors. For five minutes, the intense flames burned their way through the thick steel doors, almost dwarfing the overhead sun. Finally, the flames went out.

"Hey, stand back a while. That's liquid steel on the ground there," Jason cautioned them, but everyone was already impressed with the job he'd done. Smoke rose from the bits of vegetation that burst into flame from the heat of the metal flowing over it.

Suddenly, a new factor entered the battle, and it wasn't rebel troops! From dozens of cages near the center of the facility and from strategically placed underground bunkers that survived the random shelling, packs of strange wolf-like beasts flooded out onto the ground, charging the surviving men. True, everyone had their PDS activated, that is, their Personal Defense Shields, which totally stopped most projectiles and even the energy blasts from blasters. However, they did nothing to prevent a strike from below. That is, they provided no protection from attacks coming up from the person's feet, the PDS's Achilles heel.

These bio-engineered wolf-like beasts were trained to knock personnel over and then attack their victims via their feet. Worse, each beast weighted at least a hundred pounds. Their momentum while running at top speed was more than enough to knock the soldiers over, giving them an opening for their lethal fangs, which were also many times larger than those of a wolf.

Unlike the worms, which stayed in the valley proper, these creatures continued their charge towards freedom, gaining the ridge line, attacking the gun crews! Before the last of these had been disintegrated, most of the gun crewmen were dead, as well as half of the remaining men in each battalion, each of which was now barely at a quarter of its original strength.

As a few of the wolf-creatures veered towards Martha's position, Bess's foresight saved the day. One by one, she fired off her well-placed charges, blowing the creature into unidentifiable bits. Martha took care of the last one rushing them with a short burst from Gertrude, while her men cheered both women, who had saved them all from a very nasty situation. "Okay, help Bess make some more of those bomb things, guys," she ordered. Bess grinned and began doing just that, showing four men what to do.

Meanwhile, Jason tested the entrance. "Okay, it's cooled enough that we can get inside."

"Hey, let me get some more charges set out here first, just in case," Bess ordered.

Martha agreed, but kept a watchful eye out for more of

the wolf beasts. "What kind of a battle is this anyway?" she cursed. "Where are the rebels?" No one had any answer for her.

"Okay, I have another dozen charges set, so we should have some protection out here," Bess declared.

"All right. Hats with lights on, everyone. Form up on me. In we go. Tom, you are on point. I'll bring up the rear with our engineers; be ready to blast anything you find," Martha ordered. Her nine men jumped carefully over the still hot metal and entered the dark tunnel; the trio followed directly behind them.

Inside, the temperature suddenly got much cooler. The walls were carved from the bedrock, though only the two engineers knew how that had likely been done. The ceiling was ten feet above the polished stone floor, and the tunnel was ten feet wide, more than enough to drive most vehicles inside or outside. "General, we're heading into the tunnel now," Martha reported. "So far, nothing to report."

They needed the bright lights attached to their helmets. Otherwise, the tunnel would have been pitch black. However, there were occasional lights affixed to the ceiling, so someone could have turned on the lights. Bess kept watch for switches, but found none. Instead, she saw ventilation holes at periodic intervals in the ceiling. She had no idea that a bio-agent was being released on the group as they marched down the tunnel.

A mile in, they encountered a larger chamber, perhaps forty feet square. Interestingly enough, they found six parked electric cars and a set of light switches. Bess flipped the switches. "Ta da. Thus there is light," she proclaimed to the cheers of the small group.

"Hey, boss, how about making use of these electric cars?" Jason suggested.

Bess turned to Martha, since she was in charge of this expedition, even though she outranked the sergeant. "Good idea. Everyone, mount up. Tom, radio the general what we're doing."

"Can't reach them. We're too far underground. No signal," Tom replied. "So do we go on?" he asked, slightly worried about meeting other unknown monsters. Men, those he could handle, but not what the others were facing here.

Martha had to make the decision. "Okay. We plod onward. Our mission is to find the enemy and then let the others come and take them out, but after what we've seen, there's not going to be anyone to come and take them out but us. So let's do this. If we hit any real resistance, we back out— all the way. Don't take any unnecessary risks." Martha mounted one of the cars, sitting above the driver, her giant gun pointed on down the apparently empty tunnel. She added, "We have probably nine miles to travel. Keep alert." Off they went, silently. The electric cars were perfect for this action. The enemy wouldn't even hear them coming, Martha concluded at once.

Around every mile as they guessed, the tunnel opened up into another large chamber. Each time, they stopped so Bess could turn on the next section of lights. Also, each had a few more of the electric cars parked in them as well. However, they spotted no signs of the rebels.

A half hour later, they reached the ninth such chamber. While Bess again dismounted to turn on the next section of lights, Martha said, "Okay. We should be getting to the actual research facility on this next leg. We're about nine miles in now. So stay alert. The rebels could be just ahead of us, though maybe we will be able to take them by surprise." Several men punched their hands in the air in silent agreement with her lead. Off they went on their next leg of tunnel travel, so far wholly uneventful.

Meanwhile above ground, the horrific situation took another bad turn. Large swarms of some kind of giant bats were released. These flew straight towards any warm body, alighting on it. The PDS allowed slow moving things to pass through the energy shield. Hence, the bats landing on their bodies quickly found their way beneath the shields. Each one had huge fangs, which bit down hard. While sucking out the victim's blood, the bats also inserted a chemical, which slowly paralyzed the victim, resulting in their deaths when their heart and lungs succumbed to the chemical's effects.

The swarm was more than enough to finish off the remaining regimental soldiers. To the general's dismay, the swarm came towards his officer's group. They turned to flee to the safety of their transports, but the bats were faster. The general almost made it up the ramp of his personal transport before a bat got to him. Thus, by the time that Martha and her squad headed down the last mile to the research facility, the last of the 519th division was dead, though Martha's squad had no way of knowing that yet.

Near the end of that last mile of tunnel, suddenly the space opened up into the actual underground complex. Unfortunately, they immediately took incoming fire! Nine huge men, all absolutely identical in all physical aspects, moved out of their hiding places, and began firing their blasters at the oncoming vehicles! While their PDS shields held and absorbed the incoming blasts, the vehicles they were riding did not. Car after car piled into the ones in front of them, spilling the men onto the floor. With their feet exposed, they quickly became casualties of the battle.

Not so, with Martha who was bringing up the rear. She began firing her giant gun as fast as it could go. The huge energy beams completely disrupted one or more of these identical, giant men when it struck them. Within two minutes, all resistance ended, and a deathly silence reigned. "Sound off!" Martha ordered. From behind the remains of an electric car, she heard Jason and Bess call out their names, but none of her squad replied. "Okay, Jason, Bess, fan out ahead. Check on my men. I have you covered. Christ! What were they?"

Slowly, the pair moved cautiously over the debris, checking on the fallen men. When they reached the lead vehicle, Bess turned around and whispered, "All dead, Martha. Now what?" Jason was rather pale and chose not to say anything. Instead, he moved aside and upchucked what was left of his breakfast.

"Shit! Shit! Shit!" Martha cursed, regretting having followed orders.

"It's not your fault," Bess hastily spoke up. "General Franco should have had drastically better recon and not charged blindly into this battle. So do we head back out now? God, I feel so very tired. I could sleep for a week." Then, she thought, *Hey, this isn't like me!*

Just as Martha was about to issue the retreat order, the trio heard faint female voices calling out, "Help us. Is anyone there? Please, help us."

"Shit! Civies. Come on. We should check out what's ahead. After all, we've paid a huge price to get this far," Martha ordered. All three checked their PDS and drew both their weapons, though Martha popped in another recharge unit into Gertrude. Carefully, the trio moved on down the hall, stepping over the giant men, who had stood nearly seven feet tall. Bess estimated each identical man weighed three hundred pounds at least. Yet why were they identical in all physical ways? Her mind was no longer functioning optimally. Just now, she didn't know that Jason and Martha's minds were also not functioning properly.

Entering the main room, they saw a dozen padded cells on either side, each one holding one or more people prisoner. However, all three gasped at what they saw. True, they were human beings, that much registered, but they were severely mutilated humans, if that was even the right word choice.

One cell held two women and a man, or rather what was left of them—a head and torso, completely naked. Almost in unison, the trio spoke up, "Please, kill us. We can't live like this. I beg you, show us your mercy." Too stunned to reply sensibly, the trio moved their eyes to other cells, most of which looked more like living quarters, though they were in fact prison cells.

Another cell held three who had no legs and were also blind. On it went. At last, their eyes lighted on a cell holding an armless young woman about their own age. She too was naked, but had lovely silver hair that fell in gentle waves to her knees. Her shape was perfection in a female form and her face, absolutely angelic. Her light blue eyes, quite sharp and observant. However, her feet were a bit malformed, forcing her to either stand on her toes or wear the very tall pumps that she was wearing, her only apparel.

"Hello. Please rescue me. I'm Linda Whitney. I was protesting against the corporations on Gemma-C when they kidnaped me and brought me here to experiment on me. They did this to me. You're all in great danger just being here.

They've released one of their biogenetic agents into the tunnel system when the battle started. So you've been exposed. I don't know what its effects will be though. Can you open my cell door, please? I want to escape these madmen."

For a moment, the trio stood there stunned by her announcement. At last, Martha found her voice. "You are saying they've released some kind of agent that's going to do all this to our bodies?"

"Yes, but just what I don't know. It could be bad or not," Linda explained as best she could. "They only had those nine clone giants guarding this entrance, but released the bio agent just in case. If you drop into a coma, it's going to be really bad for you. Please, can you get me out of here? I know the others just want to die. I can't do it, but please can you help them before you pass out?" she pleaded.

"I'll get her out," Jason muttered, still struggling with his reduced mental facilities. He tried adding one and one, but couldn't. Mechanically, he set a small charge on the cell lock, but forgot to give the others any warning. Fortunately, it was a small one and did nothing more than startle the others and unlock Linda's cell.

Her mind a growing fog, Martha obeyed Linda's orders as though Linda was her commanding officer. She moved from cell to cell, blasting the prisoners, one by one, ending their long-standing suffering, though later she had nightmares about what she'd done here. That done, Linda said, "We should get out of here soon, before the men come back. Back down the tunnel?" she asked.

Once more, Martha responded as though given a direct order. "Back down the tunnel. We'll take the electric cars when we get to them. Move out. I'll cover. . ." her voice trailed off. She couldn't think of the right words to say, but walked along behind them, still carrying Gertrude. In her tall heels, Linda couldn't walk anywhere near as fast as the trio could, but then they were barely stumbling along, greatly under the influence of the bio agent in the air. Linda kept on moving on down the tunnel, figuring she'd keep on walking until she got out of it, where there might be others who could help them, especially if they fell into comas. More like walking zombies, the trio followed her until they reached the first of the nine chambers, where eight electric cars were parked.

At least, Martha still had the presence of mind to order everyone onto one of the cars. Jason lifted Linda up and got her seated, before climbing in after the others. Fighting to stay awake enough to drive, he headed on down the tunnel, Martha hanging on at the rear, though her big gun was no longer at the ready. Time seemed to flow by like ripples on a pond of a summer's hot day. Although he often banged the car into the side of the tunnel, such sudden jars kept rousing his ebbing awareness of the present.

"I can see the light of day ahead," Linda called out. "Will there be others who can help us there?" No one answered her. The electric car finally shot out of the tunnel and ran up the ridge, almost ramming into their transport before Jason realized they were out and took his foot off the floor pedal. The sudden stop jarred everyone into the present a bit more, and they climbed off, staring out over the battlefield. None of the fallen stirred. An eerie silence covered the landscape about them.

With Martha's last coherent thought, she ordered, "Everyone, into the shuttle." Mechanically, all complied with her order, though Linda wobbled trying to keep her balance going up the steps. Once inside, like some robot, Jason headed to the pilot's seat. After pressing a few buttons, one of which closed the bay ramp, he was able to get the transport to lift off Rho-C, but it got no further than into a high orbit before he finally lost consciousness. By this point, Bess and Martha had already passed out. Only Linda remained alert, though entirely helpless to fly the transport, let alone operate the controls to call for help, ignoring the fact that she had no idea whom to call.

Linda realized her rescuers were now unconscious, just as she'd seen happen to so many other bio agent victims. She had the presence of mind to study the flight controls and relaxed when she determined they were in a stable orbit being maintained by the autopilot. At least nothing bad was going to happen while her rescuers were unconscious. Hence, she carefully got to her feet and began to explore the ship, first making use of its restrooms.

Later, she found the galley, but it took her an hour finally to get something to eat out of the small refrigerator. With her hunger and thirst quenched, she headed back to check up on her rescuers. Already, she saw the two women's hair had grown substantially. Further, their facial features were also changing. One good sign, Linda thought, was that their arms still looked normal. In fact, their fingernails had definitely grown some, so perhaps these two wouldn't be losing their arms as she had. That alone gave her cause to relax a little. She examined Jason, but saw little changes in his body, which again she took as a positive sign. Finally, she sat down and dozed, having nothing else that she could really do for them, except watch over them while the bio agent did its work.

During her six months there on Rho-C, Linda had witnessed a rather large number of bio agent experiments. That knowledge gave her some solid clues about what would ultimately result when the agent finished its work. She roused herself several hours later, and once more inspected the two women. As she had guessed, their hair would probably be as long as her own was. She said a prayer of thanks when she saw that their arms were still just as solid as before, though their nails were now protruding at least an inch beyond their fingertips. One thing was certain; their physical forms were definitely altering into that of her own body, which her captors or research men claimed was the epitome of feminine beauty.

Twelve hours later, Linda surmised that both Bess and Martha would wake and become sex fiends, which was her own description of the researcher's latest experimental results. That is, the women constantly insisted and demanded sexual gratification in any way possible, a kind of insanity Linda believed. The pair would be extremely beautiful, but super-charged sexually. At least, they'd not be helpless as she was, though she couldn't yet see what, if anything, was happening to their feet. Then, she realized that if their feet mutated as hers had, they should not be still wearing their heavy boots. Linda used her teeth and feet to finally untie and get their boots off. Once done, she realized she'd done the right thing, for already, she could see that their feet were mutating similar to her own.

That done, she returned to Jason to see how he was changing. While he still looked just like he had looked when she first saw him, quite unlike the two women, his hands got her attention! They were withering up, like husks drying in the summer's sun. She touched his arms and relaxed some. At least he didn't seem to be losing them as she had. Again, she sat down and dozed off, having lost track of time.

Around a day after they first entered the tunnel, Jason finally woke up. Of course, the first thing he saw was his missing hands, and he let out a blood curdling scream, waking Linda, who jerked violently in her seat. "Silly me. I've heard that happen dozens of times so I shouldn't be so surprised," she chided herself. "Jason, are you all right otherwise?" She carefully rose to her feet and moved over to his seat in the pilot's location, noticing the dried remains of his hands lying at his feet. Jason was white as a sheet, but again, not an uncommon reaction Linda noticed.

"I've lost my hands! What the hell happened to me? I'm helpless like this!" he gushed. His entire world seemed to be crashing down upon him in one enormous collapse.

"Not as helpless as I am, Jason. You're lucky nothing else happened. God, some of them lost all their arms and legs," Linda reminded him of what he'd seen in the cells.

"What the hell happened to us?" he asked again, flushing some, realizing that Linda was right. She was far more helpless than he was.

"A bio agent they call it. I think it somehow alters a person's genetics, but that's about all I know. They have many different kinds they've been using on us victims. Look what it's doing to Bess and Martha." Linda realized she needed to get Jason attention focused outward on others and not inward on himself. She'd learned that lesson the hard way when she woke up from her own coma to find her body so altered and helpless as it was now.

Jason rose and headed back to the cargo bay seats. "Good God! Linda, they don't even look like themselves anymore."

"I know. Their hair is now like mine, as are their feet.

They are going to have to walk on their toes or get some tall heels like those that I have on. Their bosoms are as large as mine are too. Moreover, you're right. They don't even look like they did before. The research men claim we now have perfect feminine body forms, Jason. I think we're supposed to be gorgeous women, though without arms that can hardly be said of me. At least, their arms are intact."

"Well, I have to admit, Linda, you are one hot babe, but now Bess and Martha are also stunning too. Weird," Jason admitted.

"True, but Jason, I'm afraid of what their mental states will be when they wake up," Linda said softly.

"How so?"

"The ones I've seen who were given this mutation form end up being sex fiends. They have one-track minds, sex, and then more sex. I overheard the researchers suggesting this mutation was being designed for breeding many mutated children rapidly."

"So even though their arms and hands are okay, they won't be able to function?" Jason asked, trying to wrap his mind around what she was saying. He'd never seen such behavior before, certainly not in military women.

"If I have gotten the bio agent right, that's about it. So what can we do now?" Linda asked.

"How long before they wake? I'm pretty much helpless too," Jason asked and complained bitterly.

"Few hours maybe. I've been practicing using my toes some, but keeping my balance is just awful, and this impossibly long hair is the pits."

"Can't someone cut it for you?" Jason asked the obvious.

"Can't. Somehow, it has pain sensors in each strand. Cutting it causes me excruciating pain, and besides, it grows back this long very fast. I'm stuck with it being this long," Linda admitted, adding, "but it wouldn't be so bad if I didn't have to wear such impossibly high heels. So buster, you are far better off than I am."

"Okay. I best try to do something or we are all doomed," Jason declared, moving back to the pilot's seat. "Hey, come along with me, Linda. At least, you can keep me company, and maybe together we can get this ship on course."

"Okay. But where can we go?"

"Back to the space station. We can get lots of help there. It's only hours away, if and only if we can get its coordinates entered into the nav system somehow, someway," Jason explained.

After a frustrating time, Jason and Linda managed to get the numbers entered. While he called them off, she used a pen between her teeth to punch in the digits. Once verified, Jason used a stump to press the Execute button, and the shuttle left its orbit around Rho-C, heading at top speed for the space station. Jason then spent several minutes checking every readout verifying everything was operational, including having enough fuel to reach the station. Finally satisfied, he suggested they return to the two women in case they woke up. He had the sense to follow Linda, using his stumps to steady her when she needed it.

Linda had done her best to try to warn Jason about the potential reactions Bess and Martha might have when they woke up. However, both had already awakened and had torn their clothes off. As the pair walked up to the two women, both were frantically doing their best to pleasure the other, oblivious to Jason and Linda who stood close to them. Jason's face crimsoned, while Linda smiled. She'd seen these reactions before, many times. She did wonder whether she should've warned Jason that the women might well strip him and pounce on him while he was pretty well helpless to prevent them from doing so. Jason's embarrassment crescendoed when both women moaned in the sudden ecstasy of their orgasms. Only then did the two women finally become aware of Jason and Linda standing close to them.

"We need sex, Jason. Lots of sex," Martha ordered. "Take your pants off. That's an order."

"You can't give a lieutenant orders, Martha, you are only a sergeant, but I can though, since I'm his captain and superior officer. So strip, Jason. We need sex now," Bess ordered.

Linda spoke up, "Bess, Martha, think. Look. He's

helpless too. No hands. If we're going to survive, we need your hands now. Control your sexual urges a while or we're all doomed."

"Oh!" Bess flushed red as a beet. She suddenly realized what she'd both done and said to Jason, and that she was naked, just as Linda was. "Shit!" she added, hastily struggling to get partially dressed again, though her very long hair continually got in her way.

Martha stared at them for a minute and then too flushed. Hastily, she too began to get her clothes back on. "What's happened to us? Why did you lose your hands, Jason? Why is our hair so incredibly long? What day is it? Where the hell are we? Have we escaped Rho-C? Are they coming after us? Did anyone else survive the battle? Where's the general? Are we in flight? Where are we headed? Who's flying this ship?" Martha fired off all the questions she could think of in a vain attempt to hide her embarrassment. She then added, "My feet are screwed up! I can't put them flat on the floor."

"Mine too," Bess added, wobbling about while trying to get dressed. "Hell, we have to get some clothes on Linda too. Jason, go hide out somewhere." She added, "Please."

"What? And stop looking at three gorgeous, young women?" he teased them, but hastily headed back to the pilot's seat, realizing he shouldn't have said that. Either one or both of them could come tearing into him, and he couldn't do much to prevent them from having their way with him! That shocked him.

A bit later, he heard both women yelling wildly. "This isn't me! I don't look like this. My boobs aren't this big!" Bess hollered. Jason guessed right that the two had finally looked at themselves in some mirrors. *Well, they are both incredibly beautiful women now, vastly different than they were before, just like Linda is. I hope they can keep their hormones under control!*

A half hour later, the three women asked him to join them in the bay seats again. When Jason appeared there, he saw they'd gotten Linda dressed in someone's shirt and pants. All three women's hair had been brushed out some. "Okay. Can someone answer some of my questions?" Martha asked.

"It's still my mission until I get us back to the space station. I'm still responsible for you both until then."

Jason swallowed and explained a little. "Linda and I got the coordinates of the space station entered, and we're on course to get there in some twenty minutes. I think we were unconscious for almost twenty-four hours, but Linda is a better judge of that. If my fuzzy memories are right, we four are the only ones that escaped the battle alive."

Linda took over and did her best to explain what little she knew about all the genetic modifications the researchers had developed and tried out on their test subjects. She also explained about their hair somehow having pain sensors in each strand, though by now both women already suspected something like that, since they'd tried to tie theirs back in ponytails but gave up from the sharp pains from the bands they were attempting to use.

"Okay then, you best let Bess and me into the pilot and navigator's seats now. We'll take the ship in," Martha ordered. Jason was very willing to let them take over. He felt incredibly helpless now, though one glance at Linda convinced him she was far more helpless than he was. He vowed not to make such a big deal over his loss of hands, but he doubted his own resolve. He was helpless.

"That's funny. The space station isn't responding to our calls," Bess called back to Jason, who headed on up to the front to see for himself. Something must be terribly wrong. Maybe they were using the wrong frequency.

Chapter 4—Space Station Chaos

"Well finally things can get back to normal around here!" Commander West declared. He opened a comm channel to all speakers on the station. "This is Commander West. The 519th Infantry Division has officially departed on their mission. Starting now, we're going back to our usual operations here on the station. I'll be assigning cleanup crews to clean up the messes they've left behind. As soon as those quarters are back to battery, I will notify those of you who had to vacate them so you can return to those quarters. Shouldn't be more than a day or so. Glad to be back to normal once again. Thank you all for your cooperation these past weeks. That is all for now."

An hour later, every available member of his team and those of the civies began the cleanup work, going from cabin to cabin. Mostly, bedding had to be washed, and trash emptied, along with sweeping the floors, though a few mini-refrigerators had to be cleaned out. The troops left no personal possessions behind.

"Yes, it's confirmed. Rho-C, some kind of secret bio-research station," Ambassador Drina declared. Once more, her small sub-group of ambassadors were meeting in her private quarters. Already, each had shared what little they'd uncovered from their own planetary databases, and Drina had added her own discoveries. A few credits into the hands of a private yielded their destination. Her aides were quite effective.

"I have some suspicions there were also geneticists on Rho-C," put in Ambassador Alis. "That is raising red flags back home on Zeno-C."

"Why is that? If you don't mind my asking," broke in Ambassador Ancel, stroking his chin. He was under orders to find out just how much these other ambassadors knew about the corporation's activities on Rho-C. He rather hated spying on fellow ambassadors, but the corporations couldn't be ignored. He could be replaced in an eye-blink, and he knew it. Well, so could all the other ambassadors for that matter, he mused.

Ambassador Anka answered him, "Have you forgotten your ancient history? The genetic wars that nearly wiped out the civilized galaxy?"

"But my dear Ambassador Anka," Ambassador Adler spoke condescendingly, "those were barbaric times, centuries ago, the dark ages of the galaxy, the era of the mutant telepaths and mechanical men. Uncivilized ages, wholly ancient history. Everyone knows such knowledge was lost to mankind back in those same ancient times. That has absolutely nothing to do with today's modern, civilized worlds."

An annoyed look creased the brow of Ambassador Anka. She detested men, particularly those who attempted to debate by using invalidation techniques. She preferred to deal in simple facts, true statements that could be defended by straightforward logic. She spoke up. "Fact: Rho-C was founded by the corporations. Fact: they kept the installation there classified as top-secret. Fact: we know that any number of bio-engineers and geneticists were shipped there and never heard from again. Fact: that was nearly two centuries ago. Fact: the FMF 519th Infantry Division has just been sent to Rho-C. Fact: an infantry division's job is to fight a battle. Fact: the 519th members were very well armed. Fact: they even added this space station's own two engineers, one of whom is a top demolitions expert. Conclusion: obviously, something has gone horribly wrong on Rho-C. We can speculate about what that might be, but there is no denying or hiding the basic facts of the matter. Something on Rho-C has gotten far, far out of the corporations' control or they wouldn't be sending an entire infantry division to assault it."

Ambassador Drina smiled. She always admired just how well Anka put men in their place with her fiery logical arguments. Adler's face was slightly red. "I believe we are all in agreement with Ambassador Anka's assessment. What remains, while it is as she says speculation, I believe we should indulge ourselves in just that—clear the air, get our cards on the table, so we can best advise our home worlds of the situation out here on the rim."

"I say, won't the goal of the corporations to be that of a cover up?" broke in Ambassador Alis. "Won't our bosses be asking us what is actually known out here on the station so that they can better devise a cover up story? If so, speculation isn't going to matter, only what the average person on this station knows matters."

"Quite true, quite," Ambassador Ancel replied. "There's no hiding the fact that the 519th was here and has departed. As far as I can tell, knowledge of their destination is known only to Commander West and possibly a few others on his staff. Hence, the corporations shouldn't have a difficult time fabricating a cover story—infantry practice exercises is a likely explanation. However, I'm intrigued by what Ambassadors Alis and Anka believe might be going on down there on Rho-C."

Ambassador Alis hastily retracted her insinuations. "Honestly, ambassadors, I have no idea what is or has gone on down there on Rho-C. With the presence of bio-engineers and geneticists, one can substitute any number of fantasy scenarios, but I believe you're right. At this time, they would be just that, pure fantasies. I'm sorry I mentioned it. I believe a cover story of simple military practice exercises will be the likely one used and one that is quite acceptable to all. After all, as Ambassador Anka states, we simply don't have any facts." She didn't add what she thought. "Not just yet."

"Okay then, I suppose that's all for this meeting. I should make my report for Scorpi-C and get it sent in later today," Ambassador Drina said, ending the meeting. However, she nodded to Alis and Anka, who realized the significance of that tiny motion. They let the two men depart and then appeared to follow them, but as soon as the men disappeared around a corner in the hallway, the two hastily slipped back into Drina's quarters.

"I'm curious about where speculation could be leading us," Ambassador Drina said softly, knowing she was treading on dangerous waters. As the corporation's appointed ambassador, she had to be very careful about what she said, particularly to other ambassadors who would likely be reporting such to their own corporate sponsors. "It seems to me that ancient history may shine some light on the present times." She didn't want to come out and go on record as suggesting highly illegal experimentation was being conducted on Rho-C. That would get her fired in an instant.

"Well, bio-engineers have created new and improved crops and domesticated animals, enhancing world's food supplies," Ambassador Alis stated the obvious and positive side of bioengineering. After coyly glancing at the other two women, she added, "No, it's the genetics side that has me worried. Could such scientists be once again experimenting with humans?" There, she dropped the bombshell. Cleverly, she watched their reactions quite closely.

"Good god! I certainly hope not. Surely, scientists and geneticists have higher sense of ethics and morals than that," Ambassador Drina declared. "But still, I have to admit that centuries ago they did just that and nearly wiped out the human race in the process."

"Could be a distinct possibility, Drina," Ambassador Anka decided to speak her mind. "Look, we all know what the corporations want, the corporations get. They could well have ordered these scientists to do just that and any number of other horrid, disgusting things. After all, let's be honest, ambassadors. If the corporations ordered us to do something highly unethical, we'd have little choice but to carry that out. We know the penalties of crossing the corporations. Death is the likely outcome. We've all seen that happen far too often, nicely covered up, mind you."

"So you think some illegal experiment has somehow gotten totally out of control?" asked Ambassador Alis, probing a bit.

"It would have to be something quite huge to warrant bringing in an entire FMF infantry division; that much is plainly obvious," Ambassador Drina declared.

"Really, really big," Ambassador Anka added for emphasis.

"I have to agree with you both," Ambassador Alis said factually, knowing her total agreement would put both women more at ease. She accomplished her objective, and both began speculating about what these experiments could have entailed such that an entire infantry division was needed to handle the mess.

While the two were constructing their fantasies, Alis sensed something in the air, something foreign, and something she couldn't analyze. She slipped into and out of the two's conversation, but began noticing their behavior. Both women were no longer making clear sentences, more of a muddle. Drina was saying, "So we can state engineered creatures plowing farmer's cattle works wonders on the canning industry or even the pilot's guild." Alis sensed something was affecting both women's mental faculties. But what? Was it the foreign substance in the air?

"Gosh, I feel so tired," Drina yawned. "It's only—it's only, well, it must be early." In fact, it was 11:00. As Alis watched, both women slumped over, resting their heads on the table. She rose and examined both women. While Alis was not a doctor, she sensed something was very wrong with the two women. She reached a decision, rose, and left hastily.

A few minutes later and now quite shocked, she reached Dr. Gisa Wolfgang's medical lab. She found the doctor was yawning too. "Doctor, could you please come with me? Something has happened to Ambassadors Drina Celestina and Anka Polonia. It might be serious."

"Of course. I don't know why I'm so sleepy myself. Must be those silly poker games we've been playing. Staying up too late at night, I guess. I have my bag. Lead on, Ambassador Alis." Dr. Gisa stepped out of her lab following behind Alis.

"My god! What's going on here?" Dr. Gisa exclaimed. They'd reached one of the open areas. Hundreds of people were lying about on the metal floor. All the usual hustle and bustle around the kiosks was gone. A deathly silence hung over the spacious area.

"I know. It's like this all over. Please, check on the two ambassadors first. They will perhaps give us a clue to what is going on," Ambassador Alis insisted, pulling the shocked doctor along with her. She most definitely needed a medical opinion and immediately!

"My god, Alis! They are both in a coma! How can this be?" cried a shocked doctor—the significance of her examination of the two women forced her more awake than she shoud've been, Alis noted.

"I believe there is something in the air. Probably it's all over the space station. Can you do anything for them?" Alis asked what she desperately needed to know.

Dr. Gisa yawned heavily. "No, not until I can determine. . ." She slumped over mid-sentence. A quick check yielded the same conclusion. Alis decided all three women were in comas. She acted, sending an encrypted burst of data off the space station. That done, she set about spot checking as many of the others that she could find, focusing on making her way to the command center to notify Commander West of the situation. Long before she reached the command center, she had ascertained two key details. One, the women were uniformly in comas, assuming their unconsciousness was identical to those of Drina and Anka. Two, the men were uniformly dead, including boys. She'd not yet seen any baby boys, however.

Reaching the command center, she knocked. Nothing. She knocked several more times before opening the door. She inhaled sharply. Dozens of men were slumped over their workstations. She spotted Commander West and rushed to him, feeling for a pulse. None. Mechanically, she went from man to man. All dead. Two women in the Command Center did have a pulse and were unconscious, likely in the same type of comas as her two ambassadors. For a moment, Ambassador Alis slumped into a vacant chair, trying to grasp the totality of what she'd observed, mind-boggling at the very least.

Terrorist attack or an attack on the space station? That was what Ambassador Alis first had to resolve. She ruled out a mere terrorist attack. Look, all the men on the station are dead, and the women, in comas. Someone is launching an attack to capture this installation and intact as well, without firing a shot. Okay, could it be related to the 519th in any way? Had it come yesterday, most all the division would have been wiped out. Still, I wonder if there is any correlation. How can I find out? I need to hack into the 519th video stream. They record their combats.

Hastily, Alis moved some of the dead men from their chairs, sat down, and began typing away. Her fingers flew across two adjacent keyboards and soon tapped into the master recording computer on General Franco's deep space transport. For a few minutes, she watched the initial march into the valley and gasped at what she saw. Wisely, she recorded the entire video stream on a small, portable drive. Rather than watch it now in its entirety, she let it download and headed off to make further plans.

Ambassador Alis reasoned that at any moment, a band of armed men could well land to take over the space station, since there wasn't anyone left to defend it. Then, she sensed the air. Ah, the foreign matter was still present. She reasoned they wouldn't dare land until the air was cleared of this agent, whatever it was, though she couldn't rule out the use of some form of protective masks or gear, such as a full biohazard containment suit.

Thus, she decided she needed to depart the station before the attackers could land and take over the station. She alone couldn't defend this giant space station, not remotely. She headed to the docking bay zone, where her personal deep space transport was kept in a side hanger, rather than out on the deck taking up valuable landing space. She experimented with the hanger computer controls and figured out the necessary sequence to get her ship out of storage and onto the deck, prepped for flight. She made sure her ship had a full load of fuel cells as well.

That done, two hours later, she headed back into the main portion of the space station, checking every cabin along the way. Soon, she concluded that everyone on the station had been impacted. She stopped at the armory and strapped on two blasters, before continuing her extensive searching mission. Hours later, she check on the three women in Drina's quarters. No change. She headed back to the command center to check on the download.

It had completed. After retrieving her small drive and stowing it away for safekeeping, she began fast forwarding through the video. Before long, she realized the bio-engineers on Rho-C had somehow created several new and intensely deadly species of animals! Further, the entire 519th Infantry Division had been killed, down to the last man, including the general! She let the video run, while she pondered the immense significance of what she'd just seen. Ten thousand men and women, heavily armed—all dead, and not one single rebel man had even been seen! She had no clue who was behind this disaster.

Just as she was about to turn the video off, she spotted movement near the Class G blast doors. She watched and saw Martha, Bess, Jason, and another woman coming out of the tunnel, riding on an electric car that almost smashed into their transport ship! Not everyone had been killed! She watched as they stumbled into the transport, but her attention turned to the new young woman with such incredibly long hair and gorgeous body that had no arms. Somehow, that woman was taking charge. Yes, the others were acting much as Drina and Anka had just before they passed out, but this new woman didn't seem to be affected. What was going on?

Hastily, she began typing on the keyboard and soon got the online video stream of that deep space transport activated. Now she had a realtime view of the pilot's seat at least. Were they trying to take off? Yes, Jason was trying to do just that. As she watched, he managed to get the shuttle going and lifted off Rho-C before he blacked out. Hastily, she punched in the transponder code for the ship and activated the ship's controls by remote control, getting it into a stable orbit around Rho-C.

Alis had to make a decision. Did she fly them all back here to the space station? If she did that, would they be safe? Jason surely would not. Every man here was dead. No, she decided to leave the transport in its stable orbit for now. No sense in getting Jason killed. With nothing else she could do just now, Alis headed back to Drina's quarters to check on the women. No change.

Well, that wasn't quite true, she noted. Their hair had grown considerably while she had been away! And their nails were longer. Drina had hers painted red, but around the cuticle there was a quarter inch gap in the paint. Her nails had grown a quarter of an inch in just a few hours! In addition, their bosoms seemed larger, threatening to burst out of the tops of their fancy gowns. At last, Alis realized the women's bodies were somehow being altered!

Once more, she sat back and sent off a very lengthy data burst, and after a very long delay, she received a massive encrypted data burst. She spent several minutes reviewing the data, comparing it with what she could observe with the three comatose women. The only conclusion was that the space station had undergone a bio agent attack, somewhat similar in nature to those that had happened many centuries ago! Alis sent back another short burst of data, verifying what she was observing.

"At least now I know what I'm observing and have some better ideas of what to expect. Observe, Alis, observe the women carefully," she said to herself, breaking the complete silence of the station. She carried each woman to a bed or couch, and then undressed them fully, so she could observe their bodies in detail. Now, she took a seat and watched over them as the hours passed by. She did have a sensor watching for incoming transports, which would give her plenty of advance warning so she could escape. Already she had her cover story prepared. She'd left before the attack came to check out a rumor of rebel action on a nearby moon. The corporations would buy that. At least, normal transport ships wouldn't land until they received official confirmation from the command center. However, after waiting a day or so, they would likely raise the alarm that something was terribly wrong here. Alis waited patiently.

Twelve hours since the attack, Alis noticed the three women's feet were slowly mutating. She wasn't sure if that was the right terminology for what she was seeing, but their feet were definitely changing. She experimented a little and realized what was happening to their arches, based upon the detail data burst she'd received earlier. She also kept a close eye on their arms and hands, but was greatly relieved to see no withering of those limbs, rather unexpected she thought. Further, their anatomy remained unaltered as well. However, Drina's facial features were definitely changing. So were those of Dr. Gisa and Anka for that matter. Certainly, Alis reasoned, this was a new form of bio agent at work, not those that had been used in ancient times.

Alis was also a very practical person. Knowing the likely

outcome of their foot modifications, she headed off to see if she could find suitable heels for the three women. If she couldn't, she knew they'd have a terrible time walking, what with only their toes on the ground. Ambassador Alis had long ago explored every inch of the station, including its Red Light district. Hence, she knew just where to go to find what she needed: proper footwear. Based on the sizes of their feet, she found precisely the heels she estimated would be needed. Then, she added three more pairs, figuring that if somehow Martha, Bess, and the unknown woman returned to the station, they'd need proper heels as well. She brought up images of the three and estimated the sizes of their feet, though bracketing that estimate. She carried a dozen pairs back with her.

Around the eighteen-hour mark, Alis realized this bio agent was going to be vastly different in its results on the female bodies. That is, they wouldn't be having enormous breasts, but rather simply large ones, far larger than their current dresses would allow. Hence, she again headed off in search of appropriate dresses, tops, or gowns that would fit well-endowed women, estimating a D cup as their final breast sizes.

That done, she again rechecked her monitors. Still no incoming invasion fleet. She re-sensed the concentration of the foreign matter in the air. Comparing it to what she initially sensed, she rightly concluded it was slowly going away, probably being filtered out by the massive air filtration system. Enough time had passed for Alis to estimate how long it would take to eliminate the foreign matter completely. She guessed another twelve hours at most, maybe less. The variable was just how low a concentration would be safe for humans to breathe without ill effects.

At this point, Alis had to make additional decisions. How long could she dare stick around? Surely, those who had executed this attack would soon be arriving to take control of the space station. She didn't want to have to fight her way off the station. Then, there were the three women she was watching over. Alis decided she was going to save them, if nothing else. One by one, she carried each through the station to her private shuttle in the docking bay, bringing all the new apparel with her on the last trip.

Then, she checked on her ship's food and water supplies. Too low. She made numerous trips, restocking her ship. Now she again could only wait it out, hoping the women would rouse from their comas soon. Okay, she thought, now I'll need a plausible cover story for why I'm not affected as they are. She donned a pair of the extreme heels and practiced walking in them. She found a bio agent mask in the armory and brought it back to her ship. Now she had her story straight. She'd donned the mask and had avoided most of the mutations.

Just then, an alarm sounded. Ah, she noticed Jason and the others on the transport were waking. With a slight assist from her, Jason and Linda got the space station's coordinates entered and were now on their way. At this point, the three women woke from their comas, and Alis had her hands full.

Alis anticipated screaming and shock, based upon her database. Shock occurred, as each woman looked at the other, hardly recognizing them. Each woman's physical form had been altered into that of an extremely attractive, gorgeous woman—super-models might be a better description. Then the unexpected struck. All three went crazy, demanding immediate sexual gratification. A three-way women's orgy followed, a rather frantic one at that. Only when they finished was Alis able to get them coherent enough to explain what had happened here on the space station.

That did the trick. Telling them every male on the station was dead brought the two ambassadors into the present with some force, as well as the good doctor. At last, they looked themselves over in the mirrors, commenting on how their bodies had been modified, while Dr. Gisa rattled on about genetic mutations and such. All three were eternally grateful for the dresses and heels that mostly fit their new body forms. "I can hardly walk in these, but it sure beats trying to stand on my toes on this cold metal floor," Ambassador Anka declared.

"Can we see the video? Can we check on the others?" asked Ambassador Drina.

"I should get my medical bag and check on them. Crap! How can I check on thousands of women?" Dr. Gisa declared, her mind finally taking in the magnitude of the disastrous attack.

"I've a copy of the video. The dead are starting to decompose. Awful stench. Probably it's not safe to leave the shuttle. I anticipate the attackers arriving anytime now, since the bio agent is likely cleared out. Someone wants to capture this entire space station without firing a shot or damaging any of its equipment," Ambassador Alis pointed out. "Besides, we need to be here, because the only survivors from Rho-C are due to arrive anytime now. Yes, Bess, Jason, and Martha made it out alive, and they're bringing another young woman with them. However, Dr. Gisa, Jason is going to need your help. He has lost both of his hands at his wrists. Probably a different bio agent at work." Once more, Alis was wise in shocking them, which helped keep their minds off the powerful sexual urges that the three felt.

While the three shocked women watched the strange worms rising up and swallowing the soldiers whole, Alis kept an eye on the incoming shuttle. Finally, she relaxed. Martha was in the pilot's seat, not Jason or the unknown armless woman. Five minutes later, Martha made a perfect landing. All four headed out of Alis' transport to meet the survivors. "My god! Going down this ramp in these heels is incredibly difficult!" exclaimed Dr. Gisa. The others had similar statements.

When they reached the shuttle, Martha had the ramp down and called out, "Hi ya. We made it! Just don't ask me how! Walking is a bitch! Our toes are frozen! God, you all look stunning too! Hey, why didn't the command center respond to my calls? Crap, how do we get down the damned ramp?"

"Very carefully," Bess called out. "Hold on to the rails, like this." Slowly Bess made her way down, followed by Martha, leaving Linda and Jason behind them. Jason put his arm around Linda and supported her as they stumbled down behind the two women.

"My god, Martha, Bess, you both look absolutely ravishing! So different!" exclaimed Ambassador Drina, as she welcomed her friends back.

Ambassador Alis took charge. She had to, because at any moment, the attackers might arrive in force. "Come on; get into my shuttle. We have clothes and heels that should fit you. Walking in the heels is lots better, but not easy. Martha, the space station was attacked with some new kind of biological agent. All the men on the station are dead, and all the women are just now coming out of comas and look more or less like Drina, Anka, and Dr. Gisa do. I think the attackers are coming here shortly, and I want to get us safely away, unless you want to stay and try to fight them alone."

"Good God! Dead? Everyone? Holy shit! What the hell happened here?" Bess cried out, tremendously shocked.

Just then, a piercing, warning beep began sounding. "That's the attackers coming in on a docking approach. Everyone, get inside my shuttle now!" Alis ordered, rushing as best she could in her new heels up to the pilot's seat.

While she fired up the shuttle's engines, Martha yelled, "Bay door is closed! Get us out of here!" Ambassador Alis did just that. She expected the arriving transports wouldn't be expecting to see a transport lifting off, but what worried her was there any armed ships coming, light cruisers perhaps? Her only defense was to drop into hyperspace as fast as possible. Hence, she allowed the autopilot to navigate the ship up and out of the docking bay, while she punched in some hyperspace coordinates as fast as she could. Alis was an expert at such coordinates and chose a location not too far from the space station. She had no idea where they would ultimately decide to go, rather right now, they just needed to disappear and be un-trackable. Once clear of the docking bay, she saw several dozen transports lined up to dock! She hit the Execute button, and the field of view went utterly black, the void and safety of hyperspace. Finally, Alis relaxed. Now would come the needed explanations. She headed back to the cargo bay where the others were.

She found Dr. Gisa busily examining Jason's stumps, with Linda sitting waiting her turn with the doctor. Anka and Drina had taken Martha and Bess back to a cabin to change into the new dresses and heels. Wisely, Alis sat down and remained quiet, observing the doctor and the new young woman, comparing her physical form to the ancient records of known genetic bio agent mutations. Her lack of arms and long hair fit some of the criteria, but her bosom didn't. Alis also saw she didn't have male genitalia as had Jason. She concluded some new type of bio agent had been used on this woman.

"Well, Jason, it looks like your description is an accurate one. Your hands just withered up and fell off at your wrists. I'd need my lab to determine just how this has happened. There's some hope though. If I can get you to a medical facility, I can reform your stumps to take the fancy prosthetic hands, the kind that activate via your body's electrical impulses. Now, are you sure you don't have an overwhelming sex drive, like we women seem to have? Nothing else has changed with your body?"

"Nope, I'm just plain helpless now, that's about it. Guess I'll never be able to make any more explosions, doc," Jason lamented, fighting from becoming too emotional, not with Linda sitting beside him. Her plight was far worse, and Jason wanted to appear brave for her, though why he should feel this way eluded him—something about her silver hair and incredible blue eyes.

"Okay then, I should look at Linda now," Dr. Gisa declared, turning her attention onto Linda. A few minutes later, the doctor pronounced Linda perfectly healthy, but asked, "So do you have that same overwhelming sex drive that we do?"

Linda sighed. A tear formed. Hesitantly, she glanced at Jason and then replied, "Well, yes, but I have to keep it suppressed. Who would ever want a helpless cripple as I am now, totally helpless, barely able to walk?"

"Don't say such silly things, Linda. You are a stunning young woman," Jason spoke up for her, trying his best to convince her otherwise.

"Well, we should get Linda changed too," Ambassador Drina called out. She and the others had just returned. Bess and Martha were now able to walk somewhat better and looked quite beautiful in their new gowns Alis had stolen for them from a store in the Red Light District of the space station.

"Wow! You look incredible, both of you," Dr. Gisa gushed.

"Come on, doctor. It's Linda's and your turn," Ambassador Drina commanded. "Then, we all should sit down and have a lengthy talk."

A half hour later, Dr. Gisa and Linda made their appearance, receiving just as many compliments as the others. Jason, however, chose to sit beside Linda. Somehow, he was determined to look after her as best he could, since he was useless for much of anything else.

Ambassador Alis began, explaining how she'd donned a protective mask and had avoided most of the horrific effects of the attack. She explained how she'd managed to capture the video of the division's attack on Rho-C. She told of what little she knew about the attack, telling them that she'd checked on the men and found them dead.

Then, Martha outlined how the attack had gone, while Alis replayed the video so Ambassadors Drina and Anka, along with Dr. Gisa could see the awful scenes. Once they got into the tunnel and were attacked, Linda told them her pitiful story as well, adding much to their overall understanding of just what kind of secret bioengineering research and genetic modifications were being done on Rho-C. Naturally, all found this beyond appalling! Further, the corporations had been behind the research, funding it!

By the time they all finished sharing what they knew and answered questions as best they could, everyone was hungry. They adjourned to the small galley, where Drina and Alis whipped up a light supper. Linda did her best to keep from breaking down. "Someone's got to feed me," she whispered. "Jason too."

"Of course, dear. Think nothing of it," Ambassador Anka said soothingly. "We are here for you both."

Later over coffee and tea, Ambassador Alis brought up, "So the question we now face is just where do we go and what do we do? I think it wisest if we all sleep on it and be prepared to discuss it together in the morning. Also, perhaps you can pair up and satisfy your sexual urges tonight. It's obvious to me that all of you, except Jason, are fighting hard to keep that drive suppressed. So my suggestion is to let it out at night when you are in bed, as well as perhaps when you wake up in the morning."

Bess paired up with Martha, while Drina took Anka with her. Just as Dr. Gisa was about to suggest that she pair up with Linda, Jason spoke up. "I'd like to take care of Linda, if you don't mind. We are almost alike now, something that we share."

"Sure, I'll help Dr. Gisa," Alis volunteered, seeing the wisdom in Jason's request. Of everyone, Linda was bound to have the most difficulties adjusting. Having Jason with her just might give her back some self-confidence, some self-respect. It was a long shot, Alis knew, but one worth trying at least. She added, "But Dr. Gisa and I will help get you both ready for bed, okay?" The two nodded.

A bit later, both sat on the edge of their shared bunk bed. Linda's long, silver hair had been nicely brushed out and was draped over her shoulders. She'd explained she could feel with her hair, like a newfound sense of touch, which Dr. Gisa already knew, though Alis only suspected. Finally alone, Linda bravely said, "Jason, I have to tell you something. I'm," her voice faltered, and she tried again, "I've never done this before."

Jason flushed. He swallowed hard. "I'm a virgin too, so I suppose we have to tell each other what we desire as we go along. You're the most beautiful woman I've ever met, Linda. I just love your silver hair and your light blue eyes. You're so alive." Their lips met and passions swept over them. Sometime later, Linda rested her head on his shoulder, while his other stump lay on her silver hair, stroking it gently as she had asked.

Linda whispered, "Jason, I can't begin to tell you how desperately I needed that. I've gone six months with this massive urge and with no way to satisfy it. Several times, I thought I was going to go mad. Now I feel so relaxed, actually for the first time in six months."

Jason whispered back, "Linda, do you believe in love at first sight?" She giggled.

The morning brought a new round of pleasure making before anyone rose. After that, cleaning up and handling such long hair took care of an hour, before they finally sat down for breakfast. Finally, over coffee and tea, Ambassador Alis focused the group on the present and what they should and could possibly do. In her mind, she needed a destination, for they couldn't hover in hyperspace forever.

Ambassador Anka said, "Well, I suppose we should make a full and complete report of everything and send it to our corporate sponsors. Maybe sending along a copy of that video of the battle," she added. Drina agreed in principle.

Linda spoke up, "I don't know if you want me to say anything."

"Of course, Linda. You have as much a say in this as we do," Ambassador Alis countered.

"Well, look. I protested against the corporation, and they simply kidnaped me and did this to me. If you report all that happened, they are going to have to silence you permanently, all of you. The corporate bigwigs aren't about to let you ever tell your stories to anyone else. They can't possibly take that chance. Good God! If the worlds out there knew all that you do, there would be massive uprisings everywhere. I'm sure that once you've made your reports, your lives would be terminated in some manner."

Linda went on, "Right now, all of you have one thing going in your favor. The corporations believe everyone in the 519th and the space station have been lost to the rebels, whoever they are. Hence, you are more or less 'dead' right now. If you make your reports, they'll know you aren't and will probably come after you, as they did me."

Ambassador Alis relaxed. This was precisely her own conclusion and was greatly relieved that Linda had both thought of it and pointed it out to the others so she didn't have to. Thus, she said, "Linda, that's a very keen observation. I do believe she is quite right. If we report it, they'll have little choice but to silence us permanently. I don't know if they have other secret facilities where they could take us and genetically modify us as they did to Linda or not. If they don't, they'll probably just have us murdered when we aren't looking."

"Well shit!" Martha spat out. "She's right about that. We know way, way too much for our own good. Hell, now that I think about it, what the corporations are doing to humans— this genetic modification stuff, why that's utterly criminal. I mean we all went in there to fight these rebels, but now that I've met Linda and know what horrid things these corporations are doing in secret, why, I might have sided with the rebels, whoever they are!" Again, that was precisely what Ambassador Alis wanted to hear, and she watched the others reactions closely.

"Good point, Martha," Ambassador Drina spoke up. "Knowing what we do, I too have to say outright that I'm wholly against such things. So that makes me a rebel too, doesn't it? I mean I could never condone what these corporations are doing on Rho-C, not ever."

"How could any of us condone such barbarism?" Ambassador Anka added. "So we are now rebels. Still, I don't know if I want to be associated with those who used such hideous monsters to eat and kill all those soldiers. They were innocent pawns."

"I'm just an engineer," Bess spoke up. "All I ever wanted to do was build things to help folks out. But this, this is going too far. The corporations have crossed the line. They have to be inhuman animals to have done what they've done on Rho-C. So I guess I am a rebel now too, though I surely can't support the ones who butchered the 519th."

Linda said, "I agree with her. You see, when they first did this to me, I wanted just to die, but I couldn't even do that on my own anymore. Then maybe a month later, I changed somehow and wanted to fight back. Now I want to fight these corporations more than ever, but obviously, I can't fight back, not really. Still, we just can't support those who destroyed all those men and women in the army. They are just as bad as the corporations are. Now if it had been all the corporation leaders out there being devoured by those strange worm-like things, then I could back them for turning their own hideous things back on them, but they didn't. They used them to kill innocent soldiers. So yes, I so want to fight back at the corporations, but as I am now, I surely don't know how I possibly can."

Dr. Gisa spoke up next. "Look, the first thing that simply has to be done is to get us to a good medical lab. I need to see about getting some prosthetic hands for Jason, and I simply have to analyze our DNA and see if I can find out what they have done to us all. That should be our first priority. Who knows what side effects we may all suffer from in the future? Maybe the mutations are not finished, just because we've come out of our initial comas."

Hers was a very sobering thought, one that brought total agreement from everyone. Ambassador Alis decided it was time for her to make her pitch. "Okay then, first stop, medical lab. It seems to me we all agree we want to join the rebels fighting against the corporations, just not those who butchered the soldiers and murdered all the men on the space station. Those are our enemies as well. Are we all in agreement on this?" They were.

"Okay then, I do have some contacts out there. While we are dealing with the medical lab, let me see what I can uncover. Perhaps, there is a safe rebel base somewhere that we can go and help. Is that acceptable to everyone, assuming I can find such a place?" It was.

Ambassador Alis added, "Of course, from this point onward, it isn't safe to use our ID cards, not anywhere. We all know the corporations can easily track us by ID card usage. Except for Jason and me, the rest of you don't look like your recent selves, so with a name and ID card change, you're not likely to be recognized."

"Hey," Martha spoke up, "I can use Bess's last name, and she can use mine. That should work. Drina and Anka can exchange last names too, so can Dr. Gisa and you, Alis. Same with Linda and Jason. Some of us can't remember wholly new names." Several chuckled, but her idea was accepted for the present.

"Well then, does anyone know how to make fake ID cards?" Ambassador Alis asked. She certainly could, but hoped another would be able to do it. The less she had to reveal about her skills set, the better.

"I suppose I can," Bess volunteered. "After all, it's just really a simple engineering task, given a computer and stuff."

"Say Alis," Ambassador Drina asked, "Don't you have some ID card blanks onboard? Usually we ambassadors have to provide replacement cards to others from our worlds."

"You're right. I forgot about that. Yes, Bess, I have some blanks. Let me get you set up, and then let's figure out what medical center we need to visit so Dr. Gisa can do her work," Ambassador Alis answered, again relieved.

While Bess set to work on the new id cards, Dr. Gisa pointed out, "Look, we just can't show up at any med lab on any world, not without a whole lot of questions being asked. Shoot, as off-worlders, we would have to go through a lot of red tape to get the kind of access I'm going to need."

"So what are you saying?" asked Drina, growing concerned again. Her world was being turned upside down, confusing enough without the genetic modifications she'd endured.

"If we go to Bellatrix-B, my world, I have access to the Arcon Med Lab facility, where I used to work before I accepted the corporation transfer to the space station. No one will ask any questions of me. Still, that could be risky for us, if anyone is looking for us," Dr. Gisa explained.

"Well, we can't go busting into some world's med lab," Alis stated. "I think she's right, but we should be on guard, just in case someone gets wise to us." The others agreed, and she headed up to the pilot's seat to insert the coordinates and get them on their way to Bellatrix-B.

Chapter 5—Trapped

While the others were occupied, Alis fired off another encrypted data burst. Much later, she received a reply. Now that Bess had made them all new ID cards, Alis noted the new account numbers and fired off another data burst. As they approached Bellatrix-B, she announced, "I've managed to get ten grand deposited into each of your new accounts. We're going to have to go shopping for proper clothes and heels, you too, Jason. So this way, we have some funds to spend and not draw undo attention to ourselves."

"Thanks, Alis. I pay you back when I can," Drina replied. The others volunteered to do so as well.

Alis had purposely stretched the day's flight time out to two days. Why? This gave the others time to prepare the video that they wanted to release to the entire galaxy. Anka and Drina spent nearly two days working up a five-minute summary video, outlining all the known details. Meanwhile, Bess and Jason put their heads together to work out the easiest way to get the video shown across the galaxy, by hacking into one of the comm relay centers and streaming it live. Once that was done, all manner of interested parties could re-record it and use it in all sorts of ways. Their hope was that it would help bring the corporations down or at least increase the general level of hostilities towards those in power and just maybe the corporations would change for the better. Alis held out no such hope, though.

The two military engineers had little difficulty hacking into the relay center close to Bellatrix-B, though Bess had to do all the work, while the mostly helpless Jason did his best to keep his wild emotions in check, if only for Linda's sake. In fact, Jason later admitted it was Linda's presence that kept him rational and focused, instead of becoming a basket case. Linda suggested most of the captions the pair used with the video. Thus, she too was allowed to contribute. They planned to release the video when they departed from this world.

Thus, on the fifth day from the initial attack, Alis

prepared for a landing on Dr. Gisa's home world of Bellatrix-B, whose dim red sun cast a ruddy light into the deep space transport as it slowly descended onto the spaceport of Bregenheim, a sprawling city of ten million inhabitants and home to the Arcon Medical Laboratory.

Dr. Gisa took charge, handling the docking fee, and handling their entry through customs, passing the group off as some of her associates from Space Station Gamma-629 in this, the Abelard Sector. Customs bought her explanation and granted them temporary visitor passes. That done, she led them out of the spaceport and arranged transportation to a fancy hotel, chosen because it was within walking distance of the med lab and many fancy apparel shops. Once getting their rooms, Dr. Gisa took Jason with her, while the others headed off to purchase clothes and heels for everyone, along with something for Jason as well.

"Wow, Dr. Wolfgang, you sure look different," the entrance clerk commented, remembering her from several years back when she interned here.

"In a good way I hope," she teased him back, knowing he was quite impressed with her new look. The tall heels only added to her appearance, though they slowed her walk way, way down. She wore a brown gown that mostly matched her knee length, now wavy, brown hair. After affixing their temporary passes, Dr. Gisa led Jason into the heart of the lab facilities. Several more times, she had to stop and chat with others who recognized her, well mostly that is. Her new stunning appearance caused many to stare and then wonder if she was the Gisa that had once worked here.

Finally, she was able to get sole use of one of the many medical machines in the lab. Jason sat before the machine and stuck his two stumps into it. "You will feel tiny pin pricks. That's the anesthesia. After that, you won't feel anything as I prepare your arms for the prosthesis. Okay?" Jason nodded and held his breath, wondering if perhaps with artificial hands he could still prepare explosive devices.

Twenty minutes later, Jason looked at his stumps. Where his wrists had been, he saw two conical tips. She'd tapered his bones and muscles down smoothly, ending with small, one inch ends where his wrists had been. Next, she produced a pair of prosthetic hands, showing him how to put them on and take them off. "They work by suction. You stick one on and align it. Then press this spot here. Here that? A small vacuum pump is sucking the hand onto your stump. Press it again and the vacuum releases so you can take them off. They operate by translating your body's electrical impulses into corresponding hand and finger motions. You just pretend you are doing something with your real hands, and these should mimic that, at least somewhat. As I understand it, much practice is required. So while I'm working on the DNA analysis, I want you to wiggle fingers and anything else you can think of doing. Practice. Practice. Practice, Jason."

While he struggled mightily to get a finger to wiggle, she took a blood sample from both of them and disappeared into the next room. A bit later, she had him join her, since someone else needed to use the medical machine. "Okay, I have the analysis running. One thing I can say with certainty. Our DNA has most definitely been altered."

"What does that mean?" Jason asked.

"For one thing, they can't identify us by our DNA any more, not unless they get new samples," she explained. "Of course, I won't know the full results until tomorrow. So I'm taking supplies home to get a blood sample from everyone else. That way, tomorrow, I can run all the rest of them. Let's head back to the hotel now. I don't want to risk being out and about more than necessary." With that, they two left the med lab and walked back to the hotel. By then, Dr. Gisa's feet were throbbing, and she just had to sit down a spell.

A half hour later, the others arrived, followed by many packages. "We bought out the store," Drina teased Dr. Gisa. "Anka had a good idea. Since we're forced to wear these extreme heels all the time, we should dress elegantly to match them. It would look silly for us to wear jeans and these heels. We got you some too," she added.

Not to be left out, Linda said, "I picked out some things for you too, Jason. I hope you like them. Can I see your new hands? How do they work?"

"Only sort of work. I can't feel anything with them, but

maybe I'll eventually be able to do some things for us, Linda. Thanks for the clothes. Let's see what you got me."

While they were going over the clothes, Dr. Gisa went around drawing their blood. When she got to Alis, she said, "I hate needles. Mind if I draw my own blood for you? I don't trust others to do it right." Dr. Gisa laughed and handed her the syringe. She hadn't pegged Alis as being so squeamish. Alis went into the bathroom and filled it with some blood stored for such a situation as this.

"Okay, I'm off to the lab to run these samples through. Back in an hour, then we can get supper," Dr. Gisa explained.

***

Back on the space station, the Master and several hundred of his rebels landed in the docking bay, but not before observing the fast takeoff of another transport. "Who the hell was that?" he asked. "Something went wrong. Fan out and find out what. We need the identity of that transport and who was on it."

An hour later, the Master relaxed. All the men here were dead as planned. Further, all the women were reacting as expected, totally oblivious to everything around them, while furiously trying to pleasure themselves and other women, though they soon began to pester his men, as they began the massive cleanup work. The bodies of the thousands of dead men were hauled into air locks and shot out into the void of space. Meanwhile, his electronics men began establishing control of the space station systems, hacking passwords and redoing them. He put ten of his men onto the identification of the lone transport that had somehow escaped, confident no men were involved. The bio agent was terribly effective with the men.

Hours later, the transport was identified as being one used by one of the ambassadors. Knowing that, the Master sent out his ten men to locate the female ambassadors that were still here. Much to his surprise, Anka Polonia, Alis Anrhod, and Drina Celestina were all missing. That three powerful women had somehow escaped bothered him. Combined with the apparent escape of Linda Whitney and a couple of the 519th soldiers who had entered through the tunnel system caused the Master considerable worry. That wasn't supposed to have happened, and certainly, he didn't want the genetic experimentation that was being done there to be broadly known, not just yet. Worse, the clock was ticking. He summoned his top medical doctor, Hermann Meinenger, the lead geneticist at these facilities on Rho-C.

The doctor checked his watch. "Okay, we still have fifty-five hours left. We'll need to give the chosen women their antidote before that time is up."

"Don't worry. My men are going to start sorting them out as soon as they get the dead men dumped into space. What about those who invaded the tunnel, killed all our samples there, and took off with one of them?" the Master asked.

"They have about fifty-five hours left as well, Master, same as those who escaped from the station."

"Yes, but what if the changes hit them when they are out among the broad population of one of these nearby worlds?" he asked.

"Well, any doctor worth his salt will quickly be alerted to genetic modifications, if that's what you mean."

"So the cat will be out of the bag, if the process continues on their bodies and if they have landed on some world?"

"Aye, that it will. Now if we could get to them before that happens, we could either give them the antidote or kidnap them and allow the rest of the changes to occur," the doctor suggested.

"Good thinking. We know the names of three of those who fled this station. From all the evidence, those who escaped the tunnels met up with those three women and left together in one of the ambassador's deep space transports. Excuse me, doctor. I'm going to have to move fast on this one, if we're to keep our secrets for the time being."

He summoned ten of his top men and explained the situation. "We need to contain this if we can."

"So we're going to give them the antidote?" one asked.

"Hardly. No, we're going to kidnap them, let the modifications run their course, and then put them to good use. Now then," the Master continued, "I would suspect these ambassadors would likely try to land on one of their home worlds or perhaps one of the deceased ambassador's worlds. Each of you, take ten trusted men and go there at top speed. Start with customs. Surely, you will be able to identify them, once they pass through customs. You are going to Gemma-D; you have Taurus-C; you, Bellatrix-B; you take Zeno-C." He rattled off the rest of the ten major nearby worlds and sent them off, reminding them they now had fifty hours tops to find the group and get them out of sight.

***

The next morning, Jason felt really ill and didn't get up for breakfast, and then drifted into a coma. Dr. Gisa became very concerned, since his symptoms were quite strange. Hastily, she raced off to look at the lab results, hoping they would be back by now. Maybe they contained a clue to Jason's illness. At least none of the others had any symptoms. She felt terribly restricted by her heels, moving like a snail, she kept thinking to herself. She wanted to run to the lab, but simply could not. Once there, she made a bee line to the lab and brought up the results.

As she examined them, her stomach knotted into a tight ball! There was something foreign in all their blood, excepting that of Alis. Further, Jason's sample seemed to be somehow active. Then, it hit her: a DNA drug bomb! Each of them had some kind of time-release bomb in their blood stream, probably inhaled with the original bio agent, and it had then made its way into the blood streams via their lungs! Jason's had gone off! She knew she had extremely limited time remaining before her own and the other women's bombs went off, and there was only one possible cure: a complete blood transfer! Hastily, she called Alis with the awful news.

After explaining what was going on, she ordered, "Get all the others here to the lab as fast as possible. I'll arrange for complete blood transfusions right now. I have everyone's blood types already. You can thank your luck stars, Alis, that you had the sense to don that protective mask when you did. Your blood is clean, so you can watch over Jason. Linda's blood is clean as well. Lord knows what mutations will happen to his body now. Get the others here faster than fast!"

76

A bit later, she pulled every string, every favor ever owed to her here at the med lab. "Yes, I know, but there is a foreign compound in our blood streams. I believe it's a bio agent, but you can sort that out later, once we get our blood replaced. Yes, yes, I think it is about to activate. Lord knows if it will spread to others, but I seriously doubt it. It must have come from something we all breathed in back on the space station just before we all left," she explained to the head administrator. At least, he took the time to look over her blood work results. Then, he too sounded the general alarm.

Once everyone arrived, they and Gisa were rushed into a quarantined zone. A team of doctors and nurses, all wearing heavy bio containment suits, entered and began the slow process, doing all five at the same time, but making sure every drop of the contaminated blood was contained! Once done, they were then kept in a locked room under observation for another twenty-four hours, periodically quizzed about what they had inhaled. Fortunately, they all stuck to the same story. They'd noticed nothing unusual before they left the space station. Somehow, Jason's case was overlooked, much to Dr. Gisa's relief.

"Okay," the head administrator explained to Dr. Gisa and her friends the next noon, "your current blood work shows no more than a trace of the bio agent. You're free to go, but you're ordered to remain here in town for the foreseeable future. Apparently, Space Station Gamma-629 is not answering our authorities' calls. A light cruiser has been sent to investigate matters. So until they report back, you're ordered to remain here in the city. That is all. You're welcome to come and help us research this new and potentially deadly bio agent, doctor."

"I'll see. I should see to my friends first. Thanks for the offer," she replied. A half hour later, they finally entered their hotel room, but not before noticing there was now a pair of armed guards watching the entrance. Another pair of guards had followed them from the med lab.

"He's in a coma as best we can tell. How are all of you doing?" Linda asked the others the instant they entered the hotel room.

"We're fine. We caught it in the very nick of time," Dr. Gisa replied. "I best check on him now."

"It's awful," Linda whispered, following behind her into the bedroom where Alis was watching over Jason.

"Oh my God!" Dr. Gisa gushed. "What's happening to him?"

"Well, his arms are withering up. Linda expects them to fall off by tomorrow. His hair is like yours."

"Ah, they have neurons and axons in them, full sensory perception by feel," Dr. Gisa relayed one of her findings.

"Plus, his feet are going to be like yours as well, and he's developing good sized breasts as well," Alis pointed out the obvious, and then tried to be polite. "However, Linda and I have been checking on his reproductive organs. He is still male. No signs of a sex change, in spite of outward appearances. This is truly weird."

"Dear god, what have those monsters done?" Dr. Gisa exclaimed, wondering if this would have happened to all them had she not spotted it in time.

"I surely don't know, but we need to get out of here as soon as possible," Alis pointed out.

"Can't. They can't contact the space station and have us confined to the city until further notice. Two guards followed us back here from the lab, and there are two more watching the entrance. We're so screwed," the doctor lamented.

"Well, Linda had the good sense to get all our packages sent to our ship for us before all this happened," Alis explained. "So now we're just going to have to get inventive, but I suppose we can't do anything until Jason comes out of his coma."

One by one, the others peeked in to see the terrible changes in Jason's body. Then, they ordered a late lunch and began to think of ways out of this mess. Martha was ready to blast their way to the spaceport. The only flaw in that idea was her guns were back on the ship. As they talked, Alis realized if they were to get out of this one, she would have to devise a workable way.

***

78

At the same time, Tao reported in to the Master. "Boss, I found them. They're on Bellatrix-B. Complications. One of the escapees was Dr. Gisa Wolfgang. She brought them to the med center here in Bregenheim. They discovered the secondary bio agent and have undergone complete blood transfusions. Now that whole med center is on to this new bio agent. They have the group confined to their hotel for now."

"Ah, so that's why the authorities have been trying to reach us here at the station. I best answer their calls quickly. We don't need a battleship on our doorstep just yet," the Master replied.

"So what do I do about the group? Too late to kidnap them."

"Find a way to kill them outright. Got to go."

***

The next morning brought consciousness back to Jason, though he let out a muffled scream. "What's happened to me? My god!" He stopped mid-thought, startled by his own voice, which had raised an octave into the alto range, quite similar to that of Bess! Further, his hair was thick and fell to his knees when he finally got up. His cries came from his initial observation of no arms and of his bosom, which nearly identical to Linda's and the others as well. Hastily, he attempted to feel for his privates but his arms were gone.

Linda whispered, "You are still a man. At least that hasn't changed. Your feet are like ours too. See if you can get up and just let your hair fall down." She tried to help him get his balance on his toes, and she nearly began crying, because she felt so useless to help him when he most needed it. Just then, the others came running into their bedroom, expecting the worst.

"Help him to the mirror so he can see he's still a man," Linda insisted, feeling that alone might help calm Jason down. It did, at least a little.

"What's happened to me?" he asked again.

"Well, Jason," Dr. Gisa began, explaining about the delayed reaction of the second bio agent. She ended with, "So as you can see, your body is now that of a very attractive young woman, but you still have your manhood intact, so that's something. We have been thinking about this, and there's really no other option except for you to dress like us. It's not too terribly bad. You'll see. However, we're in a really bad situation right now."

This was too much for Jason. No longer could he withhold his raw emotions. He began sobbing, though Linda continued to encourage him, while Dr. Gisa worked on getting him into a gown that would fit his new shape properly, and more importantly, heels that helped them all walk significantly better. At the same time, Bess brushed out his hair. Holding a washrag in her teeth, Linda kept wiping his tears for him.

By the time that they had Jason dressed, room service arrived, and the group ate a somber breakfast, Bess feeding him, while Gisa helped Linda. After that, Drina explained in detail all that had happened while Jason had been unconscious, ending with their current plight. "So we're trapped here?" Jason sighed. "You should've just left me here and saved yourselves. Before I was darn useless to everyone, but now I'm completely helpless."

"Well so am I, Jason. They should just kill us and take off somehow," Linda broke in. Her own despair when she awoke to find herself armless was once more quite vivid in her mind. She knew precisely how Jason felt. Yet, she also had fallen in love with him and knew that he had fallen for her. That was also very real to her. Somehow, she had to help him over this intense despair, which is why she said what she did.

"No!" Jason snapped out of his misery. "I love you, Linda. I don't want you to die, not ever."

"I love you too, Jason, and I don't want you to die either. Somehow, we have to survive."

In a flash, Jason saw just what Linda had done. A bit of a smile creased his lips. "You rascal!" he teased. "Okay, okay, what are we going to do?"

Seeing Jason slightly more alert, Alis spoke up, "I've a plan. Dr. Gisa is going to take us all to see the Natural History Museum. It's not too far from the spaceport where we left the ship. Of course, the guards will be following us, but with some luck, we might be able to ditch them at the museum. Gisa knows of a back door we might be able to use to sneak out and make for the spaceport. Worth a try."

Drina added, "One of us will keep our arms around you, Jason, and also around Linda. We can't risk either of you taking a nasty fall. Walking in these extreme heels isn't easy or fun. We go slow and careful. Take no chances. If we can't lose the guards this trip, we'll try another place, but according to Dr. Gisa, this site is the closest to the spaceport. So let's get ready and give it a try." She hoped her pep talk was encouraging enough.

A few minutes later, the group walked towards the main lobby exit. Here, Dr. Gisa paused briefly by one of the guards. "I'm taking my friends on a tour of our Natural History Museum, in case you lose track of us. Back around noon, we hope." The guard nodded, but eyed all the women, definitely admiring their stunning beauty. Outside, Dr. Gisa spotted a tourist bus and quickly arranged for it to take them to the museum. Already Jason was complaining about how hard walking was for him, though Linda kept telling him he'd soon get used to the heels. Just before the bus left, two guards hopped on the bus, joining them, but staying at the back of the bus. There weren't any doubts now that they were being kept under a very close watch.

As they began wandering the marble floored halls of the museum, Dr. Gisa began chatting, telling them about how she used to come here once a week when she was a little girl. Jason and Linda soon began to enjoy her lighthearted banter, taking the acid edge off their plight. Fortunately, the guards stopped near the entrance to wait for them to finish their tour.

After walking around for an hour and finding the side rooms and the stairs that led to the exit, they found themselves on the second floor, here sort of a balcony overlooking the main entrance area. The two guards were down there by the entrance, but two more had joined them, a bit disheartening to the group. Just then, ten other men walked up to the guards. Without warning, the ten men fired blasters, dropping the four guards in seconds!

The group stood there stunned for a moment, trying to grasp just what had happened! "Quick, back up. Into this side room," Alis whispered her orders, keeping an eye on the ten men. Fortunately, they had not yet spotted the group. Inside, they found themselves in a janitor's closet.

"They just murdered our guards!" Dr. Gisa exclaimed, shocked and surprised.

"I know. Okay, they have guns and we don't. Obviously, they mean to kill us, so ideas?" Alis asked.

Jason looked around, and a big smile appeared, but then vanished as quickly as it came. Bess saw it and asked, "Jason, you had an idea?"

He sighed. "Well yes. There's more than enough stuff in here to make a nice explosion, a bomb, or two, but now I can't do it."

"Okay, tell me what to do," Bess ordered. Jason started explaining, but then decided to tell her what to grab. Before long, everyone who could carry something had their hands full. "Now we should get to that exit door and make the bomb there," he explained.

Carefully, the group opened the janitor closet door. All clear. Dr. Gisa led the way, cursing the noise their heels made on the marble floor, but there wasn't any way to muffle that. When she reached the back stairs, she stopped. Jason said, "Okay, everyone but Bess and me, get down and ready to open the door. I know; it's going to sound the alarm." He gave Bess step-by-step instructions, making sure he wasn't rushing her, but also not wasting a second, which he figured would be precious.

With the mixtures made, he had her place the reused containers of janitorial supplies along the sides of the hall just above the steps. The tricky part was stringing the critical trip wire, but Bess had explosives training and handled this aspect with ease. That done, she helped him down the stairs where the others were waiting very nervously.

"Ready?" Alis asked, and Jason nodded. Dr. Gisa opened the door. A loud alarm sounded, but the group headed out onto the street, where soon the sounds of police vehicles coming to the museum drowned out the museum's alarms. They hadn't gone ten feet before the ten men discovered their location and dashed down the stairs after them. Boom! A brilliant explosion shattered the glass on the doors they'd just left, sending shards flying outward in a rain of death. Fortunately, no one was around the area.

They continued to walk from the museum, but Jason said a quiet, "Boom!" Linda chuckled. After going a block, Alis hazarded a backwards glance. No one was following them. A mile later on, they walked into the spaceport and on out to their transport. Luck was with them. No one thought to post a guard on their deep space transport. Alis entered her security code and opened the bay doors, ushering everyone inside. While many helped Jason and Linda get buckled in, Alis fired up the engines, but didn't bother getting takeoff clearance. She knew she'd not get it, but she was clever. Before lifting off, she entered hyperspace coordinates that would locate them perhaps a hundred feet from this location, but in hyperspace. As soon as the transport lifted off on its own power, she hit the Execute button, and the ship lurched into the safety of hyperspace.

Alis yelled, "We made it! We're in hyperspace. Bess, fire off our video. The galaxy must see what happened on the space station and on Rho-C!"

"On it now!" Bess yelled back. "Wow! That was close. Good going, Mr. Boom Boom," she teased Jason.

Linda whispered to him, "See, you can still create explosions. If you hadn't, we'd all be dead." She leaned over and gave him a loving kiss.

"Maybe it's not completely hopeless," Jason admitted.

"I'm in!" Bess relayed from the transport's comm center. "Sending now." A few minutes later, she called out, "Done! Now the whole damned galaxy will have a firsthand view of just what the corporations have been doing and done! Take that, you fiends!"

A bit later, Bess rejoined the others in the passenger seats. "You know," she felt like chatting some, "my nose isn't slightly offset any more, and my left ear is the same size as my right one now."

"Hey, my eyebrows are even," Drina admitted. "Before, one was slightly crooked, kind of embarrassing. I got teased about that when I was a little girl."

"My ugly mole is gone," Anka admitted. "Must be this

new bio agent they used on us was designed to make us all look like perfect women. But what I want to know is why? Why go to all that trouble?"

Linda answered her. "I read a psych study once that said that more attractive and perfectly formed females attracted better husbands, but I don't know if that psychobabble is really true or not."

"Well, if it is, why turn five thousand women in the space station into fashion models?" Anka asked. "Have they got five thousand men desirous of such women? I hardly doubt that." The group chatted about this aspect for a time, but no one had the slightest clue.

Dr. Gisa then said, "What I wonder is what would have happened to our bodies if we hadn't gotten that bio agent thing out of our blood streams?"

Linda was pondering what Anka had asked. When Dr. Gisa's subsequent words registered, an overlooked, insignificant memory surfaced. "I bet I know!" she exclaimed. "I once overheard the men discussing how they were going to make use of thousands of armless, but gorgeous women in their breeding program. I bet anything you would have ended up just like me, armless and helpless. Now I wish I knew what they meant by their breeding program. What are they breeding? Surely not more helpless women."

Dr. Gisa spoke up, "Well, our DNA has been altered, so our children will likely inherit from us. Question is, will our children be as gorgeous as we are? Don't know on that one. Say, wait a minute. What will male children look like? Damn, I wish I could see what they're actually doing." She felt frustrated.

Drina added, "You and all of us too. That's a very good question. Breeding means having babies. So what will those male babies look like? I bet they won't be armless as we're supposed to be. Damn, what were the corporations trying to do on Rho-C anyway?"

"Make super-good looking women," Jason teased.

Martha put in, "I hope they don't come out looking like those giant men we had to shoot!" That was a sobering thought. "Anyway, my feet are killing me. Can we take a good long break for a while? Bess, anything for a foot massage!"

Alis sensed the adrenaline rush was long gone and fatigue was setting in. It had been a near-death experience. "Okay, why don't we all turn in early? I'll make some supper later on. Tomorrow we can decide where we go next." She got no arguments.

A bit later, Linda and Jason lay side by side, facing each other on their bed. "See how wonderful we can feel with our hair?" Linda pointed out.

"That's not what I really want to do just now, but I wonder if I still can?" he whispered back. "You sure you don't mind that I look like a woman now?"

"Hardly. Come on; we have to do it! I really, really need your love, Jason," she whispered back. She knew this would be a crucial time for them, if only they could manage without having to have the others come help them. An hour later, neither had any further doubts.

After breakfast the next day, the group met to discuss their next move. Dr. Gisa tossed out her wish, "I would like to have the chance to study our DNA and what's been done to us and the others, but I'd need a fancy labs."

"Well, I just want to have a chance to use Gertrude on the bastards," Martha voiced her desires. "How about you, Bess?"

"Well, I really love construction work, though I know it's going to be hard trying to work as I am now. Still, I'd like to try," Bess said, adding, "But if there's a fight, you can count me in, if Jason will direct me in making bombs."

Drina and Anka looked at each other, and then Anka spoke for them. "We both look so different than we did before, so we would like to see if we can't do some covert spying. You know, gather intelligence on these corporate bigwigs and such. Someone's got to help stop them—somehow, someway bring them to justice."

"What about you two?" Alis asked Jason and Linda.

Linda answered, "Jason wants to help make explosions that count, and I want to help anyway I can, only I really don't know how I can honestly help anyone much. Back I my cell, I was teaching myself to use my toes as fingers. Perhaps, if I could somehow do that, and Jason too, we'd be more useful. Still, we need so much help with nearly everything."

Alis reached a decision. "You know, in ancient times, when they unleashed those terrible bio agent attacks, some of the geneticists worked on partial cures for the victims. Maybe we can get some together and do just that for all of you."

"Count me in on this!" declared Dr. Gisa without any hesitation.

"Well, my contacts tell me there might just be such a place. I would caution you all, there may well be far, far more going on that we've just seen. I think Drina and Anka have a point. We need to do much more investigating," Alis cautioned.

"I agree," Martha spoke up. "Look, that's what the late General Franco failed to do. No recon. He just charged in there like a bull in a glass factory. If I was in charge, I'd of done a full recon of the area, learned about the beasty wormy things, the giant wolf-like creatures, and so on. Then, take the right countermeasures. Hell, if he'd just dropped a few giant bombs on the area first, he could have killed off those wormy things and saved half of the regiments. So yes, we really need to do much more investigating, if we can." She liked the way Alis put it and echoed her words.

"Okay then, let's go check out this potential, secret rebel base, shall we?" Alis asked. Everyone agreed, and she headed up front to set the coordinates.

Chapter 6—The Devil's Resistance

"So where are we going?" asked Ambassador Drina. Alis returned from the pilot's seat, suggesting they would be arriving in eight hours.

Alis smiled at the ambassador, and then answered, "Scorpi-C," knowing the reaction she'd get, since Drina Celestina was the Scorpi-C ambassador on the rim space station.

"What? My world? But," Drina failed to complete her thought. *I'm their ambassador. There's nothing on my world except the many corporation headquarters.* "This can't be right, Alis."

"Trust me, but I've been told we're going to have to switch transports before we get there. This one is logged out to me and is now on the corporation's hot list. If I land it on any civilized world, we'll be arrested immediately, so we've got to ditch it. The resistance is going to handle that for us. We're to swap ships on a remote moon in two hours."

"You're kidding me? The resistance is on my own world?" Drina asked incredulously.

"That's what my sources claim. They've arranged a meeting with us when we land at Malagena, along the seacoast," Alis answered.

"Yes, Malagena is on the coast, our second largest city, twenty million or more at last census. Alis, I just can't believe this. Malagena has at least fifty corporation headquarters there, at least the Scorpi-C branches of these giants. Are you sure your sources are right?" Drina complained, quite unwilling to believe such a thing as this.

Right on schedule, they landed on what appeared to be a deserted moon. However, as they began the landing sequence, Alis spotted a small domed structure and smiled. "Well, this is interesting," Drina commented. Alis had her sitting in the navigator's seat beside her. "Clever and impossible to detect unless you know where to look."

The domed zone, the only inhabitable area on the

atmosphere-less moon, was about a mile across, with a small landing bay and some fifty metal, first-contact type of buildings. Drina saw an older transport close to where they were setting down, presumably, she thought, their new, untraceable ship, and she was right. Once they lowered their bay ramp, a masked man called out, "Alis?"

"That's me," she yelled, making her rather slow walk to the bay from the front, Drina on her heels.

"Okay. That one is your new ship. Need help transferring any cargo?" the man asked. She replied that they did, and four other masked men joined him, moving the recently purchased apparel and a few other items over to the new ship. Meanwhile, the group made their precarious way down the ramp, with Bess and Dr. Gisa assisting Linda and Jason, for whom going down the ramp in their extreme heels was even more challenging. By the time they were settled in their new transport, which was definitely an older model that had seen much use, the men had transferred their packages. Alis thanked the men and headed up to prepare for takeoff, with Drina right behind her.

"Yep, those are the right coordinates for Malagena," Drina confirmed, adding nervously, "I sure hope you are right about this. If not, we could be heading into the lion's mouth!"

Six hours later, the large coastal city of Malagena, Scorpi-C, loomed large on their monitors. Scorpi was another yellow main sequence star, and the planet was sixty percent covered in oceans. Magnificent cloud banks were visible, as they neared this world, one of the more populace of these outer rim worlds, and one of the wealthier too. Here, many of the top corporations of the galaxy maintained sector headquarters, from which they ran subsidiary branches on many of the other rim worlds in this sector. So yes, Ambassador Drina had good cause to be concerned and downright worried about this move.

Alis got landing instructions and followed them, touching down on Pad 1023. Some fifty other transports were in the queue for landing or takeoff, for this was a very busy spaceport city. Once down, Alis opened the bay doors and waited. Presently, a handsome, tall, thin man with black hair and moustache came walking up to them. He wore an immaculate black business suit, typical of corporate leaders. Drina inhaled sharply as she saw him, recognizing the man at once!

"Ah, ex-ambassador Drina Celestina, I do believe. My, how your appearance has changed, and for the better I might add. So pleased we're able to meet once again. Oh, forgive me. I'm Diego Hastas, corporate legate for the Galactic Dynamics Corporation."

"You know him?" Martina whispered to Drina. "Should we shoot him? Is this a trap?" She still carried Gertrude, even though her arms now had half of the muscles she used to have and was only barely able to hold the massive gun up in a firing position.

"Yes, I know him well, but I don't understand," Drina replied. She stood there confused, while the others looked around for security guards, expecting to be shot or arrested.

"Please everyone. No cause for alarm, not just yet. I've come to get you through customs, bypassing all security measures. Believe me, the corporations have their forces out looking for you, but they don't expect to find you here on Scorpi-C, of all places. This is their home base in this entire sector. Very heavy security and all that. Please, if you will follow me. Oh, I'm told that you have some packages with you. I'll have a man pick them up directly."

Carefully, the group descended the ramp, while Diego's eyes studied each woman carefully, but he couldn't tell which one was Jason. They all looked like top super-models, but then he expected that they would. They walked a short distance to a waiting airbus with the GD logo on it. Diego opened the doors for the women and watched them enter, paying close attention to Linda and Jason though. He shut the doors and entered the driver's section. "I'll be taking you to a secret staging area. There I am to question you. If all is acceptable, then you'll get to meet the boss of this operation. Settle back. Drina, you can point out the sights as we travel."

Nervously, she did just that, though she soon began enjoying pointing out some of the more famous sites of her home city to her friends. She also kept track of just where they were going, in case this went south and she needed make a fast escape. Soon, though, any hopes of an escape were dashed in Drina's mind. They were heading towards the GD headquarters building itself, a hundred-story structure with a massive GD logo that revolved on top, along with numerous antenna for communications. The base of the building occupied an entire city block!

Diego lowered the airbus and slipped on down the sloping ramp that led to the underground parking decks. He stopped before a set of basement doors. "We're here," he announced. Drina became even more nervous, but she didn't see any security guards, only the secure doors. Blast doors, Jason observed, estimating they were likely also Class G, almost impossible to breech. So no need of security men here, a point that eluded Drina just now.

Once everyone was out, Diego swiped his card, and the thick, steel doors opened. "We're in Meeting Room One. This way." Soon, they entered a plush room with the typical modern decor of glass see-through chairs and giant table. Pitchers of water and glasses sat on its top. Subdued lighting filtered from the ceiling. Of course, there were spy cameras in all four upper corners, but Diego flipped a switch, and they turned off. Then, he took out another device, showed it to Drina and Alis. For the benefit of the others, he explained, "This is a scrambling device. No one can possibly listen in on our conversations or even spy. If anyone has a recording device on them, it will fail to operate. Hence, here we're totally secure. Please have a seat. Some water, perhaps."

He sat down and watched the others, noticing who was helping Linda and Jason. He then asked for formal introductions, which Drina provided. That formality done, he explained, "Well, you seven have certainly shaken up the corporations! That video of yours has gone viral, in spite of the corporations' attempts to squash it. All sorts of clandestine Net sites are replaying it. Let me tell you, you've certainly gotten the attention of the corporations, and us, as well. I should explain the us. We're called La Resistencia del Diablo, or simply RdD for short. Yes, Drina, our group operates within the corporations themselves, trying to bring them to justice.

Hence, all the secrecy. If you pass my test today, then the local head of the RdD will be meeting with you later on. Now then, I believe you have also attracted the attention of another resistance movement, one that we call El Contrario, for lack of any other information on them."

"Let me explain further. You see, the 519th Infantry Division attacked the new stronghold of El Contrario and were defeated, except for a few of you. These secretive men are using tactics that we in the RdD find despicable, inhuman, highly unethical, and downright illegal. We know very little about their organization, except they're dedicated to the total destruction of all the corporations in the galaxy. Frankly, we estimated it was a million to one odds that you were even able to get off Rho-C, and another million to one odds that you could avoid the genetic bombs you carried in your bodies, and we're all stunned you were able to avoid their ten man hit squad there on Bellatrix-B. They outright murdered four guards there at the museum, but they managed to get killed or wounded and captured when your makeshift bomb went off— another million to one odds that you could have escaped El Contrario's hit squad. So you see, you definitely have our attention as well as two others. I'll be frank with you; El Contrario wants you terminated, while the corporations want you interrogated and probably then terminated. You've made some remarkable adversaries in such a short time."

He went on, "And yet, you've managed to expose to the galaxy just what the corporations were doing for close to two centuries there on Rho-C. Simply amazing. Now then, we've done a thorough background check on each one of you. We want to know just whom we are dealing with, you see. Can't be too careful in our situation. Now then, Drina, Anka, and Alis, for you three, there is no going back to your former positions as ambassadors for your worlds. If you make any such appearance, the corporations will have you arrested, and well, I need not elaborate. Bess, Jason, Martha, your official military careers are over. There's no chance you could return to your positions, obviously. Dr. Gisa," he explained.

She interrupted him, "I know. If I show my head again, I'm as good as dead, but all I want to do is to study these genetic bio agents and try to find cures and such."

Diego grinned, "As I suspected. That can be arranged, if you so desire. Finally, we come to you, Linda Whitney. You were a senior in the Academy, studying astrophysics, and hyperspace navigation."

"Well yes, but then I found out what the corporations were hiding from general knowledge and began protesting. You can't believe the vital information they're suppressing about our galaxy and navigation," Linda blurted out.

"Yes, we can, Linda. I take it that you were kidnaped?" he asked.

"Yes, and then they did this to me and kept me locked in my padded cell for six months. I had to watch the suffering of so many others. Thank heavens that Martina here did as they begged her and put them out of their misery. Honestly, no human should be tortured like that—I mean no arms and no legs. It was awful," she explained in a rush of words.

"So do you still want to help bring the corporations to justice?" Diego asked.

"More than ever, but I'm so helpless now. Still I want to help somehow," Linda answered, "just as Jason here does."

"Okay then. Are you all willing to join the RdD and help us in our fight to bring the corporations to justice and not by using the evil means that El Contrario is using?" Diego asked. Everyone agreed. "Good. I accept all of you into the RdD. Now then, it is time that you met our leaders and learn a bit more about what has been going on with the corporations and Rho-C. Please wait here while I bring them to you."

They helped themselves to some water and waited patiently, though no one said anything. Each was lost in their own thoughts, none more so than Drina. Her surprise and shock was even greater when Diego returned with the two leaders. "These are our leaders, Alfonso and Carmela Vega," he announced as they entered. Drina gasped. He was her boss and had hired her! She'd never met his wife before though.

Alfonso looked the image of a top corporate bigwig. Tall, thin, handsome, with short brown hair and small goatee, he wore a very expensive light grey suit with polished black shoes that reflected the diffuse light. He was thirty-seven. His wife was thirty-four, but she cut a shocking figure. Like Linda, she had no arms, and her wavy blonde hair fell to her knees as well. She too wore the extreme heels, and she was gorgeous, just like the others! Linda gasped, as did Jason. She wore a light red, satin gown and black nylons. Her tall heels matched her dress, and she wore light makeup that added to her stunning image. Alfonso helped her get seated and then took his place beside her and Diego.

He began by saying, "Well, Drina, I take it our secret has most definitely been a secret."

Drina's mouth opened a bit before she found her voice. "Yes. I had no idea, none. I just can't believe this. You, the resistance."

He chuckled. "In our game, looks can be very deceiving. Now then, considering that all of you have been genetically modified, I'll share what little we know about this. Mind you, it cost ten brave men and women their lives to get us this much key data," he said very seriously.

"Research on Rho-C, the genetics research, began long ago. Corporate honchos wanted only the finest looking wives. We believe that initially the researchers were charged with finding ways genetically to modify normal women into stellar beauties. Lord knows who established just what a stellar beauty actually was, though obviously they must have had some pretty good ideas." He glanced from woman to woman, as he said this, while his wife merely smiled.

Carmela added, "Part of a woman's powers over a man lies in her beauty, though obviously beauty is transitory. We all age."

"Yes, and that was their initial hurdle. Once a woman becomes the equivalent of a top model, she begins to get her way with men. In order to weaken their control over men, the geneticists hit upon the genetic removal of their arms. The scores of years of experimentation have yielded their final product, which is called a UFB. In their lingo, it stands for Ultimate in Feminine Beauty. Please take note. This is critical, these UFBs. Linda here is one, as well as my charming Carmela. Mind you, most all the top brass in most all corporations now have a UFB wife, by either marrying one or having their wife genetically modified. It cost the ten their lives to find out why."

He went on; his audience was listening intently. "The UFB was only half of the picture. They also wanted to have super-men running or working within the corporations. Apparently, two distinct male models emerged from their think tanks. One has a powerful fighter-type of body, well-muscled, and burly. The other has a brilliant mind or very high IQ. We surmise, but it is as yet unverified, that these high IQ men are being bred to ultimately run the corporations, while the fighter types will be their top enforcers."

"Now here comes the wild part. They have to breed these two types. While we also first thought the whole genetic engineering project was just to create the UFB women, we were so wrong! Ten died to get us this next bit. There is also a UFBMD! I hate to tell you this, but Jason, you are officially a UFBMD. That is their designation for Ultimate Feminine Beauty Male Donor. These are reproductively men, but the rest of their bodies are nearly indistinguishable from a UFB, as you can all see right here, just looking at Linda and Jason, a UFB woman and a UFBMD man."

"So what is the significance of these two genetic modifications? This we have only recently learned at great cost. It is a breeding grid. Further, as you all have probably already observed, you have an intense sexual drive. That's part of the genetic modification, an incredible urge to breed to create more children, which you will see why now." He drew up the following chart on the whiteboard so everyone could see it and memorize it.

```
     Female    +    Male       =    Female Child or
Male Child
     UFB       +    Normal      =         UFB      or
Super Fighter
     Normal +    UFBMD       =         UFB      or
Super IQ
     UFB       +    UFBMD       =         UFB      or
UFBMD
```

"You see, the UFB female can have either a super fighter type of male child or she can have another UFBMD male child. Breeding a UFBMD man with a normal woman yields one of their super IQ men. Plus, breeding a UFB and a UFBMD together yields more of the same. By the way, twins are not uncommon. So what the corporations are doing is establishing a breeding program to perpetuate their powers in major ways."

Martha barked, "God damn! So does this mean I'm one of those UFB women now? Shit! What do they think we women are? A bunch of cows or pigs?"

Carmela answered her, "Martha, we're not totally sure in your case. You see, you, Bess, Drina, Anka, and Dr. Gisa were likely given one of the earlier versions of the genetic bio agent. Thank heavens you discovered the real UFB bio agent in your blood streams and got it out of your bodies before it could work its magic. So to be wholly honest with you five, we just don't know. For sure, though, your children will inherit your beauty traits, probably very beautiful girls, and perhaps handsome men. Time will tell on that one. I seriously doubt your children will give rise to their super type men, unless you mate with a UFBMD. Then, all bets are off, since we lack any genetic data about such unions."

Carmela flirted with her eyes a bit and then teased everyone, "Of course, if you are all willing to experiment with Jason and Diego here, we could see what your various offspring will become." Martha growled, but several laughed. Jason didn't though. She added, "So we're at least a century behind these genetic engineers and have to play catchup. Dr. Gisa, your help will be most welcome indeed, if we are to get any kind of handle on this situation."

"Hey, just how far have they carried this hellish thing?" asked Drina.

"Ah, good question," Alfonso answered. "We do know this breeding program is widespread, though obviously kept very secret. We do know or suspect many major corporations have their own in-house programs in full operation. Carmela is an example of this. I had to accept her as my wife, before I could have my position at GD. We have fifteen-year-old twin girls, Chita and Gabriella, both UFB, like Linda and Carmela. We have twin fourteen-year-old boys, Salvador and Tristan, who are definitely going to be burly, strong men when they finish maturing, and we have a twelve-year-old son, Velasco, who also promises to be like his older brothers."

Diego spoke up, "I'm married to Consuela, who is a UFB as well. We have twelve-year-old twin UFB girls, Estrella and Gracia, and a ten-year-old son, Tonio, who will likely also be a strong fighter type. So you see, we have living proof of at least one line in that breeding chart."

Alfonso continued, "Until this moment, we have never gotten our hands on one of the UFBMD men, like Jason here. Thus, we have no proof of the workability of the other two breeding unions. As I understand it from Alis, Linda and Jason are in love. If so, we might get some data down the line. We could get more, if Jason is willing, or if you women are willing to mate with Diego or me, but that's not a requirement. You're free to choose your own mates. We're not the corporation men."

"Count me in on this research!" Dr. Gisa exclaimed.

"We already have, doctor. Now then, this El Contrario group," Alfonso continued. "We just don't know much about them at all. We do know they have some outside connections and by force have taken over the research station on Rho-C. However, we do know all the major research data and a fair amount of samples were evacuated before the planet was lost to El Contrario. That happened about ten years back, which is why I sent you, Drina, to Space Station Gamma-629, Abelard Sector. I had hoped you would have uncovered relevant Intel on this group, but they are extremely secretive and apparently made little use of this nearby station."

"Now, we know they attacked the station, but we didn't know they had a bio agent that targets male bodies only, killing them in short order. That's shocking news indeed. Believe me, news of that has shocked the corporate leaders. We've been in a dozen meetings about that in just the last few days."

Martha interrupted, "So they think these El Contrarion men will use it on them, wiping out the corporate men? How appropriate is that, eh?"

"It would throw the galaxy into chaos. Not so good,"

Alfonso replied. "Then, there are those incredible new animal-like species you caught on your video. We know nothing about them or such bioengineering that occurred on Rho-C. Do they represent a serious threat or not? No one knows or they aren't saying during the corporate meetings."

He went on, "Drina, you weren't the only spy I had in place on the space station. Unfortunately, six of my men perished, but five women likely survived. Each has a locator chip in their neck, so we're hopeful we can at least learn their locations. Best case scenario, we might be able to rescue them and learn much more about El Contrario and their plans."

"Now then, let's talk about what each of you can do. Mind you, we will be setting up new disguises for you, along with substantial bank accounts and housing. Dr. Gisa has already volunteered to work in our genetics program. Drina, Anka, you both have much experience dealing with others as ambassadors. We'd like you to consider doing more of the same, that is, spying for us. Alis already has her next mission worked out by her employers, so we don't have to worry about her."

"Well yes, I would like that very much. I used to think I was good at that," Drina replied.

"Same with me. If I can mingle with the right crowds, I should be able to find out key information," Anka added.

"Good, good. Martha, Bess, let's come back to you in a minute and focus on Linda and Jason first. Jason, I know you're an explosives expert, and that is your passion. Let's face facts though. Right now, you are severely restricted along that line. I know with Bess's help, you can still operate, as witnessed by your handling of the ten assassins there on Bellatrix-B. But you and Linda are in very unique positions, as a UFB woman and a UFBMD man, you could easily be inserted into GD's headquarters and uncover far more intelligence about what is going on with their breeding programs than I or Diego can. Honestly, if you choose to go this route to help us, I assure you that you would be treated like royalty by other corporate heads."

Linda answered, "Well, we aren't good for much else. I say that we should do it, Jason. If we can find out more, that has to help everyone. This way, we won't always feel so darn helpless."

"Okay with me, as long as I don't have to make love to anyone besides you, Linda. Maybe we can be married. Will that help?" he asked.

"Absolutely," Carmela spoke up. "At least, the corporations are still honoring marriages, though how much longer they will, remains to be seen."

"Excellent, Linda, Jason. I'll work on the arrangements soon. Now then, Bess and Martha. If they are going to stick their necks out this way, I'd like them to have some backup protection. Would you two like to volunteer to be their guards and helpers? You might like to carry a slightly smaller gun though, Martha."

"Sure. That way, I can blast anyone who tries to harm them," Martha declared. "Hell, all I really know how to do is shoot well. Besides, if we need an explosion, Jason can direct Bess. That worked to perfection before. What's ya say, Bess? You game too?"

"Well, I like to help others, but I'd prefer construction details. Maybe sometimes I could help out repairing things too?" Bess added. "Don't get me wrong, I can fight too, but I wasn't a combat engineer though."

"Good. I'm sure there's plenty of repair work to keep you busy too, Bess. I think this is going to work out well for all of us," Alfonso declared. "Admittedly, things were a whole lot simpler when we only were facing the corporations. This El Contrario mess is turning out to be very nasty indeed."

He added, "Just before we walked in here, I received a coded message from a spy on a light cruiser out of Bellatrix-B. They arrived at the space station and found it completely deserted! No men, no women, but the armories were looted, and some of the computers and comm equipment were missing, but no trace of the tens of thousands of people who were there before the attack. We're talking about animals who stoop to genocide. That's what I call the mass murder and genetic mutations," Alfonso barked angrily.

"Gone? All those women?" asked Drina.

"That's not possible," Anka declared. "We saw them

making love to each other, insanely though. There were thousands of women and dead men everywhere."

"That's the latest report I have," Alfonso justified. "Something is going on out there that we know nothing about, but we damn well better and soon."

Diego then spoke up. "There's one last detail to discuss, though I'm not sure how you're going to take this, but here goes. We do have some partial genetic cures available, though none for Linda and Jason, I'm afraid. We have no idea whether they'll affect your children or not. It's possible for the neurons and such in your hair to be removed, as with your nails. It's also possible to undo the super arch in your feet so you could wear normal shoes again. This can't be done for Linda or Jason, though. We just don't know the full ramifications on the rest of you, who have been exposed to the old genetic bio agent. It certainly won't undo all the other changes in your bodies."

"Well, not having to deal with this hair and these impossible heels would be terrific," Drina declared. "The hell with the rest. I can live with it. It's unfortunate Linda and Jason can't have them. Lord knows how hobbled up they are."

"True, true, but if they are to do their spying work, they have to remain pure UFB and UFBMD," Alfonso justified.

"Well, fix me up, baby!" declared Martha. "Then I really can do a good job protecting Linda and Jason. You too, Bess."

Quickly, Anka, Drina, Bess, and Martha accepted the offered cures. Linda and Jason kept quiet, valiantly keeping their wild emotions at bay. Observant Carmela saw how hard they were suppressing their emotions and spoke up, "Linda, Jason, I've some good news for you as well. Since you are going to play these roles, I want you to know the corporations do supply some very useful devices that each of you can use to help get by better. Some are pretty darn cool. I'd be lost without them. I know, doesn't make up for your arms, but they do help me feel far more human. I'll show you how to operate them, once we get you settled in." Both were able to smile a little. She'd given them a wee bit of hope that their lives wouldn't be so dismal. At the very least, the group understood much better what had been going on and why. That was precious to them.

Chapter 7—In the Lion's Den

Six months ago, two best friends, Melissa Whitehall and Jackie O'Riley, both twenty-two, had joined the RdD, hoping to help make a difference against the unethical corporations. Why? They'd watched the insensitive corporations devour their parents' small business, the manufacturing of replacement ball bearings. The dual-family business was a small one, but provided a nice life for the two families, that is, until corporate greed struck them. After that fiasco and bout with corporate lawyers, their parents sold out, but died within a few months, devastated by the loss.

Blonde Melissa and the fiery redhead Jackie joined up and were given an assignment on Space Station Gamma-629. By day, they worked as maids, cleaning the quarters of Commander West and other top officers. Thus, they did their best to keep the RdD informed of station activities, though after six months, neither thought much at all was truly going on. This space station had seen better days. Besides, there wasn't much to report that they thought significant, just a lot of ambassadors chatting and the fact that one of them was holding card games with some enlisted personnel and civies.

Then came the terrorist attack. When the pair awoke from their comas, the inbred lust nearly drove them mad, as they did their best to pleasure each other sufficiently. Only then were they able to get up and see what was happening beyond their cabin quarters. What they saw shocked them. Everywhere they looked, the men were dead, and the women were acting as they had, sex starved maniacs. After that frightening shock, they returned to their cabin and used their tiny communicator to relay what was happening to the RdD. That done, they waited for a rescue.

Much later, strange men appeared on the station, armed men, hostile men. From their cabin, they ventured a peek at what was happening. At first, the men worked on removing all the dead men from the station. Jackie was brave enough to ask one what they were doing with the dead. "Out the air lock," came the reply. They returned to their cabin, very much afraid.

Later on, other men came by and inspected them. Already their hair had grown and thickened. Melissa's blonde hair was somewhat wavy now, reaching her knees and very much sensitive to touch. Jackie's fiery red hair was slightly wavier, likewise reaching her knees. Both noticed small facial feature changes, Jackie more so, since her freckled face was now clear of all freckles. In fact, they looked much like supermodels, something that they chatted about in their cabin. They spent some time studying their new features in their mirrors. The man said only one thing to them, after eyeing them up and down. "You're to remain in your cabin. You will be UFBs." Both asked what that meant, but the man merely left them in mystery. Not long after that, both slipped into a coma, along with half of the surviving women. They didn't know the others had received a shot that prevented the genetic bio agent in their blood streams from activating.

They awoke and screamed, just as thousands of others did. They were armless, but had no idea if there had been any other changes. This was shocking enough. They were together in a small room, but entirely naked. Someone had slipped the needed extreme heel pumps on their feet. They were lying on a soft, wide bed. Across from the bed were a small table and two chairs. To the right was a sink with a single lever to control the water flow, a toilet, and next to that, a shower, again with a single lever control. Overhead, soft lighting provided a pleasant illumination. There was one door, but armless, neither could turn the knob to open it.

After crying their hearts out, they got up and inspected their new surroundings. A bit later, a man entered with a food tray. "Food," he said, placing the two plates on the table, along with two glasses with straws.

"But we can't feed ourselves now. What is going on?" Melissa wailed.

"Pretend you are dogs. Eat." The man was gruff and promptly left.

Much later, the lights dimmed, and another pair of men entered. "Lie down on the bed. We're fucking you," one ordered. Both screamed and protested, but armless, they were helpless to prevent the rape. Besides, their bodies seemed to crave the sexual satisfaction. When they finished, the same man said, "We'll be back until you are pregnant."

Both women cried "No," and then sobbed bitterly, helpless to do anything about it. Each morning before breakfast, a man came and tested them, pronouncing them pregnant on the third day. After that, they were spared further rapes, much to their great relief. However, each day was the same as the next. Thrice daily, a man brought them food, their only outside contact. The rest of the time was theirs to do with, as they desired. At first, they took long showers, trying to wash off the filth of the rapes. After that, they relaxed and tried to figure out what was going on, especially since they were now being wholly ignored.

Tremendously bored, Jackie decided it was time to find out what was going on. "Look, we use our feet to get the doorknob turned and opened. We work together and get out of this place," she suggested. Escape was far easier said than done. Still, they worked with their feet and finally got the hang of how to do it. Working together was essential. They slipped on their heels and headed out of their cell room.

They were in a very long hall. Glancing up and down it, they saw countless doors just like theirs. Looking back on their partially opened door, they saw two red tags with the word 'pregnant' written on them. Glancing at some of the nearby doors, they spotted several more. "They must have put many of the other space station women in here with us," Melissa whispered.

"But where's here?" Jackie wondered, her curiosity pricked. Down the long hall they walked, thankful it was carpeted, muffling the clicks of their heels. They reached the door at the very end of the hall. It was locked, but they could see through the upper glass portion and saw they must be underground. Stairs led upwards. Rebuffed, they turned around. Far down at the other end was another exit door. "Let's count the rooms as we go," Jackie suggested.

When they reached the second exit door, each had counted forty rooms on their side, making eighty all told. "If they have two of us in each room, there must be a hundred sixty of us down here," Melissa estimated. Looking through the glass of the door, they saw several push carts, probably used to distribute the food plates. One held a pile of dirty breakfast plates. To the right of the carts, they saw an elevator. Beside the only button marked 'Up,' they saw a small sign that said 'B-5.'

"Does this mean there are five levels like this one? That would make eight hundred of us down here," Jackie asked rhetorically, since they had no way of knowing just now. "Let's see if this one is locked." It wasn't and a few minutes later, they had it opened, their heels back on, and were standing before the elevator. Jackie used her nose to push the button, and they waited, fully expecting some guard to come and toss them back in their room. None came. The doors opened, and the two stepped inside.

Looking at the array of buttons, they had many potential choices. Labels listed B-5 up to B-1. Those were followed by G, and then the usual numbers up to twenty. "Gosh, this must be a very large building," Jackie suggested. "What now?"

"Let's not go to Floor 2, since it says Laundry beside it, nor Floor 3 which says Kitchen," Melissa replied. "Why not go to the top?" Jackie giggled and pressed the topmost button with her nose. Up they went.

When the door opened, they saw a long hallway with giant windows at its end. Along the way were four very large office suites. Since the hall was empty, the two headed down to the windows to see what they could see. Again, no one stopped them. When they reached it, they gasped. Before them lay an entire city. As far as they could see into the distance, skyscrapers rose up, but at varying heights. Tiny people were on the streets far below. Shuttles darted about some of the buildings. However, neither woman recognized the city, but from its size, they presumed it had to have at least a million people or more living here. "We're not in the space station anymore," Jackie whispered, awed by the city. Freedom was just beyond the glass, yet so unreachable.

Reluctantly, the pair retraced their steps and returned

to the elevator. On a whim, Jackie pressed G and then B-5. "Hey, we can get a peek at what's on the ground floor." Melissa giggled and held her breath. Down they went, but stopped on the ground floor. When the doors opened, both women were shocked by what they saw. It was the office entrance of some company! Ahead they saw doors that led out into the street. Just as the doors closed, they glimpsed an emblem off to one side, the insignia of the Galactic Electronics Corporation! Both swallowed hard.

Minutes later, they entered their own room and shut the door. "We're in the GE Corporation's headquarters building? How can this be?" Jackie gushed, no longer afraid of being silent. Now the two really did have something to ponder and discuss. Had the corporations been behind the terrorist attack of the space station? The women were more confused than ever.

***

Twenty-three year old Captain Juanita Lia had been Commander West's Communications Officer when the attack came. She bunked with their twenty-four year old cook, Corporal Marita Cruz, who ran the kitchen staff for the commander's small officer's crew. Both had been on duty when the attack came. When Juanita came out of her coma, she screamed, not because of her suddenly knee length blonde hair, but rather because Commander West and all the other men in the comm center were dead. Walking on her toes rather precariously, she began searching for survivors and finally found Marita in the kitchen, just coming out of her coma.

After some discussion, both decided to make for their quarters and try to figure out what to do. Should they break into the armory and arm themselves? Prepare for a fight? However, once there, their unnatural sex drives took over, possibly from having seen so many others madly trying to satisfy anyone around them.

Later when the men arrived, they were told to remain in their cabin, which they did. After that, both fell into their secondary comas. This time when they awoke, they screamed loudly, shocked and terrified to find themselves armless, naked, and lying in some strange bed. Yes, their subsequent experiences were pretty much the same as with Melissa and Jackie. Their room layout was quite similar, as was their treatment. They too were repeatedly raped until they got pregnant, a week later. Finally, they were left entirely alone. Several days passed until the two were convinced they weren't going to be raped any longer.

"So what are we going to do, captain?" Marita asked, deferring to Juanita's higher rank. After all, she was the officer, not her.

"Well, we sure as hell can't fight back, not like this. We've already resisted the men as much as we could." She shuddered. It had been utterly futile on their part. They couldn't even stand up much without wearing the extreme heels, let alone impact the men in any productive way. Kicking them in their nuts only brought hard slaps to their faces.

"Reconnoiter. Find out where we are. Find out what is going on. Then we escape," Captain Juanita declared forcefully, though just how they could accomplish any of those objectives eluded both women for several days. The doorknob posed their first major hurdle, and they stared at it for hours at a time.

"Captain, I can't live like this—helpless I mean. We can't even open a goddamn door. Hell, I can't ever cook again, so why are we even bothering with all this? Besides, even if we escape, then what? How can we possibly live? We should have just died like the men," Marita asked and then broke down once more.

Juanita sat down on the bed beside the sobbing cook. She couldn't even put comforting arms around her fellow soldier. "I know. We can't live like this, Marita, but maybe we can live just long enough to get justice for those who did this to everyone."

"I want revenge, but I know I can't possibly get it. Hell, captain, I can barely walk," Marita continued to sob.

Captain Juanita couldn't think of anything else to say and merely repeated herself. It was either that or give into the swelling grief building up inside her. "Reconnoiter. Escape," she said. "Come on. First step: door." She walked slowly and carefully to the door.

She tried opening her mouth wide and turning the knob by biting down on it and twisting her head. After a dozen failed attempts, she succeeded. The door opened. That singular action temporarily snapped the cook out of her grief fit. She too rose and joined the captain, looking out into the long hallway filled with many identical side doors. "We're not alone," Marita whispered.

Since the hallway was empty and silent, Captain Juanita decided to reconnoiter further. "Down the hall to the far door," she whispered. Once more, walking slowly and carefully, the pair moved silently down the carpeted hallway. When they reached the door, through the glass they saw an elevator. Once more, the doorknob barrier took Juanita several minutes to manage, but her will was now steeled. Minutes later, the two stood before the elevator. A small placard read B-5. She pushed the lone button with her nose and waited.

She flinched when the doors opened, half-expecting to see a man with a gun pointed at them. The elevator was empty, and the pair stepped inside and looked at the control panel as the doors closed. There were six buttons, five of which had B-numbers, and one simply had a G on it. She used her nose to press G and up the pair went, more or less holding their breaths, expecting the worst.

The doors opened revealing another long hallway, again carpeted. This time, the carpet was badly stained and long overdue for a thorough cleaning. Nearby stood a row of pushcarts, one of which held a pile of empty plates, just like those that they were given three times a day. Still, they saw no one and headed on down the hall. They passed a set of swinging doors. They stopped and peered through the small windows and saw a number of women working in a giant kitchen. The two recognized one of the women, having seen her about on the space station. They moved on down to the next doors and peered inside. Here other women were washing dishes. They moved on.

At last, they reached the lone exit. Once more, they peered out and saw there was a world outside. Beginning to get the hang of how to turn the doorknobs, Juanita opened the door in half the time that she had on the previous ones. The pair stepped outside and saw what appeared to be some kind of military camp. Being soldiers, their first reaction was to hunt for cover. To their right, they spotted an airbus, currently empty and resting on the ground.

Walking on the relatively uneven ground was difficult, and the two wobbled wildly to keep from falling, but their efforts paid off. They reached the airbus and stepped behind it. A concrete wall was just behind them. "Acceptable concealment" raced through the captain's mind. "Observe, Marita," she whispered. The pair each took a different direction and began doing just that.

In the far distance, Juanita spotted a huge kennel housing a large number of what looked to her like giant wolves or dogs. Then, she spotted a number of poorly dressed troops milling around. Certainly, she thought, these can't be real soldiers. They are a disgrace to the uniform. She spotted another building and recognized the symbol on it: munitions dump.

"Over here," Marita whispered. Juanita joined her and peered around this edge of the airbus. She saw what looked to be a medical laboratory of some kind. At least, it had the universal medical symbol emblazoned on its front doors. The building stood five stories tall, a stone and glass structure. Next to it was some kind of dormitory. Beyond that structure, she saw a Class V Portable Field Power Generator. Just past that lay an airfield. A number of two-man shuttles were parked there, as well as a couple of deep space transports.

"There's our way out of here, Marita," Juanita whispered. "We need a distraction. If we could blow up the munitions dump, that might tie everyone up."

"Duh, aren't you forgetting something, captain? No hands," Marita brought her back to reality rather hard. Tears trickled down Juanita's cheeks. Oh how she wanted to blow up that ammo and perhaps take some of these "animals" with them. She turned her head back towards the transports, mostly so Marita couldn't see her crying. "Someone's coming!" Marita whispered, attracting her attention. Carefully, both women backed up a bit and ducked down so they were as hidden as possible. They heard voices.

"The Master has ordered the pregnant women to be moved over to Facility B tonight. We'll use the airbus there. 18:00, that's when we're to do it."

"Crap. Why move'm? Whole lot o' work for nothin'. Must be a reason."

"I think the doctors are over there in B. I heard they're bringing in some more women for us to knock up. This sure is a cushy job. We get to mess with them as much as we want until we get 'em knocked up. I hear we'll get to do it again just as soon as they have the babies."

"That's what I heard too. What I don't get is what the Master wants with all these babies."

"Haven't you paid any attention at the meetins'? Their babies are going to be special—something about super-fighters and all. Mind you, I ain't seen one of them. They keep the ones that are ready somewhere secret. I heard they can't be stopped by a blaster shot, but that's got to be weed talkin'. Super strong might be more like it."

"Hell, we'll be old men 'fore these babies grow up."

"Hey, don't worry. The Master takes good care of us. We didn't lose a single man when the 519th attacked the old center couple days ago."

"Damned worms got most, I heard. Wolfs too." Both men laughed and moved away from the airbus. "Say, where's the Master at these days?"

"Heard that he's with the others stripping the space station." The two women couldn't hear anything else the men said, as their voices faded off.

Juanita returned to looking towards the airfield. "Okay, we make for those green dumpsters next. Is the coast clear on your side?" It was, and the two walked carefully, but pitifully slowly across the space to the two tall garbage bins, ducking behind them. While Marita kept watch the way that they came, Juanita plotted their next move.

Just as they were about to head off to get to the back side of the windowless building they were next to, a man walked up close to the bins and took a leak spraying the wall, before zipping up and walking back out beyond the airbus.

Adrenaline was flowing in both women, who kept as still as possible. When he disappeared, Juanita nodded, and they again made their way across the rough ground, ducking behind the backside of the building.

Luck continued to follow the two soldiers, as they continued to move from cover to cover ten more times, finally drawing close to the airfield. Hiding behind four large barrels, they peered out onto the airfield. Two guards were patrolling the outer perimeter, quite some distance from the pair. Juanita decided they needed better cover. She spied a maintenance shack. "When they turn around and walk away from us, make for that shack. We'll hide in there for a while until we can get to one of those transports. Idiots have left the bay ramps down. Guess they want to move out in a hurry. Okay, they've turned. Come on. We have to get inside it before they turn back this way or we'll be spotted for sure!"

They made the shack but ducked behind it. There was a padlock on the door. Peering cautiously from either backside edge, for a time, the pair spied on the two bored guards. By now, their stomachs were growling. "Hey, maybe they'll leave to get lunch," Marita suggested, wishing that she had some right now. For her, this whole body modification had cost her close to twenty pounds. She felt skinnier than she'd ever been since she was a child. Then again, perhaps she was feeling the effects of being pregnant, which she'd never been before and wished she wasn't now.

She guessed right. Within a few minutes, the guards headed off, leaving the airfield unguarded. "Fools!" whispered Juanita, and the two began crossing the tarmac, moving between shuttles, using them for cover. Ten minutes later, they approached the nearest transport. Taking deep breaths, they made their last dash, heading up the ramp, though a dash is a gross understatement. They could barely walk and then only slowly. As soon as Juanita got up the ramp, she used her nose to press the Close button and headed on up to the pilot's seat. Marita followed right behind her.

"Shit! This would be trivial, but not now," Juanita cursed.

"Maybe we can use our toes. They're just buttons and

switches after all. But what coordinates do we use?" Marita asked.

Juanita knew that they had to act fast. The instant she fired up the engines, the entire base would react, probably shooting them down. Worse, she didn't know any particular hyperspace coordinates. They were just long series of abstract numbers, which, when she needed them, she looked them up. Inspiration struck. "Hit the Current Location button. When the numbers appear, hit Set." She began using her toes and nose to flip the startup sequence switches, knowing for good or ill, this was it. Either they made it or they would be killed. Well, just now awkwardly struggling to do this with her toes and nose while her long hair constantly interfered, she was ready to be killed. Life was almost impossible.

The engines came online. "It's set, but what does it mean? Oh shit! Here come dozens of men running towards us!" Marita yelled.

Using a foot, Juanita hit the liftoff button. Unable to hold onto the flight control joystick, the transport began moving around rather wildly, alternately touching the ground and lurching upwards to the left or right. At the same time, the computer drolled out, "Warning: force field above preventing takeoff. Warning: force field above preventing takeoff."

Instantly, Juanita knew what that meant and now the purpose of that Class V Portable Field Power Generator! It was powering a miniature-domed force field protecting this entire base. No ships could pass in or out through the field, preventing any sudden assault by outside forces. It also prevented her from flying away from here, assuming she could somehow regain control of the stick, which was moving about as the transport bobbed this way and that.

Marita sighed. "Okay captain, I'm ready to die. We can't possibly live like this."

"Hit the Execute button!" Juanita yelled, her body bobbing wildly from side to side as the ship lurched around, totally out of control, all the while trying to lift itself off the ground. Neither had anyway to fasten their safety belts to hold their bodies more or less still nor did they have the arms to grab onto something, let alone the stick itself. Only with great effort was Juanita able finally to bang her head into the Execute button.

Both women felt a lurch that threw them backward solidly into their seats. Then, the world outside the windows went entirely black, the deep void of hyperspace. "What just happened?" the cracking voice of Marita wailed. "Is this what being dead is?"

"It worked!" Juanita yelled excitedly, and then calmed down, seeing the startled look on her friend's face. "We just made the jump into hyperspace. We're safe. We've escaped! Marita, we made it!"

"What? Safe? Escaped? Really? Where are we?" Marita asked, trying to adjust her racing mind over from certain death, dead, now alive, and even free.

"We are still just above the ground at that base, only we're in hyperspace."

"Huh? Then, we've not really escaped?" Marita asked growing even more confused.

"We are free. Actually, that's about the only way we could have gotten away, Marita. That force field would have prevented us from manually flying away from there, but instead, we bypassed the field entirely by jumping into hyperspace. Now all we have to do is figure out the coordinates of where we want to go, enter them, and we're off, assuming we have enough fuel, food, and water to get there. Why don't you see if there is anything we can eat, while I try to find some coordinates?" Juanita asked, giving Marita something useful to do. She didn't dare mention if she couldn't find coordinates, they'd be stuck here and have to land right where they'd taken off.

What should have taken her minutes to do, a thorough search of the ship, its computers, and its memory unit, took Juanita well over an hour, as she struggled with her toes and sometimes her mouth and nose to look around. Finally, she got a computer up and lists of coordinates being displayed. A glance at their fuel status told her that they only had half left, but that was more than enough to get nearly anywhere in this rim sector of space. Just where to go was her big question.

Juanita knew she couldn't return to her base on the

space station. With everyone dead or kidnaped, there wasn't any help there, and besides, if what those men said was true, their leader was on the station stealing equipment. She decided to head to their home world of Scorpi-C and report to her previous boss, Major Garcia de la Vega. At least, he might recognize her, though she knew she and Marita looked very different now. Even their facial features had changed. Carefully using her toes, she entered the long numerical sequences and then verified them. Satisfied, she hit the Execute button again. The ship lurched a little, and she used a foot to slide the throttle up to maximum speed.

Marita joined her, carrying an entire loaf of bread between her teeth. She dropped it in the empty navigator's seat. "I got a block of cheese too, but only one mouth. Might be easier if we ate in the galley."

"Great. I'm starving. We're heading for home, Marita, Scorpi-C. Be there in two hours. Come on; I'll bring the bread."

A bit later, they were sitting around the small galley table with the bread and cheese before them. Marita whined, "We got bread, but we can't get it out of the damned plastic sack!"

"You hold it with your feet, and I'll rip the plastic with my teeth," Juanita suggested, too hungry to pass up the bread. Just smelling it made her stomach ache even more. Together, they began to succeed.

They'd just finished eating when an alarm sounded. They were receiving an incoming call. Automatically, the comm system put the call on speakerphone, since often the comm center personnel would be away from their positions. The two rose and made their way to the comm center, listening to what the voice was saying.

"Hello deep space transport thieves. This is the Master calling." His voice was deep and mellow. Something about it seemed to transfix both women, who listened to his every word. "I know you are both pregnant and armless. Please, by now you must know you simply can't fly the ship. Your safety and that of your unborn children are most important. I don't want anything bad to happen to either of you or your babies. Please, switch off the autopilot. Then, my men here can fly the transport safely back to the base, where you will be well fed and cared for, and your babies will get the very best of care. Do it now. Turn off the autopilot."

His voice was hypnotizing. If the autopilot switch was here in the comm center in the middle of the ship, Juanita would have done so at once, but it wasn't. It was up in the pilot's area. His voice was soothing, compelling, and irresistible. Juanita knew he was right. She couldn't fly this ship, just look at her bungled takeoff. Her baby would be safe.

Baby? Safe? Raped! Those three ideas drifted into her mind in that sequence. Raped brought both women out of the mesmerizing spell the Master had woven over them. "Raped! God damned bastards! You'll have to kill me first!" Marita screamed, his spell over them broken. The transmit button wasn't pressed, so the Master didn't hear her outburst, but Juanita did and shook her head from side to side, shaking off the spell-like voice.

"The hell we will, Marita! No way. We're going home," Juanita declared and struggled to get a foot up to flip the disconnect call switch. Finally, after nearly falling over, she turned off the call. "Take that and stuff it!" she barked angrily.

As they approached Scorpi-C, the ship dropped out of hyperspace, hovering above their home world nearly stationary, since that was their initial speed when Juanita had tried to liftoff from Rho-C. Using her toes, she got the comm center turned on and began making frantic calls.

"Emergency. Emergency. This is a transport ship in orbit calling Major Garcia de la Vega at the Military Base 1492 at Malagena. We need help now. Emergency assistance requested. This is Captain Juanita Lia assigned to Commander Bill West's Communications Center on Space Station Gamma-629. Please, anyone, we need emergency assistance. Come in, anyone." She repeated the message before she received a reply.

"This is Scorpi-C Command Center to unknown deep space transport. Captain, state your ID number and the nature of your emergency. Your call is being routed to Major de la Vega. Over."

She answered hastily, adding, "We have lost our arms and can't fly the ship, except on autopilot. We were kidnaped, our bodies somehow modified, arms removed, and raped on Rho-C. We escaped in this transport, but I can't fly it. Everyone on the space station is dead or kidnaped. Help us. Over."

A new voice appeared. "Captain Lia, this is General Vasco Manuel. We know about the space station and the assault on Rho-C. Turn off the autopilot, and we will take control of the transport and land it safely. Can you do that? Over."

"Yes. Give me a few minutes. It's hard to do. Over," Juanita answered. "Marita, you stay here and talk to the general, while I see if I can turn it off." She lunged to her feet and made her slow, careful way up to the front, while Marita sat down, identified herself and began a running account of what had happened to her. The cook talked as fast as she possibly could, figuring if they were about to crash and die, the general should know what they did.

An hour later, the transport was safely on the ground at Scorpi-C Command Central, Malagena. It was surrounded by six security vehicles and an ambulance. The general and many armed soldiers stood waiting the appearance of the two women. A man had already opened the bay doors, watching as the women made their slow way to the bay. When they appeared, several gasped, but some whistled. The men saw two stunningly beautiful young women with knee-length, wavy, black, and tangled hair, naked, but wearing the tallest heels most of these men had ever seen.

The general ordered, "Get them into the ambulance. Get them covered. Hospital pronto. We'll question them there." Seeing the extreme difficulty both were having trying to come down the ramp, two medical men moved up, picked them up, and carried them to the ambulances. They were whisked off to the base hospital, where a team of doctors began examining them.

The general did allow the doctors to finish a cursory exam before he and his staff moved them aside. "Okay, Captain Lia. I must insist on a full report immediately. Are you aware the entire 519th Infantry Division was wiped out during their assault on Rho-C? What do you know about the attack on the space station? Details, captain, details!"

For an hour, Juanita relayed all that she knew and what they'd discovered on their own, with Marita adding bits here and there. She gathered the general didn't know of this Master fellow, and he asked far more questions about him than she had answers for. When the general was finished, he ordered the doctors to do a full medical examination on both women and a complete DNA analysis, but he was not to give them their requested abortions, not just yet. "And find them some suitable clothing," he added.

By 19:00, the women had been thoroughly examined and found to be in perfect health and pregnant. Initial DNA results showed they had been genetically altered, but were ninety percent likely to be the women they claimed to be, even though facial recognition software didn't match their current faces to those on file. Someone had found dresses that fit reasonably well on them, plus they'd been fed a hot supper. Now, they were ushered into another meeting room, this one, extremely fancy.

When the two walked in, they saw General Vasco Manuel again, but he also had two men dressed in very expensive, black suits: corporation executives. Of that, neither woman had any doubts. The general began the briefing.

"Captain Juanita Lia, Corporal Marita Cruz, on behalf of Scorpi-C's FMF, I wish to thank you for the incredible job of intelligence gathering and reporting that you've done at grave risk to your own lives. You will be receiving the Distinguished Service Medals soon. That said, considering your current physical situation, I've no choice but to medically discharge you from the service with appropriate discharge pay. Without arms, you can't fulfill your duties, obviously. As of now, you are both civilians, but very special civilians, I'm told. I turn the meeting over to you, gentlemen." He rose, saluted the two women, and left the room.

"I am from the GD Corporation. He's from the GE Corporation. We're executives. Now then, as the general just said, you are both very, very special young women. You have been exposed to a genetic bio agent that has drastically altered your bodies, in very good ways, we might add. If you haven't yet noticed, you are both now extremely attractive women; top super-models would be most envious of your physical forms, perfect in all ways, like one in ten million women, that is, except for your arms, obviously," the man from Galactic Dynamics explained.

He continued, "Any babies you have will naturally inherit your genes, and thus your female children will also be unimaginably perfect as well. That said, you can see why we wish you to reconsider having your current pregnancies aborted. While the circumstances of their conception were deplorable, your children will be fabulously beautiful and have so very many more doors open to them when they reach adulthood than the ordinary children. Please, give your unborn children this incredible opportunity for life that is denied to most women."

The man from the Galactic Electronics Corporation interrupted before the two could respond. "That said, we should focus now on your futures. You see, as two genetically modified, perfect women, many, many new doors of opportunity are open to you. Many executives at Galactic Electronics Headquarters would give anything to date either of you, with the goal of marrying you in mind. Yes, you both most definitely can be married to nearly any executive in almost any of the major corporations, though we would prefer it if you chose executives here on Scorpi-C, rather than moving off-world. We'd like to keep your beauty here on our world."

"So you see, ahead of you both is the luxury life as a corporation executive's wife, a luxury denied to nearly all women, but one that is fully open to both of you. You would have servants to attend your every need, the finest living accommodations to be found anywhere on our world, the finest foods, the finest entertainments, and the finest husbands. All that is asked of you is to have many beautiful children by your husbands. How could you possibly turn down such a fantastic offer, eh? After all, if you don't, on your minor military severance pay, you won't even be able to hire a servant, let alone be able to work and earn a living. You are both entirely helpless now. We corporation executives are offering you a grand life."

The executive from the Galactic Dynamics Corporation broke in, "One other thing we're obligated to explain to you is there are some limited genetic cures available for victims of genetic bio agent attacks, which you both are, no question of that. It may be possible to undo the genetic changes to your hair and to your feet, but little else can be undone. Certainly, there is no way to regain arms again. I'm afraid those are gone for good. However, I must also point out if you opt to have any of these two cures, then you will most definitely not any longer be desirable in any way by the corporation executives. You would then have to make your own way in the world, which as helpless women would be next to impossible to do. So you see, you really don't have any choice but to accept our offer and become wives of some corporate executives. How could any woman turn down such a golden opportunity for a life of utter luxury?"

Some of what the men said greatly appealed to both Juanita and Marita, neither of whom had time to come to grips with their situation. Events were unfolding at too rapid a pace for them to grasp. They'd just been kicked out of the FMF minutes ago, and now this offer seemed too good to be true. However, some of the phrases the two men used stuck in these two independent, military women's minds. They had just done the unimaginable and escaped their captivity. Somehow, that didn't quite jive with "helpless" and "impossible." "Have many children" sounded more as if they'd be breeding cows or something. That there were some cures, but that they couldn't have them, also bothered both women. In short, the offer just didn't sit well with either woman.

"Look," Juanita spoke her mind, "we've just endured nightmare traumas, have somehow managed to escape, have just been discharged from our careers, and need to have abortions—we don't even have clothes or a place to stay yet. This is all just too much too quick. Besides, having this hair handled and our feet not screwed up would make our lives vastly easier to endure. Are you executives a bunch of sadists in not wanting us to have better lives? You have to give us time to think about all this. We're not a couple of brood mares for you executives. Hardly."

"She's right. I'm not some cow," Marita added testily. She didn't like some of what the men were implying, though the life of luxury did appeal to her, and yet she was far too independent, well had been at least.

"Sorry you feel this way. It doesn't matter. You don't actually have any choice in the matter. You will become a wife of a corporate executive and bear him many children, period. You'll come with us now. We'll be taking you to a temporary safe location and be seeing to your immediate needs before the execs decide who will be marrying you. Come on; up you go," the executive from the Galactic Electronics Corporation ordered, grumbling and whispering that all this pleasantness had been a waste of his time.

An hour later, the protesting women found themselves in a penthouse suite on the top floor of a skyscraper in downtown Malagena. A young servant woman joined them and began bathing them, while room service brought up a late night snack. Although the two protested, there wasn't anything they could do about it right now, especially when they saw the men locking the exit doors when they left them in the care of the servant.

At least the woman was kind. She washed and de-tangled their hair and was quite gentle with them. She proved skilled at feeding them as well, before tucking them in for the night. Juanita guessed she'd done this before, probably working for other women like themselves, and she was right, though the servant said very little and didn't answer their questions.

The next day, packages began arriving over the morning hours. Dresses and extreme heels, nylons, and undergarments galore came, and their servant insisted on getting the pair properly dressed. "You want to make a good first impression on the important men," she said, but nothing further.

"Well, Marita, looks as if we're going to have to escape a second time," Juanita whispered to her friend, when their servant was in the other room.

"No kidding, but this time where will we even go?" Marita countered. "Maybe we should play along. What else can we do? We're helpless, really."

"I'll be damned if I will go down quietly, Marita. Men. Always thinking with that thing in their pants!" Marita giggled, so true she thought.

Chapter 8—The Musician and the Dancer

"We got trouble, boss," Diego reported to Alfonso. He'd been the GD executive interviewing the two surprise escapees, Juanita and Marita, along with Mr. Corazone of Galactic Electronics, a man Diego detested. He went directly to GD headquarters when the brief interview was finished, and Corazone had whisked the protesting women away to the safe house, one of their corporation's penthouse suites for visiting executives. "They balked at Corazone's offer. Kind of figures. They are or were quite independent women. Had to be since they were in the FMF forces."

"I figured that might be the case. Did you tell them some cures are available? How did they react to that?" Alfonso asked. For him, that was the key reaction he needed to be able to make the decision he knew he had to make.

"I think they want them. It was rather interesting. After hearing the execs wouldn't want them if they had the two known cures, Juanita called him a sadist. It was all I could do to keep a straight face. Plus, both want abortions. Hell, I can't blame them for that. Who wants to have a rapist's child?" Diego answered and grimaced.

"Okay then, I hate to do it, but we're going to have to whisk them out of GE Corporation's hands and into ours," Alfonso reached his decision.

"That'll be risky. GE knows they are UFB women, and they aren't about to let go of them, not without a fight," Diego advised.

"I know, I know," Alfonso lamented. "Yet, there's one angle we can still use. Marriage. GE execs won't touch them if they are married. Our task will be to extricate them from the safe house, explain the situation to them, get them quickly married, and the cures done, if they truly want them—all before GE finds them again. Tricky business. We'll need acceptable young men to pull this one off. You devise a way to get them out of that safe house, and I'll see what I can do about the rest." Diego nodded and left. He had planning to do and fast. He was certain the GE execs would pounce on these defenseless women in short order.

***

The servant woman had both Juanita and Marita bathed and their hair washed and dried the following morning. The arrival of the apparel was perfect. She proceeded to dress each as befitting a corporate executive's wife, complete with fancy nylons, ignoring the women's constant protests. She even resorted to slapping Juanita when she continued to wiggle in a useless attempt to stop her from putting the nylons on her. By noon, she had both women properly attired. Once the noon room service came and she fed them, she could leave and go home, since the GE executives were due to drop by in the early afternoon to inspect the "packages."

Hearing the knock on the door followed by, "Room Service," she unlocked the door and let the busboy push the cart into the suite, turning her back to the open door. She felt a pinprick in her neck; her hand went up to touch the spot and then blacked out. The busboy caught her and carefully laid her on the floor.

"Juanita, Marita, we're here to rescue you out of the clutches of those corporate men. We're offering you complete freedom of choice. Will you come with us now? There's no time to lose. The executives will be coming by to pick you up and add you to their harems in less than an hour," Diego explained to the two women, confused by the sudden collapse of the servant woman. "Don't worry about her; she'll only be unconscious a few minutes."

"Okay. We don't want any part of those corporation men. Real freedom? Who are you anyway?" Juanita took charge, still playing the captain's role.

"Part of the resistance movement. We have doctors waiting to handle the abortions if you wish that done and to deliver the known genetic cures if you want them, but we must hurry. Are you game for this?" Diego asked. His companion entered the room, but stood guard waiting to see what the women wished.

"All right then. We don't have any choice but to trust you. You don't look like the grubby men that the Master man

122

had and you don't look like those corporation men who questioned us yesterday. No, wait a second, you look," Juanita suddenly recognized Diego, even though he was wearing a busboy's outfit today and not his executive suite.

"Keen eye, Juanita. Yes, that was me in disguise. We had to find out if you wanted to become a harem wife of the corporation men or not. Coming?"

Juanita smiled. *If he can do that, surely he is cunning. Either he wanted to abscond with me for himself or he is being truthful. I sure as hell don't want any part of that GE Corporation man.* "Okay, we're coming."

Diego and his helper brought out two cloaks and fastened them over the two women, hiding most of their hair and their bodies. "This way, you look like ordinary women for now. We're going out the back service elevator." He put a steadying arm around Juanita, while his helper did the same with Marita.

They left the room's door wide open and headed down the hall to the service elevator. Five minutes later, the four flew across Malagena in a large shuttle. They stopped at Orchestra Hall, of all places, rather startling Juanita, who recognized the building, though she'd never been in it. After helping them out and getting them in a back door, Diego took his leave. "I have to change and make an appearance with the corporation executives when they find you're missing. He'll take you inside to the boss man. Perhaps I'll see you later on. Best of luck, ladies." He turned and headed back to the shuttle.

The assistant said little, but led them down a hall to one specific room. After opening the door, helping them inside, and removing their cloaks, he assisted them to get seated, moving their hair out of the way for them. "He'll be here shortly." He then left, and they never saw him again.

Alfonso stepped into the room and introduced himself. "Now then Juanita, Marita, let's talk business. I'll tell you what all I know about what's going on, and then you can better judge the situation." He outlined just what the resistance, the RdD, was doing, and what the corporations intended to do with the UFB women and their breeding program.

"Oh my God! So that's what this is all about! Freaks.

They want us to breed bunches of freaks!" exclaimed Juanita. "Shit! All those women back on Rho-C—that's why we were raped. They're nothing more than cows to be bred! Marita, we definitely want this thing in us aborted!"

Marita shuddered. "Shit yes! Get it out of me soon! I could kill them if I could, the filthy bastards. So the corporations are doing this to us too, not just that Master fellow. Shit, shit, shit!"

They talked some more before Alfonso explained his plan to save the two women. "First, about the only thing the corporation men still acknowledge is marriage. If you both were married, they would forever leave you alone. Single, you would still be targets."

"But what if we got those cures?" Juanita asked. "He said the execs wouldn't want us if we did that."

"He was right; they wouldn't. However, what they would do is simply kidnap you, expose you to that genetic bio agent a second time, and then you'd be whisked off to be someone's wife," Alfonso explained.

"Bastards! All them are lying bastards!" Juanita declared.

"Indeed. So here's the plan. I've lined up two young men about your age. With your permission, of course, they will marry you, officially, but at the same time, divorce papers will be signed, but just not filed. That way, if later on, you find you want out of this pretend marriage, you can do so simply by having the papers filed. In the meantime, once you're formally married and your status updated, then the corporations will leave you alone, forgetting about you both," Alfonso explained the heart of his plan.

He added, "What you do with these two young men is up to you. They aren't married now and haven't been, but honestly, both are quite nice. They are artists, and they work for the resistance as well. They will honor your wishes in this pretend marriage, whatever they might be. You have nothing to lose and everything to gain. Will you go along with this plan to put you forever out of the corporation's reach?"

"Sure is a funny plan, but absolutely I'll go along with it. I don't ever want anything to do with those sadistic bastards,"

Juanita agreed. Marita did so as well.

"In that case, let me introduce you to your new 'husbands,'" Alfonso said, flipping a switch on a small comm device, which Juanita recognized was a simple electronic signal, nothing more.

Two young men walked in. Both were a couple years older than the two women. They wore normal street clothes, nothing fancy. Neither was particularly handsome, but both had an air about them that Juanita couldn't quite put her finger on. "Juanita Lia, this will be your husband. He is Gervasi de la Roche. By day, he's the first violinist of the Malagena Symphony Orchestra, but by night, he is a major in the resistance movement. Marita, this is your new husband, Guilermo Torres. By day, he's a dance instructor at the Malagena School of Dance, but by night, he is a captain in the resistance. Ladies, are they acceptable to you?"

"Sure," Juanita said looking Gervasi over and giving him a smile. Marita agreed as well.

"Good. Time is critical. I've a minister who will perform the ceremony immediately. We have the papers ready to be signed, officiated, and filed. Doctors are at the ready to handle your needs as soon as we're done here. After all that is handled, they will escort you to your new homes for now. With any luck, by tomorrow the corporations will leave you both alone for the rest of your lives," Alfonso explained.

The ceremony took all of five minutes, but the paper signing took ten, with two witnesses brought in to sign the document for the women. Both men also signed the divorce papers as well, but Alfonso held on to them for the women. "Okay, you fellows know where to take your new brides. Get them safely to the waiting doctors. I guess you'll have to wait and see how long the doctors will want them in the medical facility. Ladies, I leave you in very good hands." He rose and left.

"I'm sorry, Juanita. I've never been around someone like you, so I don't know what you need. Please, just tell me when you need something. We have two small shuttles waiting outside."

The two found the men were very considerate of their

needs, bending over backwards to help them, but they were observant, and the two seldom actually had to ask for help with something. Twenty minutes later, they walked into the secret medical lab of the resistance, where a doctor and his staff were waiting for them.

"Yes, I want this foul thing growing in me removed immediately," Juanita replied to his first question, rather emphatically so. Likewise, Marita.

"Good, good. Now about the cures. Our geneticists are only able to reverse two things that have been done to your bodies. We can get your feet turned back to normal, and we can get the neurons and axons out of your hair so that it can be trimmed to whatever length you desire. I'm afraid that nothing can be done about your missing arms. Total arm prosthetics are hardly worth bothering with, completely useless in my opinion."

"We can hardly walk like this, so we want our feet fixed up," Juanita declared. She looked at Marita and added, "We're not so sure about the hair just yet. Can we get it done later on or do we have to decide today?"

The doctor smiled. "Any time, ladies. You can have it done any time you choose."

"Okay, feet fixed for now," Marita spoke up, and Juanita agreed.

"Gentlemen, they will need to be here until about this time tomorrow. You are welcome to stay with them or you can return tomorrow and pick them up. Your choice," the doctor explained.

"I'd like to stay with you, Juanita, if you don't mind. We can chat and get to know each other better," Gervasi suggested. Both women liked that idea, somewhat worried about being alone and so helpless.

Two hours later, the women were in their recovery room, and their new husbands joined them. They had to remain off their feet for twenty-four hours while the bio agent worked its alterations to their feet. So both remained lying in their beds, while Gervasi and Guilermo pulled up chairs and sat beside their wives. At first, the fellows just allowed the women to talk and soon got to hear about everything that had happened and what the pair had done.

When Juanita finished relating her lengthy story, Gervasi said, "You know, I could use a good captain for my Comm Center. I've a friend who tells me he can set up a voice-activated system you could use to run my communications setup. Are you game to give it a try?"

"Well, sure, but I don't know how useful I really can be, not anymore," she replied.

"I think we just have to make some adjustments to how we live life. I never expected to be married. I spend much time practicing my music, but this is so much more important. So I promise to do my best with you, Juanita. Many of us have lost much to the greedy and unethical corporations. They wiped out my parents. Dad worked for them for years, but they assigned him a dangerous job, he was severely injured, and they just dumped him because of his medical bills. He died after losing his house, and mom, well she took a bottle of pills. I was at the Music Academy, and when I found out what was happening, it was too late for me to do anything, though looking back on it, I'm not sure I could have done anything useful for them. Instead, I joined the RdD and am doing what I can to counter the works of the corporations."

"I'm sorry for you," she whispered, sensing the grief that he was still holding onto and realized she was holding on to her own massive grief, as was Marita.

"We have to adjust and get on with making our lives go the way we want them to go. It's like a moving symphony. As you experience it, parts are so sad, but often if you just keep on going and keep true to your goals, why, it can become triumphant once more. So I think you and I are just like that now. We're in the sad, terrible part, but we just have to keep on going, working to be true to ourselves and what we want. The cheerful times are just ahead of us. So what I am saying, Juanita, is that it's more than all right for you to cry your heart out over this right now. Tomorrow is another day, and we'll make it, if we keep on trying."

Her suppressed grief seeped to the surface. Big tears formed. Finally, Juanita let it out. "I never wanted this. It's horrible," she sobbed, and he encouraged her to let her emotions run, hoping and praying this was what she needed most right now.

Nearby, Guilermo was talking with Marita, telling her about how he loved to teach others to dance, both ballroom styles so popular with the wealthier crowd and modern styles the young favored. "I heard you were the station's cook. Is that right? You must be a good one."

She cracked a brief smile. "Yes I *was*, that being the operative word," she retorted, using as big a word as she could manage. Some of Juanita had rubbed off on her. "Was," she stated again.

"Well, once I have taught someone to dance, they never forget how. I had a man who hadn't danced in years come in for lessons. Said he hadn't danced in twenty years. Funny thing, after one lesson, he had it all back again. Unless you lost your mind too, I don't see how you could forget how to cook, Marita."

"How can I peel a potato now, silly man?" she sighed, fighting back from breaking down in front of him.

"Not in any way that you used to peel them, I expect. You're just going to have to find different ways to do all those things. Heck, I have lots of time. Together, we'll figure them out, one at a time. They make a potato peeler machine. I saw one advertised once. I know what we're going to do, Marita. We're going to make you your own special kitchen fixed up just so you and you alone can cook in it, though we'll also fix it so I can make my morning coffee. Can't live without that, you know."

"But it's not possible—I mean for me to do those things—without arms and hands, is it?" she asked, as her own grief surfaced once more.

"Look, if I can teach some of those folks who can't even feel a beat and have four left feet to dance, then I'm sure working together, you and I can find ways and means for you to cook as well or better than you ever did. Mind you, it isn't going to be easy. Patience, patience, patience, but as long as you don't give up, I won't either. Together, we will succeed." That boost of hope did it. Marita broke down and let her own grief pour out in buckets of tears, just as Juanita was doing.

For the women, this was the first time since it began that they felt both safe and ready to face the intense grief they'd been keeping totally suppressed in order to survive. The young men were wise enough to recognize this and allowed their new wives to express and emote their pent up grief.

The next evening, they took them to their new homes. Some years ago, Diego had purchased a duplex in the artist district not far from the symphony hall and the dance studios for the two men. Thus, they lived side-by-side and had already put in a door in their living rooms that connected the two separate homes, though it was usually kept open anyway. "Tomorrow, we have to go shopping for clothes," Gervasi suggested, while showing Juanita around the home. "One step at a time."

"Hey, at least I can take a descent step now!" she teased him.

Thus began a steep learning curve for the two men and a relearning curve for the women. Trial and error, coaching, and encouragement went a very long way for all four, who began to see they were in this together, which meant everything to the women, who no longer felt alone and terribly isolated. Doorknobs were changed to latches so they could never become trapped in a room. Gervasi's friend installed a voice-activated security door that responded only to the two women's voices. They only needed to speak "open," and the system unlocked the doors and automatically opened them. However, that was so convenient that the fellows had his friend add their voices to the system as well.

In Marita's case, Guilermo began from scratch, working with her to figure out totally new and workable ways for her to cook again. Sitting on a chair, she had the use of her feet. Quickly, both saw that everything she would need to cook and bake had to be very low to the ground, quite unlike the current kitchen setup. While it took them a month of experimentation, they did succeed. Marita was back cooking and baking once more, though it did take her far longer to do it. In addition, he began to teach Marita ballroom dancing. She'd never danced before, but soon found that she loved it. Slowly, her own life was becoming more complete than it ever had been before.

Once Juanita was more or less comfortable in daily living, Gervasi took her to his secret RdD communications center and introduced her to his four assistants. When they learned she was a real captain and had been in charge of the space station's comm center, they cheered and insisted she take over control of the operation. Thanks to the voice-activated software his friend installed, Juanita was able to continue doing what she loved to do; only this time, her work would make a real difference. She was fighting back against the evil corporations.

A few days after they moved into the duplex with their new husbands, one evening as he was helping get her ready for bed, Gervasi asked her, "How come you kept your hair like this? I know it looks fabulous on you, but I can see how much trouble you have with it."

She giggled. "Silly. I can feel with it. I have a good sense of touch with each long strand. It's sort of like having a hundreds more hands dangling down, though I'd rather have hands. I can feel so much more via my hair." Marita felt the same way about hers. They had deprived her of her sense of touch in her hands, but had indirectly given her a whole new arena of touch, though sometimes it was a bit annoying, especially on windy days.

***

One of the tasks Alfonso assigned Gervasi and Juanita was that of monitoring the GE Corporate Headquarters building. Specifically, they were given two ID codes to search for.

He explained, "As you know, we had a number of secret agents working on the space station for us. The men died, but we know some of the women survived and were taken somewhere, just like you and Marita were. We have been looking for any trace of these two women. We got lucky a while back. For a few minutes, their embedded ID tags showed up on our monitors! For that to happen, they had to be emitting a very strong signal and that meant they were in this very city! We zeroed in and found the brief signals came from the GE Corporate Headquarters building in downtown Malagena. The signals were present for about five minutes before they again blacked out. We figure they must be being kept underground, since that would prevent the signals from being received by us. So I want your people to continuously monitor them. If at any time, night or day, those signals reappear, contact me immediately."

***

Melissa and Jackie were crushed when they discovered they were trapped in the basement of the GE Corporation Headquarters building. They spent a sober but bored week lying around their room. At least, they were being well fed, though they complained constantly that they had to eat like dogs. The man who dropped off the plates and drinks never commented though.

"I've had enough of this, Jackie," Melissa complained bitterly. "We're not birds in some cage."

"No, we are pretty and naked birds in a cage," Jackie retorted. "But what can we do? No one is going to rescue us. Hell, no one knows we're here. Besides, no one dares go up against the GE Corporation."

Melissa giggled. "I like that one, Jackie. Pretty, naked birds in a cage. No, we're going to have to rescue ourselves."

"Well, we know where the front doors are. But Melissa, we can't just walk out of the elevator, not in their main entrance lobby. They'll be on us before we can take two of our pathetically slow steps," Jackie declared.

Melissa sighed, knowing her friend was right. A daytime escape was impossible, not unless they had clothes on. Maybe then, it might be possible. Hence, the two spent a couple of *outings* from their cell looking for clothes. There wasn't any to be found that they could see, unless they could knock out some of the cooks and steal theirs, a ridiculous idea they concluded. Days passed while the two brooded and envisioned all manner of ways to escape their prison cell.

Then it struck Jackie. "You know, we should check out what's around here during the night hours. Maybe we can steal some clothes to use during the daytime." That evening after they thought everyone was asleep, they headed out of their bedroom cell. Only security lights were on, dimly illuminating the hallway. Minutes passed before they again stood by the open elevator doors on the ground floor, looking out onto the foyer of GE Corporation Headquarters. Freedom lay some fifty feet in front of them. A dozing security guard and locked doors barred their way. They stood there observing for a couple of minutes before heading on up a floor.

One by one, the two quietly checked the other floors. Many doors were locked. Those few meeting rooms that they could enter contained no clothes, not even a forgotten raincoat. All they could see were a number of white aprons in the kitchen area. For several minutes, the two women stayed on the top floor, thinking about how they could possibly get past the guard and get the main doors unlocked. Clubbing the guard was no longer an option, and once more, they cursed their near total helplessness.

"We could try to seduce the guard. One of us could distract him," Jackie suggested. "Then, the other somehow knocks him out. We could get his keys and let ourselves out."

"Brilliant, Jackie," Melissa declared, then frowned. "So how do we knock him out? I suppose if he is unconscious, we could maybe somehow get the keys off his belt—maybe using our teeth, but could we really find a way to use the key in the lock before someone else comes along?"

The two thought long and hard on just how they could render the man unconscious. Slowly, a plan materialized, as each tossed out ideas that perhaps they might be able to accomplish. Their best idea was to both come at him seductively while he was still in his chair. Then, lean over him enough to make his chair fall over backwards. With themselves on top of him, maybe they could use their feet and heels as deadly weapons, at least enough to disable him.

"Look, even if it fails, I'm all right with him killing us. I don't want to live as we are now. Death will be a welcome relief to this—this—this nightmare we're forced to live," Jackie admitted. Melissa agreed, and they continued to work out their plan.

Over an hour passed while they tried to work out every detail of their escape from the building. Finally, they took deep breaths and entered the elevator. "Freedom or death," Jackie whispered.

"Freedom or death," Melissa echoed back. Down went the elevator. They found the guard still dozing in his chair. Even though their heels clicked noisily on the granite floor, the man didn't wake up, not until both women stood seductively before him, their long hair tossed behind them.

"What the. . ." Astonishment appeared on the man's face, followed rapidly by a look of lust! Two stunning, naked women stood inches from him. Both leaned over as if they were about to passionately kiss him. Wham! His chair fell over backwards. He hit the floor hard, aided by both women falling down on top of him. Because they were on top of him, when he tried to use his arms to break his fall, their bodies were in the way. The back of his head hit the unforgiving granite floor with an awful cracking sound.

"Well, that was easy. He's out cold, maybe for a long time," Jackie whispered, as both women struggled mightily to regain their feet somehow. They didn't, but managed to get to sitting positions, tangled up in their long hair. "Quick, find his keys!"

A minute later, they stared at his key chain, fastened to his belt by a long golden chain. For a time, it seemed a hopeless task for them to undo it, and they tried all manner of things to get it free.

***

"Call Alfonso!" Captain Juanita spoke clearly. It was 22:00. She was just about to call it a night when a small window opened up on her monitor and began flashing. Two ID tag locators were active and being received! It had to be the two women whom she was supposed to watch for. She recalled him saying to call him at once, day or night, so Juanita did just that. "Alfonso, those two ID tags that you asked me to watch for—they are active right now. Signals are coming in quite strongly. What does this mean?"

Alfonso sat up in bed, disturbing his wife slightly. "Location?" he asked.

"GE Corporation Headquarters. That's what the message box is saying," she relayed what was on her monitor.

"Okay. Stay on it. Keep me posted if there is any change." Hastily, he dialed Diego. "Their locator chips are active again. Yes, same place. Take a bunch and check it out. They have to be above ground right now. Yes, break in if you have too. I'll keep you posted if there is any change. Maybe we can catch a break this time."

Diego grabbed two friends and took off in an untraceable shuttle, one that had been stripped of its built-in ID chip. He sat it down just outside the corporation building in the middle of the street, which would not have been very unusual in the daytime, but was this late at night. Since Alfonso had not called him back to tell him the signals had vanished again, he ordered the two men to stick GE Corporation logos onto the side of the shuttle just as they left. Thus, the security cameras would photograph a shuttle but it would be identified as one of their own craft.

As he and his men moved up to the front doors, Diego broke into a broad smile. Just inside, he saw the two women sitting beside the unconscious guard, struggling to get his keys off his key chain. One of his men took out a can of liquid nitrogen and sprayed the lock with it. The other took out a hammer and punch. One tap and the metal lock shattered, freeing the doors. Diego stepped inside.

"Ah, Jackie and Melissa. Good to see you are making your escape. Would you like some assistance? We've missed you both."

Both women looked up when they heard the lock breaking, prepared to be shot. They heard Diego's voice. "Diego? Is that you?" Melissa called out.

"Yes, we must hurry," he replied.

"Little help here. We're helpless," Jackie added.

A minute later, with his two helpers carrying the women, they boarded the shuttle and took off, landing ten minutes later at a safe house. Again, the men carried the two inside, sitting them on a bed, before leaving.

Diego stepped in. "Ladies, we can't begin to tell you how glad we are to have you back. Brilliant move on your part. We've been monitoring your ID signals and were able to get to you in time tonight. Alfonso will be by in the morning and get you all the help you need. I'll see you have some clothes and a helper first thing in the morning. Will you be all right by yourselves here tonight? If not, I'll send someone over shortly."

"We need help, Diego. We can't do anything anymore, not like this," Melissa said, trying very hard to remain emotionless. She knew that if she didn't, she'd begin bawling like a baby. Jackie too.

"Okay. I'll send someone over in a few minutes. Have to make a call. See you tomorrow. Very well done on your escape, by the way. Damned impressive. Doubt if I could have done that," he complimented them, bringing a slight smile to their faces. He could tell they were about ready to breakdown, and made a hasty exit, allowing them private time. He called another friend, the same young woman who looked after other women who were rescued. She arrived nearly an hour later.

Thus, when Alfonso arrived mid-morning, the women were bathed, had their hair washed, dried, and brushed out, were nicely dressed, and full with a nourishing breakfast. Once more, he praised them for their work, their brilliant escape, and their huge personal sacrifice on behalf of the RdD. In return, they explained in detail everything that had happened to them and all about the estimated eight hundred other women being kept in the small bedrooms beneath GE Corporation Headquarters. Once the intelligence was relayed, he then discussed what could be done for them.

Both wanted abortions at once and all known cures. "The abortions will be done in a few minutes. Might we discuss these cures a bit? I know how badly you both want to help the RdD and how much you have already sacrificed. However, at this point, I want to make you another offer. Mind you, after all you have been through for us, I have no right to ask anything further from either of you. No matter what you choose to do, I give you my word that you both will be well taken care of."

"What are you talking about?" Jackie asked, curiously. She knew that look on his face. He had something diabolical in mind; she just sensed it. He explained fully what they now knew about the UFB women and their purposes. Suddenly, much began to make sense to the two women.

"So what I had in mind, if you are game, is to *marry*

each of you to one of our GD executives, ones on our side, and insert you into the corporate executive group, where you can mingle with all the top executives, not just GD's, but many other corporation men and women as well. You could become incredible sources of intelligence. Later on, you could be officially divorced and receive all the genetic cures available. Actually, at any time you desire, both can be done. Such would be your calls. What say you? Game for some top espionage?"

Both women loved this idea. "You mean we get to mingle with all these other corp execs? Wow, what we could overhear or weasel out of men could really be invaluable," Jackie gushed. "Count me in, especially if we can get the cures whenever we want them."

"Excellent Jackie, Melissa. I will do my best to find you good men to be your pretend husbands. Trust me a little longer."

Chapter 9—Melchior Mining Corporation

"Someone is here to see you, sir," an assistant interrupted Fritz Melchoir, the CEO and founder of the Melchoir Mining Corporation, Abelard Sector. The fifty-five year old pioneer executive had carved this giant mining company out of bedrock. Here in this desolate rim sector, planets galore were just waiting to be discovered. That's what his company did: find new rocky planets and extract the valuable ores from them, marketing them to the insatiable Galactic Federation. Rare earths were exceptionally valuable, but also quite rare. Gold, platinum, and to a lesser extent silver, copper, and iron were handled by his corporation, which now spanned ten civilized worlds and with extensive mining operations on two dozen rocky planets or moons.

Fritz was an example of the pioneering spirit so often found out here on the very edge of the galaxy. Yet, he slavishly followed the unwritten, but widely known and more importantly enforced GF Rules of Operation that all Galactic Federation corporations followed without fail. Corporation versus corporation was a cutthroat business, quite figuratively, held together by these rules by which they operated and more or less cooperated, as they expanded and ruled the entire galaxy.

One of these unwritten rules was: Anything goes if it promotes corporate profit. Another one was: When dealing with another corporation, plan for the worst and you'll be successful. Fritz slavishly followed the first rule; it was the secret to his success. He hired workers for low pay and terrible benefits, overworked them, and saw to it that they had accidents if they complained or caused trouble. Whenever he had to deal with other corporations, he made damn sure his people had dug up all the *dirt* possible on that company so he had bargaining material when he met with them.

The result: in forty years, his Melchior Mining Corporation was the largest mining operation in this rim sector, with local headquarters on nine worlds and his main corporation headquarters here on Taurus-C, in the capital city of Tesla. So yes, Fritz was a rough, tough, self-made CEO. He was not pleased his assistant had allowed someone to pay him a visit totally unannounced and unsolicited. He was about to chastise the man, when a tall, dark stranger followed his assistant into the room, without waiting to be announced. Before Fritz could react, the assistant politely stepped back out of the office.

Fritz was sitting behind his oversized desk on a chair twice the size of the chairs on the opposite side for his visitors. He wanted no mistakes to be made, no misunderstandings; he was the important man, not whoever came to see him. Always know your place was his motto. This man, whoever he was, was upsetting the way he ran his business. Fritz fumed and was about to press the silent signal, which would bring a dozen security men busting into the room to toss the man out, but his hand somehow wasn't moving.

The stranger was well dressed, perhaps a bit overdone with a cummerbund and a suit that resembled a tuxedo. The man wore a felt hat with a wide brim, black, and befitting a businessman, and he also wore white gloves, which he began carefully removing, pulling on one finger at a time, slowly and deliberately, while eyeing him with beady, piercing eyes. At last he spoke. "Fritz Melchoir, I presume."

"Well, yes, yes, of course. How dare you," he began to protest, but found his voice quietly trailing off for no apparent reason.

"Excellent. I'm now your new boss. From now on, you will follow my orders explicitly and without question," the man's soothing voice spoke slowly and deliberately, but with a hypnotic quality about it and totally certain of the results.

"You are now my boss. I will follow your orders explicitly and without question," Fritz found himself robotically reciting back, against every ounce of strength and will-power he could muster, both of which seemed almost non-existent at the moment.

"Excellent, Fritz Melchoir. I'm sure we'll get along splendidly," the man said with a slight smile.

"Yes, I'm sure we'll get along splendidly," Fritz found

himself repeating. He had no such thing in mind, but was helpless to say anything different.

"Good. You may call me the Master. I now own your company."

"Master. Yes, I must call you the Master. You own my company," Fritz repeated, fighting with every ounce of strength he had to avoid saying those words. Yet he failed miserably.

"Good. You may continue to handle your usual daily operations. I will not normally interfere with those. Right now, I need your local Taurus headquarters building at 10494 Tesla Boulevard. Have the building vacated by tomorrow morning. There's plenty of space for those people here in this building. Perhaps on the lower floors," the Master said politely.

"Yes, of course. By tomorrow morning. Vacated. Yes, they can move into the ten lower floors here," Fritz replied against his better judgment. He wanted to ask why, but simply couldn't.

"Very good then. My people will move in tomorrow morning. That will be all for now. I believe you have quite a bit of work to handle today," the Master insinuated.

"Well, yes, of course. Much. Personnel to move in both buildings, equipment, yes, much work to be done," Fritz replied.

"Excellent, Fritz Melchoir. And remember, you can't double cross me and expect to live."

"Of course not, Master."

"Good. I'll leave you to make the arrangements," the Master added. Calmly, he rose, turned, and walked out of the room, though he slipped on his gloves before touching the doorknob, and replaced his hat meticulously onto his head, before stepping out into the foyer area, where the assistant was staring at him. The Master tipped his hat to the man and departed, heading for the elevator.

An hour later, from across the street, the Master watched the frantic work going on at 10494 Tesla Boulevard. He smiled and headed off for his next meeting. By late afternoon, he'd wrapped up the day's work. Another corporation would send eight hundred fifty beds with linens and a similar number of baby beds to 10494 Tesla Boulevard in the morning. Another corporation would send two expensive medical machines there, along with three resident doctors and their nursing staff. Yet another corporation would send periodic food shipments and a dietician. Finally, GE Corporation would have twenty, fully fueled deep space transports waiting for his use the following day, all nicely lined up on the giant spaceport just at the edge of Tesla.

He hopped into his private transport at the spaceport, after verifying the requested twenty transports were on their way. Just after supper, he arrived back on Rho-C and met with his ten Seconds. Tao asked, "Master, did all go as planned?"

"Yes, of course, Tao. Why should we spend our money on such things? It is vastly cheaper and more convenient to have other corporations provide for our needs," the Master replied, a curling smile upon his lips as he sat down to a late meal.

After eating, he added, "Make ready. Tomorrow, you must see to the arrangement of the furniture arrivals as we have planned. Exit day will be the day after tomorrow." Tao bowed and left to make the arrangements.

Long ago, Tao and his other Seconds had stopped wondering just how the Master could always succeed with his plans without the slightest setbacks. It never ceased to amaze them that this man could walk into any corporation anywhere and get precisely what he asked for. They now had no doubts they would one day rule the entire galaxy, not the corporations, which would be under their direct control. The last lingering doubt was dispelled when the entire 519th Infantry Division had been wiped out without a single casualty on their side. Further, that they were about to depart this forsaken rocky, worthless planet in the middle of nowhere meant everything to the men. It was icing that they were going to reside in Tesla, Taurus-C, a very wealthy planet, full of prospects. From the Dark Ages into the Modern World, one Second had pronounced when he heard the plan.

Nearly eight hundred pregnant UFB women had to be moved, along with all the Master's forces and acquired equipment, much having come from the secret bases here on

Rho-C and from the space station. Plus, the Master was moving his fifty-man SMP, Super Man Platoon, to Taurus-C as well. These powerful, robust, burly men were all taller than the average man and twice as strong, a product of the research bioengineering here on Rho-C, breeding normal men to the originally created UFB women.

Tao was also pleased the Master was leaving behind the fighter clones those research engineers had created years ago. Nine of them had already been killed while on guard duty in the underground cell area, taken out by the only members of the infantry division who had gotten out alive. Those clones were worthless. Tao would rather put one of his bungling guards on duty, even the pair who had somehow allowed two UFB women to escape in a transport, than make any use of the SMP clones. He thought, those things are dumb idiots, without any personality or ability to think. True, they were giants and incredibly strong, but that didn't make up for the other total deficiencies. Tao was very pleased to learn they wouldn't be coming with them.

Already the worms and the wolves had been moved to a desolate rocky world, uninhabited by humans. There, they were released into the wild, but with containers and the necessary recall machines present, should they need to be caged and taken elsewhere. Tao suspected that one day, the Master would unleash them on other populated worlds. One thing made Tao happy and that was that he didn't have to stick around to help the others pack everything for the big move. He was given the easy assignment to make sure the new supplies were delivered and properly setup.

Late the next day, the Master visited Tao at their new headquarters and was given an inspection tour. The lower floors were now equipped for the Master's men, including a fancy comm center, taken from the space station. The middle floors housed the pregnant women. One floor above that held the new medical facility and staff, along with the nursery, kitchen, pantry, and housing for the few servant women. The uppermost floors were reserved for their supplies, their men, with offices for the Seconds and the Master on the top floor of the hundred-story building. The roof landing bay held ten shuttle craft, compliments of Fritz Melchoir.

"Perfect, Tao, perfect. The world provides to those who ask," he said calmly. "The move is on for tomorrow." Tao smiled. Life was taking a giant step for the better. He was only too pleased to be off that forsaken Rho-C.

Poor Fritz Melchoir. He tried valiantly to countermand the orders the Master had given him, forcing him to give up so many of his hard-earned assets, including one entire skyscraper. However, each time he even had such a thought, a massive migraine stopped him instantly. Soon, he realized he simply couldn't go against the Master's requests. However, Fritz wasn't defeated, not yet. "He didn't say I can't do that," he said aloud to the walls. Quickly, he ordered ten men to spy on the old local headquarters and report what this Master fellow was doing to his building. He ordered his staff to research this man.

"Find out who he is. Where did he come from? What is he trying to do? I want to know all about this Master fellow, and I want it yesterday!" he barked angrily, but did notice that he wasn't getting a migraine and smiled coyly.

Unfortunately, his top research staff found absolutely nothing about this man. Fritz very nearly fired the lot of them, so angry was he. He even brought in a CSI squad to search his office and the building for the Master's DNA, hoping to identify the man this way. None was found. The man wore gloves.

Worse, when he quizzed his ten men about what they had seen, they stared back at him with blank eyes. The Master had spotted them and somehow wiped their memories, as far as Fritz could tell. In desperation, Fritz resorted to his old, tried and true method, ordering the assassination of the Master, using his best Cleaner Squad of men. The following morning when he arrived at his skyscraper office building, landing his shuttle on the roof's docking pad, there lay his ten men, brutally slain. Plus, the Master stepped out of the shadows.

"Good morning, Fritz Melchoir. I'm returning your men in a worse condition than you sent them to me in. If ever anyone makes any attempt upon my life or that of my men, I'll see that your skin is removed from your body while you are alive and experiencing it." With that, he moved over to his own shuttle and departed, leaving Fritz standing in a pool of his own urine. He'd lost control of his body for a moment.

Fritz desperately wanted to alert all the other corporation executives about this ruthless Master, but realized that if he said anything, he would be a dead man walking. He decided to keep quiet and think of some other way of dealing with this man. Somehow, he needed to get the Master's DNA. He was certain that would provide him with the answers he desperately wanted, but he could think of no way to get it.

***

Three days after the Master abandoned Rho-C, a battleship, three heavy cruisers, ten light cruisers, and a host of deep space transports arrived in orbit around Rho-C. Admiral Cusak's orders were clear. If inhabited, destroy the entire world. If void of people, retake the top-secret research facility, and find and remove the valuable research data.

IR scanners revealed that Rho-C was now uninhabited, somewhat surprising the admiral, who was ready to drop a hundred nukes on it. Grumbling, he sent down the requisite search parties. A day later, he and his fleet returned empty-handed. The Master had left nothing of value behind, not even the bioengineered new species. The world was once more desolate. Many local corporate execs found this news highly disturbing indeed. However, news of this whole fiasco finally reached to the very top of the corporate ladders, something that the local execs definitely didn't want to have happen!

In the corporate hierarchy, those at the very top delegated the responsibility of the running of the local corporation offices and enterprises to their local corporation headquarters staff. These elite men ran the entire galaxy via top-down management. That is, they made the major decisions and ordered the local branches to implement them, all the while monitoring the profits and results, which in itself was a gargantuan task, considering that there were close to a thousand populated worlds. Hence, they seldom interfered in *local affairs*.

This time, they had lost a top-secret bio-engineering

research station, along with their highly desired breeding program, to say nothing of the loss of an entire infantry division, though that could easily be replaced. No, what bothered those at the top were two things. One, that someone known only as the Master was in charge in the Abelard rim sector, and two, that they'd lost their genetic research station and their access to the UFB and UFBMD program, though if the truth be told, it was the latter that most alarmed those at the very top of the corporate ladders.

Thus, word came down to all the local corporate branches. A special envoy would soon be arriving to inspect the damage and to obtain a complete report of the local situation, particularly with regard to the breeding program. Non-cooperation would result in instant removal, though most believed that innuendo actually meant death. Further, all local CEOs were summoned to a follow up meeting to be held in three months' time on Corporate Prime, the new name of Cass-C, located in the hub of the galaxy, and the most populated world in the Federation's part of the galaxy, home of all the top corporate leaders. All this made the local CEOs very, very nervous.

Even Fritz Melchior was extremely worried, since he too was so summoned, even though his corporation was tiny with respect to the major ones and though he had no contacts beyond the Abelard Sector. He had no *dirt* on these hub people and felt particularly vulnerable, especially since the Master totally controlled him.

He decided that if he was going down, he'd bring the Master down with him. Hence, he asked the Master to pay him a call, which the immaculately dressed man did. Nervously, Fritz showed him the official summons. "I—I have to go to this meeting."

"Now this is indeed fortuitous, Fritz Melchoir. Of course, you must go. I shall accompany you, since you have given control of your corporation to me. I will make our arrange arrangements. Thank you for the notification," the Master replied.

This was not how Fritz believed the Master would have reacted. Rather, he'd hoped that the Master would have been so afraid of these top men that he would relinquish control of Melchoir Mining back to him. Instead, the man wanted to go, something Fritz couldn't believe possible. No one wanted to be under the direct eye of these kinds of men, the men who ran the whole galaxy, powerful men who could have you killed in the blink of an eye. No, Fritz was even more nervous about the whole affair.

Chapter 10—Creeping Cold

Smith stirred from her dormant, three millennia doze. One by one, she tested her eight legs, stretching them fully before slipping out of her cozy silken chamber. Sliding down a silken thread, she landed upon a life support unit and gazed hungrily at the preserved human body within. Juicy, she thought as her intense hunger triggered. Deftly, two of her legs tapped the controls. A hiss of escaping air echoed in her dark chamber far underground. She slipped her body down on top of the morsel and began sucking in the life-giving bodily fluids that she'd gone to such pains to preserve for three thousand years. Ah, this was the last one, she thought. Perhaps the galaxy had progressed some by now. Smith certainly hoped so, for she had some hunting to do.

An hour later, her many-faceted eyes looked at the now desiccated body and then felt her own bloated body and burped. She moved over to her nestlings and began to rouse them, depositing a portion of the nourishing fluids for them to devour as they woke. Thousands of tiny scampering feet quickly responded, greedily consuming their portion. While her many offspring were regaining their vitality, Smith moved up the long tunnel to the surface of this long abandoned world. The humans had called it Zeta-9-C, but that was three millennia ago. Back then, it was a tiny rocky world on the rim of the galaxy in the Rossiter Sector. Uppermost in her mind was the answer to the simple question: had humans finally returned to this world?

When she had decided to go dormant so long ago, she'd done so because the supply of juicy humans had all but dried up. No longer did spaceships come to this world. No longer could she send her children off on them to visit other worlds and return with the things that made their life a living luxury. Smith breathed in the fresh, clean air and sighed, so hoping that humans had once more grown populous throughout the galaxy.

Her hypersensitive olfactory senses picked up

hydrocarbons, something that she had not detected in three thousand years, a sure sign that humans were back. Invigorated, she focused and sent an electronic signal to her brood of thousands. Shortly, tiny little feet scurried up the tunnel, their little bodies swarming over the barren rocky surface. Her orders were simple: go scout for humans and report.

The sun was up, and she crawled upon a rock and basked in its warmth for a time, waiting the news she was certain to hear. She wasn't disappointed.

The Rossiter Sector bordered the Abelard Sector, there on the rim of the galaxy. A mining crew from Kappa-C had discovered this abandoned world a hundred years ago. Now they had a large mining colony working the valuable rare earth deposits, and to a lesser extent those of gold and platinum. Population: ten thousand men and women, more or less, scattered in ten major mining centers around Kappa-C.

In addition, a team of archaeologists had been called in some ten years back. The miners had uncovered signs of human cities. While now ruins, they warranted investigation, since the people who used to live here had space travel. Several corporations hoped to uncover any valuable secrets this civilization might have had, particularly in the technology arena. To date, however, nothing truly significant had been unearthed.

Before long, Smith began receiving reports. Indeed, humans were here once more. Even more significant, they had spaceships. Finally, Smith could begin to plot and plan once more. She summoned fifty of her brood to her. While she continued to sit upon the rock, her tiny companions hovered around the base listening to their marching orders.

In a burst of electronic signals, Smith said, "My little ones, our long wait is finally at an end. I want you fifty to hitch a ride on a human. Fan out across the galaxy as we used too. Gather intelligence on where the humans are, what their technology now is, where their densely populated planets are located. But be careful. They may have more sophisticated weapons than before. Above all, avoid detection if you can. We don't want to alert them to our presence just yet, not until we know their numbers, distributions, and technology advancements, if any. Go now and have long overdue freedom to explore."

Pleased with their unique assignments, the fifty chosen ones scampered off to carry out their mother's orders. Meanwhile, many others continued to report to her via short electronic bursts. Smith felt elated. Her playground was filled with action once more. It had been far too long this time. She vowed not to be so darn greedy this time. Best start preparations to begat more children, she thought, but stayed in the warm sun a while longer. There was plenty of time now, plenty of time and food.

***

At Base One, the foreman looked up at the wild yelling coming from the entrance of the mine. He'd gone down to inspect the progress of the rare earth dig. "Spiders! Little beasts!" one man screamed, swatting his hands around the back of his head wildly. Joe headed up the tunnel to see if he could help. He stopped short, gasping.

His ten men were all swatting at spiders, but more importantly, Joe saw hundreds of the little devils racing down the tunnel towards his men and himself! "Squash the beasts!" he yelled his order. As they approached him, he began stomping them right and left. He expected each footfall to eliminate one of the beasties, but when he lifted his foot to go after another, the darn thing got up and continued scampering towards him!

"Boss, I can't move," the man next to him began to say, but then ceased mid-sentence, standing perfectly still, like a statue in a natural history museum. Joe saw one of the spiders clinging to the back of the man's neck. Then, mysteriously, the spider seemed to disappear, melting into his neck! Joe was startled, but now felt tiny feet climbing up his legs beneath his pants! Now he too began to frantically jump about, hoping to dislodge them. He felt the skin on the back of his neck tingle and tried to swat the spider off, but failed. He felt it biting him and slapped it as hard as he could, to no avail.

Now his feet felt like lead. Paralyzed. That thought raced through Joe's mind and he tried in vain to move his feet, but they were immobile. Then he lost all feeling in his hands. He too was completely paralyzed. He watched in horror as hundreds of the devils swarmed on top of one of his men who had fallen to the ground. The spiders were sucking the bodily fluids out of the man right before his eyes! He tried to scream, but simply couldn't move a muscle. He had to breathe and couldn't even do that!

Just when he thought he was about to black out, to pass out, his body gasped and freedom of motion returned. Something inside his head ordered him, "Return to work. You saw nothing." Joe shook his head. His eyes no longer saw the small host of spiders still finishing off the fallen man. Instead, he turned and headed back down the tunnel to inspect the rare earth dig. He had no idea he was now totally under the control of the spider that had fused itself into his spinal cord, just below the base of his neck, invisible beneath the skin.

Words, memories, orders, places, things, people flashed by in his mind as his parasite gathered the requested intelligence. Joe thought nothing of all this, however, and continued to look over the find.

The fifty spiders with their special orders scampered over the planet, searching for spaceships, especially ones that could travel long distances, the deep space transports, not the local shuttles, though several lazy little ones hitched rides to the spaceport on Zeta-9-C on some shuttles. Once they found the major spaceport, the fifty small spiders easily slipped onboard and hid themselves nicely, preparing for the exploratory trips. A sense of excitement filled their little minds.

Now it so happened that one of these little beasts had a mind of her own. She'd been denied much by mother Smith the last time out, and she wanted her own freedom, the hell with the brood. She called herself Jones. *This time, I'm going to be the master, not mother Smith!* She hid in a dark corner of the transport, hatching her own plans for the future, plans which did not include Smith.

Jones knew two facts. One, if she ate sufficiently, she too could grow larger, perhaps as large as mother. Two, if she ate enough, she too could have her own brood of tiny children.

No, it was mother Smith's force of will that kept her brood in line, kept them from overeating and growing as a spider should, to say nothing of having their own offspring. No, this time, things would be different. She, Jones, was going to have her own brood and no longer answer to Smith, not ever.

***

Jascar Wells, thirty-two, was the junior executive in charge of overseeing the small mining operation on Zeta-9-C, an operation of the GE Corporation's Rare Earth Mining Division. Rare earths were absolutely vital in the production of so many products in widespread use throughout the galaxy. Hence, his direct oversight was deemed invaluable. One could never trust the miners, who were known to slip a bit of the rare earths in their pockets, later selling them on the Black Market for a small fortune.

Thus, Jascar had installed numerous spy cameras throughout the mines, barracks, and other buildings, in an effort to cut down on outright thefts. Today, he was reviewing some of the video feeds, when he spotted the invasion of the tiny spiders. At first, he was merely amused at the frantic antics of the miners trying to get them off their bodies. Soon, however, his mirth changed. The men seemed frozen to the spot! He rewound the video and watched more closely this time. "Yes, stomp them. Squash them!" he yelled at the monitor. Then, he noticed that no matter how hard the men seemed to stomp the spiders, the spiders seemed wholly unaffected by it! In fact, not a single spider was killed.

As the video advanced further, he saw the grizzly sight of the fallen man being reduced to a dried out husk! After that, the men seemed to ignore the spiders completely and returned to work. Startled, he called up the foreman of that crew, Joe.

"What spiders? We haven't seen any spiders around here," Joe answered. "No, I've not lost a miner. All is just fine here." This couldn't be! Only minutes ago, Jascar had seen Joe just as frantically trying to get the spiders off him too. Now, Joe had no memory of the attack. Further, Joe was talking somehow strangely, more like a monotone, devoid of emotion, not like the hardy foreman Jascar had hired! Something was very wrong here.

He rewound the video and watched Joe very carefully. Suddenly, Jascar paused it and stared hard at the monitor. He knew that he needed image enhancement software to see what was going on better, but he swore that he saw a spider on Joe's neck. He moved forward a bit and the spider was gone. He backed it up and moved through it frame by frame. The spider did not fall off. Rather, it just seemed to go invisible!

Jascar sat back, pondering the significance of what he'd just seen. To the best of his knowledge, such spiders did not exist. He decided that this warranted further study and made copies of the video to send on up the corporate lines. However, when he finished, he had recorded attacks at every one of the working mines! After making nine other calls, not one of the foremen reported seeing any spiders nor any such attacks!

Just as Jascar was about to leave the spaceport headquarters and go check the men out personally, he saw men running down the hallway. One yelled, "Spiders! Lots of 'em!" Jascar cursed and ran too. No way was he going to get caught by these tiny beasts. He headed to the storage room and ducked inside. As fast as he could, Jascar donned a space suit. Now enclosed entirely, he moved out into the hallway again. Here and there, he saw men and women frozen to the spot, and at least one was on the floor covered in spiders intent on sucking his bodily fluids!

Carefully, Jascar made his way out of the headquarters and over to the row of deep space transports. He entered his private code and opened the bay door. He walked up the ramp, but didn't notice a tiny spider scampering in with him. Quickly, he closed the door, feeling certain that inside the sealed ship, he would be totally safe. He double-checked his pocket to make sure he still had his video copies and then headed to the pilot's seat. Minutes later, he took off, heading for 9-Sigma-C, where his immediate seniors had their headquarters.

He then opened a comm channel and asked for his boss. "Sir, we have a dangerous situation on Zeta-9-C. You have to watch these videos. Sending them now. Over." Jascar waited patiently, anticipating his boss's reaction, once he saw them all. However, he didn't quite anticipate the reaction.

"My god, Jascar! This is vitally important. I want you to go directly to my boss with the videos. I will relay the video you sent, but you are ordered to make a full report to him. How soon can you get to Malagena on Scorpi-C? Over."

Jascar did a quick check of his fuel levels and did a time estimate. "Sir, I can be there in eight hours. Over."

"Good. Good. I'm marking this find as top-secret, level ten. You are ordered not to show this video to anyone but my boss on Scorpi-C, nor are you to even mention this incident to anyone but him, under penalty of death. Got that? Over."

Jascar swallowed hard and cursed. Something like this should be broadly known. At the very least, Zeta-9-C ought to be quarantined, even though that would severely cut rare earth production and profits. Still, he replied, "Yes, understood. Top-secret, level ten. Over and out." Jascar decided to end the communication, fearing that his boss would say even worse things, such as he was to report to be mind wiped or something! He stood there a minute, half expecting his boss to call him back and order him to get mind wiped once he reported in. The call didn't come, much to his relief.

After altering course, Jascar headed to the galley to fix something to eat and to calm his shot nerves. With still seven hours to kill, he laid down for a nap, confident that his ship would wake him if he overslept. He dozed.

Jones finished her survey of the transport, noting the many improvements since the last time she'd been on such vessels, three thousand years ago. Now she sought out the pilot and found him sleeping. So much the better, she thought, and scrambled up onto his bed. A minute later, she was in position and sunk her fangs into his neck, injecting her paralytic agent. Jascar involuntarily slapped at her but then ceased all motion. She focused, slipped beneath his skin, and injected the antidote, sensing the man was breathing once more. Now she began surveying his memories, learning his language as well. Seven fruitful hours passed, giving Jones the time she needed to get a handle on current events with this man named Jascar. More importantly, she knew he had sounded the alarm about the spiders. She decided she had to attempt to squash that knowledge.

Right on schedule, Jascar landed at the sprawling spaceport on the edge of the huge city of Malagena, Scorpi-C. After turning off his engines, he made his way mechanically to the bay doors and opened them. Standing before him were a dozen security guards and the GE Corporation top executive here in this sector, Esteban Trujillo, a forty-year-old veteran corporation exec. "This way, Jascar. Don't say anything," the stern looking man in a fancy business suit stated dryly.

Jascar fell in line, surrounded by security guards. Before long, he found himself on the top floor of the GE Corporation Headquarters skyscraper. The view was spectacular, and Jascar stared out of the windows, while Esteban took his seat and began questioning him. "So you took these videos. Excellent idea to monitor the theft of rare earths, but these spiders are something quite alarming. Please, tell me in your own words just what you saw. The video is somewhat fuzzy. There's nothing like a firsthand account, now is there?"

In a monotone, Jascar found himself saying, "What spiders? I haven't seen any spiders. Why am I here? I should get back to work now."

Esteban looked sharply up at Jascar, who wanted to scream out all about these hideous beasts, but simply sat there like a statue.

"You mean to tell me that you haven't seen the spiders?"

"Yes sir."

"But these videos your boss sent me—he claims you sent them to him."

"What videos? What boss?" Jascar's dull voice responded, rather dumb-like.

"These videos! Damn it, man. What's wrong with you?" Esteban fumed. Hastily, he hit a button and the videos began playing on the monitor back of Esteban's huge desk. "Those spiders!" he yelled. Jascar looked dumb and didn't say anything.

Esteban had not risen to his position by being kind and considerate. Hastily, he pressed another button, stopping the recording of this interview with Jascar. He dialed up Jascar's boss. "Yes, he's here, but he denies ever having seen a spider and claims to know nothing about these videos. Check this out. Over." He sent the brief recording of this interview back to 9-Sigma-C.

"What the hell is going on there? That doesn't even sound like Jascar, though it looks like him. Something is going on with him. Give him a thorough medical exam and mind wipe check. Perhaps someone has already gotten to him. Over."

Jones saw she couldn't contain this situation any longer. She didn't want to risk what their medical procedures might entail. She could be harmed. Hence, she slipped back out of Jascar's neck, becoming visible. She heard one of the security guards cry out, "Spider! There, on the back of his neck!"

"Well shoot it, man! Blast it to kingdom come!" Esteban raged.

Jones scampered beneath the giant desk as rapidly as she could go, which was incredibly swift. The men hadn't even been able to draw their guns before she was out of sight. Hastily, she moved from there to beneath Esteban's chair and hid once more, while the security men looked all around for the spider.

Jascar moaned. "God, my neck. What happened? I was lying down and now I'm here? Oh. Sir, I didn't realize it was you! Sorry. Have you seen the video?"

"Damn you! You had one of them spiders on your neck! Now it's running loose around this office. Keep watch. It has to be here somewhere!" Esteban yelled, getting up from his chair and looking all around the nearby floor. Since no one saw any trace of the spider, after a time, they calmed down. "You men, keep a sharp eye out for this spider. Send for the research department. I want that spider either shot or captured and studied. Now Jascar, tell me what you saw. This time don't tell me you saw nothing."

"I couldn't help myself. That thing—that thing was forcing me to say what I said," Jascar shuddered. Hastily, he began relating all that he had seen and done, particularly his miraculous escape in the space suit, which had kept the spiders off him. "I was fine until I laid down to sleep for seven hours. It must have gotten to me while I was asleep, sir."

"Okay then, Jascar. Normally, I'd have you mind-wiped and sent back to work. However, considering the magnitude of this discovery, I'm sending you down to the med lab. I want them to see if they can find traces of the venom it injected into you. From the videos, it must be highly potent. Those tiny spiders can't be producing much volume. Mind you, don't say a damned word about any of this to anyone but me or you will regret it, Jascar."

"No sir. I won't." Quickly, a guard escorted him off to the med lab, just as two men entered wearing biohazard containment suits, hopefully impervious to the spider and its venom.

"I want this office scrubbed. There's a spider in here. Either kill it or capture it. Seal off the office on our way out. Those two don't get out of here until they find that thing!" Esteban barked his orders. Looking down at his legs nervously, he walked swiftly to the door, followed by the remainder of his guards. Once outside, one activated the sealing codes. The doors made a hissing sound as they sealed.

However, Jones was too clever for Esteban. When she heard what he had planned, she carefully zipped over to his pants, slipping down in his right pant legs cuff, where she was darn near invisible. Thus, she went out of the office with Esteban. Jones also knew that she was making progress. This Esteban man was obviously wielding great power. Thus, he warranted further study, so she resolved to stay with him instead of heading off to further explore this new world.

Jones silently experienced mirth. These humans were just like the ones she'd known three thousand years ago. They believed they were the masters of the galaxy, the most intelligent, powerful creatures, but in fact, Jones knew that it was her race of spiders, which was all that and so much more. *Mother Smith only wants to dine on these humans and go about her own life. Stupid mother anyway. I'm much smarter than she is, the old fool. No, I aim to be the ruler of the galaxy. Already, I am making great progress. I wonder who is above this Esteban fellow?*

Esteban stood outside his sealed office watching the two

men ransack his office, or so it appeared, but they found nothing. Then they unleashed a fume bomb before reporting. "Mr. Trujillo, we found no spiders in here or any bugs. However, we are fumigating with a Class Nine extermination gas. It is guaranteed to kill all insects, bugs, and spiders. In an hour, we can say for certain your office is clean."

Esteban fumed. "Damn it! I saw it with my own eyes! You telling me that it can also go invisible?"

"Boss, maybe it came out with us?" one security guard suggested. Immediately, the group of men began shaking their clothes and such, looking for the spider, but no one thought to look inside Esteban's pant cuff, were Jones was continuing to smile in her own unique way. *These new humans are just as dumb as their predecessors had been.*

"All right. One of you go down to the med lab. As soon as they are finished with Jascar, I want him locked up for the night. No one talks to him. No one. Total silence. Have the lab send me the toxicology reports at home. I've had enough excitement for one day," Esteban ordered. They acknowledged him, and he headed on up to the roof where his shuttle was parked.

A half hour later, he landed on the roof of his fancy mansion estate, the finest on Scorpi-C, as befitting the most important corporate exec in this sector or so he believed. He headed down the elevator stepping out into his living room, where his wife and many children rose to greet him. Eighteen years ago, when he assumed his position here on Scorpi-C, his boss had given him a fabulous gift, his wife, Lita, now thirty-six. She was a stunning blonde UFB woman, whose wavy locks fell to her knees. It was at that time that he learned of the genetic breeding program, though he was warned that if he ever revealed anything about it, he would be assassinated at once. Considering how gorgeous his new wife was, Esteban wasn't about to say anything to anyone.

She was the love of his life. He got aroused every time he even saw her, so great was her beauty. Later on after meeting many other such UFB women, he realized they all aroused him; that was their purpose. Further, unlike the women he had met before, she had a sex drive even greater than his own, and that pleased him even more. "Ah my lovely Lita. You look fabulous! What a treat to come home from a bad day at the office to feast my eyes upon your incredible beauty."

Lita smiled demurely, making her slow, careful way over to him, trying hard not to wobble. The plush carpet and her extreme heels didn't mix well at all. She pressed her body into his and with her hair, felt his arms as they gently surrounded her, giving her a feeling of ecstasy. Their children were right behind her so he had to let go of her for a moment.

A big grin on her face, his eldest daughter, Luisa, now eighteen, made her precarious way up to him, pressing her body into his as her mother had done. All of his daughters were themselves UFB women, but had inherited his jet-black hair, thick and luscious, and also falling to their knees, as expected of a UFB woman. "So have you found me a husband yet, papa?" she whispered in his ear. Ever since she turned eighteen, this had been her nightly ritual, knowing that one day he would answer yes. Then, she would no longer have to seek her pleasure gratification from her mother and sisters.

"Not yet, but soon I promise, dearest Luisa, soon. Ah, my dear Marisol," he moved from her to the now arriving sixteen-year-old, who likewise pressed her body into his, her hair feeling his arms encircling her. As always, he gave her a kiss on her forehead, though she wanted very much more than that. Two more years, she kept telling herself.

He moved over to greet his youngest daughter, Herminia, who had just turned thirteen, giving her a hug and kiss as well. Behind them, his three boys, all burly young men, strong and powerful, stood waiting to greet him. They were inches taller than he was, and their arm muscles dwarfed his. Bernardo was seventeen; Cleto was fifteen; Emedio was fourteen. Bernardo said, "Hi papa. Guess what? I pressed two hundred today!"

Cleto added, "I got to one-fifty, papa."

"Well done all of you. One day soon, you three will become great men, great fighters, great protectors of our family," Esteban declared.

Just then, their older maid, Gracia stepped into the room. "Sir, supper is ready for you. Will you be taking it now?"

"Yes of course. Lita, children, let's eat and chat. I have missed you all today. Papa's had an alarming day, but as usual, I can't talk about it," Esteban replied, his arms slipping around Lita and Luisa, helping them balance better on the thick carpet. The man, no matter his other faults, treasured his family above all else and was extremely kind to them, especially his UFB daughters. Few other men on Scorpi-C could boast having four stunningly beautiful women in their lives. What he found amazing about the UFB women was that after having six children, Lita still had her utterly remarkable figure! He also had long-range plans for his super strong sons.

He helped Lita arrange her hair before sitting, while he kept an eye on his boys. Good, they minded their manners well, doing the same for his daughters. While he fed Lita, they did the same with his daughters. Again, he was thankful that he had as many boys as girls. Otherwise, he would have had to hire more women servants, which he did not want to do. Even one was more than he would have preferred. Less people to spy on him and his family.

As they dined and chatted, Jones crawled up Esteban's pant leg and cleverly slipped onto the table, hiding beneath the edge of Lita's plate. Jones was enchanted. Here was something new, something very different in humans. These women. Long did Jones study Lita while she ate. Did all human females now lack two appendages? Perhaps not, since the other older one still had hers. Still, Jones thought this was rather a remarkable change in human bodies and decided this warranted further investigation. Attempting to move on up the human control ladder would have to wait a while longer.

She decided to return to her secure location in his pant cuff and darted off the table when no one was looking down. Soon, Jones was back in her comfortable, warm location. Now all she had to do was wait. Humans bedded with each other, which she knew from her last outings so long ago. Patience, she told herself.

Sometime later, Gracia had Lita prepared for bed. Her blonde hair lying across her naked front, Lita sat on the edge of their bed, waiting for Esteban to get undressed and join her. Oh how she longed for these minutes every day! However, she'd long ago given up the idea that he'd spend all day with her in their bed. Soon he too was ready and he turned out their lights and came to her.

Jones crawled out of the pant cuff and made her way over to the bed. A couple of minutes later, she slipped up to the neck of Lita, who was completely engrossed in passionate love making. She didn't even feel Jones on her neck or her bite. As soon as Jones entered Lita's neck, she got the shock of her long spider life! For several minutes, Jones was overwhelmed in sensations coming from Lita's body. Each of her long hairs was sending touch sensory perceptions up to her brain and mind, intercepted by Jones. Combined with Lita's seemingly huge sexual drive, poor Jones was simply stunned for quite some time. She discovered she really enjoyed the sensations coming from this new model of human female, very much so. Thus, Jones changed her plans, relaxing her control over Lita's body. Jones had some serious thought to do now.

When they finally fell asleep, Jones was able to think clearly once more. She decided she simply had to study these new human forms. Thus, in the morning, she didn't leave Lita to go back with Esteban to his office. That could wait. Lita was far more interesting to Jones right now. In fact, she didn't even think about leaving Lita for well over a week. Jones didn't realize it at the time, but she was also being hooked on the overwhelming sensations coming from Lita's body. She wanted more and more of it.

There and then, Jones decided she had to find out all about these new human forms that Esteban called UFBs. Perhaps it would be these women who would ultimately control the worlds and the galaxy, she mused. They would, if she had anything to do about it.

The next day, Esteban received the toxicology report on Jascar. His people found traces of a highly toxic neuro-toxin in his system, one that was totally unknown. Thus, he had proof positive that something new and strange had been discovered on 9-Sigma-C. These spiders were both intriguing and frightening at the same time.

That they were blindingly fast, highly toxic, easily

controlling human bodies scared him deeply. If these things got loose on a world, havoc would result. Still, if their toxin could be harvested, a tiny drop could immobilize anyone, quite beneficial. Thus, that next day, he composed a lengthy document outlining what he'd discovered, attached the video, and sent it on up the line to his superior, via a secure communication. He had added his recommendation that they maintain a total blackout of this whole incident. Keep it top-secret within the GE Corporation.

However, by the end of the day, he sighed. The cat was out of the bag. Several other corporation execs had discovered the spiders. In fact, the spiders had apparently spread to several other worlds via the transports leaving 9-Sigma-C. Other execs wanted answers, and as the supper hour approached, his superior replied, ordering him to assemble the other corporate execs on Scorpi-C and brief them fully on the spiders, which were now being viewed as a very serious threat. Five other men had died, their bodies drained of all fluids. Further, he was to encourage inter-corporation cooperation on devising a plan to deal with these spiders before the average person found out about them.

Before heading home, he placed fifteen secure calls. One was to Alfonso Vega. "Good evening. I'll be quick. Something has come up that affects all of us and all our worlds. It's critical, and I don't dare say anything, not even over a secure line. I'm calling a corporations-wide meeting tomorrow here at my office. Nine o'clock. Say, Alfonso, would you mind dropping by a bit earlier? I've a small proposition for you."

"Of course. Will 8:45 be acceptable?" Alfonso asked. It was, and he was left in mystery about both topics. That evening he put the RdD on high alert and had them go over everything they could to see if they could find any clues about what this was all about.

Juanita called him back two hours later while he was at home. "Boss, it seems that a junior officer from a remote mining colony in the neighboring Rossiter Sector arrived a couple of days ago and was met personally by Esteban at the spaceport. Since then, his ship has been quarantined, but no one is saying why. The tower did have two men in bio containment suits there today going over his ship, but they didn't lift the quarantine. Does this help?"

"Captain Juanita, you are a real treasure. Yes, yes it does. It gives me something to think about. Thank you for putting in the extra hours," Alfonso replied, hanging up. *Now just what is going on in the nearby sector? My hands are full already with this Master fellow and the corporations. Is this in anyway related? I doubt it.*

Alfonso arrived at the GE Corporation headquarters fifteen minutes early and noticed extremely tight security was in place. Something certainly had Esteban's full attention, but what? He took the elevator down a floor and passed through the line of his security guards. Entering Esteban's office, the older man rose, "Ah, Alfonso. So good of you to come a bit early. I wanted to feel you out about something dear to my heart. My eldest daughter, Luisa, is eighteen and in need of just the right husband. Of course, she's a UFB as you know. I was thinking. Isn't your eldest son about her age?"

"Ah, Emelio. Yes, he's nineteen now. My first wife died during his childbirth. Like yourself, I was asked to marry a UFB when I took this position with GD. Carmela is a wonderful woman, UFB naturally. All my other children are by her. In three years, I'll have double daughter trouble, since the twins are both fifteen now. So I know what you mean. We dare not marry them to other male children from UFB wives, not yet anyway, and we certainly don't want to marry them down the corporate ladder. That isn't fair to these admirable, beautiful young daughters," Alfonso played the role that Esteban expected of him.

"So you would consider such a union?" Esteban pressed the issue.

"Of course. We'd be honored by such a union. Of course, she would need to move in with Emelio, and I'd have to get them their own home," Alfonso replied, faking financial concerns.

"Excellent. Far cheaper than being the father of the bride, let me tell you. My three daughters can certainly run up a clothing tab in the blink of an eye. Shall we shake on this?"

Esteban agreed. The men shook. "I will tell her about it tonight. What with what is going to be said at this meeting, we should push their wedding up as soon as we possibly can. Stick around, and we can firm up a date." Alfonso agreed to do so, knowing that soon he would have another set of eyes into the GE Corporation, albeit a distant set.

Still, this was a fortuitous union in his eyes. While he waited for the other men to arrive, he mused about UFB women and marriages. No longer did the men even need to see their bride-to-be, since every UFB woman was the epitome of beauty, ravishingly gorgeous, and highly motivated for sexual involvement, perhaps too much so. From a man's point of view, any of these UFB women would make a good partner, especially since they were so darn helpless. One didn't have to deal with their having careers to interfere or even likes and dislikes or even personality conflicts. The UFB women had only one thing always on their minds, bedtime. Somehow, this was all very, very wrong as far as Alfonso was concerned, yet it was the currently demanded practice among the corporate executives. He had no choice but to play this game if he wished to remain an exec at GD.

The meeting took everyone by complete surprise. No one had any word about the invasion of these spiders. "Yes, they are about the size of your little fingernail. And I can vouch for just how fast the things can move," Esteban elaborated after showing them the video. "One came into my office on the neck of the 9-Sigma-C executive who took this video. Look at how Jascar responded with that beast inside his neck and then afterwards." He played the initial meeting with Jascar and then a bit of how he reacted once the spider had left his body. The men were shocked at the drastic behavioral changes. Next, Esteban outlined the latest intelligence, which suggested that these spiders had already spread to a dozen other worlds, including Scorpi-C.

He went over the toxicology report, and now the men began to realize just how important capturing one of this new species of spiders actually was. All could see covert uses for such a powerful paralytic toxin. Still, that these spiders were extremely dangerous wasn't lost on them. Images of the host of spiders draining the poor miner were burned into their minds. No one had ever seen anything like it.

Alfonso asked, "So could these spiders have been part of the top-secret research on Rho-C, where all the bio-engineers were located, and where those worm-like beasts were, along with those giant wolves?"

"No, I have it on good authority from someone I trust that the bio-engineers on Rho-C had nothing to do with spiders," Esteban answered, knowing that many probably wouldn't believe him, but that hardly mattered.

"We are charged with figuring out a way to stop these spiders before the general public finds out about them. We have to stop their spreading to other worlds. So I propose you take this to your top research men and discuss ways and means. Let's meet at this time tomorrow and put our collective heads together on this one. We all have everything at stake on this problem," Esteban finished up and the meeting broke up.

As requested, Alfonso hung around until the last man left. "In light of this, Esteban, perhaps we should move the date up to just as soon as you can make the wedding arrangements. I'll see about housing yet today, once I talk to my staff."

"Excellent, excellent. I'll let you know tomorrow what date we can manage." Esteban looked very pleased indeed. He looked forward to having another set of eyes looking into the GD Corporation.

Alfonso called in all the GD staff to meet with him and arranged a video conference for those who couldn't cram into their auditorium, which he also recorded. Then, he relayed all he'd heard about these spiders. He asked everyone to work up ways and means of detecting them, capturing them, or killing them. He also asked those in research to see if they could find out anything about such spiders. After the meeting was finished, he replayed the recording for all those who were in his RdD group and not part officially of the GD Corporation.

Later that afternoon, while he was on his way to meet with his son, who was still at the Academy studying chemical engineering, Juanita called him on his private line. "Boss, I did as you asked and did some digging—well, the computer did the work, following my orders. There is an archaeology team from GE Corp there on 9-Sigma-C. I think that warrants a closer inspection."

"Hey, once more, good work, Juanita. I'll see what I can find out about that later today. Bye." He hung up, but decided to bring that up with Esteban as soon as possible. *While it just might be a coincidence, it should be checked out. Lord knows, no one should dare trust a corporation, not ever.*

He found his eldest son between classes. "Glad I caught you, Emelio. I have a proposition for you. It seems that old Esteban Trujillo wants to marry his eldest daughter, Luisa, to you and as soon as possible. She is a UFB of course, just as your sisters are. I told him I'd check with you about it. Son, what do you think? There are pros and cons." He decided to treat Emelio as an adult, especially seeing him here on the campus. He looked so grown up. Memories flashed of when Emelio took his first steps while he was holding his tiny hands.

"Wow. Rather takes me by surprise, dad. Sure are a lot of pros and cons. Hell, being married to a UFB is like a ticket into the big leagues no matter what route I take, isn't it dad?"

"Certainly is. Only the wealthiest men and the corporate execs generally have UFB wives. Of course, if you marry, I'll get you your own place pronto and handle finances until you graduate and get employed," Alfonso added.

"Well, that would be great. I do need your backing, at least until I get established. You know I have no intention of being a corporation executive, don't you?"

Alfonso laughed. "Son, that I do know. Have known that for a long time. Your heart is into this chemical engineering stuff. The galaxy needs more like you, if any new things are ever to come about. Still, having a UFB on your arm could certainly not hurt your standings."

It was Emelio's turn to chuckle. "No kidding. I know the UFB women usually aren't interested in much of anything except looking pretty and having sex, but I have met Luisa several times. She seems brighter than her mother, almost as sharp as mom is. Okay, I'll do it. I really want to get into a key research position when I graduate, and this should help me achieve that next year, don't you think?"

"Absolutely, son. All right. I'll get the wheels going on this. It needs to happen soon. Son, I have to tell you something I don't want you to tell to another person, at least not until we have a chance to get the situation under control. You'll understand why when I finish." Alfonso then told Emelio about the spider situation, adding, "Come by the house tonight and see the video for yourself or drop by the RdD since it's closer to here and ask for Juanita. She'll show it to you. Just don't say a word about it. We can't have the population panicking. That'll only make matters far worse than they are."

"Okay. I'll drop by the RdD, but are you sure this doesn't have something to do with that Rho-C mess? It's been on the news a lot," Emelio asked.

"Right now, we don't think they are related, if you can believe anything that GE Corporation says about Rho-C. I'm inclined to believe them this time, however. I'll phone you more details about the wedding. Any preferences for a home?"

"Close to the campus here would be nice. Oh, we should make sure all the doors operate automatically for her sake too, dad," Emelio added, thinking of Luisa.

"Right. I'll get on it. Bye for now." He rose and left, remembering his old Academy days and how bright the future seemed to him back then, before he discovered the real world of the corporations. Perhaps the premature death of his first wife also had something to do with his outlook. He shrugged and called up Esteban, confirming Emelio had agreed to marry Luisa as soon as possible.

As he then headed back to his office to search the online home listings, he realized something else about his son. Emelio hadn't mentioned love at all! Alfonso began to wonder if the modern generation had forsaken marrying for love entirely. Well, he couldn't fault Emelio for marrying a UFB woman. That alone would almost guarantee him his desired research position at GD. He had married Carmela under similar circumstances as Emelio was about to do with Luisa. He and Carmela had become very close. Perhaps it would all work out just fine.

He spent an hour reviewing homes that met the necessary requirements, printing out two addresses for Emelio to check out personally. Then, he made an appointment to interview a lady's maid for Luisa, since she would certainly need one. After that, he settled down and focused his mind on the very serious spider mess. Alfonso soon gave up. Besides being far beyond his knowledge, he had far too little information about the spiders to do more than mere speculation. The key, he resolved, involved getting far more information about them. Know thy enemy came to mind, and he jotted that saying down, intending to bring that up at the meeting tomorrow.

Later that night, Emelio called up to tell him which house he preferred and to thank him. Alfonso promised to see to the details in the morning, which he did as early as possible, handling them before he headed off to Esteban's meeting. The meeting went as badly as Alfonso believed it might. No one had any hard data on these spiders, so all ideas offered were essentially mere speculation, leaving Esteban in a precarious position, which every exec present knew quite well. He was given this problem to solve. If he failed, he would be facing severe repercussions from higher up GE Corporation execs.

Esteban also anticipated severe fallout from the spider mess. Hence, the wedding was set for the next morning. After the other execs left, he took Alfonso aside to tell him that detail. Then, Esteban did the unexpected. "Alfonso, we've known each other for what—some eighteen years?"

"True, ever since I was appointed to my position at GD."

"Right. How time flies. Anyway, I count you among my friends, though corporation rules prohibit too much interchange between us. Still, I consider you my friend, Alfonso, though we've not seen eye to eye at times."

Alfonso wondered what he was trying to say. Had he said *acquaintances*, he would have been more comfortable with Esteban's declaration. *Friends* was carrying their association a bit too far. Nevertheless, he was polite and nodded.

Esteban continued, "This spider mess. Alfonso, it has all the makings of a fiasco for me and my position here at GE. Look, we both know the situation is likely to get far worse before it gets resolved and that could well mean my head will be on the old block, as we say. My bosses will need a scapegoat, and I'll be it. We both know that."

"Corporate politics are brutal, Esteban. We both know that," Alfonso replied, still wondering where this was going.

"Right. Okay I'll just come out with it. If my head gets put on the block, my sons are old enough to make their way in the world, but not my wife and other two daughters. I've no right to ask this of you, but I will anyway. If my head goes on the block, I would like you to step in and take good care of Lita, Marisol, and Hermina for me. Do it fast before the corporation execs get other ideas for my girls. I'd do the same for you. They are the treasure of my life, Alfonso. If you'll do this for me, I'll make sure funds are available for all three of them. Plus, I'll owe you a big one if you'll agree to do this for me."

Alfonso stood there stunned by what Esteban proposed. Alfonso had a keen interest in the UFB women, one of deep sympathy and compassion. In his mind, they represented just how evil and immoral the corporations were. No sentient human being would do such a thing to a woman, turning her into a UFB woman and thereby ensuring that her daughters would inherit and be born as UFB women, helpless and utterly dependent. In fact, it had been his discovery of the UFB women and the breeding program that had turn him into the RdD in the first place. Women should not be objects, things of pleasure for men, breeders of genetically modified offspring. He was forced to marry one, Carmela, and overnight that had changed him into a resistance fighter.

"I will accept, Esteban. I have strong feelings about our UFB women. They deserve the best we can provide for them. If something happens to you, I'll quickly step in, but I'll need your security codes, and they'll need to expect me coming for them," Alfonso stated factually.

"Granted. If the time comes, I'll see that you have them and that they are so prepared. I owe you for this. I always pay my debts, Alfonso. Don't be afraid to call in your favor, anytime." He shook Alfonso's hand vigorously. Alfonso smiled, if only because he fully intended to use that chip! Esteban didn't know Alfonso knew what was being kept in total secrecy in the basement levels of this very building! Now he began to think of ways that those women could be rescued as well, though the potential number of UFB women being kept there was staggering.

The wedding went as planned, a private ceremony held at the Trujillo mansion. Only Alfonso, Carmela, and Emelio attended, since the situation was so unusual. Emelio wasn't disappointed though. Luisa was radiant! She wore a beautiful white satin, strapless gown. A small tiara contrasted sharply with her long, thick black hair. As the three entered, Lita carefully walked up to Alfonso and Carmela, as Alfonso kept a secure arm around his wife knowing how difficult walking on such plush carpeting was for her.

"Carmela, you look so lovely today. I'm so proud of my little Luisa. Emelio, she is getting a handsome young man, just what she needs most. I best keep from crying. Esteban will have a fit if he has to dab my eyes all through the ceremony," Lita chatted away. She added, "My husband speaks so highly of you both. I'm so glad you could come today. I'm going to miss my beautiful daughter so."

Alfonso had met her several times, usually at formal gatherings, such as the theater or concerts. She was never this emotional, he thought, and he kept an eye on her. Marisol and Herminia stood on either side of their older sister, looking as radiant as Luisa did, though Marisol did seem a bit envious of Luisa. *Well, she is sixteen after all,* Alfonso thought, *and soon my daughters will be this excited too. My how time has flown.*

The ceremony was over in just a few minutes, after which the formal documents were signed and sent off making the marriage official in the eyes of all corporations. This was the one detail that most concerned Alfonso, and Esteban was aware of it as well, for once the documents were sent off, no one could later come along and steal Luisa away from Emelio. For his part, Alfonso believed Emelio was very pleased with Luisa and happy. Esteban's three boys stayed in the background the whole time, completely disinterested in the whole affair, though Bernardo was happy that he would no longer have to be looking after Luisa, especially at meal times.

Emelio pleased Alfonso. As soon as the ceremony was

finished, he continually kept an arm around Luisa, steadying her on the thick pile carpeting, just as he was doing with Carmela, though Esteban wasn't doing the same with Lita. Certainly, the other boys were not around their sisters. In fact, all three boys headed off to the gym for a workout the moment the ceremony was over.

The three men and women then sat around the living room chatting for a time. The excitement of the moment was gone. Alfonso noted Lita now had a sort of blank look on her face, quite uncharacteristic he thought, but now wasn't the time to say anything. Luisa chatted with Emelio. "Dad has gotten me my very own electrostatic hair machine. It's the kind I can run myself, so you won't always be having to brush out my hair. You can't believe how wonderful it feels. Did you know that I can feel things with each strand of my hair? It is so exciting."

Emelio laughed a little. "Yes, I have two sisters, you know. They are fifteen now. I hate to be in dad's shoes in three years—a double wedding for sure."

Luisa giggled. Then, she whispered, "I can't wait to see our new home. When can we go?"

"Everyone, we are going to take off now and go check out our new home. Thank you all for everything," Emelio said politely. After shaking hands with Esteban and giving the women a hug, the pair left. Alfonso noted Emelio still had his arm around Luisa, steadying her and felt rather proud that his son was being so considerate of Luisa. As Luisa said her farewells, once more Lita was overly emotional, but as soon as they left, her face became expressionless.

Esteban noticed Alfonso noticing that and took him aside, whispering, "She's been a little up and down these past few days."

Alfonso decided to take a gamble and whispered back, "You told us the spider that was in your office on Jascar's neck was not found in your office. Could it possibly have been on your clothes when you came home? Could it possibly be on her neck? Look at her. She reminds me of the way Jascar appeared when you first interviewed him."

A shocked look suddenly appeared on Esteban's face.

Clearly, he hadn't thought about this possibility. Suddenly, her behavior began to make sense. "Oh God! You might be right! What should we do?"

"We need to get her into a quarantine room at your headquarters, that is, if your corporation has one," Alfonso suggested.

"Right. Right. We best both go and bring our wives with us. Less suspicions that way. We'll need an excuse for our wives," Esteban thought swiftly. "I know, we can pretend to be giving you and Carmela a tour. Come on. Brilliant observation, my old friend."

When they rejoined the women, Esteban suggested, "Lita, you and I should take Alfonso and Carmela here on a short tour of my office building. Kids, you behave yourselves now and do what Gracia tells you. Come my lovely Lita; let's show our good friends where I work."

"Oh. Well if you insist," Lita replied in a monotone, convincing both men that perhaps the spider really was inside Lita's neck! Interestingly enough, Esteban kept some distance between himself and Lita, while Alfonso continued to keep his arm around Carmela, giving her the support she needed, in contrast to the wobbling of Lita, who struggled to keep her balance while walking in the extreme heels.

A few minutes later, the four stepped out of the shuttle. Esteban handled the security guards, allowing the four to enter the elevator, taking it down from the roof to the seventieth floor, where the bio containment room was located. Both women had never seen such a room before and were naturally quite curious, particularly when Esteban ushered Lita inside and quickly stepped back outside before Alfonso and Carmela could get inside. He hit the Execute button, sealing Lita inside.

"Okay. She's contained. I'm calling my research team in now. Keep an eye on her please."

"What's going on, Alfonso? Why is Lita in there all by herself?" Carmela asked, quite worried.

"We believe she might be infected by some kind of nasty spider, dear. I'll tell you about it when we get home. Right now, talk to Lita. Keep her calm. Yell if you see a small spider on her," he answered his wife.

A bit later, Esteban returned. "They are on their way now. Lita. We think that nasty spider is in your neck. Don't worry dear; we're going to get it out of you very soon now."

Jones was having a hard time this day. Her host's emotions were very strong at times. Well, from what Jones could tell, her offspring was leaving the nest, which is what Jones felt should be happening. All offspring should leave the nest and fend for themselves in the world. Now she was inside some sealed room. The man's words registered, and Jones knew the man knew she was inside this woman's body. More importantly, he said he was going to remove her. *Well, I have much more work to do,* Jones declared. Quickly, she backed out of Lita's neck, dropping onto the floor, and scurrying out of sight.

"There! Look, there it goes!" Esteban exclaimed, suddenly wild with excitement. Lita screamed and shook visibly.

"You have to get her out of there!" Carmela yelled.

Poor Esteban was torn. He desperately wanted Lita out of the containment room, but if he opened the door, the spider might rush out as well. Worse, it could hop on anyone of the three! Just then, six researchers came running in. "The spider thing. It was in Lita's neck. It's out of her now. It ran to the back of the room. Can we get her out of there and not release the spider too?"

"Well, it's possible to gas her and knock her out, but no guarantee it will knock out the spider, sir," one replied.

"We can't keep her in there. No telling what that spider will do to her next," Esteban complained.

"Quarantine protocols dictate she stays in there until we have the spider contained," another countered.

"But that's my wife and a UFB woman," he protested.

Alfonso spoke up. "Look, the spider is hiding. Let's open the door and quickly get her out of there, but stand by with blasters and shoot the damned thing if it comes out of hiding." His idea was accepted.

Five security guards came. Everyone but Esteban stood back, while the five men trained their guns on the floor before Lita, as he entered the unlock protocol. A hissing sound indicated the seal was broken. "On three, we get her out," Esteban called out and counted down. He yanked the door open and moved inside, grabbing Lita and carrying her outside the containment room. He no more than got clear of the door when the spider shot like a bullet across the containment room floor and out the door. Simultaneously, several blasters fired, partially destroying the containment center.

Men yelled. "Did we get it?" someone shouted, but in the confusion that followed, no one was certain of anything. At this point, everyone there was looking around, frantically trying to spot the spider, but no one saw where it had gone.

"It's damnably fast, I'll give it that," Esteban commented, holding the terrified Lita tightly. She finally broke down and began sobbing.

"It was inside of me, telling me what to do and say some of the time. Esteban, I was so helpless," she wailed. He did his best to console her.

"We have to file a report, sir," one of his researchers said quietly.

Esteban merely nodded. "Take a blood sample now and test it for the toxin. I'll take her home." Ten minutes later, a somber four flew back to his mansion in his shuttle. No one said anything, but Lita continued to sob softly to herself.

Once home, Esteban had no choice but to explain about the spiders to his entire family, but did swear them to secrecy. Carmela insisted that Gracia make them some hot cocoa, and she more or less pushed the sobbing and shaking Lita on into their kitchen. Her daughters carefully followed after her, more worried than they ever had been in their lives.

Finally, the two men were alone. Esteban ran his hands through his short hair and sighed. "Alfonso, I think that day we were talking about has come much sooner than either of us expected. After tonight, I expect to get that call tomorrow morning."

"Hell, do they think that badly of you? Damn it, Esteban, it was your wife in there. What choice did you have?" Alfonso backed his decision.

"Between you and me who love our UFB wives—none. But the higher execs are likely to see it differently. If it does happen, I'm prepared. Come with me." He led him to his wall safe and opened it. "Okay, take these documents. They officially transfer ownership of Lita, Marisol, and Hermina to you, Alfonso. With any luck, the execs will honor the transfer. Keep them. If the call comes, I'll text you. My guess is you'll have maybe an hour to get here and get them to somewhere safe. Then, file the documents. Thank you for saving Lita tonight." Alfonso shook his hand and promised to look after them.

Later on, Carmela made her slow, careful way back into the living room. "Lita has calmed down, and Gracia is getting her ready for bed now. We should go, dear." They did just that. On their way home, Alfonso alerted Carmela to what he had agreed to do, just in case. In his gut, Alfonso suspected that Esteban was right. The GE Corporation was utterly ruthless.

Once home, he called Emelio and told him what had happened, asking him to prepare Luisa for the potential shock. Then, he alerted the RdD and asked them to monitor what they could of GE Corporation's current communications, knowing that in all likelihood, anything important would be sent over secure lines. Finally, he took a long shower with Carmela and went to bed. Time enough to alert his other children if it actually occurred.

Alfonso was just leaving for work the next day when he received a cell text message from Esteban. It was only one word: Now. He changed course and headed directly to the Trujillo mansion, where Lita and her two daughters were just finishing their breakfast. "It's happened, hasn't it?" Lita said when Gracia opened the door and she saw him standing there. Alfonso merely nodded.

"Girls, we must leave right now. Come on. I hope later on we can return for our things." Alfonso stepped inside and slipped an arm around Lita, who gave him a grateful smile. Once he had her on the more secure concrete outside their front door, he returned and slipped an arm around Marisol and Hermina. Both were wobbling trying to keep their balance on the soft carpet. They whispered their thanks, as they felt his supporting arms.

A half hour later, Alfonso helped each into his home,

where Carmela was waiting for them, along with Chita and Gabriella, who were very happy to have Marisol and Herminia staying with them. Alfonso said, "Okay, I'm off to work. I'll keep you posted on what I can find out about Esteban." Lita thanked him, and he left, doubting that he could actually learn much. Once at his office, he dutifully filed the documents and kept his fingers crossed. UFB women were valuable, but then GE Corporation had hundreds in the basement of their headquarters, so perhaps they would ignore these three, particularly Lita who was thirty-six and near the end of her reproduction days.

At his office, Esteban received orders to take the next deep space transport and report to his boss directly. Jones had picked up a hint something might happen with him, had cleverly darted into his pant cuff once more, and had gone back home with them the previous night. Cleverly, she inserted herself into the cuff of the pants he put on the following morning. Thus, she heard him being ordered on up the line to his boss and decided to follow along. When Esteban boarded the transport under heavy guard, Jones did as well, nice and cozy in his cuff. She was ready to see more powerful men. Besides, she was highly intrigued by these new kinds of human females, whose emotions were so strong. She wanted to know more about them and perhaps to occupy another one for a time. Never had Jones had so much fun as she had these past few days. *Perhaps,* she thought, *the humans have something to offer us beside juices.*

Like Jones, forty-nine others continued making their way up the corporate ladders across numerous planets. All except Jones, reported periodically to mother Smith. Jones kept her reports to the bare minimum and didn't mention these new types of human females. She didn't want mother Smith to interfere with them, not just yet anyway.

Chapter 11—Changes

Emelio and Luisa moved into their new small home, close to the Academy. Surprisingly, though perhaps not knowing Alfonso's mind, they discovered that their close neighbors were Jason and Linda Mott-Whitney, who had Captain Bess Fontana and Gunnery Sergeant Martha Spelling as their housemates and helpers. A fellow student at the Academy, Antonia, was Luisa's helper. Antonia dropped by in the mornings before her classes began, and then dropped by several times during the day as well. All this was quite new to Luisa, who until now had led a very sheltered life, rarely leaving her home. Now, she found herself surrounded by many others around her own age and students as well.

Antonia explained cheerily, "Okay Luisa, on my first break this afternoon, we're going shopping. You need more appropriate clothes. Your gowns are fine for dress up, but not for every day. Besides, I'm sure Emelio will be taking you to the beach on the weekends. All of us students go to the beach at least once a week. You'll see."

When Emelio returned home with their supper in hand, Luisa carefully rose from their new couch to meet him as he entered, holding her breath wondering what he'd think of her new outfit. "Wow! Luisa, you look great, just like one of us," Emelio exclaimed, sitting down the food sacks and embracing her. She wore tie-dyed jeans and a tight fitting tee shirt that left nothing of her more than ample bosom to the imagination. Her outfit outlined her perfect curves extremely well, and her long jeans mostly hid her extreme heels from view.

"Antonia picked it out for me. Do I really look like the other students?" she asked. "Do you all really go down to the beach on the weekends?"

"Double yes, dear. Got us Arbies for tonight," he replied.

While they were eating, Luisa asked, "You know Emelio, I was wondering if I could possibly study something at the Academy too. I don't really want to just be a pretty caged bird like mom is, but I don't suppose that is remotely possible because of the way I am, right?"

"Hey, sure you can. Being a student doesn't require arms for the most part. Many of my courses were online. Just need a computer, and they have voice-activated ones too. What are you interested in learning about?" Emelio asked, extremely pleased she suggested such a thing. He was becoming more and more impressed with her by the minute.

"Well, I always wanted to know what is and was going on in our world and galaxy. How about history?" she asked.

The next day, both had to deal with the sudden recall of her father and the realization that meant he'd probably be killed. They planned to make a quick trip to her home to get the rest of her things, but Alfonso had already handled that. His men went there and moved the women's possessions to Alfonso's mansion. Later that night, men brought Luisa's things over to her new home. She was elated to have her old electrostatic hair machine and just had to show Emelio how it worked. "Glad I don't have to try to handle your beautiful hair any longer, dear," he teased her. That had been a nightmare for him so far.

Emelio got her a voice-activated laptop and enrolled her in two history courses, Scorpi-C History I and Galactic History I. A very excited new student began her studies the next morning. When Antonia stopped by between classed to help her with lunch, she found her sitting on the couch with her laptop on the floor, her toes going to town. "Look at me, Antonia! I'm a real student now!" Luisa exclaimed, very excited and proud of what she was doing. This was the first thing t she had ever done on her own.

"Coolest! Now you are one of us. I'm studying engineering. One day, I want to help design modern labor saving things for homes," Antonia explained, sitting down beside her. "Oh, good. You have Professor Ortega. He's good. I had his lectures for Scorpi-C History last year. Everyone has to take that course." The two chatted before Antonia dashed off to the kitchen to make their lunch.

On Saturday morning, Emelio explained, "We usually spend Saturday afternoons on the beach. You know, a little R and R from studies, bask in the sun, go for a swim, and all that. You game to try it? If not, I understand. We don't have to go."

"I've never been there, Emelio. Antonia got me a bikini, which I've never had before either, and some beach mule heels, so I'm willing to try it, but I don't know if I can manage it very well. I don't see how I can swim, though, do you?"

Emelio got her into her bikini and then slipped a robe over her and changed himself. Together, they took a public shuttle to the golden sands of the beach on the eastern side of Malagena, where thousands of younger folks were partying, sunbathing, swimming, and simply having fun. Both soon found Luisa couldn't walk on the beach without Emelio holding her and supporting her all the way, but neither minded that at all.

After spreading out towels, they sat down to bask in the warm sun. Before long, others came by to chat. Soon, many young women spotted the UFB woman and before long, Luisa became the center of attention, much to Emelio's frustration. Luisa was truly happy and gaily chatted. That she too was now an Academy student lowered many social barriers, and she suddenly had many offers of friendship. She'd had none ever before. Both had many offers to come to parties that night. He had to explain to her that many of these were drunken orgies and that some students only went to the Academy to party all the time. Still, she enjoyed a freedom she'd never had in her life, treasuring every minute of their outing.

That evening back home, Alfonso called and asked them to drop by and pay a visit with four others who were still adjusting to their new lives. Besides, they lived just two blocks away: Jason and Linda Mott-Whitney. Around seven, the two stood at their door, his arm securely around Luisa. Captain Bess Fontana opened the door and announced to the others that they had company. Of course, ever the protector, Martha insisted on checking on the two before allowing them inside.

"Hi Jason, Linda. Dad asked us to drop by and see how everything is going for you two," Emelio explained. "Gosh, Jason, you do look like Luisa and Linda." He was taken by surprise at how he looked, even though he'd been told about

Jason.

In his alto voice, Jason replied, "Yeh, I do. How are we doing? Miserable. I look like a woman, but I'm not, not where it counts anyway."

"We are bored out of our minds," Bess added. "Oh, congratulations. Alfonso told us that you got married."

"Thanks. Yes, I've never been so happy in my whole life!" Luisa bubbled. "I'm a student at the Academy now too! Can you believe that?"

"What? You can't be, can you?" Linda exclaimed, very much surprised. Luisa was just like her, a helpless UFB woman.

"Yes. I'm taking Scorpi-C History I and Galactic History I. Just started this week. Emelio got me a voice-activated computer and enrolled me. I can use my toes too. It's so cool!" Luisa explained to the silver-haired Linda.

Linda sighed. "I wonder if I could continue my studies of astrophysics and galactic navigation."

"Sure, don't see why not," Emelio spoke up. "I can get your school records transferred here and get you set up with a computer and everything. Heck, you could come over to our place and study together."

"Really? You think it is really possible for me to continue?" Linda asked, some hope in her voice.

"Sure thing. How about you, Jason?" Emelio asked. "Or you, Bess, or you, Martha?" Both Bess and Martha had both genetic cures and now wore their hair the way that they used to have it. Bess kept hers shoulder length, while Martha had hers quite short so it didn't interfere with her fighting skills.

Jason volunteered, "Just what would I study, Emelio? I've never been a bright student. All I ever was truly interested in was explosions—making things go boom."

"So why not peruse that? I'm in the chemical engineering program. Let me see what I can dig up for you, Jason." He agreed to let him try. "So Bess, you could pick up some courses on engineering and constructions yourself," he suggested.

"Hey how about physical therapy?" Martha broke in. "I could use a regimen to get my body built back up. Hell, I lost twenty pounds of muscle." The group chatted, and Emelio got the distinct impression Jason and Linda really did enjoy having them over for a visit.

On Sunday morning, Emelio searched the Academy catalog and found courses that might appeal to Jason, Bess, and Martha. He then arranged to get Linda's records transferred. After that, he and Luisa headed to his parents mansion for a family time. Lita, Marisol, and Herminia wanted to see how Luisa was faring. Plus, with the sudden loss of Esteban, Lita wanted to at least keep the women together as a family. The boys were another matter and were being looked after by the GE Corporation, who always had big plans for these new super-fighter types.

When Marisol, Herminia, Chita, and Gabriella heard all about what Luisa was doing at school and even going to the beach, the four became highly excited, even jealous, begging their parents to let them do some of these things too. Alfonso rubbed his hands through his hair, and said, "I'll be honest with you, girls, it never crossed my mind that you could even do any of these things. Luisa, I'm floored by what you've done in just a week. Emelio, what you are doing with her is flabbergasting to me. I don't think any corporation execs ever thought their UFB women were able to do any of these things. Girls, give me a few days to look into this for you."

"Hey dad, I can see if I can get the older girls into the Academy and the younger ones into a high school program," Emelio volunteered. He knew that his father knew practically nothing about the educational programs available here in Malagena.

On Monday morning, Jason and Linda, with Bess and Martha supporting them while they walked, joined Emelio and Luisa, who led them into the registrar's office to get them signed up for classes. Admittedly, the counselor was startled to see the three UFB women and even more startled to find out that one was in fact actually a rare UFBMD man. Nevertheless, she got them signed up as official Academy students.

A quick trip to the bookstore yielded four new laptops, two of which were voice-activated. After that, they returned to Emelio's new home, where he and Luisa got them all started.

Later on, when Antonia dropped by to fix Luisa her lunch, she was astounded to see so many other new students with her and was intrigued to learn that Jason wasn't a woman, but a UFBMD man!

When Emelio returned and ordered supper for everyone, they began discussing the spider situation, which had gotten Esteban in so much trouble. It was Luisa who made the initial suggestion, "Say, I have been thinking about the spider mess and how badly some need to be captured. I think there is a way. Freezing cold. Don't spiders hibernate in their silky nests during the winter? If so, if they had some way of blasting them with cold, maybe that would slow them down so they could be captured and studied."

"Hey, you are on to something, but how could it be delivered?" asked Emelio.

"A simple boom would do it," Jason broke in. He outlined the proper chemical mix. "It could be put into a hand grenade with just enough charge left in it to get the proper reaction started. Of course, you could add some extras to add a bit of color to the flash, like blue or red or yellow. If I had hands, I could probably make one for you."

Suddenly, everyone was all ears. Bess verified that his idea could well work, as far as the grenade alterations were concerned. She wasn't familiar with his chemical reaction, however. Emelio quickly phoned up his dad to tell him what they'd come up with. When he hung up, he exclaimed, "Jason! You are on! You and Bess are to report to GD headquarters first thing in the morning and make one of these. Dad says that if this actually works, he might be able to use it to somehow save Esteban's life!"

"My God, Alfonso! You are letting a helpless UFBMD man into the lab to build a bomb? Are you nuts?" his top research engineer complained. At eight, Alfonso met Jason and Beth at the main entrance, signed them in, and took them to the research lab, where frankly the scientists though the "old man" had finally lost it completely.

"Look, Jason may now be a UFBMD man, but he is still a top explosive engineer. Trust me. He knows what he is doing. Captain Bess here is also a construction engineer or was that is. So let them work in peace. This is important," Alfonso replied. They had no choice but to allow this nearly helpless woman-man work in their lab. Soon, they saw that he only gave Bess detailed instructions and that it was Bess who did the actual work, convincing them that they had been right. He was helpless. Nevertheless, Jason and Bess constructed six of his new Ice Grenades as he called them.

Alfonso now had a choice to make. He could arrange to get them to some personnel on 9-Sigma-C, test them, and very likely capture a number of the spiders for corporation research or he could use it as leverage to free Esteban. The latter was fraught with risks, especially since he had no idea if this new Ice Grenade of Jason's would actually work. Do the right thing came to mind. While he was a local leader of the corporate resistance movement, he knew that unless he did the right thing, he'd be no better than those whom he was fighting against.

He placed a secure call to the temporary head of the GE Corporation in Malagena. After introducing himself, he said, "I want to speak to the GE Corporation exec who has taken Mr. Esteban Trujillo away. Esteban asked us to develop a way to capture these spiders, and it has taken some brilliant minds to come up with a way, but my people have. The credit belongs to Mr. Trujillo, who informed us of the spiders and begged all of us corporation execs to lend a hand. Hence, I need to speak to that person or else the GD Corporation will step in and test our new invention unilaterally. Otherwise, the credit will fall with Mr. Trujillo and GE Corporation. It's your choice, sir." There, he'd laid it out plain enough. Now he waited impatiently drumming his fingers on his desktop.

A half hour later, he spoke to an unidentified, off-world GE Corporation executive. Once more, Alfonso explained the situation clearly, giving this exec the choice. "No, it is not yet tested, but per our agreement, it is officially Mr. Trujillo's right to be the first to test it and take the credit for capturing some of these nasty spiders. If GE Corporation doesn't want Mr. Trujillo to do this, then I assure you the GD Corporation will send a transport to 9-Sigma-C today, test it, and bring back the captured spiders to study in our own labs. Your choice. Bring

Mr. Trujillo back so he can oversee the project that he initiated or let GD do it." For once, Alfonso rather enjoyed the conversation, even though he had no idea who he was talking right now. Again, he was put on hold with stupid music playing in the background.

Then, another voice appeared, forcing him once more to repeat everything, which he rather enjoyed. He imagined the fits he was giving these GE Corporation executives, but began to wonder if they had already murdered Esteban. Well, in all likelihood, they probably had, he thought. Why else would they be passing the ball among executives? He was about to just hang up and forget it when yet another voice took over the conversation.

"Mr. Vega, this is indeed very good news. At the moment, Mr. Trujillo is rather indisposed and cannot come to the phone. I assure you that he is quite alive, just indisposed, and will be for a few days. Nevertheless, GE Corporation does appreciate what Mr. Trujillo has done, eliciting cooperation among the corporations there on the rim world of Scorpi-C." From his choice of words, Alfonso knew he was far distant from the rim, but was he in the hub worlds? The man continued, "If you will coordinate the test with the temporary head of GE Corporation there on Scorpi-C and *if* it is successful, then we will return Mr. Trujillo back to his family in a few days. That's the best counteroffer I can make at this time."

"That is most acceptable. In times like these, we need inter-corporation cooperation against our common enemy, the spiders in this case. I will arrange for the test as soon as possible. Thank you." Alfonso hung up, but allowed an hour for these people to relay word to this temporary head here on Scorpi-C.

Before the hour was up, a very enthusiastic man called him back, ready to conduct the field tests. Alfonso headed over to the GE Corporation headquarters with the box containing the six Ice Grenades. Bess had written very clear orders on their use. It was simple. Pull the pin and roll the grenade at least a hundred feet out in front of the personnel and into the swarm of spiders. Too simple really, but he hoped it would work, at least enough to save poor Esteban's life. At least, the temporary head allowed him to send along a GD representative with the GE Corporation crew.

All manner of precautions were in effect. As soon as the transport landed, every crew member put on a deep space suit, hermetically sealed. Then, the six testors opened the bay door and walked out onto the surface of 9-Sigma-C at a location where the spiders had last been seen in some numbers. A dead, desiccated body of a miner was visible proof the spiders had been here. They waited. Sure enough, shortly a host of the little devils came scurrying out of hiding places, heading for the men. One by one, they pulled the pins and rolled the grenades out into the scrambling, fast moving, spiders. Boom! Six small explosions shook the ground. Small clouds of bluish smoke appeared and vanished.

The charging spiders stopped and took note of what had just happened. Several dozen of them were frozen to the ground. A flurry of unheard electronic data occurred, and Smith ordered a retreat. She needed time to analyze this new weapon being used against her brood. True, they were not dead, but they were inactive somehow. Smith needed data. Several spiders picked up some of their fallen ones and scampered off at top speed.

The men cheered and move forward, scooping up the frozen spiders, placing them in sealed, transparent boxes. All told, they retrieved thirty-three of them, before returning to the transport. Next, while still wearing the suits, they lifted off and left the atmosphere of 9-Sigma-C behind and then stopped. The bay door was once more opened, and all the air was allowed to escape. For twenty minutes, they sat there motionless, kept alive by their deep space suits. Then, the door was closed and the ship re-pressurized. This way, they presumed, any spiders that had snuck onboard the ship would be quite dead. On their return trip, the crew members thoroughly searched the ship and did find four dead spider bodies, which were also collected for study. Alfonso watched all of this happening via real-time streaming video, as did all the other corporation executives on Scorpi-C, compliments of GE Corporation.

Alfonso then called Jason and Luisa to tell them that their plan worked to perfection. Then, he called home to Lita, telling her that he may have just found a way to save her husband from death. That brought her back to life, as he knew it would.

When Emelio's last class was done and he returned home, Jason told him the good news. Emelio smiled and said, "See, Jason, you are still able to create good explosions and highly valuable ones at that. You are far from helpless, just with some things." That brought a true smile to Jason's face.

The next day, Alfonso received three of the spiders for GD's studies and was thankful for even that many. He put his entire research lab to work studying them. Now all he could do was wait and see if GE Corporation lived up to their agreement and return Esteban alive. Alfonso estimated the odds at being fifty-fifty. Now that they had their spiders and an effective weapon against a few of them, there wasn't any reason to honor the deal further. Hence, the low odds.

Two nights later, someone knocked on his door around ten at night. Alfonso opened the door and stared out at a UFB woman standing before his door. A soldier was walking away, back to a small shuttle. He turned around and yelled, "Mr. Trujillo as ordered, sir." He then got in the shuttle and left, leaving Alfonso staring at the gorgeous woman with knee-length, thick black hair, armless, wearing the extreme heels, and with a knockout figure. Vaguely, she looked like Esteban.

"Esteban?" Alfonso whispered in disbelief.

Suddenly, the woman began sobbing hysterically, while nodding yes. "It's me. My life is over now," she said in an alto voice. Alfonso swore a silent curse, put a steadying arm around Esteban, leading him into his home, where everyone had managed to get to the front room, trying to see who was at the door at this late hour.

"Lita, it's Esteban. They've turned him into a UFBMD man, I'm afraid," Alfonso said softly and sympathetically.

"Oh Esteban!" Lita cried, while others gasped and stared at the sobbing woman who was apparently really a man. She moved as fast as she could to her husband and pressed her body into his, while Alfonso supported both of them.

Still sobbing, Esteban said, "Oh Lita, I never thought I'd see you and the girls ever again. I love you so, but now I'm as helpless as you are." Together, they cried for some time, as well as his daughters, Marisol and Herminia. Carmela merely cursed a lot.

After helping Esteban to a couch and helping him get his hair out of the way, Alfonso got him seated. Lita and his daughters carefully sat down beside him, leaning into his body, all the while still crying, though softly now.

Alfonso took a seat across from them with Carmela at his side. "Esteban, can you tell us what happened? Did you hear how I managed to get you away from them?"

"This is the price for failure. That's what they told me. They made me into a UFBMD man and were about to make me bed any number of normal women. Then at the last minute, they pulled me out of that whorehouse and told me that I was being returned to you. Alfonso, you have saved me from a terrible fate, but now I'm completely useless to Lita, the girls, and everyone. I don't understand how you did this."

Quietly, Alfonso outlined what had happened, that his own daughter Luisa came up with the original idea, that the UFBMD Jason had invented the Ice Grenade, and that Captain Bess Fontana had built it. He described the field test, promising to show him the video of it tomorrow.

"My Luisa? She had the idea? My UFB Luisa? How? I don't understand," a very confused Esteban struggled to grasp this unbelievable announcement.

"Yes, she's enrolled in the Academy now and studying history. You, I, and probably everyone else have totally and completely underestimated our UFB women, Esteban. In fact, we've just gotten Marisol and Herminia enrolled in highschool, an online one that is. My daughters too. We've completely missed the boat with our UFB daughters, Esteban. They are brilliant and able in their own ways. Tomorrow, you can see for yourself."

"But I'm completely helpless now and completely useless. I can't do anything for myself, and I'm a total freak," Esteban sobbed.

"Dear," Lita whispered, "What about me and the girls?

185

We've been this way our whole lives, and we've done very well don't you think? We will need some servants, that's all, dear. Besides, I've missed you terribly. I didn't think I could go on living without you with me, Esteban."

"Don't worry, papa," Marisol spoke up, valiantly trying to cheer him up. "We can show you how we do some things too. You'll see."

"But Lita, I look like a woman now," he sobbed.

"But you are still a man where it counts," she whispered back, "aren't you?"

"Well, yes, that's still the same, but it's the only thing that is," he continued to sob bitterly.

"That's all that really matters to me, dear," Lita replied, again pressing her body into his a little.

Marisol added, "Papa, now you can feel with your hair just as we do. It's really great to be able to do that, isn't it, Herminia?"

"She's right papa. Now you can feel things, just like us," his thirteen-year-old daughter added, still trying to grasp why her dad looked like her mom.

Carmela suggested, "Everyone, it's getting late. Why don't we get everyone ready for bed, and let Esteban and Lita have some very private time together." Alfonso suddenly realized what she meant and ushered things along that route.

A while later, Alfonso helped undress Lita and Esteban and got them sitting beside each other on the bed. "This is so utterly humiliating, Alfonso. Just look at me. Every inch of me, but one, is a woman." Alfonso had arranged their long hair out in front of them, just as he always did for Carmela when he got her ready for bed.

"I know, Esteban, but both of you need to lie together just now. Trust me, things will get better." He carefully helped Lita down on her side and then got Esteban on his side facing her. "I'll leave the nightlight on. Lita always wanted it on while you were gone. Call out if you need anything during the night." He closed their door and kept his fingers crossed.

"That's horrid, what they did to him," Carmela whispered to him as he crawled in beside her, pulled her close to him, and began stroking her hair the way she loved it done.

186

"I know. I just hope they can manage it. If they do, I think things will work themselves out in time," he replied.

In the morning, he went to get them up, but Esteban asked him to come back a bit later. When he finally entered to get them dressed, Esteban flushed and whispered, "Alfonso, that was the most incredible sex that Lita and I have ever had. Kind of hard to do at first, but by God, beyond belief. Our hair is the key. I'm so sorry we are imposing on you."

"Think nothing of it, Esteban. I'm just glad that we were able to get you back. I know Lita was going out of her mind while you were gone. Even your daughters were very upset and missed you badly. Come on; we've a lot to do today."

Two hours later, Alfonso, his arm around the wobbling Esteban, who had not yet gotten used to walking much at all in the extreme heels, walked up to Emelio's door. "Come on in. Emelio is off at class. Jason and the others aren't here yet," Luisa called out. When they entered, Esteban saw his eldest daughter dressed in her provocative tee shirt and jeans, sitting on the couch manipulating her laptop on the floor. "Oh hello Mr. Vega. Who is she?"

After Alfonso explained who he was, a shocked Luisa exclaimed, "Dad? Is that really you? Oh papa!" she cried, lunging to her feet and pressing her body into his. "I thought you were dead or being tortured."

"I'm being tortured dear, just like you and your mom and your sisters are," he replied, fighting from emotionally breaking down once more.

Luisa laughed, "Papa! We're not being tortured. Did you know I'm now an Academy student? I'm a history major." She began chatting about her two courses and all the marvelous things she'd been doing. "We even go to the beach on Saturday afternoons with all the other students. A lot of them like me. You have to see me in my bikini, papa." She chatted away as if this was the last time she would ever see him. Esteban had tears of happiness streaming down his cheeks.

When he finally got an opportunity to get a word in, he said, "Luisa, I'm so terribly sorry. I never knew you were able to do any of these things. I always thought you were completely helpless, and I so wanted to protect you."

"Papa. I'm not all that helpless, not really. Emelio showed me I can do lots of things I never dreamed I could. See, my laptop is voice-activated, but I can also use my toes to do some things. Come sit and watch me."

Just then, the other four arrived. When Alfonso introduced them to Esteban and explained what had happened to him, Jason grinned and said, "Well, now I don't feel so all alone. Esteban, you are like me. I know, it's hideous and awful, but somehow, I'm getting by, but I sure couldn't if I didn't have Linda with me always."

"Say, I have a lot to arrange today. I'll leave Esteban here for a while. Antonia will be around by noon. If you need to return, let her know. She can arrange it," Alfonso took his leave, hoping that Jason and Esteban would bond a little, comfort in shared misery.

As he was leaving, he heard Esteban ask, "So Luisa, Alfonso told me you got the idea of how the spiders could be captured?"

"Yes, papa. It was my idea, but Jason here, he figured out a way actually to do it." Alfonso smiled and left them to chat, knowing one thing for sure: Esteban was realizing his UFB women were hardly helpless sex dolls. Besides, now he had quite a lot of new ideas to explore and had to find suitable living accommodations for Esteban and his women. He figured the man's boys would want nothing to do with him now, and he was right. They even refused to see him.

By noon, he had acquired a vacant home a block from his mansion. He made the arrangements to have it altered to more meet the needs of the Trujillo family and rehired their old live-in assistant, Gracia, and offered her sister a job as well, pleasing Gracia who had yet to find replacement work. He increased her salary as well.

The afternoon, Alfonso spent in his office exploring ideas that had surfaced with the return of Esteban. He knew that right now Esteban knew just what the UFB women being held in the basement of the GE Corp building were feeling. He planned to make use of that somehow to get all those captive women rescued and into better lives. He faced two dis-related problems.

First, he had to find a way to break into that heavily guarded building and get some eight hundred or so women out of there. With Jackie and Melissa, it had been easy. They were only two, and they'd already taken out the night guard. Since then, his spies reported a significant buildup of night guards. Rescuing them was going to be a big challenge.

Second, he had to find a way to make new lives for eight hundred darn near helpless women, along with dealing with their medical issues. He doubted very much all eight hundred could get genetic cures. That alone might take years to handle fully. So where could that many women be taken where they could be safe and live better lives?

At least, he believed Esteban would now want to tell him about the women being held in his old building, perhaps offering some ideas on how they could be rescued. But what to do with that many dependent women afterwards was the major hurdle that Alfonso could not get a handle on.

Best-case scenario, he thought, would be for the women to marry a corporate executive. At least with these men, they could afford the servants and apparel that the women needed to survive well. Besides, as UFB women, in Alfonso's opinion, they demanded the best that society could offer them, as their sacrifice had been huge. However, presuming he could rescue them, GD Corporation couldn't be seen as the ones rescuing them. That would bring down higher GD Corporation wrath on his own head, ending the whole game. No, he needed a far more clever idea.

Certainly, there were quite a lot of corporate executives here on Scorpi-C who would love to have the opportunity to have a UFB woman with them. Just not eight hundred. No, if he rescued them, the majority would of necessity have to be taken to other worlds where corporate executives there would want and provide for them. What appealed to him the most was depriving GE Corporation of the eight hundred women and doling them out to other corporations. GE was obviously trying to corner the market in UFB women. Why? He had no idea. Still, this could set them back significantly in whatever they had planned.

He thought, if somehow GD Corporation could be seen

as somehow making eight hundred of these invaluable UFB women available for all the various corporations, then that would be quite a coup. Yet, it has to be done such that no one would remotely suspect GD as having a hand in stealing them from the GE Corporation. Tricky indeed. *Still, I can't think of anything better for these women, whose lives right now must be utter hell.*

He thought of all that Jackie and Melissa had told him and an idea struck him. The press! They would be the barrier that he needed, a buffer of public opinion! He called up Juanita and gave her a new assignment, one that she loved.

That night, he decided to interrogate Esteban about the women. After supper, he took him into his study for a private chat. After explaining he'd arranged for them to have a new home nearby, Alfonso approached the topic rather gently. "Okay then, Esteban, at least you can fully appreciate just how terrible a time our UFB women have just trying to live life."

"Shit, Alfonso, that in spades. I was never so terrified in my entire life as I was when I woke up naked and like this!"

"I can't imagine. You know, there were thousands of women who woke up in the same situation there on that space station, surrounded by all the dead men. And then somehow they were all captured and taken God knows where," he hinted.

Esteban flushed noticeably. "Alfonso, you have saved my family and now me. Plus, you haven't forsaken us and are even helping us somehow survive this awful mess. I owe you, but you didn't hear this from me." He leaned over and whispered, "GE Corporation made a deal with a man who only goes by the name Master. It was this person and his organization that kidnaped all those women from the space station."

He paused a moment, sighing. "I'm ashamed to say that GE Corporation made a deal with him to acquire some eight hundred of those genetically modified UFB women. The Master executed the attack on the space station, and GE Corporation just turned the other cheek, saying it was almost beyond repair and ought to be junked. Alfonso, the women are being kept in five basement levels of our very headquarters building!"

"My God Esteban," Alfonso feigned surprise, thankful that Esteban admitted all this. "What on earth for? Those poor women."

"Oh, it's worse than you might think, Alfonso. They got them all pregnant too."

"Why?"

"GE Corporation has some grand ideas of building up a huge army of the super fighter men the UFB women have when they breed with normal men. My god, Alfonso, they were going to breed me, as if I was a bull or something, to all these normal women, trying to get super-genius sons from them. I can't possibly tell you how terrified I was, so utterly helpless to do anything about it!"

"Those poor women. UFB women ought to be treated like queens or something, Esteban. This is intolerable. My God."

"I know. I wish there were some way to help them, but they have them under tight security now. Apparently, two of the women managed to escape, though how, we don't know. It's just awful. They are kept two to a room, locked away for their lives, having baby after baby. Beyond hideous, Alfonso. I'm ashamed I had anything to do with that, but I had corporate orders. Well, you know how that is. Oh yes, the older women were only partially genetically modified and are the caretakers for the UFB women."

"Thank you for telling me about them, Esteban. I don't know what I could do about it, but I promise you if I ever had a chance, I'll try to do right by those women," Alfonso declared, putting Esteban at ease.

The next day, Juanita gave him a call around noon. "Boss, I think I have found something useful. A giant sewer line runs under the building in question. Sending you the plans now. Hope it helps."

He looked over what Juanita had uncovered and silently blessed her! He began working out the myriad details of his plan. He would need to make use of every available RdD man he had for this one.

That night, he received an emergency call from the

night security guards at GD headquarters. "Sir, there are hundreds of naked women out front of the building. They are all very beautiful looking, but don't have any arms. I think they might be like your wife. What should we do?"

"Open the doors. Get them inside. I know, take them to the auditorium for now. Call the day shift guards. Tell them this is an emergency, and I've ordered them on duty tonight. Also, call Channel 5 news. Let them know something major is going on. I'll be there as soon as I get dressed."

He was already dressed; he kissed Carmela goodbye, and dashed out to his shuttle. As he descended onto the roof, he saw hundreds of the women standing forlornly on the street just outside the main headquarters doors, waiting to get inside. He took the elevator down to the main floor and watched his guards for a moment, making sure this was working out as planned. While the women were wobbling precariously, they were making their way inside and to the elevators, where guards were taking them up three floors to the giant theater. Alfonso slipped among them and got outside.

He saw the last of his men bringing up the tail end of the eight hundred women. Just then, the Channel 5 news crew shuttle landed and a reporter and cameraman stepped out. "For God's sake, start shooting!" the reporter ordered, trying to grasp the scene before his eyes.

"Excuse me," Alfonso moved up to the reporter and knowingly becoming on camera. "Do you know perhaps what is going on here?"

"Say, aren't you the GD Corporation CEO?"

"Why, yes, I am. Alfonso Vega. I just got a call from my night guards that all these women were standing outside our building. I came as fast as I could. What's going on here? These are all UFB women. Where did they come from?"

"Sir, that's what we wanted to know. Yes, these are UFB women, but no one has ever seen so many in one location before. Usually, we're lucky to see just one. You have a UFB wife, correct?"

"Why, yes I do, but I'd never have her parade around naked in the night, not like this. This is criminal. Where did they all come from?"

"We don't know yet, but we will find out. Tell me, what are your people doing with them?"

"Right now, I've given my men orders to get them all inside where it is warm. We're using our corporate theater to hold them. We at GD can't tolerate such treatment of these most rare and precious young women. I can't imagine who would have this many and so mistreat them. They must be animals. Anyway, at GD, we'll do our best to get them clothes, food, and find them a safe place to live, somehow, though right now I'm more worried about their health. Perhaps you could alert the local medical centers that we may have a crisis on our hands, if these women are ill or something," Alfonso planted yet another idea.

"Sir, would it be possible to interview some of these women? We need to get their stories," the reporter asked.

"Of course, I want to know what's going on as well as you do, but let's not interview them naked. Let me see if any clothes have been found for some and bring them out for you," Alfonso answered and ducked back inside.

A few minutes later, he returned with an arm around each of two of the women. They were wearing lab coats and sobbing. The reporter and cameraman zoomed in on the pair. Alfonso stepped back and allowed the reporter to do his work for him, since this was absolutely crucial.

"We were on the space station in Abelard Sector when the terrorists attacked us with some kind of gas. When we woke up, the men were all dead, and we women all had screwed up feet and this strange, long hair. Then more men came and took us prisoners. Then we all fell into comas; that's what everyone says. We awoke without any arms, just as we are now. Someone told us that we were all UFB women. We were put two to a room somewhere. None of us knew where. We couldn't get out of our rooms. A man came by with plates of food, but made us eat as if we were dogs. Then," she faltered, but Alfonso knew why.

The other woman took over, "Men came and raped us repeatedly until we got pregnant. Then, they stopped raping us. They told us we were going to have lots of babies—that's what our lives would be until we died."

"Shocking, shocking," the reporter couldn't help commenting. "How did you escape? Where were you being held?"

"We don't know. Some masked men came, told us they were rescuing us, and carried us out of the sewers to this place," she answered.

"And you have no idea who these men were?" the reporter probed.

"I do," a naked woman about to enter the building called out. "I saw an emblem on one of them that said RdD. Probably the resistance freed us." Others rather pushed the woman on inside.

"Well, if you will excuse me, I have a whole lot of women to care for right now. I will hold a press conference later this morning and let you know what we are doing to help these unfortunate women," Alfonso interrupted the reporter, leaving the two women to continue to chat with the reporter.

He took a service elevator up to his office and fired up his computer. Alfonso sent off several dozen emails, some to all the other corporation executives on Scorpi-C and some to his immediate superiors. The emails outlined what had happened and what he was doing about it, namely offering any executive a UFB woman, if he would promise to treat her right. The one to his superiors also said, "I'm taking this unfortunate situation to enhance the position of the GD Corporation, who will be seen to have been compassionate to these women and magnanimously providing many other corporation executives with a golden opportunity to acquire a UFB woman for themselves. Hope this meets with your approval, since we are certainly going to get a whole lot of press out of this incident."

By 8:05, he began receiving calls from dozens of corporate executives. He also had the news coverage on his monitor in the background, keeping tabs on this developing story. "Yes, this is for real. You are welcome to come by now and pick out a UFB woman. She will likely need a bit of medical attention. I would like them all to be checked out. Some are saying they've been raped and are possibly pregnant, something that can be quickly handled. Just give them a good home and love." Many times, Alfonso continued to repeat his speech.

By nine, many dozens of executives and their assistants were milling around the auditorium, checking on the women. Choosing a UFB woman boiled down mostly to choice of hair color and to a much lesser extent their age. The Master had only genetically modified the younger women and some were still in their late teens. Alfonso shuddered to think about what that man had done to the even younger girls. So far, no one knew.

By noon, over a hundred of the women had been taken away. Alfonso trusted that they would be very well treated by the new men in their lives. He was taking a gamble this would be so, but a safe one, since the executives who already had UFB women brought them to all the social gatherings and many to public events. Now these men would also have a trophy woman to accompany them and were therefore not likely to mistreat them. In any case, their lives would have to be better than what GE Corporation had intended their lives to be.

Surprisingly, several GE Corporation junior executives dropped by to pick out UFB women for themselves, though none had any comments to relay from GE Corporation, other than a thank you. Around noon, he received word from his boss. Those women who were left were to be clothed and taken to the spaceport, where he would be arriving around four. He insisted on holding a press conference at that time.

Thus, around four, Alfonso greeted his boss and listened in to his brief press conference. "We at GD Corporation are going to see that these incredibly beautiful and valuable UFB women are given new and proper homes. Yes, we will be following the lead set here by Mr. Vega. We will be offering them to worthy executives of all corporations." He had other words to say, including that GD would not rest until they uncovered who was responsible for these women. However, Alfonso knew that was mere publicity and that GD would soon drop the issue.

When he left for home, he found a commendation for brilliant thinking from his boss sitting on his desk. Alfonso headed home with a happy, satisfied step. He had made a difference in these women's lives, a good one, he sincerely hoped, perhaps the best that could be expected under the circumstances. All of his own junior executives who wanted a UFB woman now had one. He expected they would be behind his leadership even more strongly than before.

When he returned home, he received many accolades and thanks for what he'd done. Everyone had been watching the news all day. More importantly, Esteban said, "I can't express how grateful I am for what you've done. Finally, I can sleep a bit easier at night. I should never have gotten mixed up in that fiasco."

Alfonso replied, "Dear friend, did you ever have a choice?" Esteban shook his head no, his long hair flying about his face some. Alfonso carefully adjusted it for him.

***

Quite some distance away, the Master also caught the news coverage being streamed across the galaxy. His comment to Tao was simply, "Stupid GE Corporation. You can see why they aren't fit to run the galaxy, Tao, but we are."

***

Unknown to all, three spiders cleverly latched on to three of the UFB women as they were being transported to other worlds.

Chapter 12—Reactions

New Briton, Gamma Prime (official designation: Gamma-C), Helios Sector in the left mid-spiral arm, was the centralized based for all the major corporations outside the actual hub sectors, where those who ran the galaxy resided. From this location, the corporations ran countless lesser headquarters on the more distant worlds on out to the rim in the Abelard and other nearby sectors. These top executives wielded vast powers over those farther out from the hub. Although they had ultimately to answer to their superiors residing within the hub, these men were privy to far more information and intelligence than the local heads, such as those on Scorpi-C.

When the Central News Service carried the spectacular events of the rescue operation of nearly eight hundred UFBs by the GD Corporation, many executives here took notice, but none more so than two close friends. While they worked for different corporations, long ago they found it mutually beneficial often to share key intelligence and other information. Frequently, something that adversely impacted one corporation would also do the same to the other or others.

Forty-five year old Hector Ambrose was the CEO of the GD Corporation on Gamma Prime and charged with oversight of all other GD Corporations farther out from the hub in this region of the arm. His wife of some twenty-two years was the UFB woman named Lisa, who was now forty and past her child bearing age. Their many children were already married, and their UFB daughters now formed family alliances with five other executives.

His close friend ran the GE Corporation. Albert Vice was forty-four and his UFB wife was forty-one and no longer able to bear children. Like Hector, he had carefully chosen husbands for his daughters, strengthening alliances with other executives here on Gamma Prime.

Meeting with the two top executives was Hector's right-hand man, Felix Middleton, thirty-five, who was married to the UFB woman Mandy, a year younger. Unlike his bosses' wives who no longer could bear children, Felix and Mandy had decided against having more children, because they had four UFB daughters in a row, each a year younger than the other. Sally Ann was sixteen. Then came Lilly Ann, Mary Ann, and finally Lisa Ann. When the couple reached their decision not to have more children, Felix was not honest with Mandy. He didn't tell her that his mother was a normal woman while his father was very special, a UFBMD man. That meant that he was genetically superior to most all people, and his IQ was off the charts. No one had successfully been able to measure it. Further, Felix kept his *breeding* a secret from most people. Here at GD, only his boss knew his lineage.

Years ago when the GE Corporation began serious genetic experimentation on Rho-C at their ultra-secret laboratories, the GD Corporation not only knew about it, but helped finance the operation, a fact not known below this level of corporate organization. Thus, when the early research showed such promise, both corporations were intimately involved in its further development. Their bosses further up the ladder didn't want to risk breeding with the newly created UFB women and later the UFBMD men. That task fell on these middle management CEOs.

When the news of the miraculous rescue of nearly eight hundred of the UFB women broke, both men and Felix began holding top-secret meetings. In fact, it had been Albert Vice who had ordered the arrest of Esteban Trujillo for gross incompetence with the spider affair. Rather than have him killed, Felix suggested that he be turned into a useful UFBMD man, which the two executives accepted and had done, only to discover that the local GD Corporation's CEO, this Alfonso Vega, insisted that Esteban was behind the special formula that might allow them to capture some spiders and that Esteban be given due credit. Well, he couldn't very well be returned to his former position as head of GE Corporation on Scorpi-C, not as a helpless UFBMD man. However, Felix pointed out that this Alfonso fellow only wanted him returned. As a joke, Esteban was returned to Alfonso personally and as a warning to Alfonso that he was treading in hot waters.

Now that this mess with the eight hundred UFB women

broke, once more it landed on this Alfonso Vega's plate. "Well, yes, he does make very valid points," Hector argued. "Our corporations are being seen as great benefactors, treating these UFB women as they should be, quite true. From what I can tell from the news and what little I hear from other contacts, somehow the resistance merely dumped them on his doorstep. The newscasts appear to back his story completely."

"Yes," Albert said, "I agree. I'm having the temporary head there at GE Corporation removed from his post. It does appear that this Alfonso Vega is merely acting as a responsible CEO in this matter."

"Gentlemen," Felix interrupted them, as he was wont to do, considering them both imbeciles, "several key questions must be asked. First, how did the resistance know that there were any UFB women being held at the GE headquarters? Second, how did the resistance know that the underground sewers were so close to the basement? Third, how did the resistance know precisely where to dig their short tunnel to gain access to the basement level? Fourth, why did the resistance choose to bring the women to the GD headquarters? Why GD? Fifth, just how did those two UFB women manage to escape?"

Albert spoke up. "Obviously, someone within the GE Corporation there leaked that Intel to the resistance, probably that incompetent fool I appointed to take Esteban's place."

Felix shook his head in disbelief, wondering how could these CEOs be so stupid? "Look, that idiot, as you call him, had to know he would lose his head over the theft of the UFB women. What fool willingly commits suicide over UFB women? Besides, the theft ruined your grand plans for them."

"Well then, someone else at the GE Corporation on Scorpi-C alerted the resistance," Albert replied hastily.

"Yes, yes, that is a possibility, but if you recall your own plan's details, the number of men in the corporation there who knew about the women was kept to just ten, well trusted men. Not even that night guard who was somehow overpowered by the two UFB women who escaped knew that women were being kept there below ground," Felix pointed out. He added, "You yourself told Esteban which men to use. Didn't you have those ten men thoroughly checked out?"

Albert squirmed. "Well, yes I did."

"So unless you totally botched that one, the leak didn't come from those ten men," Felix suggested.

"Then who?" Albert tossed it back to Felix.

"We must consider the answers to the other questions as well. I submit that the answer to the first question is answered by the miraculous escape of the two UFB women, who somehow managed to overpower the guard. The second one is also easy. Anyone could study the city underground facilities and discover the sewer system was so darn close to the basement. Since the resistance acquired the two escaped UFB women, they would also know of the basement level, since your report indicated that they were being housed in a room on the very lowest level."

"So you are implying Esteban screwed up the whole thing by not having sufficient security in place, allowing the two women to escape?" Albert asked pointedly.

"That is plainly obvious, Albert, unless you are completely blind." Albert didn't like Felix and his sometimes condescending attitude, but the man had a point. Felix continued, "So we're then left with the final two questions. Just why did the resistance choose to bring the women to the GD headquarters? Why GD and not one of the other corporation headquarters there in that city, Malagena?"

"What are you implying?" Hector spoke up. "GD and GE are two of the largest corporations in the rim worlds."

"Yes, but there are others as big as well. General Goods and Swan Mining come to mind," Felix countered.

"Are you saying that this Alfonso Vega was somehow involved in the theft of the UFB women?" Hector asked directly.

"Perhaps, boss, perhaps. He certainly has gotten the attention of upper management with his little gifts. He's made an indelible impression on many executives in many corporations. One could say he's just enlarged his own power base tenfold," Felix pointed out.

"Yes, but I assure you he had no idea that GD was in on the plan involving those women and their future children, our secret breeding program," Hector advised. "No one beyond me knows about that."

"Hector, haven't you heard a damned thing I've just said?" Felix barked sarcastically. "This Alfonso fellow has just enlarged his own power base at least tenfold, maybe more. Duh Hector. Do you suppose your boss might be considering replacing you with him? Obviously, right now, this Alfonso Vega is widely known and respected. Can we say that about you?"

Hector flushed. He'd spent his career trying to maintain a very low profile. Suddenly, he saw just what Felix was insinuating, that Alfonso was gunning for his job! He flushed a second time.

However, Felix changed the topic, "We must not discount it was Esteban who spilled the beans about the UFB women in the basement. After all, he would certainly desire revenge for what you did to him, Albert."

"My God, man, you could well be right!" Albert suddenly flushed, suspecting he'd made a grievous error returning Esteban. "I had him sent back to Alfonso Vega! I bet anything he blabbed all of it to Alfonso Vega!"

Felix smiled, thinking how hard it was to get these men to think clearly and analyze situations properly. He'd spent minutes talking baby talk just to get these two finally to grasp the situation, at least as he saw it when he first caught the event unfolding on the news.

"Now combine that with just where the resistance brought the women and you have a far clearer possibility," Felix pointed out. "The flaw is Esteban was only there a day or so before all this happened. That doesn't give Alfonso much time at all to have arranged the whole thing."

"Hey, if Alfonso was behind it, then was it really the resistance men who conducted the breakout or was it GD men in disguise?" asked Hector, struggling with all these new ideas.

"Or is Alfonso in the resistance?" Felix continued his speculations. "Gentlemen, we can speculate on Alfonso as much as we desire. Either Esteban told him or he didn't. Either he is somehow tied to the resistance or he isn't. But one thing we do know, he has increased his power base many,

many times, and Hector, that doesn't bode well for you. Have you heard anything from your boss about this? What is the scuttlebutt going around in the hub worlds?"

Hector shrugged his shoulders. That he didn't know. Well, his boss didn't praise him, but he had praised Alfonso. "I guess the question we should be asking ourselves is what should we do about Alfonso Vega?"

"We need to be darn careful, Hector," Albert answered. "Don't forget; it was his people who came up with the first way to catch those damned spiders. Upper management also knows about that as well. I agree with you, Felix. This man has suddenly acquired far too much power and influence with upper management. I'm just not comfortable with that. We've a nice arrangement going here, Hector. I'd hate to have to start all over with this Alfonso fellow." Albert also didn't say what he truly felt, namely that this GD man was putting him to shame. After all, he was partially responsible for the escape of the UFB women and for the failure to capture a spider. It was his man on Scorpi-C who had failed so miserably. Quite why he hadn't been replaced already was a mystery to him. He'd been sweating that one out since the news broke. If he could help convince Hector to get rid of him, then he'd have one less GD executive in the rim.

Felix noticed that he had both men thinking hard about what he'd suggested, so he didn't tax them further with answers to the last question—just how did those two UFB women manage to escape? Certainly, their story of overpowering the guard held up. He had received a concussion when he and his chair fell over backwards with the two women landing on top of him. However, what both men had been overlooking was the unique way that the main door lock had been broken. The women hadn't used the guard's key. No, the lock had been frozen and punched out, something that couldn't have been done by either woman or from the inside. They obviously had outside help, which led to the next question, just how did the unknown party know the women were attempting to escape at that precise moment? Their timing was impeccable, Felix concluded. That wasn't a chance encounter. More was going on than either CEO even suspected, but he, the brilliant, super-intelligent Felix, did see it.

Further, Felix reasoned, if by chance this Alfonso, who appeared to have a spotless record, was in league with the resistance, then with him gone, the resistance would suffer tremendously. His idea was to have Alfonso removed and then monitor the level of coordinated resistance to the corporations on Scorpi-C and on the other Abelard sector worlds. If it dropped off significantly, then Alfonso was in the resistance, probably leading it. If it was unaffected, probably he wasn't, but he had far too much influence now. There was a good chance that Hector would soon be replaced by this Alfonso. After all, Hector was forty-five, past his prime, and this Alfonso was in his late thirties, in a prime position to move on up the corporate ladder. In fact, Felix wondered why upper management hadn't made the move already.

"We could have him assassinated," Hector suggested.

"No good. That can be traced. It's the most common form in use by all corporations," Felix pointed out the obvious. "Upper management is aware of the usual men who are used for such things. Have you got a death wish, Hector?" he punched in bluntly. The man was an idiot, he thought.

Albert chuckled, "Why not make him into a UFBMD man like I did with Esteban? Then, he can be just like his supposed friend."

Hector smiled sadistically. "Albert, sometimes you amaze me. Yes, that is altogether fitting, quite appropriate. It could be done during a terrorist attack on GD headquarters," he proposed.

"But you want to be careful, Hector. Just how many there do you want to eliminate?" Felix pointed out. "A selective terrorist attack on one target should be the plan, if you are convinced this is the way to go. Just be careful. Right now, this Alfonso may well be the *darling* of your boss. If he's wiped out, your boss could well become suspicious of you."

"Best let Albert handle the details then," Hector replied, tossing his dirty work over to his friend. "Just get it done soon. I don't want to risk getting replaced by Alfonso Vega."

Albert smiled. "I'll see to it this afternoon. You will owe

me one, Hector." Hector laughed nervously, knowing Albert was precisely correct. Felix now had more observations to make a few days from now, interesting ones, the genius thought.

***

That evening, long after the staff had departed from the headquarters, a janitor-maid made her way up to the top floor and began cleaning the rug, just as she always did. However, it wasn't the real woman who was there; rather it was Alis Anrhod in disguise. After she helped Dr. Gisa, Jason, Linda, and the others get settled in, she'd resumed her own personal spy work. The moment she heard about the escape of the two UFB women from GE Corporate headquarters, she dashed off to Gamma Prime. She knew about Hector and Albert, though little of their plans, save that they were working together. After some digging, she uncovered the woman who cleaned up the top office floor. Conveniently, the woman was *ill,* and Alis took her ID card and disguised herself as the janitor-maid, cleaning the office each evening. However, the first night there, she installed a miniature listening device. It was very short range, so she had a power booster hidden in her cleaning cart.

Thus, by day, she listened in on what was said. Thus, their entire conversation was heard by Alis! That very afternoon, she fired off a secure and coded message to Alfonso Vega, warning him of the plot against him and promising to call him tomorrow. That night, she returned to clean as usual, but removed her device. Then, she paid a call on the ill woman, injecting the proper cure in her arm, warning her not to mention that she had been ill because they might fire her.

Alfonso replied via a secure call. "Alis, I can't thank you enough for this timely warning. If I get clobbered, I suppose it will have been worth it. I've saved eight hundred UFB women from a horrible existence, so my actions will not have been in vain."

"True, Alfonso. But think of the resistance. You are needed there on Scorpi-C. Besides, the GD Corporation needs your guidance," Alis protested. "I don't know if it will be possible to avoid this *terrorist* attack or not. I don't have any more data about what Albert intends to do or when, just soon.

If he is successful, any chance you can insist on keeping on running either the resistance or GD?" she asked what she most wanted to know. After all, this awful genetic mutation virtually wiped Jason out, and Esteban had simply given up everything he had been doing and was now just trying to survive somehow. Could or would Alfonso even consider trying to continue the fight? Certainly, he'd be damned helpless, to say nothing of the utter humiliation that he would experience when his body was so drastically altered.

"Until recently, Alis, I would have said the UFB and UFBMD people are completely helpless and virtually useless. However, from what I've seen some of these people doing recently, I'm not so sure that is true any longer. Certainly, Esteban is crushed by it and has more or less given up. On the other hand, Jason is doing vastly better than I ever expected, and I've now seen Luisa and others doing things I thought impossible."

Alis replied, "You'll have to show me the next time I'm on Scorpi-C."

"Deal. So to answer your question, Alis, you know, if I got turned into a UFBMD man and if I could somehow still hold my GD post, why, that would certainly up the stakes considerably, wouldn't it?"

Alis laughed appropriately. "Yes, that would certainly shake things up considerably. If you are of a mind to try this, I can arrange for both of their bosses in the hub sector to *discover* the recording that I made. I have everything recorded."

"Alis, I love you! Yes, that would be fantastic! If I can't avoid the terrorist attack, wait until I recover from the coma, and then get the recording into their hands. I'll fight to keep my position here. With any luck, given that incriminating evidence, the higher executives will go along with me or at least let me try to run things here. I best make contingency plans pronto."

Alfonso suspected he had at least one full day before the terrorist could possibly get here and make his attempt. Quietly, he doubled the guards at headquarters and around his home as well, though those men were seldom seen. That evening, he explained to Carmela what might be happening to him and what he proposed to do if that happened. She backed him totally. The next day, he got his finances in order, such that things could run nearly on automatic, bills paid electronically and such. He hired another live-in maid, using the pretext that the girls needed more help now that they were going to online high school.

He spent several hours going over the plot with Diego, who wanted him to go into hiding until this was all over, anything but to become genetically modified into a UFBMD man. However, he swore to go along with Alfonso no matter what happened. "Look, boss. You can still lead the resistance, even if you aren't the head of GD anymore. Just look at what Jason is able to do and Luisa too. I would never have thought she could go to the Academy. Then there is Linda who is back continuing her Academy education in astrophysics, and even Captain Juanita. They have totally amazed me, boss. The real question is will the hub GD CEO go along with you?"

"Yes, that's the real question. If by chance he believes I've proven myself sufficiently, there's a chance of that happening. If not, well, I will still do everything possible for the resistance. The RdD will not die if I am laid up. One day, the corporations will fall, even if I don't live to see that happen," Alfonso declared with some passion.

***

What Alfonso didn't know was that Alis was heading back from Gamma Prime as fast as her deep space transport could go. Once she landed and refueled, she again took off, but only apparently so. Once she reached orbit, she activated the transport's secret invisibility cloaking device and descended planet-side again, totally hidden from view. Her objective: attempt to spot the terrorist before he could carry out the attack. She made a calculated guess the attack would come at GD headquarters and not his home, since he arrived home at often unpredictable hours. The hired man would want to get the job done as fast as possible. Since his office was on the top floor and since he would be there most of the daytime hours, that was the most likely place to strike without also affecting many other people. Certainly, those executives didn't want so suddenly create a whole bunch of UFB and UFBMD people, for that would really raise the ire of their hub bosses.

Alis flew around the building, being careful to avoid other shuttles, and looking for the right vantage point that the assassin might use. Twice, a shuttle nearly flew into her ship! But Alis found what she was looking for, the ideal vantage point. It was on the roof top of a building two blocks away from GD headquarters. She shot back into orbit, turned off her cloaking device, and landed again. She strapped on her PDS and PID, that is, her Personal Defense Shield and her Personal Invisibility Device, and took a shuttle downtown from the spaceport. She then landed it on the building in question, activated her devices, and abandoned the rented shuttle by activating its homing device. She watched as it flew itself back to the spaceport. Now, Alis merely waited, hoping that she was correct in her guess.

There were also two other likely spots the assassin could use, though this one was the best. The real question for which she had no answer was just how the terrorist would get the genetic bio agent into Alfonso's office. A sharpshooter could perch here and take him out easily. But how would they get the bio agent in there? Of that, Alis had no idea. She could only wait and see, perhaps being able to react in time to save Alfonso.

The rest of that day, Alis waited patiently from her perch. Shuttles landed nearby, men got off, men came up to the shuttle landing area, boarded some, and departed. Always, she kept close watch on them, but saw nothing suspicious at all. All night, she sat there. The sun rose on the next day. From her perch, she admired the beautiful sunrise and then focused on the office two blocks away. Glancing at her watch, she guessed that Alfonso, a creature of habit when it came to work, was probably just now walking into the building. She focused and soon saw him entering his office.

The attack took even the totally prepared Alis by surprise. It was ingenious, almost unbelievable. The man certainly was a professional. A shuttle swung by his office window, momentarily blocking her vision of Alfonso. From the shuttle, a blaster fired, shattering the glass pane on the wall.

Puff! A gun fired a canister of the genetic bio agent into the room. Alfonso had no chance to avoid the attack! He was stunned by the concussion of the blaster blast. Thus, he was unable to get up and flee the room.

Alis and many others also knew there was a bio-chemical attack detector on all floors of most all corporation headquarters to guard against just such attacks. It instantly went off, triggering a series of irreversible actions. All the doors on this floor sealed and locked. Only when the detectors sensed the biological or chemical agent had sufficiently dispersed would they automatically unlock and unseal. Further, the air circulation system shut down completely, avoiding further spread by airflow. Finally, alarms went off signaling a biological or chemical weapon attack was underway.

"Shit!" Alis swore and drew her own special gun from her left holster, aimed, and fired. A tagging dart struck the side of the shuttle as it pulled away from the building. She hijacked one of the shuttles on this rooftop landing bay and headed after the fleeing shuttle, determined to get the man. She followed him back to the spaceport, landing her stolen shuttle by his. As she got out, the terrorist saw her and drew his gun. With a blaster, one does not need to be remotely accurate. Just point and shoot.

However, the man didn't count on her wearing a PDS, which absorbed his shot. She fired back and dropped him dead. She then alerted the authorities that the terrorist was shot and activated her PID, vanishing from sight. She entered her deep space transport and sent a copy of the incriminating audio recording to two hub corporate executives, along with the suggestion that once he was out of his coma, Alfonso would be back at his post once more. That was the best that Alis could do for him. What developed next depended upon Alfonso and upon the mostly unknown top executives. While she knew of them, she had not personally seen them, not yet anyway.

She swore to get revenge if they totally sacked Alfonso and if he actually was able to continue his duties as CEO of GD here on Scorpi-C. That done, she decided to remain around here a bit longer, on the off chance that Diego might need some assistance. Besides, she was curious about whether Alfonso could actually stand up to this drastic alteration of his body and continue working. If asked, Alis wouldn't have given Alfonso much of a chance at truly continuing to do what he desired to do. The UFB women that she'd seen were virtually helpless women. Still, Alis didn't abandon the GD executive.

For three days, Alfonso remained in a coma. He'd been removed from his office when the containment locks released about eight hours after the early morning attack. From there, he'd been rushed to Malagena Medical Center, where he was placed in an isolation unit for another day while the frightened medical doctors and authorities debated whether his infection represented further threats to anyone else. Finally, they decided he wasn't and moved him to a private room, where Carmela was finally able to visit him, sitting beside his bed for hours. Diego stepped in and continued to bring her to his room each day. Both knew in advance that this was likely to happen. Nevertheless, both were shocked and frightened of the future.

"Carmela, he's really going to need your support when he wakes up," Diego whispered to her.

"I know, and I feel so helpless to do anything for him. He was always there for me—you know, simple things like a supporting arm while walking, moving my hair to the front so I could sit down without swinging my head to do it. We must make this work, Diego. I know he depends on you a lot."

"Yes, he'll need us both. I sure hope he can somehow manage to retain his post as CEO of GD here on Scorpi-C," Diego replied.

During the last hours of his coma, Carmela instructed Diego on how to measure his body for clothes and heels. His body had pretty much finished its genetic modifications. Even Diego was floored at how physically changed his friend's body had become.

Ignoring his privates, he looked like an extremely shapely, top fashion model, very similar to all the other Ultimate in Feminine Beauty women, a female-looking body that others would die to have, and yet he was still male where it mattered for reproduction. In fact, ignoring that one aspect, he appeared little different than any other of these stunning UFB women. His black hair had thickened and now had a wave to it, falling to his knees. His feet now had a super arch, so like Carmela, only his toes would lie flat on the ground; his heel was far above it, requiring he wear the same extreme heels as all the other UFB women did. In short, he was one of the rare UFBMD men.

Thanks to Diego and Carmela, when Alfonso awoke from his coma, they had appropriate clothing waiting for him and ready to put on him once the doctors finished their final examination and released him. Unlike most others, when he awoke, he didn't scream. Alfonso knew in advance what he would discover when he awoke, thanks to Alis and her warning.

"Help, attack. . ." Alfonso began to say, recalling the shattering glass window. His voice sounded strange, up two octaves, a mellow alto female voice. That caused him to stop speaking. He inhaled sharply and struggled to sit up, moving his non-existent arms before reality came crashing in on him. He gasped a second time.

"It's okay dear. We're here," Carmela said, leaning closer to him, trying to maintain a brave face for his sake. She wanted just to sob her heart out, but knew Alfonso needed her to be strong for him.

"It's happened, hasn't it?" he said, as Diego helped him to sit up. His eyes took in his new body form and shape. Wisely, both remained silent while Alfonso gasped again and swallowed hard. "God, I feel so helpless right now." He glanced at Carmela and quickly added, "I'm so sorry, Carmela. I don't want to hurt your feelings."

She smiled, "Dear, you haven't. I'm so glad that you're alive. I just couldn't go on without you. Give yourself time to learn. Remember, I've been like this all my life and you haven't. Me and the girls, we'll show you how we do things. You'll see; we can survive this."

"This is so embarrassing. I'm naked," he flushed.

"Hang in there. Carmela and I got you some proper clothing. We figured you might like at least to look like some of the professional women we have working at GD," Diego said, trying not to stare too much at his gorgeous form.

"Oh! Right, yes, that's a very good idea, professional woman. Sure can't wear my suits anymore," Alfonso replied, relieved. The two had thought ahead and that pleased him. Ten minutes later, Diego had him dressed. A garter belt held up black nylons. He now wore a black skirt, hemmed just below his knees, and a white silk blouse, with very small ruffles for sleeves. Black patent, extreme heels completed his professional outfit.

Diego helped him stand up for the first time in the heels, and he examined his appearance in the wall mirror, while Diego attempted to brush out his long hair. "Going to need to use your electrostatic machine on your hair soon. Can't do much with it here," Diego lamented. He had much experience doing these things, since his wife was also a UFB woman, as were his twin twelve-year-old daughters, now about to have their thirteenth birthday.

"Well, I look quite passable as a professional woman at GD, don't I?" he commented, still feeling a bit weird about his alto voice.

Diego laughed, "Boss, you look like a stunning professional woman. You're going to make them quite jealous of you." Both men laughed at that tease, easing Alfonso's tension some. "Let's get you checked out of the hospital and home. It's late. Tomorrow promises to be a most interesting day. I have quite a bit of business to discuss with you before then, and your daughters are dying to see you."

"Okay. Get me out of here. I hate hospitals, you know." Diego was efficient and had him checked out in short order, primarily because he was a corporate executive. As they began their long walk out to the shuttle parking deck, he whispered, "My God. Walking is treacherous. Don't let go of me, Diego!" His second in command had his arms around him and Carmela, but Alfonso shouldn't have worried, since, like himself, Diego always took care to do so with his own wife and daughters, quite unlike many other executives who didn't believe such was really necessary.

"I knew it was challenging for you, Carmela, but I had

no idea it was this bad. It's downright scary!"

"Going down steps is far worse, dear. I always appreciated your arm about me," Carmela replied.

A half hour later, they arrived at his home. Diego had them stop at the front door, while he entered some codes in the keypad. "Okay, Alfonso, speak clearly. Say 'Open Door.' I've installed a voice-activated system. Already I've adjusted it to your daughters and Carmela's voices. Now we'll add yours. This way, you can get in easily." A few minutes later, Alfonso entered his living room, only to find his daughters were there waiting for him, including his daughter-in-law Luisa and Emelio as well. Emelio was the only son who had not abandoned him.

Tears streamed down many cheeks as he entered, looking like his daughters, though if you looked closely at his altered face, you could still recognize Alfonso's face. Oh, how he wanted to hug his three daughters, but he realized he could never do that again, not ever.

"Oh papa!" cried Chita, pushing her well-endowed body into his equally well-endowed form. Soon, all four surrounded him, pressing against his body, his hair sending waves of unfamiliar tactile sensations through his body.

Wisely, Diego allowed the family some time before insisting on a brief conference with him. "Might as well let the girls listen in too, Diego."

"Okay then. I've had a number of communications from Hector Ambrose on Gamma Prime, your immediate superior. He's requested your boys be moved to a military school. They were most eager to go, I might add. I think they were glad to get out of having to help your daughters all the time. He appointed me as temporary head of GD here. I countered with the idea that you intended to continue your post when you recovered from the attack. He didn't seem too pleased with that, but I did get him to take a wait and see approach, though I don't know how long he will wait, boss. Everything else seems quiet."

"How about the attacker?" Alfonso asked, still annoyed with his far higher pitched voice.

"He was found shot to death beside his stolen shuttle at

the spaceport. The port authorities have verified that he was the terrorist. They found the equipment he used in the attack on the shuttle. They are in the process of trying to identify him. Seems the man had many aliases. The day after the attack, Ambassador Alis told me she followed him back to the spaceport and shot him for you. She also said that the recording has been sent and that you would know what that means."

He went on, "Other than that, it's been quiet. Spiders have now been detected on another ten worlds, but their presence is still being kept secret from the public. Oh yes, by the way, when you return to GD, expect to be cheered by nearly everyone. Now, I best leave you to get settled in. I'll be by in the morning to take you to the office, if you are still going to try to continue as head of GD." Alfonso thanked him for everything and watched his friend leave.

His wife and daughters then took over, showing him how they did some things, the first of which was how to operate the electrostatic hair machine, which he sorely needed right now to get his tangled hair fixed up. He found he was on a steep learning curve, trying to learn and master actions that his wife and daughters had done all their lives. He was very frustrated with his apparent helplessness, though he soon found inspiration in Carmela and his daughters and took heart. "I need time, right?" he asked.

Gabriella giggled, "Yes, papa. We didn't get this good at them overnight. I've had many years to practice. Remember, you helped me to learn to walk." He smiled, remembering how hard that had been for her and Chita to master.

Later when Gracia left him and Carmela sitting on the edge of their bed ready for bed, Carmela whispered, "We can do this somehow. Jason and Linda dropped by a few days ago and gave me some suggestions. We'll manage, dear." With some struggling and Carmela's constant encouragement, they worked it out. An hour later, both claimed this was the most exciting, rewarding, and pleasureful lovemaking they ever had. Alfonso then fell into a deep sleep, this worry forever gone.

The next morning, Gracia got Alfonso dressed in the same professional woman's outfit and fed, just in time. Diego arrived to escort him to his office. On the way there, Diego explained, "Boss, I hired you a personal assistant, Alicia. She's been setting up the needed voice-activated computers and phone system for you. She'll be your hands for now. Also, we're going to land on the street this morning and enter the main doors. As I said last night, many want to welcome you back, though just between you and me, I suspect a lot want to see what you look like, a fabulously looking woman." Both chuckled. Alfonso realized he might as well chuckle, since this was the way things were going to be for the rest of his life.

When he walked in, Diego supporting him, he was quite surprised to see over fifty men and women crowded into the entrance area. As he stepped slowly and carefully inside, they broke into spontaneous clapping and cheering, somewhat embarrassing him. When he reached the main desk, the security guard quickly photographed him and made him a new security ID card, putting it conveniently on a chain for him. At last, he had a chance to address them.

"Thank you, thank you all for your vote of confidence. I just want to let everyone know that I'm fighting to remain your boss. I won't give up my position here at GD without a fight. Thank you for your support. It means a lot to me."

A young woman wearing a similar professional woman's outfit walked up to them. Diego introduced her, "Boss, this is Alicia, your new assistant. I'll let her take you on up to your office, while I see if the higher-ups have sent anything new for me to handle. I'll also let them know officially you are back on the job."

"Thanks. Not sure how much good I'm really going to be, Diego, but I'm here and going to try. Lead on, Alicia. Crap, best put an arm around me," he added, feeling terribly insecure walking on his own, especially with fifty or more watching him.

Alfonso spent a very frustrating morning. Everything that he used to do automatically, he now either couldn't do or had to find entirely new ways to do. At least, Alicia knew what she was doing and constantly made suggestions, some of which worked out. Lunch was even more embarrassing for him, since Alicia had to get his food for him from the cafeteria and then feed him, while eating herself. He felt like thousands of eyes were staring at him while he was eating. Even bathroom visits were embarrassing, but Alicia didn't seem to mind.

Mid-afternoon, the dreaded call from Hector came. Alfonso spoke clearly, "Answer phone." The computer-controlled system responded and answered the call, putting it on speaker-phone. "Hello Hector. I'm back at work. Rather like a first day on a new job. Any news on who the terrorist was or who hired him?" Alfonso asked pointedly. *Might as well get this battle going.*

"Ah, good, Mr. Vega. Er, not as yet. The man has a myriad of false identities to sort out. So you are really a UFBMD man now? Correct?"

"Yes, that I am. However, they have me all set up with voice-activated everythings and an assistant, so I'm getting the work done. I received a very warm welcome back by my staff this morning. Rather surprising," he added, letting Hector know he was still popular here in spite of being nearly helpless.

"Good. Good. I have placed your boys in one of the finest military academies around. Now then, are you sure you don't want me to replace you? I can't imagine how difficult this must be for you. Shortly, you will receive your disability package. I believe there are enough funds in it for you and your family to live quite nicely for the rest of your lives."

"Well, that is comforting to know. I will be the first to let you know if I can't handle my work here at GD, sir."

"So you really do want to stay on, helpless as you are?" Hector asked, a note of extreme annoyance in his voice.

"Absolutely, sir, unless I'm not able to do the work. If I can't, I'll be the first to step down, sir."

"Are you sure I can't talk you out of this?"

"No, I'm giving it my best."

"Well, let us make a compromise then, Mr. Vega. Mind you, I'm very much against keeping you on as my CEO out there in the rim. I need an executive who can pull his own weight, do the job. I can't see you as being able to do that. Still, I don't want to be seen as biased. So let's compromise. We both know you're now an official UFBMD man. Further, we both know what your male children will be like if you have some with a normal female."

"You mean the supposed super IQ men?" Alfonso came straight out with it.

"Precisely. If you want to stay on as head of Scorpi-C's GD, then you get six normal women pregnant with your children. Odds are three will be males. Hell, start with that new assistant of yours. You do that, and I'll let you stay on until we find you can't do the job," Hector laid out his proposal, knowing if Alfonso were still keen on trying to keep his position, he'd do it. If he did, then he would have some valid reason to support his decision to retain Alfonso to his superior: three super IQ male children.

"But that's not ethical, sir. What if Alicia is married or doesn't want illegitimate children?"

"Hell, we all have to do our part for GD. You do this, and I'll keep you on, if or until you can't do the work. Take it or depart today. That's my final word."

"I get to choose the women?" Alfonso fought to gain some additional concessions. This, he hadn't anticipated, but now that Hector ordered it, he realized he should've considered this might happen.

"Hell, I don't care, as long as they are normal women. We both know what will result if you and Carmela have more children. Deal?"

"All right, but I'll need some time to find them. It might take some time to get them pregnant."

"Of course, but I fully expect to hear you're giving up the post soon. We both know you can't possibly do the work. Good day." Hector hung up.

"What was that all about? Getting me pregnant? Super IQ children? I don't understand, boss," Alicia asked. At the mention of her name, she'd become very worried.

Alfonso sighed. "I neglected this aspect of being a UFBMD man. Okay, this is top-secret information. Don't reveal what I'm about to tell you to anyone outside this room." She agreed, and he outlined the breeding program and what the expected results were. "So my sons that Carmela and I had are overly strong. They will very likely be extremely powerful fighter types. Heck, my fourteen-year-olds can already lift over two hundred pounds. Our daughters are UFB women. Now as a UFBMD man, if I mate with a normal woman, our daughters will also be UFB women, but our sons would be what they are calling super IQ men, men with off the chart IQs."

He went on, "As you probably know or suspect, most all the corporation top executives already have UFB wives, and as a result, have had a number of UFB daughters. However, UFBMD men are extremely rare. I only know of another one here on Scorpi-C, out of our billions. So what Hector wants is for me to have three of these super IQ boys. Honestly, Alicia, this isn't what I planned for. It's not right. I'm happily married. Don't worry about it. I'll just have to find another way around this mess that Hector has dumped in our laps."

Alicia surprised him. "Well, boss. I'm twenty-one now and single. I've worked here at GD long enough to know you run a very different corporation than the usual ones around here. I just couldn't believe how wonderfully you handled that situation with the eight hundred UFB women. So I wouldn't mind it if you got me pregnant with one of these super IQ boys. It's the least I can do to help support GD and you."

"Thank you, Alicia. I have to talk to Carmela about this as well. It's not right. We'll see. There must be some other way around Hector and his plot. We best get me back to work here. Damn, this is so darn frustrating! I'll admit, Alicia, this is a thousand times harder than I expected it would be. Besides, if I truly can't do the work, then the whole deal is completely moot anyway."

Chapter 13—Descending Clouds

New Caledonia, Corporate Prime (or Cass-C), Central Hub Sector, the heart of the Galactic Federation—here were the topmost corporate headquarters of the largest corporations in the entire galaxy. Corporate Prime was densely populated, boasting more people than any other world, estimated at one hundred billion. Every available piece of land was covered with buildings, some stretching two hundred stories tall. Its continents were y one continuous city, though there were demarcation lines separating individual cities.

Many of the very largest corporations had their main headquarters in New Caledonia, which also had a huge spaceport nearby. In particular, the GD Corporation had its headquarters here, a two hundred-story building, with thousands of personnel all reporting ultimately to the CEO, young Louis d'Armont.

Louis had only recently taken over as head of the entire GD Corporation from his step-father, Eloy d'Armont. Why? Thirty-six year old Louis was a Super IQ man, the product of a normal woman and a UFBMD man, bred by old Eloy himself, who raised Louis from age three, grooming him to take over the reins of this giant corporation. Old Eloy's legacy was to provide a Super IQ CEO for the corporation.

Louis had married a young UFB woman, Sally, imported from another world because of her particular beauty and her incredible blonde hair, which closely matched that of Louis. Already they had three children, but were taking a break from breeding at this time. Aimee was twelve, Amorette was ten, and Edmond was eight. Both daughters were UFB girls, but the real question was what would Edmond turn out to be? No one knew for sure.

He had a stepsister, Arianne, who was thirty-eight and a normal woman with blonde hair as well. She and Louis were raised together from age three and were quite close. More importantly, Arianne was married to a UFBMD man, Bastien Benoit, who was only thirty. At Eloy's insistence, she had five children in succession, in an attempt to breed more Super IQ boys. Her special boys were Bertrand, eighteen, Corin, seventeen, and Claude, fourteen. In between the older boys, she had UFB daughters, Annette, sixteen, and Alaina, fifteen. Louis planned to bringing Bertrand into the GD fold later this year. If all went well, he'd bring Corin onboard next year.

Old Eloy was a clever man, and with the support of Louis, he had installed another Super IQ man, Felix Middleton, as Hector Ambrose's second in command on Gamma Prime before Eloy retired. Louis had long-range plans for the future of GD.

However, he had just received the encrypted sound file from an anonymous sender, Alis. He easily broke the encryption and sat back, curious about what this unknown sender had cleverly brought him. He recognized Hector's voice at once, along with Felix and Albert Vice, head of GE Corporation there on Gamma Prime. How interesting, he thought, recorded under their very noses. Felix is slipping.

Partway through it, he sat up straight. Now this was interesting! When the recording finished, a woman's voice added a few more details. Louis sat back, deep in thought. Events were unfolding, that's for sure. He brought up the intelligence reports his staff had accumulated on this Alfonso Vega. His eyes skimmed down the listing, scrolling as he went. Nothing seemed out of the ordinary. Like all top executives, he had a UFB wife and appropriate children, two UFB daughters, three fighters-to-be sons. He was keeping to the GD program.

He looked over the handling of the spider situation, which was still quite bothersome, particularly since his staff continued to relay reports of spiders being discovered on various worlds, all moving closer to the hub worlds. He had one serious question about Alfonso's handling of the spider situation. Why did he go to such trouble to save Esteban Trujillo's skin? He worked for the GE Corporation after all. Red flag one went up in Louis' mind.

He scanned on down, reviewing Alfonso's handling of the UFB women's affair. True, the man had done the only honorable thing, donating the women free to all corporation executives. *The man has a sense of honor,* Louis thought, *when he should have sent all eight hundred on up the GD line. What we could have done here with eight hundred UFB women! Yet, he chose honor over corporation policy. Red flag two.*

Then, Louis re-listened to the recording, paying particular attention to the arguments Felix had put forth, knowing he was the only intelligent man present there. Then he spoke to himself, as he was wont to do, since few real people interested him, for they were just too dull and dumb for his attention. "Felix, you failed to point out the two red flags, but took another approach. I concur; as it stands, this Alfonso Vega fellow has become a prime candidate for promotion, assuming that honorable and good public opinion are the requisites. Did you intentionally hide the red flags or did you miss them, old fellow? Well, you certainly missed the recording device!"

"Well, decision time. Will it be A or B?" he said, rolling his chair several feet across his top floor office to his large comm center. Quickly, he established a secure line to Felix. After making sure Felix was alone and secure, he began issuing his new orders.

"Felix, I'm in possession of a recording," he began, giving the exact date, time, and location of the meeting, along with who was present. On the monitor, he saw Felix flinch and knew Felix had missed the fact that someone recorded the meeting. "Yes, Strike One on you, Felix. No, I have no idea who sent me this recording, but in all likelihood, it was a woman."

"Now then, Hector has made a complete mess of this whole situation. What is he doing about it?"

Felix outlined what Hector had just proposed to Alfonso, that Alfonso had returned to work, and wanted to keep on being the GD CEO there on Scorpi-C. "Yes, he has ordered Alfonso to breed six normal women, hoping to get three Super IQ sons out of it. Hector's grand plan is to salvage something of value, the boys, assuming the normal women don't all have UFBs instead. Lousy plan."

"Okay. Felix, as of this minute, Hector is removed. You are now the new head of GD on Gamma Prime. Your first action is to arrest Hector for incompetence. Have someone expose him to the genetic bio agent and let him make amends by being a UFBMD man as he planned for Alfonso. Make him disappear from society. Breed him to as many normal women as you can, but explain to his wife that he died while on duty and see that she gets his benefits plan."

Felix laughed. "Thank you sir. Serves the fool right. We can get something useful out of him yet. I will do a thorough investigation of the illegal wiretap at once. It shall not happen again on my watch, sir."

"Excellent. Now then, we have a serious situation with this Alfonso Vega UFBMD man. Did you miss the two red flags?" Louis asked quite pointedly.

After a pause, Felix replied, "Three red flags. Why save Esteban? Why dole out the UFB women? Is he connected to the resistance?"

"Ah, thank you Felix for pointing out the third. I admit I only did a cursory review of the man. Plus, I'm glad you hadn't missed them. From the recording, I had questions."

Felix laughed, "Hardly boss. It's difficult working with morons. They can only accept ideas so fast. I sometimes lose patience with the dopes. Yet, the Alfonso situation remains."

"Yes, it does. Should I look into it or should I leave it to you?"

Felix knew his new boss was suddenly testing him. Hidden behind such a simple question lay all manner of intrigues and traps, but nothing his superior intellect couldn't handle in seconds. "Boss, I can handle it from here. After all, it is on the distant rim of the galaxy, hardly something top management should have to handle, even though middle management bungled it. I have an idea that will help sort out honorable versus corporate policy." By that, he meant whether this Alfonso was likely involved with the resistance.

"Excellent point, Felix. I'll leave this matter in your capable hands. I suspect shortly you will have a new counterpart over at GE Corporation. The recording was apparently sent to them as well. I would like an update on the situation when it is appropriately handled. Also, this spider affair is getting out of hand. Please address some thought on the matter. We must take some effective action and soon. That's all for today. Good hunting." Louis signed off, satisfied on several accounts. First, Felix hadn't missed the key red flags. Second, he was contrite about having missed being secretly recorded and that it wasn't likely to occur again. Third, he was aware of the Alfonso situation and had a way to deal with it, sorting out just what Alfonso really was.

Now, Louis turned his attention elsewhere. He was so looking forward to this evening's romp. He and his stepsister, Arianne had agreed to swap marital partners. She was tired of giving birth to UFB women and Super IQ boys. Besides, Bastien was completely helpless, something that she found particularly annoying, and always had a female assistant take care of his needs. She was intrigued with just what would result from mating with her stepbrother. He was anything but helpless. Thus, she had eagerly agreed to their private affair. Tonight, they would bed together, while in another room, Bastien and Sally could see if they could even manage to have sex without help. Louis knew they were exploring genetically untested grounds, which also pricked his curiosity.

Back on Gamma Prime, Felix barked his initial orders quite clearly, "Yes, I want you to immediately arrest Hector, charges of high treason. Put him in the bio containment room for now." He then called up their medical-geneticist and ordered Hector be given the genetic bio agent as soon as he was in the containment room. Next, he called up the head of Breeding Center One. "I've a new UFBMD man coming to you in about four days. Work out a program to breed him to as many normal women as you can. Yes, women who work here at the HQ."

As soon as he had confirmation of Hector's arrest, he then placed a secure call to Alfonso Vega, noting the time difference and hoping the man was still in his office. If he weren't, the call would have to wait until the morning. "Hello. Alfonso Vega here. What can I do for you, Mr. Middleton?"

"Is your assistant Alicia present with you and can she hear us?" Felix asked.

"Yes, she's become my hands. She has been sworn to Level 10 Security, so that shouldn't be a problem, sir," Alfonso replied, wondering why Hector's second in command was calling so late.

"Okay then. First, Mr. Vega, I'm now the new head of GD on Gamma Prime. Hector has been arrested and being dealt with for gross incompetence."

"Well, congratulations, sir, on your promotion," Alfonso replied, thinking fast. Would Felix be replacing him? Did he have to fight this battle all over again?

"Thanks. Now then, about your situation. Hector claims that you wish to remain on as our CEO there on Scorpi-C, despite your physical situation. Is this correct?"

"Yes sir. I have the full support of my staff in this matter. I do hope I've done enough for GD, recently." He decided not to outline the details of the spiders and UFB women. Surely, Felix knew all about those.

"Indeed. You have certainly gotten our attention and that of my own superior I might add. I'm sorry a promotion isn't in order at this time, but I'm sure openings will come soon for advancement. The question you and I must resolve is that of your request to stay on as CEO."

"Yes, I would definitely like to continue my work here, as long as I'm able to do the work. I'll be the first to resign, if I find I can't handle everything expected of me," Alfonso replied. If he still had fingers, he would have crossed them.

"Acceptable to me under one condition."

"What's that?"

"You must realize your unique genetic makeup is extremely rare. Hence, the GD Corporation simply can't afford to ignore it. My sole condition is that you take Alicia into your home as a second wife and get her pregnant as often as possible. We need to produce more Super IQ men for the future of GD or the other corporations will leave us in the dust. So I will let you remain as CEO as long as you take Alicia into your family and the two of you make babies. If you prefer, you may have UFB female fetuses aborted. We are only interested in male offspring. Of course, if later on we find that you are physically actually unable to perform your duties as our CEO, I'll have to replace you. Is this agreement acceptable to you?"

Shit! Alfonso thought. "I believe I can somehow make

this work, but shouldn't Alicia have some say in the matter? If she doesn't wish to participate, surely, we could find another young woman who would." Oh, how he wanted Alicia to say no to this unethical, immoral deal, but he had no way to express that, not with Felix on the line. He would hear anything he said, and he had no hands to jot her a quick message!

"Sir," Alicia spoke up, "I would be delighted to have babies by Mr. Vega, but I don't have the wherewithal to support UFB girls, not on my salary."

"Excellent, Alicia, excellent. Go right ahead and have those aborted. I'm sure you will be extremely pleased with your male children. They will be incredibly intelligent and end up with extremely important positions within GD, doing you very high honors indeed. Then, the matter is settled, Mr. Vega. I do hope you're able to perform your duties. I'll be watching and monitoring you. Do report to me when Alicia is with a male child. Good evening." Felix hung up, certain of one detail. Alfonso was not following the honorable role, but had accepted the corporate line, so he put the notions that Alfonso was somehow connected to the resistance out of his mind for now.

Alicia spoke up, "Well boss, if I am to do this, it would certainly help if I had a substantial salary boost so I can afford what we'll be needing." She gave him a coy wink.

"Yes of course, Alicia. Consider your wages doubled. Now I best get home and clear things with my wife. We'll discuss arrangements that we'll need tomorrow."

He discussed this unexpected turn of events with Diego, while his second took him home. Diego promised to research Alicia thoroughly and inform him in the morning. After dinner and being fed by Gracia who alternated between him and Carmela, he finally got the chance to speak to her alone. Carefully, he explained what had happened and what he would have to agree to if he was to retain his position a while longer.

To his utter amazement, Carmela didn't break down and cry; rather she began to laugh! "Oh Alfonso, you blind fool. Of course, I know about the UFBMD man thing and what that really does mean. I knew this was going to happen, eventually. Who wouldn't desire to have extremely brilliant boys? Just as who wouldn't desire to have gorgeous supermodel girls? As long as you can keep me satisfied, it's fine with me. But I would suggest you have her come and stay with us. After all, she is your personal assistant now. She should be ferrying you back and forth to work. She should be helping care for your needs here. We could use another helping hand at mealtimes. She would be earning her children by you."

"Really? You're okay with this arrangement?" he asked dumbfounded.

"Of course, dear. You need the help. We all do. I don't really want to bear more children if I don't have to. It's terribly hard for us to have them, but at least you're spared that uncomfortable mess. No, as long as she helps, as she should, then I'm fine with it. In fact, Diego and I are surprised they didn't kidnap you, put you in some breeding cell somewhere, and having many, many women raping you just to get male children from you. This is much more acceptable, especially if she pulls her weight around here."

In the morning, Diego reported he had uncovered nothing amiss in Alicia's background. When they met in his office shortly after eight, Alfonso proposed the new arrangements to her. She bit her lip. "Are you sure Carmela is okay with this? With me moving in with you? It certainly would be more convenient and easier for me. Honestly, boss, we have to get you better outfits."

That evening, Alicia took Alfonso home. At first, she was embarrassed to be in his home with his wife and daughters, but she soon began to relax, as they accepted her as part of the family. That night when she had him ready for bed and in her new bedroom, their guest room, she looked at his naked body and exclaimed, "My god, Alfonso, you look like a fabulous model, all of you, except for that. This is incredible."

He flushed. "I know. Let's get this over with please." He allowed her to work her magic on him, though he soon found her irresistible and realized this powerful sex drive was now part of his new genetic makeup, and there wasn't much he could do about it. She roused him in an instant, in spite of his many misgivings about this whole arrangement.

True to her word, she took him shopping the next day, and when she finished up, his appearance was a hundred percent improved! He laughed heartily at his image in the mirror. He even aroused himself! Now, he understood far better his own wife and daughters and vowed to help them even more in the future.

His third day back brought more troubles. The special envoy arrived. His purpose was to inspect the various breeding programs in place at GD Corporation here on Scorpi-C. That meant, he had to pay a visit to all the various executives and their families, checking on the UFB women, UFB daughters, and now on Alfonso and his arrangement with Alicia. He was very embarrassed by having to answer such frank and personal questions, but knew he had to do so. Likewise, Alicia, who explained they were successful last night, but it was too soon to tell if she were pregnant. Even more embarrassing for her, the man had to verify she wasn't using any methods of contraception.

Further, he had to tag along with the envoy as he visited all the others who had UFB wives and daughters. Thankfully, Alicia went with him, though he had to keep telling her to keep an arm around his waist. By the end of the long day, his feet were killing him, and he realized yet another aspect he'd not truly understood before about his wife and daughters. However, the envoy gave Scorpi-C's GD headquarters a glowing report. All was perfect here. Alfonso was never so glad to be rid of a meddling fool as he was, when the man gave him his report and left GD.

The next day, Felix called him. "We have big trouble on Taurus-C!"

***

The Master wasn't idle. Once he had his new breeding colony functioning well and the building's security quite tight, he began the next phase in his plans. Once more, he began walking into the headquarters of various corporations on Taurus-C, asking to see the CEO. Once in the man's office, he had him sign over total control of that local corporation to him. The only name ever given was simply the Master. The CEOs found themselves unable to resist his request and did so, much to their displeasure once he walked out of their building. Twice, one angry CEO had ordered his security men to shoot the man as he left, but to their chagrin, he was wearing a PDS, and their attempts did nothing.

By the time Felix called Alfonso, the Master had taken control of every major corporation on Taurus-C—at least in theory he had. The papers, if presented in court would hold up, since the CEOs had signed them over to the Master. However, the courts were run by corporation men who would rule that these documents were invalid, that somehow the Master had forced the executives to sign them under duress, invalidating them. Besides, no monetary credits changed hands.

What truly got the attention of middle management was the email from the Master. In essence, it said for them to advise their local CEOs to comply with the sale and hand over the corporation to his men. Failure to do so would result in the total destruction of those in said headquarters. Middle management, Felix in this case, had ordered a massive security guard buildup, with orders to shoot the Master on sight. Unfortunately, in response to Felix's reply, two days later, the entire GD building on Taurus-C suffered a massive genetic bio-agent attack. Four hundred six men and women dropped into comas! The local medical facility simply couldn't handle that many victims at once, but they didn't even get the chance.

Instead, the Master's men, wearing bio containment suits, entered the building, removing the comatose people. Just where they were taken and what happened to them after that was unknown at this time. GD headquarters on Taurus-C was wiped out and the actual business offices on that world quickly began following the Master's men's orders. They had no choice. By the time of Felix's call, six other major corporation headquarters had been similarly attacked, and their comatose personnel removed.

Thus, Felix had quite a lot to tell Alfonso! He finished up, "So Scorpi-C is close to this Taurus-C world. Have your people go there and find out just what is going on. We need answers and need them by yesterday. Hell, go there yourself and find out firsthand. Oh yes, by the way, Rho-C is totally abandoned. All facilities on that planet have been demolished, so the Master fellow can't retreat there. Get me answers or you are fired, Alfonso. Oh yes, one other thing, we have nuked that rim world where the spiders came from. End of spider threat." After he hung up, Felix roared with laughter, imagining the helpless Alfonso trying to go to Taurus-C and investigate. Ludicrous indeed. Perhaps, he would soon have the man's resignation. Still, he would continue breeding him.

***

Jones followed a man called Louis d'Armont home, hiding in her usual place, his pant cuff. There she found more of these most unusual human females, the ones that she was fond of sharing in their extremely strong emotions. From what she'd heard, this Louis fellow sat at the top of the company's hierarchy, so she was not particularly interested in moving on just now. No, Jones decided to enjoy these strange, new females, and hopped out of his cuff, scurrying over to the adult form. As she scampered up her nylon covered legs, the woman shrieked, but had no way to dislodge Jones, and the man ignored her. Soon, she was crawling up Sally's hair, knowing that Sally could most definitely feel her. She'd already experienced other such women, who had a rather large degree of tactile perception in their hair, quite unlike anything she'd ever experienced three millennia ago or from the more recent men. Soon, she plunged her toxin into the woman's neck and then slipped beneath her skin, latching onto all the sensory perceptions sailing through the body's neuron network, and calming the woman down. Her husband totally ignored her outburst.

"Sex now," Jones made the woman called Sally call out to her husband, this Louis fellow. She made her walk over to him while he was changing clothes and even rub her body against his. Nothing. The man didn't respond as Jones desired.

"Not now. You know darn well we're going over to the Benoit place after dinner. You'll just have to wait until then, my sex doll," Louis explained, rather annoyed with his moronic wife.

Jones sighed; she could wait. Just then, she felt a gigantic power surge. Some of it trickled out into Sally's system causing her body to jerk and to fall down, unable to keep her balance. At least, Louis helped her back up. "What was that all about?" he asked quite annoyed with her.

She had a blank look in her eyes and muttered something he didn't get, so he left her and headed off to see if supper was ready. Jones analyzed the power surge and realized what it meant. To be sure, she sent an electronic data burst to mother Smith. Nothing happened. Now she knew. Mother Smith was dead. But how? That thought perplexed her, and she knew that she needed to find out.

A short while later, Louis took Sally with him to another house, while anticipation excitement in Jones grew. When they got there, she saw another woman like Sally and another normal human woman. For a time, Jones was confused. Louis was handing her over to this other UFB woman. "But I want sex," she made the Sally body complain.

"He'll give it to you, dumb broad," Louis replied antagonistically.

Sally followed this other woman into a bedroom, where a servant undressed them both. Sally gazed upon the other woman being called Bastien, who was just as shapely as she was, but then she saw his male appendage and inhaled. *What was this?* Jones had never seen such a thing before, not in the human species. An hour later, floating in utter ecstasy, Jones decided these were the perfect forms for all humans! The sexual sensations and emotions between these two strange new bodies were electrifying! Jones now had the beginnings of her grand plan. Unlike Smith, she wouldn't just dine on the humans, but rather breed these new forms and enjoy them.

Later on when Sally fell asleep, Jones slipped out of her neck, hopped onto the floor and went in search of the Louis fellow, knowing he must be an important man, perhaps one with enough power to make her grand plan come about. She slipped into the sleeping man's neck.

During the next day, Jones was astounded to learn he had ordered the destruction of the rocky world where mother Smith and so many thousands of her little ones lived. As he received field reports from men who landed there reporting on the destruction, Jones could hardly keep from injecting a lethal dose of her toxin into Louis!

Louis felt funny all day, as if someone was inside his

head, but that was, of course, impossible, he told himself. Still, he found it both strange and unusual that he would pay a visit to the lower floors of the building, strolling among all the breeding rooms, even going so far as to peek inside a few. Further, he found his mind going over everything that was known about the UFB women and the scarce UFBMD men. Quite why he was thinking about such things when there were much larger problems at hand he couldn't say. He even found himself in the genetics lab, checking on the quantity of the genetic bio agent they had. Even more shocking was his orders to the men to increase production ten times. They looked a bit surprised at the order, but complied, declaring it would be ready in three days.

Jones knew that she needed some help with her plan. She focused and sent out a summoning call to all other spiders within her rather limited range. Two answered her, having made it to Corporate Prime on their own. "Mother Smith, she's dead!" One sent back.

"Yes, I know. We are down but not defeated. Spread the world, Jones is in charge, and I have us a super plan. Tell everyone to come here to Corporate Prime as soon as they can. You guys are going to love this!" Jones sent. *Now, it's just a matter of time.*

***

"It's just a matter of time, Master, before they send another army to kill us," Tao complained. He and the Master were meeting in the former GD Corporation CEO's office on the top floor. The other Seconds were out carrying out other orders.

"They will need the right convincing, that's all," the Master explained to his most trusted assistant. "GD Corporation executives who control this small branch office here on Taurus-C have gotten the word. Now, it's time to ensure they truly understand my meaning. Tao, it's time you play janitor for a spell. The others are gathering up what we need from the researchers that we now control, combining their supplies. I have some GF Corporation engineers designing the delivery mechanisms as we speak. A few more days will see the *convincer* is ready for deployment."

He leaned close to Tao. "Here's what you and the others are going to do. First stop will be Gamma Prime. Most all the major corporations have their mid-arm headquarters there. You'll play janitor, but while cleaning, find the air circulation system. Insert one of these new devices inside it. That's all you have to do. I have the activation devices. When the time is right, poof! We add another batch of UFB women and more importantly UFBMD men to our growing collection."

"But Master, what are we really going to do with all them? They take up a lot of resources and have to have so much assistance," Tao asked, hoping to get more clues to the Master's true plan.

"Until now, the corporations have been playing god, keeping the spoils to themselves. What normal man could possibly afford to have a UFB wife? Hell, the corporations only let their most trusted executives have them. And a UFBMD man, why, they are as rare as they come. We will win over the support of the common people on any given world by giving the men their own absolutely gorgeous sex dolls, and the women, their own magnificent sex toys as well. After all, Tao, what man can resist being with a woman who looks like a super model? What woman could resist the seduction of these UFBMD men, eh? Few. Men and women would rather spend time in bed with a real sex doll than fight deadly battles against us. Weaken a world's defenses by subduing those in power and that world is ours for the asking."

Tao looked baffled. Surely, this wasn't the Master's grand plan! Suddenly, the Master burst out laughing. "Gotcha, Tao. Had you going there didn't I? Seriously, we take out all of those who wield the real power, the corporate executives and their staff, by turning them into UFB women and UFBMD men, helpless sex toys. Think about it for a minute, Tao. What will happen here on Taurus-C if every person who works for the major corporations is turned into one of those? The corporations make the laws, enforce the laws, and try those arrested. If all those men and women of a world are gone, who then controls the world? We step in and quietly take the fallen reins, and everyone is happy, especially if we can spread the sex dolls around a bit."

"Ah, now I understand. Yes, GD here was a real threat, but now there isn't any of them left to issue orders to the actual manufacturing plants, survey crews, and mining operations. So we step in and fill the vacuum," Tao replied, hoping he was saying it properly and had understood the Master correctly.

"Indeed, Tao. Our main task will be to fill the vacuum, one planet at a time. My good Tao, there are thousands of worlds out there. It'll take us years to get to all them, and we will need a goodly supply of the sex dolls. Hence our small breeding project. I also know some corporations have their own secret breeding programs as well, but I don't know if they are as large as ours is. If so, that will only aid us. Meantime, we have to eliminate all them here on Taurus-C. GE Corporation is tomorrow's target. Make sure another four hundred beds are ready in this building, please."

***

"He's setting you up for a fall!" Diego complained. Alfonso had called him into his office shortly after the surprising call from Felix Middleton. He outlined what he'd been told and what he was ordered to do, namely go to Taurus-C, find out what happened to GD headquarters there, and what this Master fellow was actually doing or planning. "Even if you were your old self, you can't do this. This isn't an assignment for top management, boss. Such things are supposed to be assigned to others in the corporation, others who are trained for field operations."

"Nevertheless, Felix has given me marching orders. I have no choice, if I want to keep my position here. As helpless as I'm now, I have to try, Diego. I can't risk taking you with me. I'll take Alicia and a few select others. Keep the party small and inconspicuous as possible, though a UFB woman isn't going to be all that inconspicuous." He was referring to how he looked to others. Besides, Diego, I sent Anka off to Taurus-C and no one has heard from her in almost a week. She's over due to report in. I must also find out if she is in trouble. I owe her that much. I don't leave my employees in the lurch, Diego."

"May I make some suggestions on who else to take with

you?" Diego pleaded.

"Of course, but let's keep the party fairly small." The two discussed the personnel for a time. Ordinarily, Alfonso would have paid a visit to each, asking them to go on this mission with him. However, as limited as he now was, he decided on a conference call, employing all security measures possible.

"Captain Bess, I need your engineering assistance. Gunnery Sergeant Martha, I need your firepower. Jason, I hate to ask more of you, but I would feel more comfortable with an explosives expert tagging along. Captain Juanita, I truly do need your comm center skills on this one." The four agreed to go without even hearing what the mission was!

He continued, "Captain Armando de Cruzas, I need your sharpshooting expertise on this one. J. D. Galling, I need your recon skills and perhaps your Special Forces training."

"Agreed boss. Love to come, but we want to bring our girlfriends along with us, Melissa and Jackie. They can't get by without us around. Besides, both of them are familiar with Taurus-C, and they can stay with the transport and guard it," Armando countered. Alfonso couldn't argue against him, for he needed both men. Perhaps having someone watching their backs was a good idea.

"All right. Here's the mission," Alfonso began outlining the situation on Taurus-C. He finished up with, "Plus we've not heard from Anka in a week. That's not like her, so we also need to locate her and find out if she's okay. My job as GD's CEO is at stake on this one. Upper management doesn't think I'm capable of doing my job anymore."

"Boss, this isn't CEO work," Armando protested.

"I know. I just think they're trying their best to get me to give it up. Nevertheless, we have a serious job to do," Alfonso countered. "So now is the time to back out, and I'll understand." None did. "Be at headquarters at 09:00 tomorrow. I'll provide all the supplies we'll need then."

Chapter 14—Tackling the Impossible

"Wow boss!" exclaimed Jackie, the fiery redhead, when she got her first look at Alfonso early the next morning. "You look just like us. Incredible." Her surprise and thoughts were echoed by her constant companion, the blonde Melissa. Neither had yet seen him after the terrorist attack. Jackie added, "Thanks for letting us come along, boss. We won't let you down. Armando and J. D. have been giving us lessons on flying a transport."

"You can fly one?" broke in Bess, quite surprised to hear that. She and Martha had been wondering just why Alfonso had invited them on this dangerous spying trip. They could understand the need for the ex-Special Forces recon man, J. D. and the sharpshooter Armando, even why nearly helpless Jason was coming along in case a bomb was needed, but these two had baffled the pair. They knew that Captain Juanita was doing a superb job as his new RdD Comm Center officer, despite being armless as well, for at least she had her feet repaired as well as her hair, now kept rather short, but attractive Bess thought.

"Look," Jackie defended herself and Melissa, "since we heard how Juanita and Marita escaped, we've been trying to learn how to fly a transport. Our new boyfriends are helping us work out ways and means. We can do it. We want to help too."

"Of course, you do. You all do. That's the point," Alfonso spoke up. "That's why I chose each one of you for this mission. I know I'm the weakest link here. I haven't even gotten remotely adjusted to my situation and am depending utterly on Alicia here to help me. By the way, she and I have agreed to try to have some children to satisfy my boss Felix, so I can stay the head of Scorpi-C GD. I want to be clear about that."

"Now then this mission has two key purposes. One, we are charged by Felix to find out what is going on on Taurus-C and with our GD headquarters there. What is this Master fellow trying to do? What does he want? Intelligence. Our second purpose is to find Anka Polonia. I sent her to Taurus-C right after she got back from the space station attack. We've not heard from her in over a week now, and I suspect she's in some kind of trouble."

"Each of us will wear a Personal Defense Shield. Those with arms, you get the armaments. I want you to carry a blaster, an automatic handgun with silencer, and a grenade launcher. You can take along anything else you desire. It is autumn on Taurus-C right now. So I've ordered cloaks for us all. That will hide our lack of arms and hide some of the guns. We want to look as inconspicuous as possible. Jackie and Melissa will stay on the transport, both guarding it and keeping it ready for a fast takeoff, should we run into trouble. Captain Juanita's post will be the ship's comm center. She'll be monitoring us on the ground, spaceport communications, and searching for Anka's chip's signal. As head of our local RdD, I simply won't leave a man or woman behind, not if I can find a way to get them out."

"Finally, Jason is our safety factor. If we get into bad trouble, we are counting on his demolitions expertise and Bess's construction skills to get us out of it. J. D., Armando, Bess, Martha, if we get into a firefight with the Master's forces, shoot to kill. Don't hold back. Questions?"

"Can we take along some C-8 and thermite charges? I prefer those," Jason asked.

"Good lord, son. You think we're going to have to break through solid steel?" asked J. D.

Bess chuckled, "You haven't seen Jason in action." Alfonso smiled and added those to their supplies.

"Do I get a gun too?" asked Alicia.

"Do you know how to use one?" asked Alfonso. He'd forgotten about her, thinking that she was merely his assistant.

"An automatic gun with a silencer would be fine for me. Someone should show me how to use it though," she answered him more or less. "How else can I protect you?" She got her gun, and J. D. showed her how to use it during the flight to Taurus-C.

Once supplied from GD headquarters, the group took several shuttles to the spaceport and got in one of GD Corporations' deep space transports, but one that did not have the company logo on it. J. D. and Armando insisted that Jackie and Melissa be allowed to pilot and navigate the transport, though they would be right there with them. Alfonso allowed it, for two reasons. One, if the two were serious about wanting to learn to fly a transport, they needed the opportunity and practice. Two, he had no idea UFB women could possibly do such a thing. Juanita and Marita had done it by using the autopilot all the way from take-off to landing, hardly flying a transport. In the back of his mind was the very faint idea that perhaps he and the many UFB women were not as helpless as everyone thought, only no one ever gave them the slightest chance to be and do anything beyond being a sex doll and baby factory.

He quietly asked Bess to monitor the pair, adding, "See if when we get back, there isn't something up front that could be modified to make it easier for them to fly a transport." She nodded and did so.

Eight hours later, they reached Taurus-C. Per Alfonso's order, Jackie and Melissa began orbiting the planet in an orbit that spiraled around the world. Via Captain Juanita, Alfonso contacted the main visitor's spaceport, requesting planet-orbiting permission. "We are just tourists visiting Taurus-C for the first time," he had her explain to the control tower, and received permission to do so, along with landing pad instructions.

That done, Juanita began thoroughly searching for the tiny chip's signal from Anka. Alfonso was very glad that he had insisted that all those working for him on intelligence gathering missions off-world have one inserted into their necks. On the third pass, Juanita called out, "Got her boss. Beginning triangulation now." Alfonso relaxed a little.

"If this location is correct, boss," Juanita called out, "she is somewhere in GD Corporation headquarters!"

Based on that, Alfonso gave the order to land at the spaceport. Armando carefully watched as Jackie and Melissa valiantly struggled to get the transport landed correctly. Even Bess wanted to just jump in and lend the struggling pair a hand, but Armando held her back, and she knew why he did. Still, her heart ached to see the pair struggling so hard to do it and vowed to see if there wasn't some redesign of the controls that would help them with this, but that would have to wait.

Once safely down, Alfonso ordered Melissa, Jackie, and Juanita to remain on the ship and have it ready for action at a moment's notice. Juanita said, "I'll be continuously monitoring all of you and Anka's locator chip. I'll keep you informed."

The rest headed down the bay ramp, though Bess and Alicia had to help Jason and Alfonso with the descent. Jason carried a backpack with their explosives hidden beneath his cloak. In fact, the weather was quite chilly, and their jeans and cloaks were definitely needed. Alfonso had chosen their apparel correctly. They blended in with the locals they saw on the streets. J. D. handled paying the tourist landing fee and got them all through local customs and out on to the street in front of the spaceport. Here, they took a public airbus into town.

Their first stop was a local diner, since it was around suppertime. Taking booths together and in the rear, the feeding of Jason and Alfonso wouldn't be so noticeable. Meanwhile, they all listened in on the local gossip. They didn't hear too much that was useful, other than strange things were going on at the GE Corporation headquarters today and that GD headquarters building had been quarantined, though only wild speculations were given as the reason behind it.

After eating, when they stepped outside the diner, dusk was falling. They made their way along the streets, heading for the corporate headquarters section of the city. The GE Corporation skyscraper was three blocks from the GD Corporation building and, as they neared that first, many onlookers were milling around on the street some distance from the building. Even a news crew was there recording the event. The group pressed in closer to hear what they could.

". . . announced that the GE Corporation headquarters building has officially been quarantined. Officials claim a deadly bio agent attack has infected everyone inside the building. Word has it that some five hundred workers were inside, including the top executives. No word on any casualties has come out from the officials."

"Days ago, the same thing happened three blocks down

at the GD Corporation headquarters. We now know that five hundred sixty-three men and women, that is, the entire GD Corporation staff here on Taurus-C, were wiped out. We've no word from GD Corporation when or even if these people will be replaced. No timetable for recovery has been reported. Earlier today, we visited one of the local GD factories to learn if they had any word from GD Corporation off world. Here is what they had to say."

At this point, the camera turned off, and the station cut away to the prerecorded interview, which was monitored by the news crew on a small portable monitor, while they prepared their next live shot of the building and the large red quarantine signs posted at all entrances. As the group watched, medical personnel wearing bio-containment suits left the building, climbed into their special transport, and left. At this point, another transport vehicle arrived and a number of armed men stepped out. One man strode over to the news crew.

"We are about to ventilate the skyscraper. Unless you want to be infected yourselves, you should move at least two blocks away. If you want to be infected, that can be arranged. Step forward, and we'll escort you inside." He turned briskly around and headed back to the main entrance, where other men were undoing the red tapes, discarding them. Wisely, Alfonso had his group move back before the stampede began.

After the confusion died down, several key windows were blown out and some yellowish vapors could be seen seeping out of them. Then, the unexpected happened again. From near the entrance of GE Corporation, a very well dressed man wearing white gloves and an antiquated top hat, felt and black as his suit, walked determinedly towards the news crew. Alfonso took note of him. From his bearing, he looked like an executive of some kind. "We stick around," he whispered. The cameras began zooming in on him, and the reporter stepped forward, eager to get a scoop.

"Hello. Are you recording this?" the man asked. They were. "Good. I have a message for the people of Tesla and all Taurus-C. I am the Master. I've come to liberate you, the common man, from the vile tendrils of the evil, wicked corporations, who have strangled you and abused you for countless centuries. These all-powerful, major corporations make the laws, enforce the laws, and try you for breaking them. You, the real people, have no say, no voice, and no opinion in these things. How many of you have been victimized by their unethical, immoral, selfish, greedy policies? I dare say there's not a man or woman on Taurus-C or anywhere in the galaxy who hasn't been victimized in some way by these vicious corporations and their evil executives who control every aspect of your lives, obliterating your personal freedom."

"They keep the best, the spoils of your sweat and blood, for themselves. These executives have the most beautiful, gorgeous women as their wives and companions. They monopolize the fabulous Ultimate in Feminine Beauty models. How many of you men have seen images of these fantastic-looking top models and drooled over them, fantasied over them, eh? Yet, is an ordinary man ever allowed to have such a beautiful wife? Nay. The executives do not ever allow anyone outside their inner circle to have or even see such magnificent women. And you women, have you not heard of the equally fabulous male models, which the corporation executives keep safely hidden away from view?"

"This abuse, this destruction of the common man and woman, this evil suppression can't be tolerated any longer. I, the Master, am here to put an end to the corporations, to remove the hangman's noose they have around every one of your necks, tightening them if you do not do as they say. Today, such behavior ends, ends here on Taurus-C."

"Soon, I, the Master, will give out some of these ultimate in beauty women and men to you, the ordinary men and women of Taurus-C, so that you may partake of the ultimate in luxury that has so long been denied you, kept captive in the hands of these evil executives. The GD executives are gone. Today, GE executives are gone. Tomorrow, more of these evil corporation executives here on Taurus-C will be gone. Your freedom is at hand."

"Starting tomorrow, any man or woman who has been harmed by actions taken by these evil corporations should report to Central Hall, where my associates will document your claim. Shortly after that, we will see that you are appropriately compensated for the corporation's crimes against you. Further, those of you who wish to have one of these incredibly beautiful women and/or men as your mate, your wife, your partner, please report to Central Hall and make your desires known. As these unbelievably beautiful men and women become available, you will get yours free of charge. No longer will these very special dolls be the sole property of the wealthy corporate executives! The Master has spoken." He tipped his black, felt top hat, turned, and retreated, ignoring the shouted questions fired his way.

Alfonso, like nearly everyone else, stood there completely mesmerized by the man's voice. Every word he spoke seemed to be the utter truth, whether it actually was. As he left, Alfonso was finally able to shake his head and throw off the hypnotic spell he'd been under, as did most others.

"Good God!" exclaimed Bess, "If he would have said shoot yourself, I would have!"

"Who is he?" asked Armando.

"Better ask *what* is he?" added Jason.

"Hell, the whole crowd was mesmerized or hypnotized or whatever!" J. D. put in.

"This is far more serious than we ever imagined. Come on; we best see if we can find Anka," Alfonso whispered. Moving slowly, the group headed on down the street, leaving the gabbing crowd to their wild speculations.

Through his earpiece, Alfonso heard Juanita. "Boss, I recorded all that. Unbelievable." He thanked her, very glad he'd brought her along in spite of her limitations.

They stopped across the street from the GD skyscraper to observe. Two men stood guard at the main entrance. Most peculiar, all the windows of the middle hundred stories of the two hundred-story building had recently been painted black! "They are hiding something," Alfonso whispered the obvious. "How do we get inside?"

If they fought their way inside, all the other guards would be alerted. That wasn't a good plan. Alfonso alerted Juanita. "Captain, can you relay the precise coordinates of

Anka to Armando's GPS device?"

"On it boss. There, he should have them. She isn't moving, if that helps," Juanita replied.

"Up there somewhere," Armando whispered pointing about halfway up the tall skyscraper.

Jason suggested, "We could bluff our way in. You all could say that you found two UFB women, Alfonso and me, and need to get us inside."

"Yes, but Jason, we don't know if that's what they did to the GD people. They could just as easily killed all them," Armando countered. "Out here, we're blind."

Alfonso suddenly had an idea. "Say, you all aren't supposed to know this, but all GD headquarters have a secret entrance for emergency evacuations. What we need is to locate this one's entrance. Juanita, are you hearing this?" She was. "Okay, use this code and see if you can get access to their building plans. It's the override code that is supposed to work. Never tried it, so no guarantee." He rattled off the numbers.

Ten minutes later, Juanita reported, "I'm in boss. Checking now. Say, this is very well organized. Ah, here it is. It's two blocks to your right, basement of Acer Hardware. Northwest corner. Blast door, it says."

"Thanks Juanita. We're off," Alfonso whispered. Again, walking slowly because of the small steps of Alfonso and Jason, the group took twenty minutes to reach the store, another tall building, but this one was more like a giant warehouse than a skyscraper. Armando circled the building and brought everyone to the rear doors.

"If we break in, alarms are going to go off. The place will be swarming with armed responders," Armando said. "So we would have to find these doors quickly and somehow get them opened fast. In all likelihood, boss, we wouldn't be able to exit this way."

"Where's a burglar when you need one," Alfonso joked. "We'll have to take our chances on this one. Break in, Armando," he ordered.

He fired a couple of rounds with the silenced gun and forced the doors open. "Okay, find the way to the basement as fast as possible," Alfonso ordered.

He was surprised when Armando picked him up and carried him inside. J. D. did the same with Jason. "Faster this way boss," Armando teased him, as the small group headed inside rapidly. Lighting was dim, and it took them precious minutes to find the stairs to the basement. Down they went, with Alfonso feeling like he was dead weight on this mission, a sack of flour thrown over the man's shoulders.

"Class G blast doors," Jason identified them behind a shelf. "We know how to handle them, don't we Bess?" reminding her of those they'd gotten open on Rho-C. While Bess got the thermite out of his backpack, Jason began telling her just where to place the charges. Armando got the shelves out of the way and took up a rear guard position.

Ten minutes later, the blinding white light illuminated the basement for a minute, also filling the enclosed area with an acrid smoke cloud. The blast doors swung open. Quickly, everyone stepped inside. "Hold on. We should block the entrance," Jason whispered.

"Already on it," Armando whispered back. He'd found some heavy metal bars and proceeded to use them to make a sort of locking barrier from the inside. That done, using their flashlights, the group moved on down the tunnel, which was barely four feet wide. Its roof almost touched their heads. "Two blocks," Armando whispered, taking the lead with J. D. right behind him.

Sometime later, they halted before another set of doors. "If we open these, an alarm will go off in the security center," Alfonso spoke up. "However, there might not be anyone left who would know what that alarm means. We'll take that gamble. There should be an elevator close by. We need a plan. How about pushing a button for a floor that you think may be too high for where Anka is? Then, keep a close eye on the GPS unit as we go up. If we pass it, we can press the next floor number and after that head back down." They liked that idea, and J. D. opened the door. All was deserted. In the dim security lighting, they spotted the service elevator and made for it.

Armando pressed the button for floor 150. Up they went, while he watched the GPS device closely. As they passed floor 101, he said, "That was it. 101." Hastily, Bess pressed the next button, and they waited, guns drawn. The doors opened and then closed without incident. Now they headed down a floor and stepped out, getting their bearings. Two guards came walking along, spotted them. "Halt! Who are you?" one said.

Puff. Puff. Two silenced guns fired dropping the men. "Shit," Alfonso whispered. "Which way?" Armando looked at his GPS device and pointed down their hall to the right. Slowly, the group began moving along the once-office suites, now turned into bedrooms. These large areas were housing many UFB women all in beds, as far as they could tell, though there were others around watching over them.

Shortly, another brief firefight broke out! At least the fire bounced off their PDS shields. Not so with the security men, who took the group's return fire and dropped. Any surprise had just been lost. The situation had just gotten more precarious. Armando continued to lead them towards the next office suite, while Bess and Martha dropped back forming a rear guard. More shots were fired and Bess called out, "A bunch is coming after us. Hurry up!" She and Martha fired another volley and then tossed a couple of grenades down the hall.

"Boom. Boom," Jason whispered just before they went off. Now the entire building was alerted to their invasion, but Bess had bought them some precious time. No guards came after them for a short while as they continued to back up down the hall behind the searchers.

"Here, this suite," Armando called out. Bang, bang. Guns fired left and right. There were six guards here, alerted to their coming from the precious shots and grenades. Against well-armed men and PDS shields, they didn't have any chance and were soon taken out. Once more Armando studied the GPS unit, leading them across the office suite filled with fifty beds and UFB women, who were now shrieking in terror, wholly helpless to do anything. Besides, they were naked.

As he drew closer, he yelled out, "Anka! Anka Polonia! Where are you?"

"Over here. Who is it? I'm helpless," she cried out, struggling to sit up. The group quickly reached her. She stared at Alfonso and blinked. "Do I know you?"

"Alfonso. They got to me too. Come on, Anka; we have to get you out of here," he said hastily, blushing some. Her body was now extremely attractive, as were all UFB women, but she was naked except for some extreme heels that enabled her to barely walk. Bess got her up and stabilized on her feet, draping her knee length brown hair around to her front, slipping a steadying arm around her. That done, J. D. led them back out of the suite, where Martha was still trying to hold off the guards.

"Good. You got her. Now what? There's a large bunch just around the corner," Martha warned them. "Can't go back. Can't use the hall. They will come at us in force if we do."

J. D. took a quick look at their position within the floor. They were cut off from the main hall, which led to the elevators. The only way open to them now was to continue to back up, but if they did so, they'd hit a dead end in the hallway. The only other option was to head back into the office suite and look for another way out, perhaps circling around the gathering forces just beyond the bend in the hallway. "Boss, we're trapped in here. Let's try backing up and seeing if we can find another way out of this office suite."

Hastily, they retreated all the way back to the far end of the suite. Martha had no choice but to fall back as well. There was a door there and Armando took it. They were in a janitor's closet, but it had another door and he opened it, peering cautiously out into another hallway. He moved out, with Armando taking a flanking position, soon joined by Martha. Down the hall the group moved, rapidly becoming disoriented. Where was the elevator?

They rounded a bend and saw the hallway ending at the glass windows once more, a dead end. "Shit!" Armando cussed, turning around facing the others, who also halted. As they started to head back, Martha yelled out a warning, firing off another grenade. Several more cussed. They were trapped again.

Martha called out, "I can hold them off a while, unless they start tossing stun grenades at us. Then, all bets are off."

Jason said, "Bess, we can blow the windows out. Will

244

that help any?"

"We could repel down, if we had ropes and harnesses, but some won't be able to do it," she answered, seeing what he was thinking. They were just too far above the ground, a hundred stories.

Just as Alfonso began to lose all hope of getting out of this one alive, Bess yelled, "There's our transport!" Everyone turned and looked out of the window. Sure enough, there it was.

Over his earpiece, Alfonso heard Juanita, "Looks like you need a backdoor. Can you get the windows blown out? If so, Jackie and Melissa think that she can hover close enough for you to jump into the ship."

"Blow the windows, Jason, Bess. Stand back. Martha, fire off a couple of delaying grenades," Alfonso ordered.

Once more, Jason told Bess just how much to use and where to place the charges. "We don't want to blow ourselves up," he teased. A minute later, a boom shattered the glass, blowing the shards outwards. The deep space transport looked huge hovering there close to the building. Alfonso wished he'd left someone with arms onboard, wondering how those three could possibly be doing all this by themselves. Shortly, the bay doors opened, the automatic controls overridden by Juanita from her position at the comm center. Once down and locked, the bobbing ramp was about a foot from the side of the building, the best the two could do from the pilot's seat, which had poor vision to the side of the ship.

One by one, they began to jump across to the ramp. However, Armando knew the three couldn't make it on their own. He picked up Alfonso and jumped him across. Bess took the hint, picked up Jason, and hopped him across. "Don't drop me!" he yelled. The fall looked bad from his sideways position over her shoulder. D. J. did the same with Anka. Martha shot off a grenade and then jumped across, bringing up the rear. She hit the close button the moment she was inside and yelled for them to take off. As the door began to close and the transport slipped away from the building, she fired off a last grenade at the men rushing towards the open window, forcing them to fall back and not pepper the ship with blaster shots, which probably would wipe them out. A second later, the door was shut, and she could only pray she'd delayed them enough, but she hunkered down, prepared for the blast, which didn't come. Finally, she relaxed.

"Now that was real fun!" Martha yelled. "Nice flying, Jackie, Melissa," she shouted towards the front. The ship lurched slightly, and she knew they'd just jumped into hyperspace and were finally safe. She joined the others now getting seated in the cargo bay, opposite Juanita and her comm center.

As soon as they were safe, Bess and Martha found a sheet to wrap Anka in, giving her back some resemblance of modesty. Anka then said, "Thank you, thank you all. That was a living nightmare back there. They got all of us in GD headquarters, boss. But what happened to you?" Jackie and Melissa joined them, with carefully measured steps, enormous smiles on their faces. The ship was now on autopilot with eight hours to kill until they arrived back on Scorpi-C. Seeing who the pilots were cause Anka to gasp in total surprise once more. She simply couldn't believe what she had seen.

Alfonso said, "Well done everyone! Just incredible. First, let's let Anka tell us what happened at GD headquarters. That, I simply have to know now."

"Well, boss, I was there gathering Intel on what they knew about this Master fellow. It seems he met with the head there, and he ordered everyone to do whatever the Master ordered. They objected, naturally and didn't do anything that his men asked. I was heading up to talk with a fellow I knew to find out more when we all began smelling something in the air. I knew at once that it was similar to what I smelled there on the space station, so I headed out of there as fast as I could go. I didn't get too far. I remember falling down. Then I woke up in that bed where you found me. Must have been days later. I sure did scream though, but then so did everyone else when they woke up. At least, they provided food for us, but made us eat like dogs. No one answered any of our questions, though."

She went on, "This morning, the Master himself showed up in our suite. What he said scared the crap out of me! My God, Alfonso, the man's voice hypnotizes everyone around him. Anyway, he said some spiel about how the corporations were evil and were keeping all the stellarly beautiful women for themselves and that was about to change. He said that soon we would be given away to deserving ordinary men and women to be their sex dolls. Disgusting, but I couldn't help myself, and like everyone else, I cheered him. After he left, the spell broke. I can tell you that a lot of us cussed a blue streak, for all the good it did us. I'm sure he plans to give us all away to anyone who wants a sex doll. Sorry I don't know more."

"So the attack, it came through the air system?" Alfonso asked the key question.

"I believe so. The gas seemed to be everywhere at once, ruling out a release on one floor, and slowly settling down the floors," Anka answered. She added, "I swear everyone has forgotten our ancient history! Remember the genetic wars nearly wiped out the civilized galaxy? I know, that was centuries ago, barbaric times, the era of the mutant telepaths and mechanical men. Uncivilized ages, totally ancient history. Still, doesn't all this harken back to those times? I sure do think so."

"Possibly, Anka. Thank you for your sacrifice in getting this invaluable intelligence for us. I best explain what happened to me and how I got like this. Officially now, I'm a UFBMD man, if you hadn't guessed," Alfonso said, flushing slightly. He outlined what had gone on and that he was still determined to retain his GD CEO post on Scorpi-C.

Then he added, "Anka, since we last talked, I've discovered the UFB women are nowhere near as helpless as everyone has been presuming! Captain Juanita has been doing a fabulous job running the RdD comm center. She located you. Even more shocking, Jackie and Melissa here are somehow able to fly this transport, which I absolutely wouldn't have believed unless I'd seen it myself. Some UFB women are back in the Academy. Linda, for example, has resumed her astrophysics and galactic navigation studies. My own daughters are in an online high school. So Anka, there is some hope for the likes of us, though right now, I'm only barely able to function and only with Alicia's help. I guess we just need time."

"You mean you aren't benching me?" Anka asked.

"Benching you?" he queried.

"Yes, since I'm like this, a helpless UFB woman now."

Jackie laughed. "Hey, so are we, and we just flew this bird to your rescue. Don't count yourself out just yet. Damned hard though. Won't say any different."

"Of course, I'm not benching you, Anka. Take some time to figure out how to do things. You and I will be back in the battle soon. I sure hope so," Afonso alleviated her greatest fear, that of being abandoned as a helpless, useless person. Several others knew precisely what he meant too.

"Okay, Juanita, open up a secure line to Felix Middleton. It's time I made my report to him, and nip this in the bud. I don't want him to get any ideas of replacing me." She laughed and began using her toes to flip a few switches and set the frequency knob. A few minutes later, Alfonso made his official report to a shocked Felix, outlining everything that he'd learned. He knew Felix had anticipated he was calling to resign his post. Alfonso took great pleasure in stymying that idea of Felix's.

That done, Alfonso took another action. Although he didn't know it, this one would have a far-reaching impact. "Okay everyone. We have eight hours to kill. Let's get something to eat, and then let's all put our heads together and see what changes should be made inside a transport so we UFB can operate it somehow. Melissa, Jackie, and Juanita have taught us valuable lessons today. Let's take advantage of what they've shown us."

By the time that they returned, Bess had four pages of ideas jotted down and ten more with rough sketches. For the first time in her life, Bess was truly excited about her construction projects, since Alfonso had given her carte blanche to do whatever she desired to modify some GD transports, among other things, so that UFB women could use them in the future.

Now, Alfonso could only wait and see what upper management would do in response to this very serious threat of the Master. He presumed, like everyone else, that the spider situation was handled. For the next week, Alfonso focused on learning all he could from his wife, daughters, and the other UFB women that he knew.

***

Felix Middleton, the new head of the GD Corporation on Gamma Prime, met with the newly appointed man for the GE Corporation to discuss how to handle this upstart Master fellow, who remained completely unidentified. They decided to stop playing games. They ordered Admiral Flak to take his battleship and the entire 409th Infantry Assault Division to Taurus-C and get rid of this man and all his men once and for all.

Ten thousand, extremely well-armed men and women marched onboard his giant battleship. The next day, he, along with two heavy cruisers, and ten light cruisers left Gamma Prime bound for Taurus-C out on the rim of their spiral arm. Unknown to them, the Master had already calculated they would be sent, since these ships and the division had been stationed on Gamma Prime. Before the fleet departed, some of his men slipped onboard on their suicide mission. The fleet was on autopilot when it dropped out of hyperspace into an orbit high above Taurus-C. However, no one onboard any of these ships was conscious. Approximately twenty thousand men and women were in a coma and would be for a few more days.

The Master's men were kept busy making trip after trip to and from the ships, bringing the comatose down to Taurus-C, housing them inside the corporation skyscrapers. By the time they began to awaken from their comas, the Master had acquired a small fleet of his own, impressing his Seconds and his men. Now, he began recruiting new personnel from Taurus-C to join him and to man these new *toys*. Each man who signed up and came onboard one of the ships was given his own personal UFB woman, while each woman who volunteered was given her own UFBMD man toy. Morale had never been so high and word of this spread to all of Taurus-C. Even more enlisted.

***

"What's happening?" Felix cried to his Comm Center captain. "What do you mean no one is answering? There's a whole damned fleet there. They have to be in orbit now. Try again!" The poor man had been trying to reach the admiral for hours and reluctantly tried all known frequencies and tried contacting all thirteen ships in the fleet. Nothing. Only static.

Suddenly, the static cleared. "Hello there. Who is calling?" a voice said. Hastily, Felix grabbed the microphone.

"This is Gamma Prime GD CEO Felix Middleton. What's going on? We've been trying to reach you for hours. Over."

"Oh, sorry. I forgot to say over. I must thank you, Felix, for giving me my first space fleet. The battleship will come in quite handy. Oh yes, this is the Master speaking. Over."

"What?" screamed Felix. This should not, could not be happening.

"Yes, I've also got nearly twenty thousand more UFB women and UFBMD men. Thank you ever so much. By the way, you will be joining me shortly. Can you smell it? Over and out."

"What's he mean smell it?" asked his comm center operation. Felix sniffed and detected something in the air. Just then, the bio attack sensors went off and many bio containment doors sealed themselves shut. Felix cursed wildly and raced out of the comm center, but found the exit doors of this floor sealed tight. Slowly he sat down and drifted into a coma, along with everyone else currently inside Gamma Prime's GD Corporation's headquarters. Nearby, the same thing was happening to all the GE Corporation personnel as well.

Further, the Master's men were just then installing more of the special cylinders into the air circulation lines at ten other major corporation headquarters there on Gamma Prime. As soon as there were enough men at least to pilot the light cruisers, the Master sent them off to Gamma Prime to begin ferrying the comatose back to Taurus-C, adding to his collection of genetically modified individual sex toys to be handed out to those who joined him. Thus far, his plans were working to perfection. His only real concerns now lay with those executives in the hub sectors, the ones with the real and ultimate power over the galaxy at large. Still, he now had a small fleet, even if no one onboard was actually trained. *Time, we need time,* he thought. *Do not go too fast.*

***

Back on Scorpi-C, Alfonso knew about the attack and waited patiently all that day for word from Felix. Surely, the Master's small forces couldn't hope to deal with an entire Assault Division, especially since they didn't have those awful worms and strange wolves with them. He and Alicia headed home for supper still having heard nothing from his boss.

By the following morning, Alfonso hadn't received even one message, so he again called Felix. No answer. Growing worried, he had his comm center people try calling every conceivable post at Gamma Prime GD Corporation headquarters. Still nothing. In frustration, he called up the CEO of Ziggy Mining Corporation, whom GD often used for more remote mining operations.

"Yes, there has been a terrible bio agent attack on GD headquarters and GE Corporation headquarters too," the man reported. "Both skyscrapers are currently under strict quarantine. Don't know what is truly going on. It's chaos around here. They are calling out the entire 214th Infantry Division to guard against further terrorist attacks. I suspect that everyone in your headquarters is a goner, Mr. Vega."

Alfonso sat back stunned. The Master's arm was indeed a long one! Slow came the realization that the situation had gone critical and that there were some protocols he should follow. "Alicia, I need your help again. That safe. Here's the combination." He hated having to reveal such top-secret things to her, but he had no choice.

"Yes, that packet. Top-secret. Open it please and spread the documents out on my desk so I can read them," he asked. If Alicia ever had any doubts that he didn't trust her, she didn't now, spreading them out before him.

"Okay. Enter these numbers in my private phone there. Good. Put it on speaker phone. Thanks. This is CEO Alfonso Vega on Scorpi-C invoking Protocol 10. Please respond. Over." He waited. Probably he would get a reprimand for overreacting, but he needed orders. Silence. He tried again, still nothing. Grumbling, he tried three more protocol

251

numbers. Nothing. Silence. He had her pick up the documents and replace them in the safe, while he sat back in his chair. Was something wrong on Corporate Prime? In the heart of the galaxy? Surely, the Master had not gotten to them too.

Finally, he recalled the CEO of Ziggy Mining Corporation and asked him to see if he could contact anyone on Corporate Prime for him. "Yes, I'll take full responsibility for the call. I'll wait here, just put me on hold. And thank you. I owe you one, sir."

A half hour later, he began talking to someone from the General Goods Corporation on Corporation Prime. "Yes, there is a full quarantine around GD headquarters. Spiders. They have control of the building. They've released some of the genetic bio agent into the building. Same thing over at GE headquarters. I'm afraid GD is temporarily out of business here. Don't worry. We will soon exterminate these spiders. Over and out."

"Good God!" Alicia gushed. Alfonso sank back in his chair. The hierarchy of GD Corporation was history. True, all that remained were subsidiary headquarters, some in the hub, some in the mid-spiral arm, and a host further on out, but his own direct chain of command was gone. He, Alfonso Vega, was on his own. That scared him.

He took a deep breath and had Alicia open a direct line to everyone in the building. Carefully, he explained the situation both on Gamma Prime and on Corporation Prime. He ended with, "We are now on our own for the time being. Spread the word." He summoned Diego and had him do the same with members of the RdD for him. Slowly, he rose, wobbling slightly before Alicia reached him. "I need to go home now," he whispered.

Just then, Alis walked into his office. "Boss, I have some shocking news about Corporate Prime. The spiders. . ." she began.

He interrupted her. "I know, they've unleashed the genetic bio agent at GD there too, and at GE Corp headquarters. Just found out."

"Right. Damn, you are good boss. What the hell do we do now?" she asked.

"Lord knows, Alis, lord knows. I'm heading home to think. Want to come with us?"

"I'll be along later. Need to talk to Diego first. This is ill news indeed. It surely can't get any worse."

Chapter 15—The Beltazar Situation

Not all inhabited worlds of the galaxy were controlled by the corporations. These were few and pioneering in their ways, home to rugged individuals, hearty, strong, and also patient. One of these independent worlds was called Beltazar, approximately eight thousand miles across and illuminated by a yellow-orange sun by day and three pale moons by night. It lay on the rim of the galaxy, but had some limited contact with the Galactic Federation, generally trading gold for older model spaceships.

The people of Beltazar had two very serious problems, both of very long duration and thus far unsolvable, much to the chagrin of the Councils who ran the world. The first problem, and by far the most serious one, could be traced back to the founding of their world by ancient colonists. Just taking a cursory glance at the people would give any educated person a strong clue to the nature of this problem. Everywhere one looked, one saw fiery red-haired men, women, and children.

Yes, their problem was one of a seriously narrow gene pool, exacerbated by the length of time since their founding. Children were being born with alarming deficiencies, most of which were stillborn. Today, one in two children never survived their first week of life. Grim indeed.

During the last fifty years, they lived under the constant fear that the corporations would finally decide to land and take over their world, turning it into another business run solely for the benefit of the companies, forsaking the people who lived here. These people weren't dumb. They had access to the Interstellar Network and all the stored data and history. In some measure, their fears were not unfounded, because recently, a corporation mining engineer discovered a huge deposit of rare earths on a northern plateau. He tried to open negotiations to allow a corporation to set up its own mining operation there. That would have opened the door to the corporations, most believed, rightly so, and thus the man was assassinated and his reports destroyed.

Their second problem had arisen only relatively recently. Since the mining engineer incident, First Counselor Bearach sent forth spies to neighboring corporation worlds, seeking to learn what they could of corporation policies and plans, facts that might not necessarily be on file via the Interstellar Network. Thus, ten years ago, one spy was able to infiltrate GE Corporation on Bellatrix-B and discovered their secret breeding program!

"I don't need eyes to see where this is going," First Counselor Bearach declared to his staff. In time, they'll be able to field an army of these super-strong fighters, led by these super-IQ men, and we of Beltazar will become like shafts of wheat in the autumn, blown away by the wind. If we're to survive, we must find a way to counter this before it is too late." Many heads pondered the problem, and many potential solutions were proposed, but all were seen as futile or folly or both.

One fact remained very clear to everyone. These genetically modified men and women were unbelievably beautiful, beauty-incarnate some suggested. Yet, they were helpless, by all reports, and had an utter craving for sex and at all hours. Many proposed that these UFB women and UFBMD men might be the answer to their first problem of genes. Thus, First Counselor Bearach had his scientists research that notion. It came as no surprise to him that they concurred. Breeding their own men and women to these UFB women and UFBMD men would greatly enlarge their gene pool and provide super strong men and super intelligent men as well. However, the sheer helplessness of both breeders remained problematical. At least, he ordered more spying on them to be done.

One red headed woman managed to obtain an assistant's position for a GE executive's family. She became the First Counselor's main source of key information about the UFB women and their actual needs. Proper shoes and the fancy electrostatic hair machines were about all they actually had to have that was in any way unusual. Thus, several years ago, he began planning. Somehow, someway, they would need a large supply of the extreme footwear, the hair machines, and of course, the actual genetic bio agent used to make these incredibly beautiful, perfect men and women.

These were patient people. Given the initial samples of the shoes and hair machine, the First Counselor Bearach ordered them into production. They simply duplicated the machine, but they redesigned the shoes, turning them into far more practical knee high boots. This way, the gorgeous women and men would not have to have someone around to help them get their shoes on. As you can probably tell, they were wholly ignorant of their actual needs. Obtaining the actual bio agent was vastly more difficult. Further, they didn't have the means of transporting the men and women here to Beltazar.

Having so many spies active in this rim sector paid off over a year ago, when the Master took over the research facility on Rho-C. When he learned of this, First Counselor Bearach sent an envoy to make contact with the Master and to try to work out some deal with him, either for goodly supply of the bio agent or for the actual modified men and women. Nothing, however, came from this initial meeting.

With the capture of the space fleet and the additional tens of thousands of new victims, the Master recalled the envoy's visit a year ago and had another bright idea. This time, he sent word to Beltazar that he wanted to meet with their envoy once more. When the man came, the Master listened to what he had to say, taking note of the real reason why they wanted to obtain so many of these freaks, as the Master privately called them.

He then said, "I do believe I may be of help to your people," mesmerizing the envoy as he was wont to do when speaking with normal humans. "I take it that you do not wish older men and women."

"Quite true. We need breeding stock. Ideally, they shouldn't be over twenty-five, but we would even accept children who can grow into maturity and then breed," the envoy suggested. The Master chuckled, but the poor envoy had no idea what he said that was so funny.

Surprising him, the Master then said, "How many can you handle at one time?"

"We are prepared to take on twenty thousand at once,

but we might be able to take more if we have time to make their shoes and hair machines, Master."

"Good. Never let it be said that the Master fails to come to the aid of those in dire plight, such as you good people of Beltazar. Within a couple of weeks, you may expect your first batch of them, twenty thousand. Let me know when you are ready to accept another twenty thousand. They shall be yours. May they solve your severe inbreeding problem. Stupid corporations and their idiotic colonization policies. Those led to your horrible misfortune. The Master shall correct their gross errors. Go now and prepare for our arrival."

The envoy couldn't believe his ears. "Don't you want something from us in return?"

"Not at all. I accept your people's gratitude for saving your race from extinction and for correcting the gross negligence of the corporations." The envoy returned with the most hopeful news the First Counselor Bearach ever heard!

"Tao, I have a new mission for you. This one promises to be quite interesting indeed. You are to go to Bellatrix-B—Bregenheim to be specific. Locate the largest high schools there and their Academies. We want to produce UFB women and UFBMD men from those who are between say twenty-five and fourteen. We need around twenty thousand of them. We'll snatch their brightest and their children. That will definitely shake them up and take them by complete surprise."

"Indeed it would, but how do we get them off-world?" Tao asked.

The Master laughed. Poor Tao, he thought, no imagination. "We make use of our new battleship and its marvelous equipment." Seeing that Tao still didn't understand, he spelled it out for him. "Once the agent has been released and they fall into a coma, we will use the teleport station on the battleship to teleport some of our men down wearing bio containment suits. They will gather up the children, and we'll teleport them to the battleship. Later when the local authorities believe that it is safe to enter, they will find the children have vanished without a trace."

"Master, I'm truly humbled. I will make it so." He bowed respectfully and left at once to handle the advance work.

A week later, the coordinated attacks took place at Bell Academy and at ten high schools. The operation went like clockwork. As soon as the authorities detected that it was a genetic bio agent attack, they properly quarantined the schools, allowing no one inside. Even the emergency responders balked at the idea of donning bio containment suits and entering, for fear of getting contaminated themselves. They knew the horrors of this bio agent and definitely wanted to wait a few days until the gas had dissipated. Thus, when they did enter, they found all the schools empty, except for the comatose faculty and staff, who were sent to the local medical facilities.

The next day, the Master sent Bellatrix-B a video recording, explaining, "I'm rectifying a gross injustice, criminal negligence on the part of your corporations. Your children are the price you must pay to rectify this hideous crime your corporations have done." His announcement sent more shockwaves through the Abelard Sector there on the rim. Even the general population on nearby Scorpi-C was appalled at this new strike of the Master.

***

At Bregenheim Academy, a sprawling campus with ten thousand students enrolled in many disciplines, a pair of recently married couples shared campus housing together. Agata and Bertran Schein were twenty-one and studying Childhood Education and Gas Dynamics respectively. They shared the housing with the newlyweds, Emil and Frieda Schultz, each twenty years old, just finishing up their general education courses. Frieda had two younger siblings, who were close to graduating high school and planning to join them next quarter, the twins Dirk and Elisa Schmidt. All six were a few of the many victims of the Master's genetic bio agent terrorist attack.

They awakened amid screams of terror, shortly adding theirs to the din. Soon, they learned they were onboard a huge battleship. When they saw high school children here, as well as Academy students, Frieda panicked and insisted that the four of them search for her twin siblings. Luck was with them, and they found Dirk and Elisa not far from them and got them moved over with the four older students.

When they arrived on Beltazar, First Counselor Bearach was there to meet the mass of terrified students, who were simply teleported off the ship into the large assembly hall. Here, he addressed them with a prepared speech. He outlined the terrible crime that had been committed on their ancestors by the greedy corporations, spelling out just how dire their situation actually was, with one of every two babies not surviving their first week. He also praised them for their incredible beauty, explained how the corporations had created this bio agent that was used on them, and just why the corporations had invented it in the first place, along with how the top executives then kept these now stunning genetically modified women and men for their own uses. He also told them about the corporations' breeding program and what their children would be like.

"Finally, I want you to know that each of you will be placed with a loving family who will care for you. In return, you must bear or father as many children as you can so our gene pool can expand enough so we of Beltazar can survive into the future and not slowly die off as we are today. You're the saviors of our people and will be treated as such, but only as long as you help us by having babies or making them possible for our women. Plus, I've been informed that some of you have brothers and sisters here with you. We will do our best not to break up families. If there are some who wish to remain with your spouse or siblings, let the administrator know when he gets to you. Once more, I wish to thank you all for saving our people."

Agata and Bertran ended up being moved into the First Counselor Bearach's home, where she was to service him and Bertran, to service his wife, Caitie. The other four were taken to a rural farmstead, the Clancy Bleager family. Frieda was to service Clancy, while Emil, to service his wife Fiona. Dirk and Elisa were to service their two children that had survived, Breanne, eighteen, and Burk, nineteen. All their other attempts to have children failed at some point during Fiona's pregnancies.

The four were terrified when they were brought to the rural farm, naked and almost unable even to stand on their malformed feet. By this time, their knee length brown hair was tangled masses. None had anything to eat since falling into their comas, but they had at least had been given a bottle of water while on the battleship. On top of everything else, the two young men were horribly embarrassed with their bodies now looking like beautiful women and their voices so raised.

Clancy brought them to his farmstead in his open-topped roadster car and helped them out, calling out, "We're here." Fiona, wiping her hands on her apron, came out, followed by Breanne and Burk. All three stopped short and stared at the four humiliated young adults.

"Well, just don't stand there gaping as if you've never see beautiful women, er men, before. Lord knows, they must be freezing, what with nothing on, and they're probably starving. Come on, Clancy. You and Burk, you carry them inside. Don't you fret, young'uns, we have two of those fancy hair machines that you need inside and the boots that will help you walk, but lordie, we need to get you all bathed first and some hot food in you. Come on; get them inside right now," Fiona took charge.

Ah hour later, the four had the new arrivals dressed, their new boots tied securely on them, and their hair de-tangled and arranged via the hair machines. Wobbling to keep their balance, the four made it to the dining room table, but couldn't pull their chairs out. Again, after an awkward moment, the Bleager's realized this and helped them get seated, but Fiona and Breanne had to show Clancy and Burk how to get their impossibly long hair out of the way.

Their plates were filled and set before them. "How do we even eat?" wailed Elisa.

"Well, we can't spend all day feeding you," Clancy decided. "I suppose you lean over and try it that way. Fiona, don't we have some straws we can put in their drinks?" After a miserable and embarrassing time at the table, it was time for bed. Each of the four Bleager members took their new mate into their own bedroom and shut their doors.

"But I've never done this before," Elisa cried, sitting

naked on the edge of Burk's bed.

"Well, neither have I, Elisa. You are the most beautiful woman I've ever laid eyes on. I think you should lie on your back, but your hair will be in the way. There, now it's over your front." Sometime later, Elisa now knew that she needed this a whole lot, for it explained the awful craving she'd been feeling since she woke up from her coma. One by one, the four finally discovered how to appease that driving, craving urge that they simply couldn't suppress. For good or ill, they each knew that they needed this frequently. Before long, the four Bleager family members realized their new additions would endure most anything, as long as they got sexual gratification at least twice a day.

At first, after breakfast, the four were left alone while the Bleager family went about their farming chores. "We have to find a way to escape," Frieda whispered to the others. "Emil, help us. We have to get out of here and get back home somehow." Her twin siblings nodded vigorously, bouncing their hair about.

Emil sighed, "How? How, Frieda? If you haven't noticed, I'm a woman now, mostly, and just as helpless as all of you."

"Well, he's got that car. Maybe we can drive it somehow," Frieda suggested.

"How do you propose we do that? If you hadn't noticed, none of us have any arms and hands anymore," Emil griped, feeling particularly helpless and failing utterly his new wife, to say nothing of hating Clancy for having violated her, though he was only disgusted that Fiona had done him last night.

"There has to be a way somehow," Elisa whimpered. "I want to go home, Frieda."

"Don't worry sis; we will find a way, won't we Emil?" Dirk spoke up for his sister, unable to comfort her physically, as he always had when she was upset.

"Maybe we can walk back into the city," Elisa suggested.

"We better learn how to walk first," Dirk pointed out. They agreed and adopted that plan. For several days, they walked all around the Bleager home, sometimes taking a spill when they lost their balance and tried to use their arms, which weren't there. Then, one morning, Elisa noticed a jar containing an herb and recognized what it was, a sedative. Now she got another idea: drug them so they could make their escape. No one believed she could actually do it, but that only hardened her will somehow to do it, if only to prove them wrong.

Using her teeth, she got the jar over to the kitchen table. Then, she had Dirk help her with their coffee canister. Pressing it tightly between them, they got it to the table as well. Not knowing how much to put in, Elisa dumped the whole jar into the coffee and used a spoon in her mouth to stir up the mixture, while Dirk looked inside, telling her how it was mixing. Finally satisfied, the two struggled to get it back in its proper location, and then hid the jar beneath a nearby couch. "Don't drink any coffee from now on," Elisa whispered.

"We're going to get it when they find out," Emil grumbled, unwilling to admit that Elisa had actually done all this. Now, they nervously waited to see what would happen next.

Around noon, Fiona came inside, dumping a load of carrots on the table. "Damn it kids, I wish you weren't so helpless, but I can see you are." She set about making lunch for the bunch. The four watched her make the coffee and held their breaths. Before long, the others joined them, again filling plates, and sliding them before the four. Dutifully, the four leaned over and ate as if they were dogs. Compared to the others, they were pitifully slow eating this way. Before long, the four were sitting back drinking their coffee and chatting about how wonderful it would be with four young children around the house.

"Lordie, it has been far too long since I heard children playing around here, Clancy," Fiona said and yawned. After finishing their coffee, Fiona encouraged the others to hurry up and told them to wash their own faces when they were done. She headed outside to help with the farm chores.

"See, it didn't work, Elisa," Emil pointed out. Elisa looked glumly at her plate.

"Maybe it takes longer to do something to them," Frieda suggested, unwilling to lose all hope just yet. This had been their best idea yet. After finally finishing, she got up and peered out the window. "Hey, come and look! It worked. They are all lying on the ground!" As fast as they could, the others joined her, though it wasn't fast at all.

Next, they faced the hurdle of how to get the door open. Emil finally solved it by using his mouth, biting down hard on it, and twisting his head around. Then, they all stepped carefully outside.

"Now what?" asked Dirk. The four looked at the beautiful topless roadster car parked in the driveway. Emil made his careful way over to it.

"Hey the keys are still in it. I wonder if we can possibly drive this thing?" he asked.

Dirk headed over to it. "Come on. It beats walking that far. Must be miles. I know, one of us steers, and the other pushes those things on the floor."

"How do we get in?" asked Elisa, when she reached the doors. None had any idea of how they could open them. Undaunted, Dirk leaned over and rather fell into one of the front seats. After a valiant struggle, he got upright. One by one, the others emulated his action. Meanwhile, he used his boots to twist the keys enough to start the motor.

Emil insisted on steering, got one foot up, and locked onto the steering wheel. Then, Dirk finally managed to get the shift level down a notch, and the shiny roadster began moving forward a little. "Press on one of the pedals," Emil suggested.

After a bit of experimentation, Dirk found one made the roadster go and the other stopped it. "I can barely steer this thing, so go slow, Dirk," Emil ordered.

"This is fun! See Emil, we are escaping. I just knew that we could," declared Elisa feeling triumphant at last.

In the backseat, Elisa and Frieda began to give them directions on which way to go. Since they were going slowly, they had time to compare memories of the route that they had followed getting here. They had no idea just how slowly they were actually going. It was dark when they finally entered the city of Bregenheim. They had no idea that the roadster even had lights, which was fortunate for no one spotted the slow moving car moving through the dark streets. Most all were in bed enjoying their new family "additions."

"Now where do we go?" asked Emil.

"The spaceport silly," Elisa replied. "It's that way." She tried to point but failed and began crying. Frieda said, "Hear the takeoff roars? Head toward them."

"Duh!" Emil commented, feeling rather foolish.

Before long, the spaceport loomed large before them. They stopped the car and mostly fell out onto the ground. After that, it took a good deal of struggling and effort for the four to get back on their feet. The ground was uneven, and they quickly found walking extremely treacherous. Yet, forward they went until they reached the paved tarmac. "Now where?" Emil asked.

"Look for a deep space transport," Dirk advised. "We need one of those to get all the way home." They looked around and saw mostly smaller ships where they were at.

"Hey way over there," Frieda whispered trying to nod in the general direction with her head. After what seemed an eternity, they neared parked rows of these larger ships.

"Now what?" asked Emil.

"How about that one?" Elisa suggested, recognizing the GD Corporation logo on its side. "Its ramp is down so we can walk right inside."

"But what if someone is inside?" Emil complained. "They'll throw us off in a blink."

"Not if they are from GD. We can tell them that we got kidnaped. Tell them that our folks will pay them a ransom or something," Elisa declared, not about to lose this chance to escape. With no other viable ideas, the four headed towards the looming ship, pausing before the ramp. With a nod, Emil led the way up. Shortly, all four were standing just inside the ship. Dim lights were on. "Maybe we should hide or something," Elisa suggested.

"Where?" Frieda asked.

"Maybe in the very back?" Elisa whispered back. She led the way, heading towards the rear, but noticed the spikes of her heels made distinct sounds on the metal floor. She tried to tiptoe, but simply couldn't. She got halfway back when a woman stepped out of the galley, blocking their path.

"Well, what do I have here? Four stowaways?" Alis said, putting her hands on her hips and staring at the four young UFB women, not realizing two were men.

Alis had heard of the abduction of the twenty thousand students on Bellatrix-B. It was all over the news the next day. Hence, she'd headed off to do her own investigation. She correctly guessed the Master had been behind the terrorist attack. When she arrived near Bellatrix-B, she saw the "lost" battleship just departing from its orbit high about the world. Hastily, she launched a tracer shot, and luckily, it stuck onto the side of the huge ship. Now she could follow it through hyperspace.

It traveled faster than her deep space transport could go, and she very nearly lost it. When the signal vanished, she brought up her galactic 3-d display and entered the ship's course thus far into the display as a curved line. She then extended it until it reached a star. Zooming in, she discovered there was an isolated planet orbiting it and adjusted her own course to go there. When she arrived, she saw the battleship just leaving orbit and concluded the children had been dropped off here. *But why?* Alis decided to do a little investigating of this relatively unknown world of Beltazar, particularly since it wasn't a member of the Galactic Federation.

Two days later and ten marriage proposals later, Alis knew the sad story of this world. Further, she knew why they so desperately wanted the young adults. Well, the Master had done the crime, but he was actually trying to aid these people, which definitely confused her. Were the motives of the Master more than just his own desires for power? She knew she had far more investigation ahead of her. She was just relaxing and recharging when she heard footsteps approaching her transport.

Heels clicking. *Ah, not men coming to try to marry me or abduct me so they could do so,* she thought. She decided to let the heels continue and heard them entering her ship. She smiled, growing more curious. They slowly came towards her, and she stepped out of the galley, prepared for action, but stopped short, seeing four UFB women staring at her, terrified.

"Well hello. I'm called Alis. And who might you four be?"

"I am Elisa. My twin brother, Dirk. She's my sister, Frieda, but she'd married to Emil there. We were kidnaped from our schools on Bellatrix-B. I think we were terrorist-attacked too and turned into these strange bodies. Please, we just want to go home and not have babies for these strangers."

"Well, you certainly came to the right shuttle. I was just about to leave. If you will have a seat, we'll be on our way," Alis said kindly.

"Whoopee, I told you we could escape if we tried!" Elisa declared triumphantly.

"I admit, Elisa, you were right. Thank you," Emil admitted. "Thank you, little sis." She beamed.

A few minutes later, they felt the ship lift off and shortly drop into hyperspace. Alis then rejoined them. "Anyone for supper?" she asked, guessing they were starving.

"No, let me feed you. It's humiliating to eat like dogs," Alis broke in, as they were attempting to eat as they had been doing, like dogs. One by one, she got them fed.

"Now then, we best have a long talk. You see, it'll not be safe for you to return to Bellatrix-B. As UFB women, everyone will know you were some of the twenty thousand students who were victimized and kidnaped. The men who did this to you will certainly find out that you're back and probably assassinate you. But not to worry. I know of a very safe place where I can take you. There are others there like you going to high school and the Academy. Perhaps your parents can move to this world and join you. Then again, as UFB women, your parents might not want to have you back. Many disown genetically modified children. We'll just have to see."

"But I'm not a woman, well only sort of," Emil complained. "And he's Dirk, a guy too. Frieda and I are married. Those two are her younger siblings. We've managed to stick together all this time."

"Oh. I'm sorry, Emil. I didn't know. There's only one way to tell, unfortunately."

Emil and Dirk both turned red as beets. "Please, don't separate us," Dirk added.

"I certainly won't do that. You have my word. I'll get you four to safety, and I know a nice man who is just as you fellows are. He will get you back into their Academy, a good place to stay, and someone to help you with things, like a personal assistant," Alis explained, much to the four's great relief, quite visible on the young faces. "So what were you two studying at the Academy?"

Once she got them talking, nothing could shut them up until they fell asleep on their seats. Alis heard their entire story, including their miraculous escape. After carrying each sleeping person to a bed, she headed to the comm center and placed a secure call to Alfonso. "Yes, I've found out what happened to the twenty thousand students. I'm bringing four who managed to escape back with me. Arriving in the morning. I'll need your help again." She relayed everything that she'd learned.

That handled, Alis focused and sent a long electronic burst of data. Patiently, she waited an hour before she received a similar electronic burst. *About time that something is done about all this,* she thought and retired to her cabin, awaiting the passage of time before making planet-fall.

***

Alfonso knew he had a busy day. Anka was being released from the medical center and need a place to stay for now. Plus, he had to work out where the four rescued young adults from Bellatrix-B could stay. Since Anka had been working for the resistance, he decided she should have the best arrangements he could make. "Call Martha," he spoke clearly to his fancy computer. "Hi, Alfonso here. You've heard Anka gets out of the medical center today. Good. Yes, you're right. She's going to need a place to stay for a while, particularly until she gets used to her situation."

Martha laughed, "So it's a situation now, boss?"

He flushed, thankful she couldn't see his face just now. "I was hoping you and Bess could take her in with Jason and Linda, help her adjust, perhaps even see if she is interested in going to the Academy."

"Sure boss. We'd love to have her with us. Want us to pick her up?" Martha asked, knowing how difficult most everything was for Alfonso, just as it was for Jason and Linda—all the others for that matter.

"I would appreciate it. Alis is landing today with four more victims, young adults from Bellatrix-B, Academy and high school students. Grim. I have to take care of them. I'll hold an RdD meeting later today and let everyone know the latest intelligence. Thanks again, Martha." He hung up, sighed, and said, "Call Emelio."

"Hi pop, what's up?" his son's voice sounded chipper this morning.

Alfonso related what Alis had found out and that she was bringing four back with her from Beltazar. "Pop, why don't you have the four move in here with us? Antonia has a younger sister who wants to help. We can hire her too, but we should have another one of those hair machines. With five of them, there's going to be a line up around it, instead of the toilet." Both men laughed, but Alfonso already faced that here at his home.

Emelio added, "I can get them enrolled in the Academy. What about having the two younger ones join up with Chita and Gabriella. They can go to the same school. It's not far from your place, if you didn't know."

Alfonso chuckled. "You're right, son. I didn't know. I've been so ignorant of my daughters and wife. I hate to say it, but it's taken me becoming like them to realize they are people too and can do things for themselves."

"Shoot pop, I always knew that, but then I grew up with my sisters. I'll get things arranged today. Can't wait to see them. Bye. Linda's calling."

Alfonso hung up and relaxed a bit. *Best start on getting ready for the day*, he thought. Sure enough, Alicia was up, had herself dressed for work, and was just finishing helping Carmela into her dress. Nearby Gracia and her sister had the twins dressed and fed. After giving Chita and Gabriella a morning kiss, he told them about the new teens who would be arriving later. Both were very pleased to play host to the four and helping them get settled in at their brother's place. That done, Alfonso patiently allowed Alicia to get him dressed in his professional woman's outfit.

After she made the final adjustments to his skirt, she said, "Your turn with the hair machine. I'll be in the living room."

He stepped up to it and activated the machine. *What a wonder this thing is!* He thought again. His body was flooded with tactile sensations from every strand of his long thick black hair, as the machine used electric charges to raise each up, separating it from all the others, only then releasing them all, allowing them to fall gently down his back. "Wow!" he whispered. "I could do this all day. No wonder the women love it! It's just that I never really knew. That's the key here. I took them for granted and never really took the time to understand or appreciate these incredible women in my life. Well, that's sure changing now. Best get going. Alis has a dilly for me to handle today." He made his careful way out to the living room, gave his wife a loving kiss, and kissed his daughters on their foreheads. Then, with Alicia's arm around him, he headed off to work.

Mid-morning, Alicia took him to the spaceport to meet Alis and her four rescued students. He found he enjoyed standing on the tarmac today. The sun was warm, and the gentle breeze jostled his hair this way and that, each strand sending him a strong tactile sense. He felt alive and alert. Was this feeling more so than before, he wondered? Had he become calloused after so many years in GD? Alicia was now pregnant with his child, and she looked good this morning, a freshness in her cheeks he'd not seen before. She was pleased; he knew that much from their private time last night, though it was too soon to tell if it would be boy or a girl. Either way, he was happy, but would she accept a girl or have it aborted, continuing to try to have a son who would likely be one of those super IQ men? He didn't know, but hoped she wouldn't abort it if it was a girl.

Alis landed right on time and didn't have to worry about landing fees or even customs, since she was using an official GD transport. Alfonso had already taken care of the customs requirements for the four students, obtaining visitor's ID cards for them. After it landed, he and Alicia moved closer to the bay, watching the ramp lower. One by one, Alis lifted each of the young folks down. They were wearing simple sack-like dresses, short and plain, but easy for them to manage bathroom duties themselves. Their knee-high boots did look a bit strange though.

"Welcome to Scorpi-C. I'm the GD Corporation CEO here, Alfonso Vega. This is my assistant, Alicia Varga. I have housing, temporary ID cards, and helpers for you, but first, let's stop off at headquarters, get you medically checked out, and see about contacting your parents on Bellatrix-B, shall we?"

"Wow! You are like us!" exclaimed Emil. Dirk nodded too.

"Yes, fellows, that I am, so you aren't alone. There are several others like us. Don't worry, I've arranged for you to continue your educations at our Academy and the high school that my twin daughters are now attending. This way," he explained and then led them to the company shuttle bus, which Alicia drove for him. So many things he now had to have done for him, and he sighed as he sat back, allowing her to drive.

Fortunately, neither woman was yet pregnant, much to their relief and Emil's as well. That handled, he listened to their entire story, allowing them to release more of their pent up grief. Then, he and Alicia took the four over to Emilio and Luisa's place, where his son took over. Later, he learned that they had gone shopping, purchased many new outfits, been enrolled in their new schools, and had new voice-activated computers and cell phones. He did understand why their parents preferred them to remain on Scorpi-C and not return home. Neither of their parents wanted to have to deal with UFB women and UFBMD men, though he personally couldn't imagine abandoning his own daughters, but he understood them. Perhaps in time, they would decide to come for a visit. That handled, he spent the rest of the day in pointless GD meetings.

The following morning, his daughters were bubbling with excitement. They had gone to their new school yesterday and began making new friends, something that they'd been denied all these years. While they did some of their work online, part of the point of high school was to develop social relationships and skills. He'd never seen his twins so vibrant and alive as they were this morning.

"Papa, can we go to the beach Saturday afternoon with all the other kids?" Gabriella pleaded with him. In the past, he'd never consider such a thing. His UFB women were completely helpless, and he would never risk taking them to a public beach. Now, his opinions had been dramatically altered. If Elisa, Dirk, Frieda, and Emil could engineer their own escape, surely they could manage going to the public beach!

"Sure you can, dears. In fact, let's all go to the beach. Getting some sun and fresh air will be good for us all. I'm sorry I never took you there before, girls," he answered. Both girls giggled and pushed their bodies into his, the best they could do to give him a hug. He smiled and gave them each a kiss on their foreheads.

Saturday was a revelation for Alfonso, Carmela, and even Alicia. Everyone wore a bikini, though Alfonso was terribly self-conscious and embarrassed about wearing a red one at first. Seeing all the young women on the beach wearing much the same and the boys wearing only shorts, he began to relax some and watched their playful antics.

To his amazement, four boys and six girls hovered around Chita and Gabriella. One girl said, "Gabriella, you and Chita are the prettiest girls in our junior class. You both should run for prom queen."

"Really? Us?" Gabriella asked, taken aback by the idea.

One of the boys piped up, "You bet. You are gorgeous, Gabriella. You too, Chita. You are a chinch to win. I know lots of boys who will vote for you."

Nearby, Emelio had brought his group too. Alfonso gazed over at them to see how the four new arrivals were faring. Again, he was amazed. While Emil and his wife Frieda were kissing and snuggling together on a beach towel, sunning themselves, Dirk and Elisa were surrounded by a number of other high school seniors, but had been separated into two groups.

Dirk had four girls hanging on to him, chatting gaily, all trying their best to become his steady girlfriend. Meanwhile,

Elisa had several girls and boys around her, and at least two of the boys were doing their best to attract her attention to themselves, trying to get her to be their girlfriend, while the girls had adopted her into their small group. Once more, Alfonso realized how much of life had hitherto for been denied to all the UFB women and now the UFBMD men as well.

He made a solemn promise to do all he could to change the way they were being treated here on Scorpi-C. No longer did he think of UFB women as mere sex dolls for the corporate top executives, but as real people, but who had a more difficult and challenging life to live. He decided to propose a new law requiring all UFB girls and UFBMD boys to go to public schools until they graduated. In addition, he would fund an assistance program to help finance the computers and phones they would need, along with a clothing allowance. Then, he decided to fund an Academy scholarship that would fully cover the costs of their higher education as well. Certainly, his viewpoint had been radically altered with his own genetic modification.

Later, Alicia whispered, "It's a girl. I'm keeping her." That pleased him immensely and he told her so, giving her a passionate kiss as well. Things were going so well here, but the galaxy around him was heading downwards at a rapid pace. Somehow, he had to keep Scorpi-C alive and prospering.

Chapter 16—Decisions

"Look Alfonso," the tall, pudgy exec from GE Corporation, Benedicto, declared nervously, "none of us wants to become like you. Good God man, we'd rather just be killed outright. And frankly, that's what has been happening all around us, Taurus-C, Bellatrix-B, Gamma Prime. Who's next? We have to do something. This Master terrorist has to be stopped."

It was Monday, and Alfonso was at a combined corporation executives meeting. He decided to host it at GD headquarters, mostly so he didn't have to deal with traveling to other buildings and be stared at by all the strangers there. Two dozen CEOs and their seconds in command were present, along with two others that Alfonso invited to the meeting, General Domingo Florencio and Admiral Enrique Gasparaldo. Alis had suggested now was a good time to hold the meeting and plan for the defense of Scorpi-C. He'd taken her advice and found the other executives more than ready to meet.

"I second Benedicto," Goyo spoke up. "Look, the Master has been systematically taking out everyone in all the corporation headquarters there on Taurus-C. God, none of us wants to end up like you, Alfonso. No offence, but we'd rather die than be turned into a helpless woman-freak as you are. We have to do something."

"True, but look," Gilberto spoke up, "we can't get a hold of our superiors on Gamma Prime either. Word has it that all the major corporations on Gamma Prime have been wiped out, our people turned into freaks as well. So we can't look to them for either help or advice on what we're supposed to do. None of my corporation protocols is now workable. What the hell do we do? Sit back and wait to be turned into woman-freaks like Alfonso? No offense, Alfonso, but you look and talk like a woman now, sexy looking one too," he teased, causing Alfonso to flush, embarrassed yet again.

Francesco, who had been silent, spoke up. "Perhaps there is some truth in what the Master is doing. After all, we executives have been making UFB women and keeping them

273

to ourselves. We do have our breeding programs going. I know our corporation has several of the super IQ men about ready to step into upper management role on Corporation Prime. Look what the corporations did to the colonists on that obscure world of Beltazar. It is probably a good thing that the Master has done for them, bringing in new breeding stock to broaden their gene pool before it's too late for those surviving colonists. Maybe the Master has right on his side."

"What the hell are you saying, Francesco?" bellowed Benedicto. "He's a mass terrorist, nothing more. Well, I do see your point, but that doesn't give us any help does it?"

"Well, maybe we could talk with the Master. Tell him we're on his side. Maybe he won't unleash our own genetic bio agent on us. I sure as hell don't want to become a woman-freak, gorgeous or not," Francesco declared.

"You are talking treason, Francesco!" bellowed Goro. "Forsake our own corporations? You should join the resistance, you fool. One day soon, we'll get help from Corporate Prime. You just wait and see."

"Yeh, maybe two years from now, after all of us are turned into woman-freaks and forced to become some worker's sex toy!" Francesco countered, sobering all. Everyone knew that way out here on the rim of the spiral arm, help, if it came, would be years from now. Corporate Prime was always more concerned about the densely populated hub sectors and to a lesser extent the mid-arm regions. The sparsely populated rim worlds had always been at the bottom of their priority lists for anything.

Goyo spoke up. "He does have a valid point, gentlemen. We all have lost contact with our immediate superiors on Gamma Prime. Other contacts there and the news reports, which we've all seen, show clearly that those headquarters and all personnel there have been subjected to the genetic bio agent. We know the Master has confiscated the victims while they were in comas. Most likely, those men and women, if we dare call them that now, are the sex dolls of low life's. We also know that Corporate Prime has its own problems right now. The spiders have infected both the GE and GD corporations. Benedicto and Alfonso have told us they can't get through to anyone at those top headquarters. Those are the two largest corporations. So let's face it, right now, we're on our own and likely so for a couple of years before Corporation Prime gets to us."

"He's right about that," Benedicto agreed. "We're on our own for at least a couple of years. But are we then doomed?"

"Well, we can't send our 509th Infantry Division after the Master. We don't want our main ground defense unit wiped out like the 519th was," Goyo replied. "He's got a small fleet now, including that battleship. We don't dare send our small fleet after his either. We only have one battleship in our fleet." He nodded to Admiral Enrique who nodded back. "We have to protect ourselves."

Alfonso laughed, "That, my friend, is like locking the stable after the horse has been stolen. Look, with all the security that GD brought to bear to protect me, they still got to me. We can't afford to sit back and hope our security measures keep us safe."

"He's got a point. I'm sure they had good security measures in place at the corporate headquarters on Taurus-C, especially after they got to the GD and GE Corporations," Goyo added. "Those didn't help one bit. I tell you, this Master fellow is far too clever for our simple security measures. Let's face it; we're doomed. Perhaps the wisest course would be to pack up and get the hell off Scorpi-C."

"What?" yelled Benedicto, "abandon Scorpi-C?"

"Well, you can't run it if your whole headquarters staff is turned into women-freaks, now can you?" Goyo replied with a snide smile.

"Gentlemen," Alfonso spoke up calmly, "we don't know that the Master intends to attack our corporation headquarters on Scorpi-C."

Just then, Diego glanced at an emergency text on his cell. "Excuse me, boss. We just got word that ten corporation headquarters on Gemma-D have been attacked with the genetic bio agent and that ten schools on Zeno-C have also been attacked the same way." Around the same moment, the other execs began receiving similar messages from their staff. The news traveled fast.

"See, I told you the Master would be coming after the rest of our corporation headquarters!" Goyo gloated. "It is time to evacuate before we get turned into helpless women-freaks, no offense Alfonso. I'm leaving as soon as I possibly can. I urge the rest of you to get the hell off Scorpi-C while you still can!"

One by one, the other executives agreed with Goyo, fear displacing all reason in the room. Alfonso shouted, "Hey, hold on. I'm not leaving my post. If you are all going ahead with this, then at least sign over the operations of your corporations to me on a temporary basis so we can at least try to mount a defense here. That is in your protocols. I know that for a fact!"

"Okay you fool. Here," Goyo declared, hastily whipping up an electronic document stating for the time being, GD Corporation had total control over his corporation. Likewise, all the others followed suit and dashed out of the meeting room as fast as they could run.

Soon only Diego, Alfonso, Alicia, General Domingo, and Admiral Enrique remained. Diego broke the silence, "Damned yellow bellied cowards, the lot of them!"

Both the general and admiral roared with laughter. "Son," the admiral said, "you can say that again, but then we always knew the corporation executives were a bunch of cowards."

General Domingo spoke up, "Well, Alfonso, when fighting a battle, you only want one man in charge, not a committee of executives who can never reach a decision in time to do any good. If nothing else, we're in a better position now than when the meeting began."

Alfonso chuckled. "Well, I do seem to be holding the reins of Scorpi-C in my very capable hands." Now everyone roared with laughter. He had no hands. Even Alicia laughed heartily at his surprise jest.

"Now then down to business. I aim to defend our world to the last man and woman. I'll not give in to this Master, not ever. Now then, let's get down to some real business. I've done a lot of thinking about the Master's strategy and methods of operation. Every one of his genetic bio agent attacks has been delivered through the ventilation systems, either those of the headquarters buildings or through those on your fleet ships."

"So my first order, Admiral Enrique, is for you to have your crew members do a complete search of every air vent system on every warship and make damned sure none of those devices has been installed in them. Once a warship has been thoroughly inspected, put armed guards on all vent access points, 24/7. Make sure those guards are wearing PDS at all times. Then, we can count on your fleet for action."

"General Domingo, you do the same with your barracks. Leave no vent anywhere unchecked. We have to make taking your division out by the bio agent impossible. Once done, put similar armed guards on all such critical access points. We will then go from there."

"Diego, do the same for GD headquarters here. Alicia, issue that order from me and send it to all the other corporation headquarters. By tomorrow, I want our fleet, our ground division, and our headquarters totally secured from these genetic bio agent attacks. We will meet at noon tomorrow to plan the next phase. Meantime, how soon can we get our planetary defense shields up?"

General Domingo answered, "Well, probably take us a day to get it up and the dispatchers ready to handle all the incoming ships. I'll have to make sure that those facilities are also locked up tighter than a drum as well. This is Monday, so I'll try to have it up and operational by Wednesday morning at the latest. Will you be implementing corporate martial law?"

"No, I'd rather not. That tends to make people work against us. They have suffered enough from the corporations and their heavy-handed tactics. It's time for a change. If we are going to stand against the Master, we need everyone on Scorpi-C working with us, not against us," Alfonso answered truthfully.

"My God, Alfonso, I never in my life thought I'd hear that coming from a corporation executive!" declared Admiral Enrique.

Alfonso added, "True, but like Goyo hinted, even if Corporation Prime decides to help us, their assistance isn't likely to get here for a couple of years. If we're to hold out that long on our own, we have to change and change for the better in our people's eyes."

"Here, here," General Domingo cheered him. "Now we do have a chance, if I say so myself. Well done, Alfonso."

"Boss," Diego spoke up, looking up from his most recent text message, "we're being asked to accept victims of the attack on Gemma-D. They want to get comatose survivors off their world before the Master gets to them, as he has done on Taurus-C. What should I reply?"

"Tell them to send all the victims they want. We'll take them all. We'll have to arrange suitable housing and assistants to care for them. Guess the war has started," Alfonso replied.

Then he asked another question. "Admiral, how difficult would it be for our fleet to destroy the Master's battleship and perhaps his heavy cruisers? I'm afraid I'm mostly ignorant of such things."

He frowned and rubbed his face. Alfonso cringed, here was another action that he could no longer do and such a simple thing. He'd been forced to ignore facial itches, too embarrassed to ask Alicia to scratch for him. "Well, that is a tough thing to do, what with only a single battleship to bring to bear on his. I'll be frank, Alfonso. Our fleet can't take on his fleet, not directly. One on one means that both sides would probably lose all their ships. However, his new crews are untrained and unskilled, so perhaps we might only lose half our fleet taking his out. Still, not good odds. However, if we stand fast on defense and make his ships attack us here on Scorpi-C, where our field batteries can also be brought to bear on his ships, then we stand a good chance of soundly defeating them."

"Thanks, admiral, that's kind of what I thought. Don't worry. I've no intention of sending our fleet to its destruction. Home defense will do nicely." The admiral smiled, greatly relieved to hear this, and Alfonso ended their meeting.

When he returned to his office, Alis was waiting to see him. "Well, how did it go?" she asked.

"Just like you predicted, Alis. Sometimes, I think you are a super genius woman. They're all abandoning Scorpi-C, fleeing like frightened rats. I'm in control of all the corporations on Scorpi-C now, which makes me in charge of our ground forces and our fleet, just as you advised me. I have everyone thoroughly checking all air ventilation systems now. By tomorrow, we should at least know the status on that one. Have you heard about the attacks on Gemma-D and Zeno-C?"

"Yes, came in a half hour ago. They forwarded the messages to Diego so you wouldn't be disturbed," she replied.

"Good. I've given the okay to accept all the victims that those worlds wish to evacuate. Seems they don't want their victims being kidnaped by the Master. Can't blame them, but I do detect an undercurrent here."

"What's that?" she asked.

"I don't think those worlds want anything to do with thousands of UFB women and UFBMD men. Well, I've a completely new viewpoint on them. I'll take all that we can get."

"Mind if I lend a hand getting them situated?" Alis asked.

"Please. Diego is going to need a ton of help on this one. I have to try to get a public address ready. I'm going to speak to the average person on Scorpi-C, tonight, if I can get it ready in time."

"Good. Like I told you, it is imperative you have the average citizen of Scorpi-C backing you in this fight," Alis commented, pleased that Alfonso was taking her suggestions to heart and following through on them. Alis altered her calculations. She had calculated there was about a fifty percent chance that Alfonso would actually accept her suggestions and follow them. Had it been the GE Corporation's Benedicto, his chances were perhaps one percent. Now, Alis had to revise her calculations and was pleased to see that given his current response, he had an eighty percent chance of accepting and following her suggestions. She sent of a short data burst and headed off to find Diego.

At one o'clock just after lunch, Alfonso received a text message from one of the men who was searching the air vents here at GD headquarters. It read: device found in Vent 13. Armed. Orders? Alfonso sat back stunned! He realized in all likelihood, the Master had one or more of his men at least keeping the place under surveillance. If he ordered a mass evacuation, probably they'd set off the device. No, he had to be smarter than them. What to do?

Then it came to him. He asked, "Alicia, open up a comm line to all personnel only on this floor, please." She did so. "Attention. There is a bio agent bomb in our air vents. I want everyone on this floor only to quietly take the elevator and stairs to the roof. Whatever you do, do not alert anyone about this. We will evacuate floor by floor so that we don't alert the Master's spies who will surely set it off if it looks like we are on to the bomb. Thank you."

Alicia looked fearfully at him. "Go now. I'll be all right. Just show me how to do this floor by floor."

"But you can't. No hands. I'll stay with you, though I'm getting really scared," she replied. His opinion of her rose. After giving them a few minutes, he made a similar call to the next lower floor. Around three, he finally got those on the ground floor to take the elevators up to the roof, which was now quite crowded with people. "Okay, Alicia, time for you to evacuate too. I'm heading down to join the bomb squad and see how they are doing. Go. I can push a button with my nose." She grinned and reluctantly fled for the roof.

He headed down into the basement and found four bomb squad members working away. All wore bio containment suits and he relaxed. If the bombs went off, his specialists here wouldn't be harmed. "How is it coming?" he asked.

One muffled voice spoke up, "Boss, we got two disarmed and are working on the last known one. Now. Couple more minutes." Alfonso relaxed a bit and leaned against a wall to keep his somewhat precarious balance better. Finally, the man said, "Clear. Got the known ones disarmed. We should recheck and make sure there aren't anymore."

"Okay, I will send everyone home now. Thanks fellows."

"No, thank you for having us check for bombs! We all could have ended up like you!" Alfonso smiled and headed up to the roof to spread the word. There were quite a lot of small shuttles parked on the roof, and kindly, everyone doubled up, taking as many with them as the shuttle could safely transport, promising to return to pick up more. A half hour later, Diego, Alicia, and Alfonso remained on the roof.

"Boss, I'm getting some texts sent to you now from GE Corp headquarters. They've found bombs there too a few minutes ago," Diego hastily spoke up.

"Tell them what we did. For heaven's sake. . ." Alfonso replied, but was cut off by a series of explosions coming from a couple blocks down, the GE Corporation's headquarters. "Cancel that. Send it to all the other corporation headquarters. For God's sake, tell them not to panic and mass evacuate. That will only alert the Master's men." For an hour, Alfonso waited on the roof, hoping and praying that there wouldn't be more explosions. There weren't.

Around five, he got the all clear word from his technicians. Four genetic bio agent bombs had been located and disarmed. He ordered all vents to be double-checked and guarded 24/7 and then checked with the other corporations. Two of them had discovered one or more bombs, but wisely had followed his advice. Meanwhile, the emergency medical responders had quarantined off the GE building. There wasn't anything more that could be done now. They would be in comas for perhaps three days. Time enough to worry about that tomorrow. His public address would have to wait a bit.

That night, he received word from the admiral that ten bombs had been found and disarmed, primarily on his battleship. He promised to continue the search. Fortunately, the general reported no bombs found. Finally, Alfonso relaxed. Today had been a very narrow escape. Had the Master been able to strike, they would have been left nearly defenseless. Ironically, Benedicto was caught inside the GE headquarters when the bombs went off, packing up his things, while getting ready to flee; his fears had come true, but then he was the one who had panicked when his people discovered the first bomb, and he'd ordered a mass evacuation, bringing doom to five hundred six workers.

The next morning as Alicia got Alfonso seated properly, many reports came to him via secure emails. Bombs defused, precautions taken, CEOs and their families fled—dozens of such emails, though none needed his attention. Hence, feeling far more secure this morning, he began working up what he would say to the people of Scorpi-C. Alicia quietly called their local news station, requesting live coverage for a special and vital press conference to be given around four this afternoon.

As the hour drew close, Alicia brushed out his hair and adjusted his blouse and skirt. "There, handsome, you look good. Knock them dead," she encouraged him. Slipping a steadying arm around his waist, she led him down to the main floor where the camera crew had setup and several reporters were waiting. Soon, he was on live news, being broadcast to the entire world.

"Fellow citizens of Scorpi-C, I'm Alfonso Vega, the CEO of GD Corporation. Yes, as you can plainly see, I have been a victim of this terrible genetic bio agent, an agent that our various corporations invented in the first place. At this time, I feel it is my responsibility to brief everyone on this terrible bio agent, particularly since it has been used to wipe out all those working in the GE Corp headquarters yesterday."

"Many years ago, the corporations began a secret bio engineering station on Rho-C, where this terrible agent was developed. Why, you might be asking yourselves? Why would they want such an awful thing that permanently alters a person's genetic makeup and their bodies? I'm not privy to all their reasons. Such is far beyond my own clearance. I can tell you what I have learned though. It was developed for several reasons."

"First, as you all know and can see, the mutations are designed to turn any female into their idea of the Ultimate in Feminine Beauty, hence the name UFB woman. Indeed, they are all incredibly perfect and stunningly gorgeous. My wife is a fine example. However, they went beyond that. They discovered that mating a normal man with one of these UFB women yielded either another UFB girl or a super strong boy. These boys are being trained to become an army of super fighters. My own three boys have been whisked away by the corporations to a military school on another world."

"However, they didn't stop there. They also discovered that when normal males are exposed to this nasty agent, their bodies also mutated into what appears to be a UFB woman, but their male organs were untouched and fully functional. They further discovered that breeding one of these UFBMD men to a normal woman yielded the expected UFB girls, but surprisingly the boys were normal boys, except that they appear to be exceptional geniuses with IQs that are off the charts, unmeasurable some say. So yes, the corporations are at this very moment breeding a crop of these super IQ men, planning to install them into key corporation positions when they are old enough."

"That is as much as I know about the program. However, as I have recently discovered, the UFB women and we few UFBMD men are neither stupid nor completely helpless. We are people, just as everyone else is. The corporations, however, have kept their UFB women back from participation in our society in any meaningful way. And yes, until recently, I too followed company policy on this. However, now that I know better, I am changing this. My own twin daughters, UFB girls, are now attending a normal high school. Others are attending our Academy pursuing all manner of degrees."

"My own folly was acutely pointed out to me last Saturday when at my daughters' insistence, I took my whole family to the beach, joining all the other high school and Academy students for a carefree afternoon. I cried to see how my own UFB daughters finally got to interact with others their own age, something that we should never have forbidden. So as of this moment, all UFB girls and UFBMD boys, if there are any, are to be given the chance to go to high school or the Academy. I'm setting up full scholarships for these students. I hope to see many more of our special children in our public schools very soon. Give them a chance. True, they need help with some things that the rest of us take for granted, but they can do some surprising things, often in unusual ways. Give them a chance."

"Now then on to vastly more serious topics. As you know, the Master has been systematically attacking corporation headquarters on many worlds, delivering these terrible genetic bio agent attacks, and targeting our young students as well. What has your ruling corporations done about this situation? As of yesterday, every CEO except myself, has abdicated their position and fled with their families off-world!"

"Yes, at this point, I'm the sole leader of Scorpi-C. I have officially declared war on the Master. I will not let him harm any more of our people. I will not allow him to take over our world, turning everyone into his slaves. We have discovered many of his genetic bio agent bombs and defused them. Some were targeting other corporations, including GD. Some were targeting our space fleet and our lone battleship. These have all been found and defused. I have ordered strict security measures installed to prevent further such attacks. Tomorrow, our ground forces will be securing all our schools so that our children can't become his next victims, as they were on Zeno-C and earlier on Bellatrix-B. Later on, other critical institutions will likewise be secured."

"Now then, in the past, I know for a fact that the corporations have operated wielding ultimate powers, that they have committed atrocities, harmed smaller companies, perhaps even had dissenters assassinated. As of today, as long as I'm in control, all that ceases. If anyone has evidence of a crime or abuse that a corporation has committed in the past, please forward a copy of it to my GD headquarters. I don't know if I will be able to obtain justice for you or not, but I sure will do my best to do so. Some of these crimes have staggered me."

"Like the situation on Beltazar, which has been in the news recently." Alfonso described what the results of the corporation's handling of that world were. "So that is why the children of Bellatrix-B and probably those from Zeno-C have been genetically mutated, kidnaped, and sent to Beltazar—a desperate attempt to save that entire world's population. I can't say I agree with the Master's methods, but I can say the corporations knew about the situation there and did absolutely nothing about it for at least a century. A simple solution would have been to begin an immigration program, offering incentives for people to move there."

"With yesterday's attacks, I have given my permission for Gemma-D and Zeno-C to send some of their victims to Scorpi-C. I promised them safety from the Master's claws. So yes, I have declared war on the Master, and I will defend our world to my last breath. I hope you will pitch in and help me defend our Scorpi-C. No one else will but us. It is up to you and to me. Don't worry. I won't be asking you to go on an offensive. That is the responsibility of the military, but we together must defend our world or we all become slaves or worse. Thank you and good night."

"No, no questions. If you have some, email them to me, and I'll reply that way. My own family is expecting me home for dinner," he responded to the sudden barrage of questions thrown at him.

As he and Alicia headed up in the elevator to the roof and his private shuttle, he said, "Alicia, I want to make one stop on the way home. Jason's house, please." She nodded. Some fifteen minutes later, she helped him out of the shuttle, which she parked on the street before his home and knocked on the door for him. Bess answered and let them in.

"Hi boss. Coolest speech ever!" Bess praised him, as they headed into the dining room, where supper was just being served.

"Thanks. I want a quick word with Jason here. Son, I've a new project for you. Figure out how you can blow up a battleship. No, not in a battle with other ships. We don't have enough to win such a conflict. No, can it be done by internal explosions of some kind? I want to blow up the Master's battleship, if possible. Think of this as your ultimate boom," he teased Jason, whose face broke into a huge smile, as he finally grasped what Alfonso was asking of him.

"Okay, I'm all over it!" he enthusiastically replied. Alfonso thanked him, and they left, heading home at last. For some reason, just now Alfonso wanted to hug and kiss his wife and daughters. They meant everything to him.

"Papa! Papa!" Chita and Gabriella gushed and tried to run to him, but were really wobbling as they tried to walk fast. "We have real girlfriends now and Gabriella has a boyfriend too!"

Seeing their radiant faces brought a surge of unexpected emotions, and he couldn't keep tears of joy from watering his eyes. "That's wonderful, both of you. Best news all day."

"And papa, they want me to run for prom queen. Do you think that I should?" asked Gabriella.

"If you want to run, then run. If you don't, don't. You should always do what you want to do, but only if it is right, Gabriella. Come on. I smell supper. You two have to tell me all about it." Carmela entered the room and gave him a big smile of appreciation. Even Alicia was pleased to hear this news, especially since in about eight months or so she would have a UFB baby girl.

Chapter 17—Fallout

Wednesday noon, Alfonso finally felt more secure. General Domingo had the planetary shields up and running. The defense shield prevented any ship or object from entering any closer than ten miles from the surface. Even if the Master brought his fleet here, they couldn't get past the shield nor could they harm those on the surface. No further bombs were found, and all air vents in the corporation headquarters were secured, as well as those at the military barracks. Earlier this morning, squads headed out to secure the many schools all over Scorpi-C. With any luck, by tonight, there wouldn't be any more worries about genetic bio agent bombs being released on Scorpi-C.

However, General Domingo had told him that it would be weeks before all the critical infrastructure potential targets could be thoroughly searched. Since the Master had not yet targeted such things, Alfonso believed this was only a distant possibility. The next decision he had to make was one of building up Scorpi-C's ground forces. They only had one corporation-provided division here, the 509th Infantry Division of some twenty thousand men. Scorpi-C had a population approaching seven billion, more than enough to field many divisions, except there wasn't enough equipment to field more than one potential division.

Until now, that was all that anyone thought necessary, the single division. In a time of crisis, Corporate Prime would send forth all the divisions necessary to fight a battle or war. Today, Corporate Prime had its own problems to face, the spiders. The second tier of support on Gamma Prime was also out of commission, thanks to the Master's clever attacks there.

Alfonso knew that to obtain more divisional support, he would need to bypass all normal lines of communication and reach out to the other mid-arm sector corporate headquarters, something he was reluctant to do at the moment. His was a rim world and hardly at the top of mid-arm headquarters' priorities. He decided to make such calls only if things deteriorated badly.

Closer to home, the comatose victims at GE Headquarters had all been identified and distributed to medical centers around the city. Their families had all been notified, and he decided that when they revived, their care would be the responsibility their respective families. Still, he established a safety net, in case there weren't sufficient able-bodied family members or staff there to help them with their needs.

In addition, he ordered production of the extreme heels and electrostatic hair machines to be ramped up. Many more were going to be needed and soon. The five hundred six victims at GE Corporation were likely to be waking on Thursday. Initial counts suggested there would be two hundred four new UFB women, while the remainder would be UFBMD men.

Today, the first of the other victims from Gemma-D and Zeno-C began arriving as well, though exact numbers were sketchy at best. During the next few days, he paid close attention to those students coming from Zeno-C. He saw a startling fact. Those who were still young adapted well to the total alteration of their physical bodies, while the older people fared poorly, particularly the older men. Since youth represented the future, Alfonso focused heavily upon them, making sure these young students were handled as well as possible.

Housing was first on his list for these students. With Alicia's help, he used corporation funds to buy up all the available housing units close to either high schools or the sprawling Academy. He placed a large order for voice-activated computers and phones, and he placed ads for personal assistants, preferably those who could be live-in assistants.

As the days rolled by, he began to watch the many steps of his plan for the students coming together. Two weeks later, the final tallies were in from Zeno-C. Approximately two thousand junior and senior high school students were added to Scorpi-C's totals, split evenly between the sexes. Well over five thousand Academy students arrived, again roughly evenly divided by sex. Scorpi-C now boasted the largest numbers of UFB women and UFBMD men of any nearby world, outside those controlled by the Master. His new scholarship program became critical, supporting all these new students, particularly those in the Academy. Alfonso's view of this was money well spent, an investment in the future. Five thousand well-educated new young adults could only help everyone.

Some three weeks later, two men wearing professional women's apparel walked slowly and carefully up to the home of Jason Mott. "This is the right address?" one asked.

"Looks like it. They said we just needed to stand at the entrance. God, I hope we don't make utter fools of ourselves, Bill."

"I already *am* an utter fool walking, Hank. Here goes. Christ, I've never been so embarrassed in my life. This is a walking hell," Bill lamented for the thousandth time. It had only been three weeks since they both became UFBMD men, while working on a top-secret project at the Academy on Zeno-C. They weren't native to that world; rather they had been sent there by GD Corporation executives on Gamma Prime to work out their invention, where the chances of espionage were drastically reduced from the mid-arm worlds.

Automatically, something that sounded like a door knock could be heard coming from just inside the door. Shortly, a gorgeous brunette with shoulder length hair appeared at the door. "Oh. Cool. Can I help you? Lost?" she said in her mellow alto voice.

"I hope not. We're looking for the residence of Gunnery Sergeant Martha Spelling and Captain Bess Fontana," Bill spoke up, his alto voice still sounding foreign to himself.

"Ah, I'm Captain Fontana. Martha's inside. Come on in," Bess opened the door wide. "Need a supporting arm?" Both men flushed but valiantly decided against accepting her offer, wobbling some as they headed into the living room.

"Oh, we got company," Martha called out, just entering the room. She had her brown hair cropped short, as she always had worn it while she'd been in the FMF. "So who are you lovely ladies?" she asked.

Both men flushed and looked very nervously about,

wishing they could sit down before they fell down. Their feet were aching from such a long walk. Without asking them, both Bess and Martha moved alongside of them, slipped a supporting arm around them, and ushered them to the couch, adjusting their knee length brown hair for them.

Bill cleared his throat and began, "Hello. I'm William Franks. This is Major Hank Feldspar, er rather ex-major. You can call me Bill."

Now Martha flushed. "Er sorry fellows. I didn't realize—well you know." Hastily, she changed the subject, "So you must be new to Scorpi-C. Haven't seen you around. Jason and Linda are off at their classes at the moment." She figured the more she chatted, the less embarrassing everyone would feel.

"Yes, we've come to see you both," Major Hank took over. "Crap, there's no easy way to do this."

"Sure fellows. Begin at the beginning," Martha suggested.

"GE Corporation saw promise in Bill's design. He was a student at the Academy on Gamma Prime, you see." She didn't, but nodded as though she did. "I used to be a major in charge of a crack assault gun unit, so I know all about the MK42."

"Hey, super cool! That's my gun. Carry it everywhere," Martha interrupted him.

"We know," Hank continued. Martha gave him a quizzical look. "Anyway, they marked Bill's design as top-secret and sent us both out here on the rim, to Zeno-C. Less chance of espionage out here, or so they claimed. He and I were charged to develop his new assault gun, the MK50."

"Wow. Even more powerful?" Martha asked eagerly.

"Different," Bill broke in. "You see, always the problem our fighters face is the PDS. The MK42 can blast a hole in the best armor, but bounces off anyone wearing a PDS—well its blast is really just absorbed. So my new design will remedy that. If it works, it will punch right through any PDS."

"Holy dingo's kidney! I gotta have me one of those!" Martha exclaimed. "How much? I'll buy one now!"

Bill grinned. "Er, that's just the problem. I had it all designed and ready for the prototype to be made when this happened to us. Hank is supposed to help me with the design and then thoroughly test it, but now, we're just a pair of helpless freaks. Yet, when a GD man heard about us, he said that we should come here and ask for you two, that you could help us."

"Hey, great. If you got the plans for it, Bess here can build darn near anything. I'd love to fire it. I'm a crack shot with the MK42, best in my unit," Martha volunteered.

To Bess's eyes, both men looked relieved. "I have the plans on my laptop. It's stuck in the pack on my back. I'm afraid that I can't even use it anymore," Bill sighed.

Martha dug the computer out and opened it up. "Oh, needs a password." She looked at Bill who turned beet red. Martha looked confused. What was so embarrassing? It was just a password.

At least Bill squeaked, "9PinkCunts. I'm sorry. Just a guy thing." Both Bess and Martha roared with laughter, adding to the two men's humiliation.

"Just like a couple of horny guys," Martha finally calmed down enough to talk, typing it in. She added, "Would you like to change that now?"

"Please! 9GreenWhales," Bill replied. She made the change.

"I have to compliment you on a good password, though. Easy to remember, hard to crack or guess," Martha commented. "Don't worry, guys. We gals in the service have our own private sayings. Now then, Bess, give Emelio a call. Tell him we need voice-activation software installed in a hurry. Sorry guys. I'm not the hottest one with a computer. Bess, you want to take over. I'll watch. I gotta see this new Gertrude II— Gertrude, that's the name I gave to my MK42, you see."

"Done. He's on his way, so let's see the design specs, and I'll let you know if I can possibly make it for you fellows," Bess explained.

While she followed his instructions to bring up his detailed drawings, he explained further. "It is built around the frame of the MK42, so if you have a spare one around, we, er you can disassemble it and make use of quite a lot of its components. The theory is quite simple. Get the force shield dropped for an instant, long enough to allow penetration of the blast," Bill explained.

"Ah, I get it. Take the shield down and shoot through the hole," Martha said.

"Except we don't actually have to take the whole shield down," Bill clarified a little. "Just a small section so the blast energy can go through it."

"Say," Bess began thinking about this, "you could use a bigger version to get through the planetary defense shield that we've got up protecting us now."

"Ahem," Hank cleared his throat purposely. "You weren't supposed to make that connection, Bess. Top-secret and all that, but hell, Bill, we aren't going to be able to do another damned thing on our project. Might as well read them both in."

Bess replied, "Actually, that was a pretty obvious connection to make, Hank. Why aren't you going to be able to keep on working on this?"

"Look at us. We're darn near helpless and freaks to boot," Hank answered, fighting to retain control over his wild emotions.

"Well, give yourselves a while to get accustomed to new ways of doing things and allow others to help you with things you can't do, and you both will be back to battery again," Bess counseled. "Jason is still blowing up things, though these days he instructs others on just how to do it, well me actually. He's right there beside me telling me what to do step by step. So you two will be still doing things, just give yourselves time and don't stop trying."

"So it's true. You both were there on Rho-C and survived it? We heard that there were only a few survivors," Hank asked, taking a good look at Bess and Martha.

"Yes, we survived it. Rescued Linda," Bess answered.

"And I got good use from my MK42, killed a slug of giants—honestly, they were seven feet tall and must of weighted three hundred or more," Martha broke in, proud of her accomplishments too. "Of course, we all got somewhat genetically screwed up, but Dr. Gisa got to us all in time to keep us from becoming UFB women, though Jason didn't make it. He got screwed, like you guys did, a UFBMD man now. Hell, I lost twenty pounds, almost couldn't carry my MK42 anymore, but I've been working out every day since I got modified, but getting the muscles back isn't going so well. I think this new body isn't building up right."

"Really? Incredible, Martha. Can I buy you a coffee sometime and have you tell me all about it? Oh!" Hank suddenly flushed and shut up.

"Oh what? You asking me out or something, handsome fellow?"

"I was, but forgot myself, sorry," Hank said quietly, still embarrassed.

"Forgot yourself? Whatever are you talking about?" Martha probed, not grasping what he was implying.

"I mean I'm like this now, not my old self. Yeh, I was going to ask you out but I slipped and forgot that I'm mostly a freakish, helpless, almost-woman now. Sorry."

"Hank, you still got your big gun down below? Does it still fire off solid rounds?" Martha teased in her usual military way.

Hank laughed, "Yes, big gun still fires. How'd you know that what we guys—oh you been around."

"Course. You think you hunks do all the look'en? Hardly. We keep sharp watches too, you know. Sure, I'd like to have ya buy me a coffee. Know a good place close to the Academy. You're on, anytime I'm not needed here to help Jason and Linda out," Martha replied.

"But I look like a woman," Hank protested, not believing her.

"No, a gorgeous dish, but you got what it takes where it counts by me," Martha explained. "So did you lose weight too?"

"Almost sixty pounds!" Hank answered, relieved that she'd changed the topic and that she was willing to go for a coffee. "I can't see how I'll ever get that back, but then I can't see that I'll have any use for it."

Emboldened by Hank, Bill asked, "So Bess, any chance you'd let me buy you a coffee too?"

Bess giggled. "Sure Bill. I want to know more about

your design and how it works. We need to get it working and then get a really big one that can punch through a planetary defense shield. I think we might need such a weapon against the Master fellow."

"Say, you two aren't a—well you know sort of a couple or something?" Hank asked Martha.

"Lezzies? Nah. Now we appreciate good looking chicks as much as anyone does, but we want the gun, if you know what I mean," Martha replied coyly, leaving no doubt what she desired. All four chuckled and got back to the design.

Before long, Emelio arrived and was introduced. Hastily, he set about installing the necessary software and then helped them get used to using it. He also doctored up their cell phones, which they presumed they could never use again. When he left them to get to his next class, the two men were amazed!

Not long after that, the door opened automatically and Linda entered, taking the men by surprise. They saw a mound of knee length, silver hair on a stunning-looking young woman who wore a tee shirt and tight jeans, leaving little to the imagination, highlighting her perfect figure. Her extreme heels were just barely visible below her pants. "Oh hi there. Didn't know you had company. Just ignore me. Home for lunch," Linda said gaily.

Bess rose. "Linda, this is Bill Franks and Major Hank Feldspar. They are developing a new assault gun and have asked Martha and me to lend them a hand. Fellows, this is Jason's wife, Linda. She's gone back to the Academy, picking back up her astrophysics and galactic navigation studies. Like you two, she thought her days were over when she was kidnaped and genetically modified, but now she's back in our Academy continuing her studies. Many men and women like you are going back to school, picking up where they left off." Bess wanted to put in a not so subtle hint that they should consider doing so themselves, especially Bill.

"You're kidding us, right? Linda is now going to the Academy?" Bill asked quite confused. Linda was as helpless as he was, or so he believed, since her body looked much the same as his.

"Well, when those two and Jason rescued me, I just knew my Academy days were long over, but everyone has shown me that is just being silly and wallowing in self-pity. Voice-activated computer and phone make all the difference. I've picked up right where I left off, which is cool because I'm into the meaty courses now. You fellows aren't interested in astrophysics are you?" Linda asked.

Hank laughed. "I don't think I can even spell it, but seriously, are you the Linda that Bess and Martha and Jason rescued from Rho-C?"

"The one and the same. Have you two got my lunch ready? I have a one o'clock class to get to," Linda asked.

"Sorry. I'm on it. You fellows staying for lunch? Can't say no," Martha replied, dashing off to the kitchen, leaving Bess to usher the three into the dining room.

"This is so humiliating. You are going to have to feed us," Bill whispered to Bess.

"We don't mind, Bill. There are some things you guys can't now do. So relax and let those of us who can help you with this. There are many other things you *can* do that we *can't* do, like designing this new gun. Martha is going ape over it, if you haven't noticed," Bess explained, trying to put them more at ease.

Linda spoke up, "She's right. It is simply a matter of working out what you can and cannot do now. Like being a baby learning to walk and such. What's so hard for us is we have been used to doing things since we were kids, and now the ball game has changed; we have to start over. I have learned to do a whole lot with my toes, using them as fingers. If you fellows can be here tonight, I'll give you plenty of lessons on how I manage some things."

"Deal. Er that is if Bess and Martha don't mind," Bill replied.

"I'll kick your butts if you aren't here tonight," Bess teased him.

Mid-afternoon, they wrapped up the session with the new assault gun design. "Now you fellows can buy us a coffee," Martha hinted. She and Bess slipped a steadying arm around the men and headed off to the fancy coffee house, partially filled with other young folks, primarily Academy students.

Over coffee, which the men drank using straws, Bess and Martha in particular related their adventures on Rho-C and several others later on. Both men were very much impressed with the rescue operation of Anka and the firefight. They simply couldn't believe that two UFB women could fly a transport. Thus, since there was still some time before they had to be back to whip up supper, they headed over to the spaceport, where Jackie and Melissa were practicing with a GD transport, under the watchful eyes of Armando and J. D.

Once more, they left flabbergasted. Two UFB women were actually operating the deep space transport by themselves. However, Jackie left them with a key fact. "Look, it is often easier for two of us to handle what one normal person does. Work together, that's our motto. It takes both of us to fly this transport. Alone, neither of us could really do it well at all."

During supper, Linda gave them something else to consider. "I'm getting the hang of how to use my feet and toes to feed myself. Pretty clumsy yet, but I keep practicing it. Each day, I get better at it. You can too, if you try."

From that long day on, Hank and Bill hung around Bess and Martha as often as they could. Weeks later, Bess had the prototype MK50 ready for trials, but by then, the ice was broken, and a close friendship had developed, leading to passionate kissing. Several months later, both men proposed, and the women accepted. In an unexpected direction, Bess found the love of her life, while Martha did too, seeing much of herself in Major Hank.

***

During these weeks, Jason poured over his new assignment with a passion. How to destroy a giant battleship from within occupied his thoughts almost to an obsession, except when he was around Linda, when entirely different thoughts obsessed him, naturally. Battleships were behemoths. Built-in redundancy was in every design feature. It had to be, since these warships carried the battle to the enemy, sometimes ferrying an entire division of ground forces, while at others, carrying fifty transports. Destroying one from within was quite a challenge, but Jason knew that anything could be blown up, if one only were smart enough to see the weakness and exploit it.

At first, he did computer simulations. When finally the simulated battleship blew up on his screen he smiled. Not good enough. It took fifty precisely placed charges throughout the ship to do that. He needed another approach entirely. No one could set fifty charges. Now he began to study the ship in detail, focusing on potential secondary explosions.

After several fruitless weeks, Jason finally hit upon it. If one could cause the nuclear fusion engine that powered the gunnery to explode, then due to the ship design, the explosion could potentially be focused or directed towards the main batteries, which in turn would also explode, providing a huge secondary explosion. He cranked up yet another simulation, and the ship blew up. Now Jason knew that he was on to the right approach, if only he could figure out what charges were needed and their precise location, since everything depended upon forcing the massive secondary explosion.

A further complication was the weight of the charges had to be small enough for a person to carry. He settled upon a combination of thermite and C-10, military grade, however the twenty pounds of explosives had to be positioned within three inches of the precise spot! Still, if done, each simulation resulted in the total destruction of the battleship. Convinced he had worked out the solution, he called Alfonso to tell him the news. To his amazement, Alfonso dropped everything and came over to his place immediately.

After running the simulation for Alfonso several times, he explained the method and what was needed. "Simply amazing, Jason! Work out a detailed, precise set of instructions. We may be able to put this to good use and soon!"

That night, he called up Alis to tell her what Jason had worked out. "The catch is that the charges have to be placed within a three inch margin of error, very precise, or it doesn't destroy the ship. Plus, the location is hard to get, deep inside the ship. So I am not so sure that this is going to be feasible," Alfonso explained.

"Well, we are going to have to try something. The Master keeps on using this battleship to teleport his new victims up from where they fall into comas and then takes them off to who knows where. We simply must take this battleship out of the equation," Alis replied. "Let me go talk to Jason and get a personal feel for the challenge." He agreed.

***

The Master had not been idle. The past three weeks, he'd continued with his reign of terror, attacking corporate headquarters where he could and schools as well on Gemma-D, Bellatrix-B, and Zeno-C, before hitting Gamma Prime schools. Many of these worlds valiantly tried to limit the number of attack victims the Master could get by sending in men in bio containment suits to pull out the comatose victims. However, few of these worlds wanted to then deal with the resultant mutants, as they called them. Most of the rescued victims were sent over to Scorpi-C, who accepted all students and a good deal of other younger men and women. Alfonso put his foot down on accepting those older than thirty, since experience continued to tell him that the older ones simply refused to adapt and remained helpless individuals, requiring everything be done for them. They'd just given up on life, as he put it.

So yes, Alfonso and Alis agreed on this point. They needed to take the Master's battleship out of the equation. Yet, Alfonso knew if he sent in someone to do it, basically, it would be a suicide mission. There wasn't any hope of the person getting out alive, assuming they could even get on the battleship in the first place or even get past all their security to the proper place to set the charges. No, in Alfonso's mind, this could only be a suicide mission. Worse, if the first bomber was caught, the Master would know the ship's vulnerability, and they'd not get a second chance at it.

Alis also knew this factor was in play, though Alfonso never mentioned it. What Alfonso didn't know was Alis had received permission to act in the matter. What she lacked, Jason had just provided, a way for a single person to take out the battleship. She spent an entire day with Jason, repeatedly going every detail, particularly the precise location of the

298

charges, their specific arrangement, and just why they had to be in this particular location and sequence.

That done, she made a quick stop, covertly acquired the twenty pounds of explosives, and departed in her GD deep space transport. Her task: find that battleship. She also had something else that no one else had or knew about: her tracking locator, which she soon found was still operational. Two days later, her cloaked transport began shadowing the battleship. She kept track of the reports of new genetic bio agent attacks, correlating them with the battleship's position. At last, she determined it probably wasn't ferrying victims right now, so Alis decided it was time for her to act.

She attached a locator to her ship, put the heavy bag of charges over her shoulder, double-checked her locator receiver, and nudged her invisible transport in close to the battleship's open transport bay doors. Ever so gently, she extended a magnetic grappler, until it touched and grabbed onto the side of the huge ship. With her ship now attached, she slipped out of the forward escape hatch and pulled herself over to the battleship using the grappling line. Soon, she was inside the giant dome. Far below her, she saw a few deep space transports resting on their docking piers; there was room for fifty of them. Orienting herself, she floated down to one of the metal docks, her soft-soled shoes muffling her landing.

No one noticed her slight noise. Off Alis went. She wore a PDS and her Personal Invisibility Shield, her PIS. As long as she avoided banging into people and having them see doors opening magically, Alis felt safe enough. It took her two hours to get to the right location deep within the ship. Another half hour passed while she meticulously set the charges, verifying each step from her photographic memory. Finally satisfied, she set the timer for two hours, hoping that would be sufficient.

Now she had to hurry and retrace her steps. Twice, she was delayed by a bunch of trainees, fumbling their way through their duties. Finally, she reached the transport bay. She knew she had only minutes to get to the safety of her ship and get away, but somehow she had to get all the way to the top of the open dome, where her lifeline was attached to the magnetic grappling hook. Just then, a transport was slowly backing out of the battleship. She grinned, raced, and jumped, landing on its topside. She hoped no one inside would notice the slight jar. They didn't. Soon it reached the giant dome opening. At the last instant as the transport cleared the dome opening, Alis leaped as hard as she could, arms outstretched to the maximum, reaching for the line. Now free of the artificial gravity of the inner dome, she floated across the space. Finally, her hands touched the thin wire and clamped down hard. She glanced at her watch. Sixty seconds! Arm over arm, Alys pulled herself up towards the safety of her transport, slipping in headfirst and slamming the hatch after her. She landed in a heap, upside down in the navigator's seat. She reached out and hit the Execute button, jumping stationary into hyperspace, just as the brilliant, blinding light of the explosion nearly blinded her, replaced with the blackness of hyperspace. That had been far too close for comfort.

She got herself upright and straightened out, turning off her devices, thankful she didn't have to float through space in search of her transport. She waited patiently for five minutes and then deactivated her hyperspace jump, appearing where she had previously been, as modified by the forward motion of the battleship and transport during the past minutes.

She saw nothing but a debris field and took several photos of the remains. She sighed; she'd killed many men and women who were onboard the battleship, which was why she'd had to get the authorization to do this mission, and why it had taken so long for that electronic signal to come. Still the greater good prevailed. Alis entered the coordinates for Scorpi-C and headed back to report to Alfonso. The Master no longer had the use of a battleship in his fleet. No longer could he teleport his comatose victims and ferry them away to who knows where. She'd leveled the playing field somewhat. But had she gotten the Master? What he onboard? That was the question uppermost in her mind.

Only later did she learn the transport that had left at that last instant and that had given her a ride up to the dome had been carrying the Master away from the battleship and hence the explosion. When she learned that, Alis began to wonder if somehow the Master knew she'd set the explosives and was fleeing just as she had. That gave her pause. Nevertheless, she sent an electronic burst of data, relaying what she'd done here.

"You did what?" exclaimed Alfonso, when she reported and showed him the photos of the debris field. "How? Unbelievable! You should get a medal for this! Please, tell me how you did this? I thought it was a suicide run, which is why I didn't order it done. My god! Jason ought to hear about this too!" Alfonso was beside himself with joy. Alis had done the impossible. Jason had done it too! "You both need medals!"

"Boss, leave me out of that. Just say a secret agent of yours did the deed. Otherwise, you will blow my cover, and I can't go on other vital missions for you," Alis insisted. Alfonso knew that was right, but he so wanted to give her the praise and validation that she deserved. Only his inner circle knew it Alis who carried out Jason's plan. However, Jason did get his medal.

Later that day, he made a public broadcast to all of Scorpi-C telling them that the Master's battleship had been destroyed. That made the top news story that week.

***

Also during these four weeks, Anka wasn't idle either. The late Adler Schmidt of Bellatrix-B had pricked her interest when he had argued against her suggestion during their discussion on the space station before the terrorist attack came. She recalled him speaking condescendingly, "Those were barbaric times, centuries ago, the dark ages of the galaxy, the era of the mutant telepaths and mechanical men. Uncivilized ages, totally ancient history. Everyone knows such knowledge was lost to mankind back in those same ancient times. That has absolutely nothing to do with today's modern, civilized worlds." To Anka, such things could well be possible. *How else can you explain all these strange things happening?*

Cursing her debilities constantly, Anka used her new voice-activated computer to search the Interstellar Network for more information on that long gone era. To her amazement, there was actually very little hard data available. The best entry read:

301

Galactic Dark Ages: [the date given was four hundred fifty-six years ago] A barbaric time for the entire civilized galactic worlds, an era of planetary genocide, where the weapons of choice were biological agents that caused horrific genetic mutations to everyone, a time when millions of mechanical men were needed to sustain the lives of the mutated survivors, and ended when a race of telepaths ended the barbarism.

That was all the online systems had from those times. Anka felt frustrated. Corporations had records dating back millennia. So where were the detailed records of that era, not quite half a millennia ago? To Anka and her devious mind, it seemed someone or someones had deleted all the key, relevant information from those Dark Ages. Surely back then, someone kept accurate records, newscasts, video recordings, anything, but Anka simply couldn't find anything in the vast Interstellar Network. That frustrated her even more than her own physical helplessness.

A few days later, Alis was again around Malagena, Scorpi-C, and decided to check up on how her fellow ambassador, Anka, was faring. "I'm a helpless mess, Alis, but so damned frustrated with the total lack of information about those Dark Ages. Remember, Ambassador Adler was chastising me about such foolishness back on the spaceport. I swear someone has gone to a whole lot of trouble to wipe the database clean of anything having to do with that mess!"

"Remind me again what it was about?" Alis played dumb, hoping her friend wasn't truly after what she thought she might be.

"The Dark Ages about five centuries ago, when they committed planetary genocide using nasty biological agents that caused terrible genetic mutations, kind of like what's happened to us, at least I think so. They had mechanical men and telepaths back then, but I can't *find* a damned thing on them. No, but I can *find* records of lost deep space exploration vehicles going back an entire millennia!" Anka griped.

Alis saw how badly Anka wanted answers and that she would probably never give up her frustrating search. She also knew where some additional data could be found. Not all traces had been wiped and what was there probably wouldn't compromise anything. "Anka, I think you should start using your feet."

"What?" Anka asked confused. "What has my feet got to do with anything?" *Has Alis lost her mind? Well, things are pretty darn bad.*

"There is the Scorpi-C Master Library here in Malagena, close to the Academy. What you are seeking is not kept online, but can be found the old-fashioned way by a manual search. So if you are up to making use of your feet, look up this reference: Zeta Scorpii-C. I think that you might find more of what you are looking for related to that world. I believe it is or was a populated mid-arm world in the ancient Federation of Planets." Alis knew that if Anka was serious about her research that she'd have to start finding new ways to do things and that would help her adjust to her genetically modified body and get back to living life again. She could do no more for her friend.

"Zeta Scorpii-C? Never heard of it. Okay, thanks, Alis, I'm on it. I'm just sure someone is covering up something vitally important, perhaps even where these corporations got their damned genetic bio agents in the first place!" Anka said with passion.

"Who knows? Well, I'm off again. I'll try to spend some time with you when I get back again, Anka. Don't give up," Alis encouraged her and left, but watched as Anka then determinedly headed off the find the library, even though she'd have to walk a mile to get there. Alis smiled, knowing Anka was at least strengthening her feet and legs with so much walking.

"Oh this is the utter pits!" Anka said, as she finally reached the library. Her feet ached and her knees throbbed. She'd nearly fallen three times and only wild wobbling had kept her on her feet. At least, someone had opened the main doors for her, and she now stood in the main foyer looking up at the vaulted ceiling and tall marble columns. Many young people were here, coming and going, probably Academy students Anka guessed. She spotted the information desk and walked up to the young receptionist.

"Oh, you want Ancient Documents. That's in the basement. Take the elevators over there. Bottom floor," she replied politely. Anka turned and walked slowly over to the elevators, managing to use her nose to push the button for down.

When she stepped off into the basement, she saw a long, dimly lit hallway, a reception area with numerous soft chairs, and small lights designed to illuminate documents by shining their lights over your shoulders, thereby avoiding the need to have costly bright lights overhead running all the time. The place was deserted. She walked up to the desk. A sign said ring bell for service. "How the hell am I supposed to do that?" she grumbled. At last, she managed it by using her chin and a downwards head motion.

A young man with wire-rimmed glasses stepped out, holding an old book in his hand. "Oh. Hello. Librarian Juan Carlos. How may I help you?" *Wow! Look at her! What a dish! She has to be one of those exotic UFB women I've heard about. Wow, here in my section. Wow.* His eyes nearly popped out of his head.

"Well I'm looking for ancient records concerning the Dark Ages and a planet called Zeta Scorpii-C, sir," Anka said clearly, but noticing the man was staring at her. She blushed, though she didn't know why. Perhaps it was because she was so deformed now, so helpless.

"Okay, that's my job, to help readers and researchers find what they are looking for. Sorry, I've never seen anyone as beautiful as you are. You must be one of those UFB women. Anyway, this is my first week on the job. Just graduated from the Academy. Got my degree in Library Science. Oh, pardon me, I'm Juan Carlos, ma'am. This way, the archives are this way."

"Thanks, Juan. I'm Anka Polonia, originally from Taurus-C some years back. Yes, I was a recent terrorist attack victim. Sorry I'm so helpless, but I really do need to do this research. The Interstellar Network has almost nothing on the Dark Ages, like they never existed or had no importance at all," she chatted, following slowly after him. "Oh!" she stopped and stared at floor to ceiling shelves filled with books and boxes. The space was huge.

"Yes, I know—kind of daunting at first. Don't ask me

why they destroyed the computer versions of all these, and made and kept hard copies. Doesn't make any real sense, does it? But then who knows what goes on in the minds of the corporation executives?" He sounded as though he had an antagonistic view of the corporations. *Well, these days who didn't,* she thought.

Thirty minutes later, Juan finally found an old volume, A Brief History of Zeta Scorpii-C. Soon, Anka discovered what Alis meant by using her feet. Juan put the volume on the floor on a slanted, wooden book reader. She sat on a chair, leaned over, and used her feet to flip the pages. Before long, Juan became as curious as she was and began reading over her shoulder.

Fascinated by the albeit one- sided account, Anka spent long hours every day down in the basement reading all that Juan could find for her. The two struck up a friendship, and soon Juan got up the nerve to ask her out, and their relationship began to flourish, though it would be another six months before Juan got up the nerve to propose to Anka.

Thus, when Alis returned from destroying the Master's battleship, Anka, with the supporting arm of her friend Alis, visited Alfonso at his home that night, armed with a rather large amount of relevant history. "Alfonso, I've really found out a whole lot of ancient history that may well be important to our current situation," Anka began, after greeting everyone and being seated beside her boss. Alicia sat on Alfonso's left, while Alis sat on Anka's right, ready to help as needed.

"You see, way back then nearly a half millennia ago, the galaxy was divided in half with two great groups controlling their half, the Imperium and the Federation of Planets, who went to war. Scientists in the Imperium, which was losing the war, invented a new genetic bio agent weapon, designed to wipe the populations of entire planets out by turning them into helpless mutants. However, the war ended before those terrible weapons could be brought to bear."

"Later on, these bio agents fell into the wrong hands. Before long, all sorts of planetary leaders decided to stockpile these terrible bio agents using them as a deterrent to their enemies. If you attack us, we will launch our bio agent weapons and wipe your entire world out. That was the idiotic thinking and before long, just that happened. Genocide occurred on a number of densely populated worlds. The story gets confusing at this point, and I'm not sure what actually to believe. Anyway, this Zeta Scorpii-C became the home of millions of these mutants."

"What struck me is the similarities of their mutants and us, boss. They had no arms, like us. Their feet were somehow malformed, perhaps similar to ours, but I'm not sure about that. Their hair was like ours with neurons and axons in it, but theirs was far longer, reaching their ankles. However, there is one huge difference, boss. Everyone was turned into hermaphrodites! According to the book, the only way to tell men from women was either a lab test or watch where their urine came out! Incredible. Plus, they all had breasts bigger than their heads, if you can believe that. So I find the similarities rather striking, boss."

"Anyway, in order to survive, they had millions of robots who raised their crops, produced their food, and helped them with daily living. I believe that our modern electrostatic hair machines came from them. Anyway, they also had some unique robot men, called humaniforms. They looked just like a person, indistinguishable the book claims. I don't believe that, mind you, but these robots got angry with humans for committing so many wars and unleashing genocide attacks. They then began to fight back, wiping out many worlds and turning the populations into these helpless hermaphrodites and moving many to this Zeta Scorpii-C world, where their mechanical men could care for their needs."

"Apparently, these robots almost conquered the whole galaxy, but were stopped at the very last minute by a group of strange telepathic people. Quite why, the book's author doesn't say, and I don't think he knew what really happened. Anyway, these robots all just vanished, never to be seen again. The telepaths apparently kept the peace for a long time after that."

Anka finished up, "So boss, I think somehow the GE Corporation discovered some of these ancient genetic bio agents and were experimenting with them on Rho-C. Plus, maybe this Master fellow is one of them telepath people or maybe even one of those humaniform robot things!" Anka sat back with a huge smile of satisfaction. She'd uncovered more than anyone else currently knew about ancient history. More importantly, she had her self-respect back, for she had made a contribution to the cause.

Alis didn't say anything. *Perhaps Anka is on to something with the Master fellow being a telepath of sorts. That might account for his fortuitous escape seconds before I blew up the battleship he was on. Did he read my mind? If so, that would account for his miraculous escape or perhaps it is just serendipity. Still, there is his hypnotic effect on masses of people to consider. Such a skill is in my data banks.*

Alfonso praised Anka for her work. "I think we need to look for some additional clues. Call Diego," he replied and commanded his cell phone. "Diego, tomorrow I have a special assignment for you and Anka." At this time, the GE Corporation headquarters was locked up. All their personnel had been terrorist attack victims. "Tomorrow morning, Diego and Anka, you are to thoroughly search their building, looking for secret documents that have anything to do with their secret research base on Rho-C." Alfonso didn't know if anything would come from this, but he needed to know, one way or the other.

As far as the Master being one of those weird telepath people, Alfonso had no idea, only that the man had an unnatural ability to hypnotize everyone around him. Instead of worrying about that aspect, he placed is trust in this new MK50 that Bess and Martha were helping to make. His only idea was for a shooter to take the man out somehow.

Chapter 18—Autumn Leaves Falling

Autumn came. Diego and Anka had been searching for secret documents for a couple of weeks, having uncovered some that were quite interesting, outlining what Alfonso considered to be criminal actions on the part of GE Corporation. However, they had not yet finished their search. On the home front, Gabriella was waltzing around their living room; she had just been elected Junior Class Prom Queen! The big dance was scheduled for Friday night.

"Papa, you and mama just have to come," Gabriella insisted. "Chita is one of my maidens too."

"Gabriella, I wouldn't miss it!" he replied. Watching his twin daughter's excited expressions brought joy to his heart and Carmela's too. *How could I ever have thought they are not real people and not just some immature sex dolls?*

"I'll make sure your Friday late afternoon is free, boss," Alicia added, making a note of that on her phone.

That Friday afternoon was hectic around the Vega home, as Gracia and her sister hustled from one to the other, getting the teens all dolled up, as well as getting Carmela ready. Now five months pregnant, Alicia handled Alfonso, getting him bathed and dressed in his professional woman's outfit. Besides, she'd just had a checkup at the medical center and wanted to share the good news with him. "I'm having twins, a girl and a boy, Alfonso!"

"Wow, that is good news, Alicia. Incredible. Well, the doctors do say that with UFB women, there are many twins. So I guess it is the same with UFBMD men as well. Have you picked out names yet?"

"Shouldn't you have a hand in that too?" Alicia asked, pleased that he was taking this news so well.

"If you insist, how about Roberto for the boy, but you name the girl, unless you want it the other way around," Alfonso suggested.

"Ernesta after my grandmother," she suggested with a smile.

Gabriella wore a flaring white taffeta gown with striking white heels. "Dear, you look positively stunning," Alfonso complimented her and then did the same to Chita, who wore a pink, satin gown, as would all of Gabriella's other maidens.

At the prom dance, Alfonso again felt very ill at ease. So many fathers and mothers were present, acting as chaperones or supporters of their children's school activities. He looked like their mothers, not Gabriella's father, and that bothered him, even more so when they announced the first dance was for the fathers and their daughters. While the other fathers had their arms around their daughters, all he could do was face her, while she leaned her head on his shoulders like the other girls were doing. It didn't matter to Gabriella, though, nor did it to Chita a few minutes later when he danced with her.

Finally, the teens split off to dance with their boyfriends and girlfriends, giving Alfonso the chance to dance with Carmela and then briefly with Alicia, who insisted she was too pregnant to dance very much. That done, most of the parents huddled around the refreshments table, and once more Alfonso felt very out of place, having to have Alicia help both himself and Carmela.

However, he overheard a couple of the men talking about his recent request for young men who wanted to fight back against the Master to sign up for the new Scorpi-C Infantry Division. He knew recruitment for the new division had been dismal so far.

"I don't know why we should send our sons off to fight the corporation's battles. Hell, we don't even own our own homes. The corporations do; they own everything around here. We're just their puppets," one man said.

His friend whispered, "Hey cool it! That's the GD CEO over there, that professional woman, that's him."

Alfonso walked up to them careful not to further embarrass himself by having to wobble to keep his balance. "Hey, it's okay to speak your minds freely. I'm curious about what you were just saying. Can you tell me more about how you feel? We all live on Scorpi-C."

"You heard him. He said I should speak my mind,

Alberto. All right then, boss man. We don't own anything, but our own clothes and personal items. The corporations own it all, so why should we spill our blood to defend corporation property? Shouldn't the corporations be fighting their own battles?"

"You have a very interesting point. I hadn't really thought much about past corporate policies. Tell me this; if you owned your own home, would you feel any differently about helping defend Scorpi-C?" Alfonso asked.

"Hell yes! We defend our property, our things. Let the corporation defend their things," he replied.

"Very valid point. You know, it's not right—the corporation owning your homes and making you pay rent all these years. Doesn't seem fair to me," Alfonso suggested.

"Damned right it isn't fair. Some of us have been paying rent for nigh onto thirty years now, more than enough to have bought the damned house in the first place!"

"Excellent point."

The other man added, "So you're not going to get many volunteers for your new army division. You should get the corporations to send in their armies from some other worlds to help out here."

"Not going to happen, I'm very sad to say. The other corporations on the other worlds could care less about us out here on the very rim of the galaxy. We're on our own, probably for a couple of years, if we can hold this Master fellow off that long. You know fellows, we need a change from the way things have always been done. Listen to the news Monday night. I think you've both given me a really good idea for change," Alfonso replied and rejoined Carmela and Alicia.

"What was that all about?" Carmela asked.

"Tell you about it when we get home, dear. Right now, I just want to watch our lovely daughters and you two beautiful women," he replied.

At ten on Monday, all the other corporate executives and their assistants again met at GD headquarters. Alfonso had asked Diego and Alicia to call them over the weekend and arranged for this meeting. "Gentlemen, things are not progressing well. Zeno-C has fallen into the hands of the

Master. We've accepted around ten thousand refugees here, including another five hundred or so UFB women and girls. Interestingly enough, the 502nd Infantry Division and the Zeno-C space fleet departed for the mid-arm region just before the Master took over. So we get a break there in that he can't add to his space fleet."

"So let there be no doubts, eventually, the Master will set his target on Scorpi-C, and we must be ready. However, our own single division can't defend the entire world. I've been trying to raise a volunteer division, but hardly anyone has signed up. Why?"

"Well, I found that out at Friday night's prom dance for the junior high school students. No one here wants to fight to defend Scorpi-C, because they don't own anything here except their clothes and personal items. As you know, the corporations own the land and built the houses, renting them out to the population at large."

One CEO broke in, "Yes of course. That's the way it's always been done. Highly efficient; keeps costs down."

"True, true, but the people don't own their own homes and as a result have no incentive to help us defend Scorpi-C. So today, I'm establishing an entirely new policy. Hear me out before you bark."

"As of now, it will be the right of every person to own their own home and the land it sits on. We will work out the value of that property. Then, tally up how much rent the person has paid so far. If he's paid its value or more, then we will give him the deed to his property and refund all excess money he's paid us. Those who haven't yet paid in full will be given a document that explains how much they have paid and how much they have yet to pay. For value purposes, we will use the value the property had when they first began to pay rent on it. Gentlemen, that will give your people a good deal to work on immediately. I'd like this project to be wrapped up in a month."

"Why am I doing this revolutionary thing? Simple. If they own their own property or see that they will soon or eventually own it, then they are going to fight to keep the Master from taking that away from them. In short, we'll have our volunteer army and a way to defend Scorpi-C. Yes, I'll take the heat later on, if the corporations try to come down on us for what I've done here. None of you will have any responsibility for it, only me. Am I clear? Now you can bark at me." Alfonso sat down, ready to hear their protests.

"What you're doing is revolutionary! Something the resistance might have demanded," one exec complained bitterly.

So it went, with most executives going on the record as opposed to this. However, they had no choice, since Alfonso was the sole leader at this time. He let them voice their objections, and then let them get on with carrying out his orders.

That night, he again held a special news conference and carefully outlined this major change and how it would affect those who were renting their homes from the corporations. When he finished, the reporters were so stunned by this unbelievable news that for once they didn't bombard him with questions.

That came the next day when the phones at GD headquarters were constantly busy! Most calls began by the person asking if this was really true. Convinced, they then provided their information, and his staff promised to get back to them with their deal later this month. They had no time to work out the actual situation for any caller, not for the next two days! Alfonso had definitely shaken the establishment's tree and the leaves were falling far more rapidly than anyone could rake them up!

By the end of the month, more than half of those renting homes from the corporations now owned their homes, with some getting rather large overpayment settlements. Morale shot upwards. During the month after that, Alfonso had far more volunteers than he could arm, and now faced the problem of where he could get more weapons and gear for the men, something that he preferred to do. *If the Master will just hold off long enough, then we can truly defend our world.*

Just as the chaos of the month wound down, an extremely worried Diego came by his office. "Boss, you'll never guess what I discovered in a secret safe at the GE Corporation headquarters. My god, Alfonso, this is just plain damming."

"Have a seat and tell me, Diego. It can't be that bad, can it?"

He sat down and looked hard at his genetically modified boss. "Okay then. Some hundred fifty years back, GE Corporation sent an archaeology team to Zeta Scorpii-C to excavate several ancient sites. The team uncovered some ancient bio agent cylinders, but they were in bad shape. When they reported their discovery, GE sent out a team of research scientists, who retrieved ten of the cylinders. The cylinders went to Rho-C, along with a dozen top geneticists, joining the bioengineers who were already there. Then GE Corporation upped Rho-C's classification to their highest top-secret level. A later document reported the discovered bio agent was degraded, but that the geneticists were able to gain some valuable clues, whatever that may mean. There are also two top security proposals among the documents. One contains the initial outline of the UFB and UFBMD breeding program, but the other is damming. It outlines how this stuff could be used as a weapon against hostile forces and planets! Boss, the damned corporations invented this genetic bio agent and have plans to use it on a broad scale!"

"Damn. Well, we know the corporations are unethical, but this is downright criminal. A weapon? What the hell are they thinking?" Alfonso cried.

"Pretty easy, boss. They don't like what you've done here on Scorpi-C, so they dump a shit load of that stuff in our atmosphere, and everyone on Scorpi-C is mutated and becomes utterly helpless. Their people come in and take over the entire world without firing a shot or fighting a battle," Diego speculated.

"Well, we best let everyone know. Set up a meeting with all the RdD members for tonight. Set up a similar meeting of all corporate executives and their people for late this afternoon. I aim to let everyone know just what the corporations have done and may do in the near future. This could lead to Anka's genocide notions from the ancient Dark Ages," Alfonso ordered, his face, grim.

***

Curses and wild exclamations shot around the room of normally conservative corporate leaders. Alfonso finished reading them the contents of the secret GE Corporation documents. He echoed their feelings, but he'd already gotten his own curses out of the way. "Gentlemen, I'll be going public with this in the morning. I owe it to every person on Scorpi-C. They have to know what GE executives have done, because we could well be a target of a massive genetic bio agent attack down the road. Meantime, put your best people on trying to find a way to prevent such airborne attacks. Hell, have them work on cures, if possible. Lord knows how long we have before the higher ups decide to unleash it on all these rim worlds, hoping to catch the Master in one of the attacks." Very sober men and women left the GD auditorium.

That night, the auditorium was filled with all the RdD resistance fighters. Once more Alfonso read the secret documents and listened to their violent reactionary curses. Anka called out, "Damn, I was right about them making use of the bio agents of the Dark Ages! Damn them to Hell!"

"So what do we do now?" one finally called out.

"First thing we must do is find out if small particles can float down through our Planetary Defense Shield. If they can't, then we are likely safe for now. We need to see if they could just dump the stuff in our upper atmosphere, have it settled down through our shield, and mutate everyone. If it can, then we need to put our minds together and find a way to stop that from happening. If the stuff can't penetrate our shields, then we are in better shape and just have to ensure they can't covertly land and then set off some bio agent bombs." Alfonso sighed. This was all that he could think of doing now, precious little.

"Going to let the public know this?" Anka asked. Many nodded, wanting to know this as well.

"You bet. I'm making public newscast tomorrow morning, spelling it out. We might get more people wanting to join the resistance movement," Alfonso answered and was cheered for that notion.

Sitting quietly in the back, Alis calmly sent off another short electronic burst. "They know about the source of the bio agent," was all she sent. There was an awful lot of meaning in that, however, none good. Anka was, she thought, on the right track with her genocide theories. Grim. Slowly, bits were beginning to fall, and none of the bits was particularly wholesome, far from it.

Chapter 19—The Corporations' Strike

The power struggle on Corporate Prime ended. Bloody, yes. Effective, yes. Nasty, yes. Conclusive, apparently. With the spider's total elimination of all the executives and personnel working at the two galactic headquarters of both the GE and GD corporations, the two most powerful or influential corporations in the galaxy and who had dominated the other corporations, a powerful political and ruling vacuum appeared. Nature abhors a vacuum. So did the corporations and their executives.

A trio of top executives formed the Trilateral Corporation, sharing the ruling of the galaxy equally between the three corporations, but really themselves: Walter Slack of General Goods, Jakob Peterson of Peterson Engineering, and Jackson Sparks of Essentials Limited. The bodies of five other top executives were found later in a picturesque lake not far from Central Park.

Of course, their first problem was the elimination of the spiders. Webs and cocoons were visible through some of the windows of the two buildings. This, they had handled by Peterson Engineering. A temporary defense shield dome was formed around the two buildings and several smaller buidlings that were unfortunately within the spherical dome being generated. Then the engineers imploded everything within the dome while the force field kept anything from leaving that zone. When the huge blast was over and the dust settled, nothing remained but a fine, pulverized dust, composed mostly of concrete, steel, and glass particles. Mixed in there somewhere were the remains of several thousand men and women and, of course, the spiders.

That handled, they forcefully took over control of the middle management levels of the GE and GD corporations, some dozen headquarters within the hub sectors, and some fifty scattered in the mid-spiral arm sectors. Of course, many of the GE and GD executives swore to regain control of their own corporations, but their infighting and deal-making was totally secondary, as far as the new Trilateral Corporation was concerned, who now turned their focus outward toward this minor annoying mess in the rim sector of Abelard. They needed to demonstrate they were competent, able, effective, and powerful enough actually to lead the entire galaxy. They couldn't have some upstart fellow on the distant rim taking over corporation-built and run planets. All Corporation Prime eyes were on them, especially after their effective handling of the spiders. Besides, this was just a trivial situation and very, very far from Corporate Prime.

Admiral Alister Atkins and General Felix Groundwaters, both veterans of several minor conflicts with war medals to prove it on their uniforms, were given the task of removing this minor situation from the news. In fact, they were given carte blanche to deal with it anyway they chose. "Eliminate them all, permanently," Walter declared when the two men queried their exact orders.

"Understood," the admiral replied with a covert grin.

They departed Corporate Prime a month later, heavily loaded and ready to fight a major war. Admiral Alister's main battle fleet consisted of three battleships, ten heavy cruisers, and twenty light cruisers. He also had two additional battleships ferrying the two divisions now under the charge of General Felix, the 2nd Assault Division and the 3rd Infantry Division. Over forty thousand men and women, heavily armed and fully supported, would make the ground assault. They were prepared to blow away all resistance in short order. These were the elite divisions normally stationed on Corporate Prime, as the space fleet was. That the Trilateral Corporation had left only the 1st Assault Division to guard Corporate Prime along with a few light cruisers was of no importance. There wasn't anyone who would or could attack the ruling planet of the galaxy, such was unheard of. In fact, Corporate Prime had never in its four hundred year history been attacked. Besides, it had a Planetary Defense Shield around it.

Late autumn, the fleet arrived in the Abelard Sector and made the short hyperspace jump to Taurus-C, the last known home base of the Master. Within a half hour, Admiral Alister relaxed. The battleship wasn't here, though he didn't know it had been blown up some time ago. The small fleet that had once protected Taurus-C was nicely within the ten mile high Defense Shield that surrounded the planet. No fleet battles today.

Of course, the first action was to eliminate the shield that prevented all ships from getting closer or even blasting the surface with their guns or dropping devastating bombs on them. There were several ways around this force barrier. One way was far too risky even to try. That was to attempt to drop out of hyperspace at a location just below the ten-mile sphere of force. That was never considered because the precise hyperspace coordinates had to be more precise than the technology worked. That is, be off by one digit and the ship could drop out of hyperspace inside the planet or be cut in half by the force field. Another way involving considerable risk to the ship trying it was to approach the shield slowly, halting as it touched the force shield. Then push through it at a millimeter per minute speed. Once the ship was completely through the shield, it could then fly freely. However, for the long duration that it took to "seep" though the shield, it would a sitting duck for ground artillery and for the fire from the local fleet of cruisers.

No, Admiral Alister took the tried and true approach: bombard the shield with enough energy that the power generators on the surface that kept it up would fail. Then, his ships could head on down with near impunity. "All cannons to bear on the force field. Continuous fire at will," Admiral Alister barked his orders from the Command Bridge. Through the blast shield, he sat back to watch the fireworks fly as the many cannons of the battleships pounded the force field, each shot resulting in gigantic explosions of multi-colors.

Amid the fireworks, no one noticed a deep space transport lift off from Taurus-C and cloak itself. The ship with the Master aboard rose up to near the firing zone and close to the location of the three battleships and the ten heavy cruisers, all firing at the shield. The Master focused and began his own work. Meanwhile dozens of other deep space transports lifted off from Taurus-C, each one cloaking as soon as possible. Many dropped into hyperspace, following the long-planned orders of the Master, confident that he would soon be joining them.

Onboard the Battleship Intrepid, suddenly crewmen began shooting other crewmen. In seconds, chaos erupted on the ship. Amid the confusion, two men walked like zombies into two of its nuclear power generating rooms. Their guns blazed, killing the operations personnel. Then, they adjusted several levers, walked out, and fired their blasters at the entrance keypads, destroying them and any easy access to these two rooms. That done, they stood still like zombies. Officers bellowed orders, and then resorted to screaming them. "Shut down the reactors!" With the keypads destroyed, ten minutes or more were needed to cut through the blast doors and gain access. However, before that could happen, both power plants blew up, knocking out all firing guns and all maneuverability of the behemoth ship, which was effectively dead in the water but with hundreds of dead and with gaping holes amidships.

The Master moved on to the next battleship. A half hour later, that one too had a pair of nuclear power plants explode with identical results. To say that Admiral Alister was angry was an understatement. How could this be happening? Was the crew members that incompetent? Traitors? Sabotage? He had no answers, but ordered the two battleships carrying the two divisions of troops to combine their fire on the planetary defense shield.

The shield collapsed in a giant ball of light. The admiral's standing orders were instantly executed, as all ships, except the two crippled battleships swooped down towards the planet. Not knowing why or how the other two battleships had been taken out, Admiral Alister reacted. Best defense is a powerful offence. Without hesitation, he issued the orders to nuke the planet. He wanted to give whoever was sabotaging his ships no further time to do so. Three battleships fired volleys of rockets, each bearing massive warheads. As soon as they were released, the fleet's standard reaction was to make the jump into hyperspace in order to avoid any possible damage to themselves from the significant EM pulses, which in this case, considering there were about to be hundreds of them seconds apart, was a very wise move.

When they jumped back from hyperspace minutes later, Taurus-C wasn't visible any longer. A roughly spherical shell of dust and debris completely hid the world below. Meantime, the battleships, heavy cruisers, and light cruisers opened fire on the remaining small fleet that had once been the pride of Taurus-C. Frantically, the unskilled men, which the Master had given to these ships, tried to counter-fire, but many of their systems failed to work, knocked out by the many EM pulses. Engines failed to function. One by one, they were destroyed.

With the ships eliminated, Admiral Alister turned the matter over to General Felix and his two divisions. "Radiation suits," the general ordered. "Recon Battalions go!" A number of transports deployed in formations from the two battleships. They were followed by an infantry regiment from each of the two divisions using twice as many transports. During the next hour, more transports came and went, ferrying the remaining pair of regiments of infantry down to the surface. Finally an hour after that, the remaining battalions finally landed.

The infantry's orders were simple. If it's alive, shoot it. It didn't matter that their targets were unarmed, dazed, and confused innocent men, women, and children. By nightfall, the few survivors of the nuke attack had also been eliminated, and the two divisions returned to their battleships. In the minds of Admiral Alister and General Felix, they had delivered a devastating blow to the Master, wiping out his known base of operations. In actual fact, they had done little more than execute a genocide attack on around six billion people, for only a few of the Master's men were still planet-side. Towing the two crippled battleships, they headed for home, albeit slowly.

While the Galactic News carried the sound defeat of the Master's forces on Taurus-C, praising their valiant men, the average person didn't see it that way. Rather, they saw an entire world destroyed, genocide of a corporation planet, though the vast majority had no idea where this world was located, just somewhere on the rim. Thus during the weeks after the attack, the biggest result was a rapid, enormous escalation of hatred against the corporations.

"How could they do that?" was the most frequent comment heard on many worlds, including the remaining worlds of the Abelard Sector.

The very next day, Alfonso received many calls from corporate executives on Gemma-D, Bellatrix-B, Zeno-C, and a number of other smaller populated nearby worlds, all demanding a meeting and soon. It was obvious to these rim rulers that their superiors in the mid-arm headquarters were not protecting them, that mere contact with the Master meant utter annihilation of their world. Alfonso was certain some of these executives were panic-stricken, while asking, demanding, and begging for a sector-wide meeting. Alfonso hastily agreed and arranged for the meeting at GD headquarters, issuing orders to his staff to prepare for it within two days. He hoped in the brief interim, he would receive some form of apology from Corporate Prime. He received none, but then Alfonso wasn't surprised by that. Thus far, he'd received virtually no communication or support or advice from those higher up in the GD corporate hierarchy.

"So what are we going to do now?" wailed one executive. Some one hundred top men who ran these more heavily populated worlds of the Abelard Sector gathered in GD's auditorium. Alfonso and the other Scorpi-C corporation temporary executives, who had been locally appointed to run their corporations after their top executives had long ago fled Scorpi-C, sat behind tables on the stage, looking out at these very frightened men.

"Yes, it's obvious we'll be targeted next, since the Master landed on our world," one from Zeno-C pointed out.

"How could they just destroy an entire world? Taurus-C has always been a loyal corporation world," another asked.

"We've not heard anything back from our bosses either," yet another top GD exec from Bellatrix-B declared. "Has any of you heard from your mid-arm bosses or even from Corporate Prime?"

No's and head nods uniformly indicated that none here had, a most sobering affirmation that they were on their own. "So what do we do?" the original man asked again.

Alfonso decided to speak up and get this meeting going

somewhere, for or against him. "Gentlemen, what can we do? Simple. We can defend ourselves. Here's how. Already, several of your worlds have sent your space fleet here to Scorpi-C to avoid the Master stealing them as he did on Taurus-C. One: everyone sends their space fleet here. We join all of our fleets together. Had that been done at Taurus-C, we would have outnumbered those that Corporation Prime sent to destroy them. Then, when Corporate Prime sends them out to one of your worlds, you simply notify us, and the entire combined fleet will came racing to your world to blast them out of the skies. Your planetary defense shields can hold them off long enough for the combined fleet to get to any of the worlds in this sector. United, we can be strong."

"Two: we build up our own defensive infantry divisions. We major worlds have one infantry division with us, but as some of you have heard, here on Scorpi-C, we have added two voluntary infantry divisions made up of local men and women who want to protect their homes. We could have more, but we are out of weapons, ammunition, and such supplies for them," Alfonso explained, knowing what many of these men would ask immediately. He wasn't surprised.

"But how? No one would join up on Bellatrix-B," one asked immediately.

"Glad you asked that," Alfonso replied. He then outlined his gigantic change in corporate policy, namely allowing those who were renting their homes and properties from the corporations to own theirs outright. He spent a half hour outlining what had been done here and the results. "So you see, when a man owns his own home, he will fight to the death to protect it, quite unlike the way he felt when the corporations owned everything but the clothes on his back."

"But that's treason against the corporations!" one man yelled.

"Hey, I say it's treason what the corporations did to the people of Taurus-C," Alfonso fired back. "Look, you can go back to your worlds, do nothing, and wait for Corporate Prime to send their forces back to wipe you out because the Master visited your world or you can stand up for your rights and perhaps lives. I don't care; it's your choice. We've made ours."

322

"Look, if we all stand together here in the Abelard Sector, we have a fighting chance of getting Corporate Prime to see reason. If we don't, one by one, we will all become another Taurus-C. The only other choice we have is to pick up and flee. We six billion on Scorpi-C have nowhere to flee to, so we are staying and fighting," Alfonso finished up. *Now let them make their own choices.*

Several men began asking for more details on just how they went about the process of allowing people to own their homes and properties. Alfonso let Diego explain the details, since he'd been overseeing that gigantic project. Diego added, "The morale of our people soared after they saw they now owned their own homes. I can't begin to tell you the difference that has made here. If we have to fight, we'll have many very determined men and women taking up arms. So you can wait around, and hope and pray that Corporate Prime comes to its senses, or you can get yourselves in the best defensive position that you can."

When the meeting finally broke up, all decided to pool their fleets, as long as Alfonso swore to send it to their defense should they be attacked. More than half decided to give Alfonso's ideas a try. The rest decided to wait and see how it worked out with the others, hoping they still had time before doom came to the entire sector.

***

The Master wasn't idle nor ever had been. "Always plan two steps ahead of the corporations, Tao," he once explained to his best Second. Thus, when the long anticipated retaliation came to his one-time base on Taurus-C, the Master's main force was long gone. True, he left some recent volunteers and converts behind, believing that they were holding onto to Taurus-C, but he'd already gotten everything he wanted from that world. The space fleet was just a decoy. He did not intend to wage a space fleet war. That would have been an exercise in futility. He had no trained men to run them. While he was able to *capture* them, he had no way actually to replace their crew members with his own. Those that he did man up were so poorly run that it was a wonder they even got a shot off when the time came for battle.

No, he'd made excellent use of the fabrication machines on Taurus-C, churning out substantial duplicate copies of the stolen genetic bio agents from Rho-C. He acquired, that is, stole, PDS and PIS devices for nearly all his personnel, that is, Personal Defense Shields and Personal Invisibility Shields. He had also obtained many more solid recruits, men and particularly women who wanted to bring down the corporations. It was these who had fled Taurus-C days before the anticipated assault actually came, thanks to one of his spies who was watching the military bases on Corporate Prime and alerted him to their sudden activity.

Purposely, he made sure these new recruits heard the Galactic News coverage of the genocide of their home world, Taurus-C, knowing this inflamed their hatred to a fevered pitch, which is precisely what he needed for the next phase in his grand plan: female suicide attackers. When the victorious fleet arrived back on Corporate Prime, dozens of the Master's invisible bombers slipped onto the three battleships, ignoring the two badly damaged ones. Besides, two of these carried over twenty thousand infantry each. His female attackers, invisible via their PIS and wearing their PDS to protect them made their way to their specific locations within the ship and opened the valves on the cylinders strapped to their bodies. Then, they proceeded to walk back out of the ships, leaving a trail of the nasty gas as they went. The Master had chosen the same bio agent that he'd used on the space station.

Eventually, bio containment alarms sounded; bulkhead doors sealed, but such was too little, too late. All but six of the women made it off the ships, where they were given the proper injection to prevent the secondary genetic mutation now in their blood streams from activating. Onboard the ships, male crewmen and infantry simply passed out and died within minutes of the exposure, while the women underwent the first genetic mutation as had those on the space station, namely modifications to their hair and feet. The women fell into eighteen-hour comas. A day after they awoke, they fell into a three-day coma during which their bodies completed the UFB woman genetic modifications. Thus, those who had committed the atrocity on Taurus-C were themselves eliminated or turned into UFB women.

Meanwhile, the male volunteers, all fired up from the genocide of their home world, headed out onto Corporate Prime, vowing to carry out their revenge attacks. Here, the Master had little intelligence upon which to direct his attackers. Instead, he replied upon these men being able to think on their feet and find what was needed for maximum attack effectiveness, though he didn't phrase it that way. "Men, your task is to slip into your assigned building and find their main air recycling center. Empty your cylinders into the air intake lines." Given that each of these men would be invisible (wearing a PIS), they had a high chance of success, the Master reasoned, just not much of a chance of staying alive. Barely a quarter of these men survived their own attack, but to a man, they died believing in the justness of their cause, which should be considered when judging them.

The result was rather dramatic. Corporation Prime was home to close to a hundred billion people. The attack on the fleet wiped out close to sixty thousand military personnel. The attacks on the corporation headquarters wiped out well over a hundred thousand, the top and key leaders of all the corporations. However, some twenty thousand new UFB women survived. In time, greedy lower level bureaucrats gave these helpless women new homes. More importantly, the Master had eliminated many of the new super IQ men who had just begun to take over key corporate positions. Much later, many realized the Master had to have acted when he did, because if those super IQ men had been given another twenty years to get their new programs implemented, the Master might well have failed utterly with his plans.

Yet, the Master wasn't finished, not by a long shot. In the ensuing chaos, his men, disguised as some of the thousands of rescue personnel, infiltrated these buildings, and confiscated more of the different genetic bio agents the corporations had on stock and used their own fabrication machines to make more of the terrible bio agents! A week later amid the total confusion on Corporate Prime, the Master and his band quietly lifted off from that world. He truly wanted to have wiped them all out, but simply lacked the means at this time. What he needed technology-wise didn't exist just yet, unlike the ancient days, the Dark Ages as noted by some historians.

Two weeks after the slaughter on Taurus-C, word finally reached those on the rim of the vicious and deadly terrorist attacks on Corporate Prime. Many cheered when they heard the military forces that had wiped out Taurus-C had been themselves wiped out by the Master's forces. Others cheered to hear that all the corporation headquarters had also been wiped out as well.

***

Alis again sent a lengthy burst of electronic data and waited patiently for the reply. When it came, she smiled; her request and arguments had been validated. She headed to meet privately with Alfonso. She needed this new MK50 his people were developing.

"Ah, Alis, just in time to watch our latest demo test firing," Alfonso greeted her. She'd found him paying a visit to one of his research labs, where Major Hank Feldspar, Jr. and his new bride, Gunnery Sergeant Martha Spelling-Feldspar, were preparing their latest test of the new MK50 assault gun. With them were the designer, Bill Franks and his new bride and constructor of the gun, Captain Bess Fontana-Franks. Alicia, as always, was there, assisting Alfonso. "This promises to revolutionize our defenses. Major, care to explain this test for Alis?"

"Certainly, boss. The dummy target yonder," he nodded towards the distant human-like torso, since he no longer had arms, "is wearing a PDS that is activated. You can see it there on the dummy's chest. The green light indicates it is armed and active."

Alis interrupted, "Isn't the dummy also wearing standard field armor?"

"Yes, good eye. This is to be the ultimate test of our new MK50, simulating battlefield conditions, where the assault troops are heavily armored and are wearing the PDS for maximum protection. Now Martha here is holding the prototype that Captain Bess has assembled, using the base of the usual MK42. The objective is to eliminate yonder dummy soldier with a single shot from the MK50. Bill?" he turned the explanation over to the gun's designer and his longtime friend, equally helpless, both now being UFBMD men.

Bill continued the explanation for Alis. "You see, we can't depend upon two shots to take the enemy out. Under combat conditions, who knows where the target would move to or what defensive actions he could take between shots. So my invention here will have to first take out the PDS long enough for the maximum penetration round to tear through the armor and eliminate the human wearing it. That's done by the unique shell that is being fired, the heart of the gun. Its tip is a maximum energy dispersal system. Its job is to overload the defense shield at the tiny point of impact for approximately a millisecond, long enough for the second half of the depleted uranium round to go on through the shield at that precise point of impact. Fired from this new MK50, which by the way has twice the kickback of the MK42 Martha claims, that round will go through any known personal body armor. Further, the head is designed to splatter into many smaller fragments upon armor penetration, thus tearing up the human body as it passes through it, creating a severe or deadly wound."

Bess added, "Since we don't yet know its full penetration power, I'm erring on the side of caution. That's why we have a standard lab test-firing bin immediately behind the dummy. Hopefully, if the fragments go through the dummy, they will be captured by the water tank. Safety first."

"Hey guys, enough talk. Let's do this!" Martha broke in impatiently. The gun was as large as her Gertrude, her MK42. She had continued to work out trying desperately to regain the arm muscles that she used to have prior to her genetic modification. Unfortunately, try as she might, her new body simply refused to add more muscles to her arms, though what muscles were there had strengthened considerably.

"Okay, okay," Hank said. "Firing one round."

Blam! Martha squeezed off the round, jerking back hard from the terrific recoil this new model had, more than twice the kick of Gertrude. The results were almost impossible to see, beyond a flash of light and a four-inch hole in the body armor, a mass of flying dummy internal stuffing, and a wave of water splashing out of the backup tank behind the dummy. However, Bess had installed a high speed camera, and after the exclamations, she played the video in slow motion.

All watched as the tip struck the defense shield with a blinding flash of energy, temporarily lowering the shield at that precise point, allowing the main body of the shell to pass through the shield. It literally tore through the body armor as though it was made of butter. The many fragments then tore a gaping hole through the simulated human torso, with most fragments flying out the backside into the water tank, but with such force that a good deal of water splashed out in a pretty, slow moving wall of water.

"Wow! Incredible. It works perfectly, Bill!" Martha exclaimed. "I need one of these with a whole lot of ammo! How about an automatic feed system too?" she suggested, thinking far ahead. Right now, she'd have to reload if she needed to fire it again.

"Working on that now," Bill replied. "That's the easy part, if Bess can do it."

Bess smiled, "If you can design it, I can build it." The construction side of this woman came to the fore once more.

Alfonso spoke up. "Okay, get it to the munitions makers as soon as possible. If we can arm our forces with these, then if we're invaded, we stand an excellent chance against the corporation's assault troops." Four very pleased inventors agreed wholeheartedly.

"Boss, I need to speak to you in private," Alis then said. After everyone stepped out of the lab giving them privacy, she explained. "The Master simply must be stopped. This new gun is the answer we need. If you can give me one of these, I will search the entire galaxy until I find him and eliminate this beast, hopefully before he can harm more people."

"But he controls minds. You won't have a chance," Alfonso protested.

"Boss, I believe I have a way to do it even if he tried to control my mind. Trust me on this one," Alis replied.

"Alis, your counsels have been invaluable to me, brilliant beyond belief. All right then, we both agree this madman must be stopped. The damage he's done is likely irreparable. Still, he has to be stopped, but I'm not sending you on this suicide mission alone."

Alis wanted to protest having to bring others along, but she also knew Alfonso well. His sense of honor wouldn't allow him to send her out on this extremely dangerous mission alone. "Acceptable, but let's keep them to a minimum."

Alfonso thought for a moment. "Martha goes. She'd the gunnery expert. Hank won't let her go alone. Bill and Bess should come in case the gun needs some adjustments. It has not been field-tested, and a thousand things could go wrong with it. Best have some along who can respond to such problems. Hell, Jason is going to demand to go as well. You might need some diversionary explosions. Take Linda. Those two can't be parted; besides, she's one heck of a good galactic navigator. She should be graduating with her degree this year. You need some backup. The best I have are Armando and J. D. Take them too so you will have an ex-Special Forces man and a sharpshooter. Wait, Jackie and Melissa will insist they come along too and pilot for you. That will make a good crew, Alis, the best I can offer you at the moment."

"Accepted. We can leave once their gun goes into production," Alis agreed. While she certainly didn't want all these people tagging along with her, complicating matters, she knew she couldn't refuse Alfonso. Besides, these men and women were highly motivated and would likely be insisting they come anyway, once they heard of her mission. Besides, she thought, this might help raise the self-confidence of Jackie, Melissa, Linda, Jason, Bill, and Hank, who truly needed a big confidence boost this may give them.

Alfonso added, "I'll let you take one of the new, modified deep space transports that GD is developing so that the UFB women and UFBMD men can operate them effectively. That will lessen the burden you have with those six. Will this be acceptable?"

"Yes, as long as the ship has a good defense shield and cloaking capabilities," Alis replied.

"Good. I'll arrange a meeting tonight with all them. Good hunting, Alis. I'm afraid if you get into trouble, there isn't going to be much I can do to help out," Alfonso tried one last time to dissuade her from this likely suicide mission.

"I knew that before I even suggested it," she replied with a wry smile.

That night, Alis looked out at the ten who had come to hear what this secret mission was all about. She looked at the six with their knee length, wavy hair, silver, fiery red, black, and brown—three UFB women, three UFBMD men—their faces eager and pleased. Jackie spoke up, "Thanks for having us along. So what's this exciting mission all about?"

"Thank you all for coming. After I tell you, each of you will have the opportunity to decline this mission. No one will think less of you if you don't wish to participate. That said, the mission is a simple one, thanks to this new assault gun of Bill's. We are going after the Master and take him out using this new MK50."

"All right! Count me in!" declared Martha, very eager to make good use of the new improved Gertrude. She had already decided to call it Gertrude II. A chorus of "me too's" echoed from each of the others.

"Hey, we're your pilots," Jackie broke in, adding, "and Linda's your navigator."

"Of course," Alis regained control of her meeting. "Here are your assigned posts on this venture. Hank and Bill, your job is to keep the guns working. If anything goes wrong with them, you fix them, via Bess. Martha, you and I will get the first shots off, if possible. Armando, J. D. your job is to provide whatever covering fire we need in order to get our chance to eliminate the Master. Jason, you are our backup. If we hit trouble, I'm counting on you to make something go boom for us. Jackie and Melissa will be our pilots. Linda, besides navigating, I need you to monitor the comm center and coordinate us five when we leave the transport."

"How do we find him? That seems to me to be the biggest problem we're facing at the start," asked Armando.

"Yes, it is. We know he was on Corporate Prime in the hub of the galaxy. So we start there. This could well be a lengthy voyage, but we're not coming home until the job is done. The Master must be stopped and hopefully before he destroys the lives of many more people." They chatted a bit longer before breaking up. No one wanted out of this mission, but then Alis didn't expect that they would.

The group spent the next week fixing up their new GD transport. Its pilot and navigator controls up front had been modified and lowered so that the UFB women could handle everything with their feet. Similarly, the comm center had been modified for Linda's use. The galley now had tables of two heights, a lower one that made using feet for such chores far easier. All the doorknobs had been replaced with latches that could be worked by feet as well as hands. In fact, there wasn't any place on the ship where the six could not go or accidentally become trapped inside and unable to get out on their own. Alfonso was definitely looking ahead to the future.

They stockpiled food supplies to last them for two months. Besides all the normal weapons, armor, and defense devices, they brought along three of the new MK50 assault guns, as well as a large box of the special ammo for them. In addition, Alis added an IR scanner and a complete military IMU, Individual Monitoring Unit, for each of them. When worn, Linda could monitor their exact location from her position at the comm center, communicate directly to them from the ship, and capture the live streaming video coming from each set. Plus, each could communicate to each other directly. Alis was taking no chances. She wanted every possible advantage she could devise; figuring with the Master, she'd need it.

Chapter 20—Strikes and Chaos

The Master's strategy became apparent even as soon as two weeks after his surgical strike on Corporate Prime. When fighting a vicious snake, cut its head off and the body merely writhes harmlessly about until dead. By eliminating all the top leaders and their support personnel at all the major corporation headquarters, the head of the snake was gone. The many other bureaucrats of Corporate Prime existed solely to service these top several thousand leaders and their military wing. Now leaderless, they simply continued to do what they'd always done, schedule shipments and the like, presuming soon someone would replace those who were lost.

Those top leaders on Corporate Prime handled long-range planning, establishment of new worlds, fabricating the laws of the galaxy, and the growth and profit of their vast corporations whose offices and plants were far flung throughout the galaxy. Hardly a civilized world did not have a local GD corporation plant or office, likewise with most all the major corporations. However, one head office at the heart of the galaxy could not possibly hope to administrate over thousands of subsidiaries, so they'd established mid-level headquarters, one in each of the galactic sectors of the hub and mid-arm regions. These in turn oversaw all the local branch offices on the thousands of worlds.

The Master had already eliminated the mid-arm headquarters that oversaw the Abelard rim sector. Thus, Alfonso and the other local executives had no one above them, no one to go to for guidance, aid, or advice. They were on their own, as Alfonso continued to drill into their heads whenever these off-world executives met.

Confusion and chaos followed, almost at once when Corporate Prime ceased to function. Now the middle level of corporate management had to act, to step up, and fill the vacant shoes of their own bosses. While some attempted to act as though nothing in the galaxy had changed, many others saw this as a golden opportunity for advancement. Some issued their own unilateral decisions to their lower branch offices, while others headed off to Corporate Prime to attempt to take over the top reins of the entire corporation. Exec versus exec became the game being played out among the millions upon millions of bureaucrats there at the heart of the galaxy. Assassinations became commonplace three weeks after the Master's strike.

However, the Master wasn't finished, not by a long shot. His plans were bearing fruit, just as he had long ago foreseen. His goal was and continued to be the elimination of the corporations' rule of the galaxy, which many individuals saw as a good thing, considering how corrupt, unethical, and greedy these corporations had become, believing they were somehow the gods of the universe. With the head of the snake now gone, the Master set out on the next to last phase of his grand plan, the elimination of many of the mid-level headquarters and their staff, particularly the super IQ new executives, who could well concoct ways and means to defeat him. Those men were the only ones he feared, but only because of their uncanny ability to solve problems swiftly and decisively.

Thus, his next move was against the four hub worlds that housed the sector headquarters of the mid-level corporations. Five weeks after his attack on Corporate Prime, he'd wiped these four out using the same exact tactics that he had used on Corporate Prime, leaving more chaos and confusion in his wake. A few more of the key mid-arm mid-level headquarters had to go before he could make his final rise to power as the Emperor of the Galaxy, his ultimate goal, the sole ruler of the entire galaxy or at least that portion the was the Galactic Federation.

***

Three of the new electrostatic hair machines were loaded onto the Nueva Estrella, the name they gave their new deep space transport, new in many ways, not the least because it was operable by the UFB women and UFBMD men. Alis looked at her enthusiastic crew. They'd gathered in the cargo hold by the ramp, taking one last look at their spaceport before departure and any final words that Alis had to say. She saw a sea of long wavy hair, as well as their bright faces. "Okay, let's do this," Alis said.

"Ah, no cool speeches?" Martha jested, "Like go smash'em boys or shoot'em dead." Several chuckled.

"No, but do you need that?" Alis asked pretending to be dead serious. That cracked them all up. "Let's get underway, pilots."

"Aye, aye captain," Jackie said jovially. Tossing her fiery red hair about, she headed up to the pilot's seat, followed by Melissa. Of course, these six had to move both slowly and carefully to avoid unsightly wobbling to keep their balance or even take a nasty spill on the unforgiving metal of the ship.

"Where to?" asked Linda, assuming her new role as galactic navigator.

"Hub sector for now. Once there, start monitoring hub broadcasts," Alis advised, and headed for her chart room. Meanwhile, Martha, Armando, and D. J. made a thorough recheck of their guns, particularly the three MK50's. Satisfied, they headed to their quarters to relax. This promised to be a long, boring trip until they actually found the Master somewhere. On the other hand, Bill continued to work on his giant version of his new gun, one that could be used to punch a hole in a planetary defense shield, allowing some form of bomb to go on through.

Bess helped Jason lay down on his bunk. "Have you heard the good news?" he asked her. She hadn't. "Linda is pregnant. I'm going to be a father." He sighed, "But I don't know how I can be much of one though, not as I am."

"Oh, I shouldn't worry about that, Jason. Just make sure you teach him or her the safety rules. Let's not have any explosions wiping out our house," she teased him. Both chuckled, and she commented, "I think we're going to be really bored for quite a while."

Jason added, "Yep. Jackie and Melissa are also pregnant too. Nine months from now should be interesting. I wonder if our child will have Linda's incredible silver hair or if Jackie's will have her fiery red hair. I rather hope so." The two chatted idly.

Alis looked over her charts. Unlike the others with her,

she'd been all over the galaxy at one time or other, though even Alfonso didn't know that. Her first task was to figure out where the Master was and then get to him in time. He'd been at Corporate Prime in the hub of the galaxy, but he certainly wasn't there now. Just where was he? Alis concluded she was going to have to work out what the Master's plan must be, and set herself that task. There were an enormous number of possibilities though.

Hours later, Linda called her to the comm center. "Captain, I've just tapped into some hub broadcasts. He'd wiped out the headquarters on Haclion-3, Diggory-C, Abel-D, and 9-Cygnus-D. Same M. O."

"Okay, so he's still somewhere in the hub. I'll relay some coordinates to Melissa now," Alis replied. After doing that, she went back to her chart room to ponder this new data. So he was continuing down the same path. What was the significance of these four, she wondered. Then, it struck her that these were the four mid-level hub headquarters, overseeing all the other local hub offices. Would he be then going after the smaller local offices or fan out to other mid-arm mid-level headquarters? That depended upon the Master's plan, assuming he was following a plan of some kind and not just acting spontaneously. No, Alis tossed that one out, for everything the Master had done to date had been very carefully arranged. Nothing was left to chance.

Days turned into weeks, as they followed in the wake of the Master's carnage. At least Linda was able to keep them abreast of the Galactic News and that wasn't good. It seemed at all corners, the corporations' vice grip on the galaxy was crumbling, leaving power-hungry mid-level men fighting each other for control of larger portions of their corporation than they once had.

Furthermore, by now word had begun to reach the mid-arm worlds about what had been happening in the Abelard Sector, namely that the corporations there had given ownership of the once corporate-owned properties and homes to their renters, turning them into home and small business owners. That further fueled open rebellion on many other worlds, where the long suppressed general population began demanding their local corporation headquarters executives do the same thing on their world.

Meantime, Linda finally heard of another attack by the Master, this time on a mid-arm world, 6-Gamma-C. At once, Alis set course for that system, realizing that the information Linda had was days old. Surely, the Master would be long gone by now. That was the case when they arrived in that system. Look, Alis thought, at this rate, we will be constantly following at least a week behind him. We will never catch him this way. I must find a way to predict where he will strike next and get there before him.

Alis wisely decided the Master must be following some predefined plan, some schedule of which worlds to strike. There had to be a definite reason behind each attack. If they were indeed merely randomly chosen, then she had no hope of catching up with him. That was a self-defeating path. No, there had to be some overall plan that she wasn't seeing. Hence, she began to review every known action the Master had taken since he first emerged on the scene. Her mind raced through the data while her hands brought up her 3-d galactic model, highlighting in red the known worlds he'd struck. Soon, she had them all glowing and sat back to examine the pattern, but just didn't see one.

Linda interrupted her. "Captain, I've picked up chat among a number of world leaders. It seems that they want to get rid of their many UFB women and UFBMD men, claiming they are too helpless to continue to support indefinitely. This is scary."

"Give Alfonso a call and tell him this bad news. Suggest that he contact these worlds and accept them on Scorpi-C," Alis advised, suspecting that Alfonso would take her advice. She put her attention back on trying to find the pattern. Over supper, she complained, "I sure can't see any pattern with the worlds that he's attacked."

"Maybe it isn't a geographical one," Linda suggested.

That took Alis by surprise. Yes, she'd been looking for some logical, physical location pattern to his attacks, which yielded nothing. What other pattern could there be? Then, it struck her, the Master was obviously trying to destroy the corporations' grip on the galaxy. She headed back to her chartroom to think this one through. Was there a pattern along these lines? Her mind raced and then it clicked! "Eureka," she exclaimed, having figured out just what the Master's plan had been all along.

"He's been systematically cutting off the head of the snake or snakes, the corporate leaders," Alis explained to her crew, whom she gathered for a quick pep talk meeting. She wanted them to know her reasoning as well. "He began with Taurus-C, a remote world at the rim of the galaxy. Why? He knew darn well that soon his initial base on Rho-C would be attacked and wiped out by the corporations. On Taurus-C, he got access to fabrication machines and made many more duplicates of his genetic bio agents. Then, after raiding other nearby worlds and wreaking sufficient havoc to encourage these worlds to rebel against their corporation overseers, he moved on, taking out their immediate mid-level headquarters, denying worlds like Scorpi-C any assistance, advice, or aid. Then, he struck at the heart of the corporations, wiping out all the top level executives on Corporation Prime. Cut the head of the snake off. Now the snake is writhing, creating chaos among many worlds. Next, he's taken out several key hub and mid-arm worlds, which are the next most powerful headquarters."

"Looking over the relative influence and power that the remaining mid-level corporate worlds have, my guess is that he will be going after three other worlds next. No telling which though, so we're choosing one and will go there and wait for him," Alis explained. "Linda, set course for 3-Scutum-D. He should strike there. I just hope we get there before he does."

"Brilliant, captain!" Linda gushed. "On it!" Relief shone on all their faces. Now they had an explanation for the Master's strikes. None knew if it was the right one, only that it fit the facts and seemed reasonable.

Two days later, they arrived in orbit above this mid-arm world. "Too late," Linda called out from the comm center. "He struck here yesterday."

"Okay, set course for Kingston-B. Top speed," Alis ordered, checking one of the three off her list. She had predicted right and felt the noose was closing in on their prey.

They arrived above this world the following day. Kingston was a small reddish star, hence the habitable world was fairly close in, compared to yellow main sequence stars, Linda explained to her friends, who gaped out the bay windows at the dull red sun.

Now the question was how to get at the Master when he showed up. Alis was confident that he would, just not when, hours from now or days. He was sure to come, if her analysis was accurate and her intelligence on the power wielded by the corporate executives here was correct. For now, the Nueva Estrella remained cloaked and silent, like a cat for its unsuspecting prey.

Alis ordered Linda to begin monitoring all spaceport communications. "What am I looking for specifically?" Linda asked.

"The Master modifies people's minds. So look for a controller challenging a ship or person and then for no apparent reason suddenly allowing them to land or something," Alis suggested. "Strange patterns of response might be our clues."

The next morning, Linda summoned Alis to the comm center. "I think I got something. A group of ten deep space transports requested landing permission, claiming to be from a rim world. They were denied it at first, but then the controller allowed them to land. Let me replay that exchange." She hit a button, and the brief exchange played back. "So what do you think? This them?" Linda asked, rather excited.

"I think so. Let's follow their landing pattern. We'll stay cloaked and see if we can stay close to them and not raise any alarms," Alis advised, heading to the front to help, if Jackie and Melissa couldn't handle such a delicate operation. She need not have worried.

"On it, moving into close proximity of the rear ship now," Jackie said, gently moving the flight stick with her feet, while Melissa used her feet to adjust their sub-light speed, matching that of the descending ship. Jackie got in close and tight. If ground control was using radar to track the ships, they weren't likely to be able to separate the two! As the ground loomed up, Jackie had to adjust a little. She couldn't land on top of the other ship. Gently, she sat the Nueva Estrella down barely ten feet from the rear of the tenth ship in this group.

Now the group watched from all available windows. Soon, they spotted the port's customs man walking out to meet the new arrivals. Bingo. A man dressed in black and wearing the familiar black felt top hat stepped out. Linda was on top of the situation, engaging an outside microphone and amplifying its signal. They heard the Master exchange words with the customs man, who repeated the words that the Master told him.

"Yes. Just a small group of rim traders. Ten credits to land for a day. Thank you," the man repeated in a monotone. Then, he added, "Public transportation is just beyond the main terminal. No need to scan your ID cards. Move along." He accepted the credits and left them, returning to the control tower.

As the eleven watched, the Master's men and women began disembarking. From the way that they walked and from the bulges beneath their clothing, Alis suspected they were carrying more of the genetic bio agent and were about to launch another terrorist attack. Decision time.

Alis realized that they could hop out now, guns blazing and perhaps stop them from carrying out this terrorist attack. However, there were just too many in this group. She counted at least fifty men and women heading off into town, far too many to handle. Alas, she knew that they simply had no way to stop this attack from occurring. Worse, the spaceport security guards were heavily patrolling the area not far from them. They'd have to defend against those men as well as fight the Master's crew. Best bide their time.

"Jason, we're going to need a diversion here. We need to get the spaceport security guards away from here while we go after the Master," Alis explained. He was looking out the bay window.

"Thinking on it. My thoughts exactly. It needs to be far enough from here so that the Master does not get worried either," Jason thought aloud. "A nice boom way on the other side of the tower should do the trick. Needs to be triggered from here when we want it. Probably should be several independent ones as well. Okay, give us a few minutes." Jason headed off to direct Bess on what needed to be done.

When the Master and the few men still here went back into one of the transports, Alis acted, lowering their bay ramp. Hastily, she got out, put a tracking beacon on his ship, and darted back inside, all while she was invisible. After the door closed, she made sure that no one noticed anything or heard her. None apparently had.

Meanwhile everyone else made their last minute preparations. Alis ducked inside her quarters with one of the new MK50 assault guns. She figured that when the firefight came, the Master would attempt to control their minds, preventing them from firing at him. Hence, she hastily added a failsafe factor, a small program that she could activate if that happened. Satisfied that this would work, she headed out, joining the others. Bess had several sacks slung over her shoulder, along with several ordinary blasters and guns with silencers on them. Extra ammo clips were strapped across her chest. Jason sat on the floor, his feet ready to flip the switches, firing off the charges that Bess would be setting in place.

Martha carried the second of the new MK50 guns, but also had three other guns on her. J. D. carried the third Mk50, while Armando was armed with five different guns, including a grenade launcher. "Are we ready?" Alis asked. Everyone was.

"Okay, listen up. Those of you remaining on the ship, if this goes south, I want you to take off and leave us behind," Alis ordered.

"We can't do that!" protested Jackie.

"Look, if this goes south, I will give you a direct order to take off, and I mean it, you take off. Live to try again another day," Alis insisted, getting them to promise to do so. She ordered, "Bess will take off first. Once she gets back with the charges laid, then we'll take action." She opened the bay doors, and Bess scampered off. Her PDS was activated as was her PIS, so no one saw her moving around the spaceport. However, Linda monitored her live video stream, letting everyone know where she was as the minutes passed. At least the Master was still inside his ship.

Fifteen anxious minutes passed before Bess returned,

having laid six charges where they could cause confusion, but not damage anything. "All set, Jason," she whispered. "So how do we get the Master out of his ship?"

"Here's how," Alis took charge. "We deploy our fire power here and here," she pointed out five locations from which they would take anyone around the Master's ship in a crossfire. Once we get into position as verified by Linda and our video stream, then Jason, you fire off one of the charges. That will get the security guard's attention and hopefully the Master will come out to see what's going on. We get him. Jason, keep on with the charges. Your job is to keep the guards away from us. Let's move out. Linda, let us know when everyone is ready."

Five invisible forms slipped down the ramp and headed to their assigned positions. Yes, seeing the open bay and insides of the ship without the rest of the transport visible was more than a bit strange. Now they waited. Alis had purposely taken up the position farthest from their ship. If this went south, she wanted the others to be able to get away in a hurry.

Boom! The first of Jason's charges went off, followed by spaceport sirens. As expected, it brought five men out of the Master's transport, including him. "Now," Alis whispered. Three MK50's and two blasters fired at the five men. Unfortunately, the Master was protected by one of his men whose body blocked their shots. All were wearing PDS, so only three went down, proving the effectiveness of the new weapon. Boom! Boom! Two more charges went off. Two more men rushed out of the master's ship, while four poured out of the other ships, firing in the general direction of the five, the flashes from their guns giving away their positions somewhat.

"Put your guns down. We won't harm you," the Master's soothing voice spoke to towards the five. He wasn't fast enough to keep the others from firing again, this time with more effectiveness, since the newcomers were not wearing PDS shields. They dropped like rocks. Guns fired back at the five, their PDS shields glowing as they absorbed the blaster hits. Armando and J. D. were very effective, dropping the rest of the Master's men, leaving him standing there, top hat and all, looking their way.

Now his voice struck their minds. One by one, Alis saw them dropping their weapons. Boom! Boom! Boom! She heard the last of the bombs going off and knew that Jason was doing his best to keep the security guards from interfering, but that he'd run out of charges. Any second now, they would come charging around the control tower, their guns blazing. "Turn off your defense shields and your invisibility devices," the Master's voice ordered. One by one, Armando, D. J., Bess, and Martha obeyed and stood like statues awaiting his next order. Though Alis fought hard to keep from doing it, she too turned off her two devices.

"Guards are coming!" Jason's voice screamed in their ears, but the five simply could not move, merely awaiting the Master's next command to them.

"Halt!" Alis heard a man yelling from far behind them, probably a security guard.

Quickly, the Master drew his own gun and aimed it in the general direction of the five, uncertain who to shoot first. The edgy security guards then opened fire on them, but fired wildly as they came running towards the small battlefield.

"I order you all to leave now!" Alis barked loudly, suddenly pulling the Master's attention onto her. He figured that she must be the one in charge and fired at her, a slug slamming into her as bullets from the wildly firing guards began ricocheting about everyone else. "Go! Go!" Alis ordered, as a number of security guards began to close in on them. Her command broke the Master's spell over the four. One glance at the fifty men running towards them convinced the four to race into the transport, all assuming that Alis was right behind them.

But she wasn't. Using the unfailing power of his voice, the Master told her, "Drop your weapon and surrender to these security guards." In a flash, she saw what he intended to do: he would use his hypnotic powers to convince the guards that Alis was some mad bomber and to shoot her, that she'd killed his men. The Master smiled at Alis, knowing from the contact with her mind that she understood his command and saw her hands starting to lower the huge MK50, and was supremely confident that he had once more total control over the humans around him, just as he always had.

That was the key triggering mechanism that Alis had installed back in her quarters on the transport. As her hands began involuntarily lowering, the special programming kicked in. Blam! She fired a direct shot at the Master. A bright flash of light caused her to blink, as the tip did its job, creating a millisecond hole in his defense shield, through which the depleted uranium back half of the bullet flew, ripping the Master's heart to shreds, killing him.

Instantly, his spell over everyone vanished. Too late for Alis. With so many guards within mere feet of the gaping hole of the invisible transport, D. J. had no choice but to slam his hand on the Close button, while Jackie hit the hyperspace jump button. The transport truly vanished, jumping into hyperspace as it picked up speed, but leaving the wounded Alis on the tarmac.

Alis had mere seconds to act, and act she did. With near super-human speed, she bolted into the Master's now empty transport, hitting the Close button as she ran to the pilot's seat. She didn't even sit down, but rapidly fired up the transport in but seconds, slamming it into hyperspace as well, just as a dozen guards reached the closing doors, pounding on them, and a few shooting their blasters at it, tearing a hole in its side, just as it vanished into hyperspace.

With the air seeping out rapidly, Alis raced back and slammed a cabin door shut, sealing the air leak somewhat, enough for some time at least. Then, she looked down at her wounded left arm. Had the other ten seen her arm, her game would have ended, but that was another reason Alis had ordered them to depart leaving her behind. She could not afford to have them see her wound.

Alis focused and sent an electronic burst of data and received back a reply far sooner than she'd expected. Another was on their way. She went back to the front and entered the coordinates she'd just received and hit Execute. Her eyes glanced at the read-out: two hours until the destination was reached. She set a timer and began a search of the transport.

An hour later, she found what she was looking for: a hundred of the genetic bio agent cylinders! Only now did she relax some. She had recovered the Master's stash of the bio weapon. Alis then headed to the pilot's seat to wait for the rendezvous.

***

"But we just left her there!" Linda fairly screamed. "Can't we go back and get her somehow?"

"D. J. tried to calm her down, "You know we can't. There were fifty guards on top of us. We wouldn't stand a chance, not unless you want us to kill those men. They're only doing their job protecting the spaceport. After all, Linda, we were the ones setting off those explosions, though they didn't harm anything."

"I know, I know, but we just left her to those men and the Master. We failed to get him," Linda cried.

"We will just have to try again," Martha declared. "I swear I will devote my life to killing that man, though I don't know what came over me, dropping all my guns."

"I do. It was his hypnotic effect," Armando spoke up. "We stood no chance, not when he used his voice on us. Somehow, Alis managed to save us all. I don't know how she was able to override his control as much as she did. I couldn't control my own body. That was the scariest thing I've ever felt!"

"Hey, we owe it to Alis to keep on with our jobs," Jackie called back from the pilot's seat. "She wouldn't want us to give up the fight because we lost the first round. Next time, take out his damned transport ship!"

"She's got a point," D. J. added, "Alis wouldn't want us to limp home defeated. What was the next planet she thought he was going to hit?"

"Got it here," Linda answered, taking heart that they weren't just going to give up. "It's 3-Leo-C. Sending you the coordinates now, Melissa. How long til we get there?"

A few minutes Melissa answered, "Eight hours. No need to rush there. The Master has to finish his dirty work back there. We have time. We'll get him next time."

"Right. We need to make some new plans," D. J. took charge. "Some of us go after him, while some of us go after his transport. He can't guard both at the same time."

344

"I'll rustle up something to eat," Bess decided, "then Jason, you and I need to make some more satchel charges. Say, can you make some that will stick to the side of his transport? Then we can set them off as he takes off. That's another way to kill him."

"Hey, we should have thought of that sooner! On it, Bess. Indeed, we can make a sticky thermite charge, which will burn through the side of his transport like it was butter," Jason explained, greatly relieved. Even he was terribly disappointed that they'd lost Alis.

D. J. ordered, "Linda, monitor the local chatter back there. See if you can find out what they are doing to Alis. Maybe we can rescue her later on, somehow, once we've dealt with the Master."

"On it!" Linda replied, thankful to have something useful to do, particularly since it offered some hope for Alis.

An hour later, Bess dished out a stew for everyone. When Linda joined them, she said, "Weird. No mention of Alis. Two shuttles took off, leaving a number of dead men. They captured a large number of his terrorist companions when they returned to their ships. They've been arrested and are being tried for high treason. They wiped out all the corporate headquarters there though. Initial reports estimate ten thousand victims all told. Terrible."

"They said nothing about capturing Alis?" asked D. J.

"Nope. Do you suppose the Master got away and took Alis with him?" Linda asked.

He shrugged his shoulders. "Perhaps holding her hostage. If so and if she's on his ship, do we dare blow it up?"

"Have to," Armando answered. "She knew the risks, as we all did. The Master must be stopped at all costs. My God, the damage that man has done! She would want us to continue, even if it means harming her, if she isn't already dead or tortured or even genetically mutated as well." That sobered them all. "Let's all get some rest before we land."

A gong announced that the autopilot had taken them successfully to the entered coordinates, that of 3-Leo-C. Two sleepy women headed up to their positions at the front to drop out of hyperspace, cloaked of course. Bess headed to the galley to make some much-needed coffee for everyone, while Linda made her careful way to her comm center post.

Soon, the aroma of freshly brewed coffee filled the ship. "Hey, send some back to me," Linda called out.

Just as Bess brought her a cup with a straw in it, Linda's comm set began crackling. A secure call was coming in on their unique emergency frequency, known only to themselves and to Alfonso. Linda snapped alert in an instant. "Call coming in. Probably Alfonso. Who else has this frequency?" Her toe flipped the accept switch. She nearly fell out of her seat when she heard the voice of Alis speaking. Bess dropped the coffee onto the steel deck.

"Alis calling Nueva Estrella, come in please." She repeated it twice before Linda was able to react.

"Linda here. Alis? Is that you? They said you were shot. I didn't want to leave you behind. Are you all right? Where are you? Over."

"Yes, it's me. Tell the others that the MK50 worked. I got the Master. One shot took him out. I'm fine. All patched up. I made it into the Master's transport before the security guards got to me and took off, jumping into hyperspace at zero velocity. By the way, I found a hundred of those genetic bio agent cylinders and have destroyed them. Stopped on an outpost and used their medical machine to patch up my arm, so I'm fine. Where are all of you? Over."

"3-Leo-C. Looking to get the Master. We figured he got away. I monitored the local news and heard that two transports got away. One was us, so I figured the Master got away too. We came to the next possible planet looking for him. Over."

"Okay, you guys wait for me. Be there in three hours. This ship took a blaster shot and it tore a hole in the hull. Am leaking air, but I can make it that far before I have to dump this bucket. Best conserve air. Will call again when I get closer. Tell everyone very well done. We got the Master! Over and out." Alis signed off.

True, this wasn't quite what had happened, but it was a logical explanation, one that would jive with what the ten knew and could accept. After her brief rendezvous, her arm was fully patched up, and the cylinders handled safely. True, there was very little air left in the transport, but enough to get her there. Alis settled back to wait.

Right on time, Alis dropped out of hyperspace and signaled the Nueva Estrella, who responded anxiously. "Linda here. We are scanning for you. Okay, Armando has you on radar. We're coming to you. Over."

"Good idea. I'm in a space suit now. Air gone from this rust bucket. We should do an emergency forward hatch dock," Alis advised. Armando groaned. This meant the other ship was so badly damage that they couldn't execute a normal docking with that ship, and Alis was planning a risky move, floating through space from her ship to theirs and then entering the forward, small emergency hatch, all while wearing a clumsy space suit; there wasn't anything he could do to help her.

Linda fired up the external video system, and the group gathered around her monitor, watching the slow moving Alis, as she made her way from the battered transport over to theirs. Meanwhile, Armando was up front by the inside emergency hatch, ready to help her inside, knowing how difficult doing anything in the heavy space suit was, particularly entering the transport via this emergency hatch, while upside down.

"Gotcha," he exclaimed, as she more or less fell into the front section, while upside down.

"Get me out of this thing," Alis teased him.

"Don't like the baggy look, eh, Alis?" Armando teased her back. He got her helmet off and helped her maneuver through the tight quarters back to the more spacious bay area, where everyone else was gathered. As soon as the red space suited Alis appeared, they all cheered, but D. J. quickly lent Armando a hand getting her free from the suit.

"Okay, let's see that arm of yours," Armando insisted, "I saw you take one there."

She leaned her left upper arm outward so he and the others could see the tiny visible scar. "Told you, I made use of a medical machine," she teased them, lying a bit, and thankful she had insisted on having a bit of a scar visible where the slug had ripped into her.

"So my gun worked on the Master?" Bill asked what everyone wanted to know.

"You bet it did. Without it, I'd not be here, and the Master would still be on the loose. You all are what made it happen there at the last second. Those guards were almost on us, and the Master had us all under his control, so I yelled for you all to get away. That did it and gave us our shot at him. He took his attention off me, turned to see you four diving up the ramp, and the bay door closing. He also saw the guards were mere feet from us. That gave me a fraction of a second to get one shot off. It worked just as it did on that test dummy, Bill. The second the slug ripped through him, his control over me vanished. You were firing up. Besides, if you opened the bay door, by then I'd be captured, and they'd be shooting you with their guns. So instead, I ducked, rolled, and raced up the ramp into the Master's transport, hitting the Close button as I ran to the front, slamming the ship into hyperspace. As I did that, the guards blasted a gaping hole in the side of the ship. I ran back amidships and slammed the cabin door shut, sealing the leak somewhat and headed off to get some help. So here I am, safe and sound, thanks to all of you," Alis explained, though some of this was a lie, a plausible one though.

"You got rid of the cylinders?" Armando asked.

"Yes, dumped them in space and used one of the Master's detonators to blow the hundred cylinders up. No more genetic bio agent attack, thank heavens. Have you heard anything about what happened back there on Kingston-B?"

Linda filled her in completely, and Alis sighed, "So many more lives have been ruined." The other nodded. "Well, we best let Alfonso know the good news. Linda, would you do the honors?"

Proudly, the silver-haired young woman made the call.

348

Chapter 21—Fallout

When the Nueva Estrella landed, Alfonso had a large crowd waiting to welcome them back, complete with full news coverage. He'd spread the word that this team of eleven had finally eliminated the Master, so this truly was big, local news. At least Jackie managed to set them down with the bay ramp facing away from the crowd. She did that on purpose, so that the six of them who needed to be helped down the steep ramp wouldn't be embarrassed by the crowd. Jason whispered a big thank you to her for this. "There are so many people watching!" he said nervously, hating this kind of limelight.

"I know," the fiery redhead whispered back, waiting her turn to be lifted down the ramp, so hard to manage in their extreme heels.

Alis got them into a line with the five putting a supporting arm around one of the six in an alternating pattern. Then, the entire group walked slowly around the side of the transport to face the wall of cameras and cheering people. Alfonso made a short speech outlining what these eleven had done, his general hung a medal on each, and Alis was asked to give a brief account of their mission.

"It was teamwork. It took all eleven of us working together as a team that allowed us to get the Master and stop him. Bill's new MK50 took him out, even though he was wearing a PDS at the time. We took his transport and destroyed a hundred more of those bio agent cylinders that he was using to destroy so many lives. The Master is no more. We can all sleep better at night now," Alis said to the cameras and crowd. "Sorry, I can't be more specific, top-secret, and all that." While it wasn't secret, she just didn't want to say more.

Finally, Alfonso and Diego ushered them into the control tower and out the other side, into a waiting airbus transport. Never were the eleven happier to see GD headquarters than today. Finally, they relaxed, out of the public eye. Here, they gave Alfonso and Diego a complete briefing and agreed to repeat it for the benefit of many other executives, some from neighboring worlds, tomorrow around one in the afternoon.

That done, Alfonso allowed everyone to head home for a much needed bath and change of clothes. Alis, however, stuck around a bit longer.

"So how many of the UFB women and UFBMD men have the other worlds sent here?" Alis asked what she now wanted most urgently to know.

"We are still having daily arrivals. Fortunately, the problem I was most worried about hasn't materialized, namely having a bunch of UFBMD former corporate top executives coming. Most all those were men and killed by the gas. Interestingly enough, many worlds not even attacked are sending some of their executives' wives and children here. Apparently, they are abandoning their breeding programs on many corporate worlds, which I'm taking as a very positive sign. However, we're getting some pretty upset newly divorced or widowed wives and their children arriving. We're doing our best to keep families together."

"So the numbers are not yet in. Okay, keep me posted on them. I'm keenly interested in the totals. We can use many more like the six that went with me this time, Alfonso. Keep on spreading the word that we're accepting them here. I believe that many are taking advantage of this chance to dump them way out here on the rim, as far from their worlds as possible," Alis replied. Alfonso agreed, and Alis headed to her home here in Malagena, Scorpi-C, though it was just one of many that she had.

***

A relatively quiet month passed. At last, transports bringing the "unwanted" people to Scorpi-C finally trickled down to none, finally allowing Alfonso to come up with more accurate figures of the victims they'd given sanctuary to. He relayed them to Alis as she had asked. Even as he looked them over, he felt a bit of pride, so many young and bright ones.

Alis looked over the final tallies and sighed. So many, she thought, but the large number of young amazed her and gave her some hope.

UFB Women over 35:   2,341

```
UFB Women 18 to 34:  15,409
UFB Women under 18: 19,305
UFBMD over 35:          91
UFBMD Men 18 to 34:    603
UFBMD Men under 18:    505
              38,254
```

Alis also knew that these didn't include the many that were taken to Beltazar and were pretty much beyond her reach. Still, so many young, that was what interested her, along with the realization that in all likelihood the corporations had ceased their *special breeding* program or put them on hold. She also felt sympathy for the ex-wives, widows, and their children who had simply been dumped now that they'd decided to end the program.

The other factor that truly bothered Alis and one that had been mentioned by Anka was that most of these women were of breeding ages. These genetic modifications to their DNA meant their children would also be UFB women or UFBMD men, depending on who impregnated who. That is, like the half-millennia ago situation, these mutations would continue to be propagated into the future generation. While the growth of these new mutations would not be as dramatic as they had been with the hermaphrodites, in which both partners gave birth making the birth rates more than double the norm, still these UFB women now had inbred strong sexual drives and would likely have more than the average number of children. Even Alfonso's family was indicative of this.

True, there were forty thousand of them now, but the next generation would likely see closer to a hundred thousand of them, and so on. While this was small compared to the approximately six billion on Scorpi-C, in time, their numbers would soon begin to become a significant percentage of the overall population. And while the younger ones were working hard at regaining some of their independence, they still needed significant assistance with life. In time, their bludgeoning percentage of the world's population would create an economic disaster.

Alis had already collected a goodly sample of just how

these genetically modified women and men felt about the two known cures, foot and hair repair. Around half of those she had talked to about this wanted only their arms back. Another half wanted their feet repaired, but only half of that half wanted their hair back to normal. In other words, at least half didn't want to lose what they now considered made them special, a partial compensation for their ruined lives. If Alis had it in her power to overnight repair everything except for their arms, that would upset more than half of the victims, adding to their misery not lessening it, for uniformly they all valued highly their uncommon beauty, their only real benefit as they saw it.

As far as the actual results from the corporations' breeding program, little hard data was known. A few records of other corporations' results were uncovered, but nothing definitive, save there was a visible pattern, which they already knew from the table that Alfonso had found. Almost no data existed on second-generation results. What would the children of Luisa and Alfonso's girls be like? She also knew Alfonso was very anxious to see how his son with Alicia would turn out, that is, would he be a super IQ lad? Their daughter would be a UFB woman, if the breeding charts were correct. No, far too many were looking forward to their children, and how and what they would turn out to be.

There was another side to this genetic modification mess Alis had to consider. If somehow the genetic modifications could be halted in future generations here on Scorpi-C, then the remaining UFB women and UFBMD men still out there among other worlds would become quite scarce. Thus, once more they would become incredibly valuable, since scarcity prompts value. There could well be future problems developing from such a scarcity. That situation could be wholly prevented if the genetic modified men and women continued to breed true here on Scorpi-C—abundance, not scarcity. For Alis, there appeared to be no real solution to the situation. Each choice had pros and cons, nearly equally balance in her mind.

However, if regeneration of arms could be somehow established, then a completely new set of possibilities could be had, for it they had arms, who wouldn't want to be a UFB woman and to a drastically lesser extent a UFBMD man? Disenchanted, Alis sent off a lengthy electronic burst, requesting further guidance.

Alis had other things to ponder as well. In all these months, no one had asked what she thought were the critical questions: Just who was the Master? Where did he come from? Were there more like him out there in the galaxy? True, thanks to Bill's new MK50, she had been able to eliminate him, taking down his attempts to rule the galaxy, but were there others like him waiting in the wings? Or was he just an anomalous freak of nature? She would have liked to obtain an example of his DNA for study, but under the circumstances, there wasn't time to collect any. For a time, she considered going back there and finding out what they did with his remains, perhaps obtaining some that way, but gave up the idea as being too risky. Undoubtedly, the authorities there would be on the lookout for her.

All that was known was that he had suddenly appeared on Rho-C. Perhaps some of his henchmen had been captured and could tell them more about this strange man. That was worth looking into, she considered, but how?

Even more worrisome to Alis was the simple fact the genetic bio agent had once again been used as a weapon by the Master. Until this happened, the corporations used it in their private breeding programs. Now, its usefulness both as a terrorist weapon and as a mass destruction weapon was widely known. Anka's ancient history suggested perhaps the cat was out of the bag once again. Would other disreputable leaders begin to use this awful stuff as a weapon? Alis gave that an almost a hundred percent chance of happening. It had been used to wipe out two entire infantry divisions, as well as the crew of the battleships.

There was one aspect of this mess she didn't have any hard data on and that was whether the corporations had samples of the particular version the Master had used that outright killed males upon exposure. Had he come across that one himself or had he just stolen it from Rho-C? If the corporations had that version, then its use as a weapon of war would be beyond horrific. If they didn't, then perhaps such attacks might be survivable as a species.

Then again, Alis wondered if the researchers on Rho-C, who had recovered those ancient bio agent cylinders on Zeta Scorpii-C, had been able to recreate fully the genetic mutations that had been used a half millennia ago? Those were even worse, since back then it turned men and women into nearly identical hermaphrodites, whose breeding rates more than doubled the normal rates, generating escalating problems as the future generations arrived. To Alis's highly logical mind, it seemed Pandora's Box had been opened. The only remaining question was would something come out? Alis could only assume that it would.

Alis finally received a brief electronic data burst, but she wasn't pleased with the answers to the many questions she'd asked. It said simply, "Working on it." Nothing more. Hence, Alis decided to stick around Scorpi-C for a while and see what happened on this world, what the new babies would be like, and to learn what she could about what the remaining corporations' executives would do.

The answer to the latter question came within a month after she and her crew returned to Scorpi-C. Some of the more distant relatives of the top executives of the major corporations on Corporation Prime attempted to step in and take control of their relation's corporations. That failed utterly, since by now the middle layer of corporation executives were fighting among themselves for more control over more sectors, and they completely ignored everyone on Corporate Prime.

At this point, the bureaucrats began departing Corporate Prime, looking for greener pastures, since the work that they had been doing virtually dried up, forcing them to look elsewhere. It would take years, but the hundred billion on Corporate Prime during its heyday would end up down to a supportable level of barely six billion.

Here in the Abelard Sector, Alfonso's power continued to grow. Whether he desired it, the man found himself the unofficial leader of the entire sector. On top of that, by now, all the corporation worlds in this sector had adopted his policy of returning ownership of land and homes to the renters. The incredible shift in local morale and thus support of the local corporations skyrocketed, precisely what was desired by these local executives, who saw their powers growing by leaps and bounds, but only as long as they followed the pioneering steps that Alfonso Vega used. That the Abelard Sector now had no immediate mid-level corporation headquarters above them certainly helped them retain their anonymity.

Other sectors soon found themselves embroiled in corporation politics, as mid-level corporation headquarters executives unleashed volumes of new rules and regulations, designed to strengthen their vice grip on all those branches in their sectors. These, as one might surmise, didn't sit well on the local world offices. As the months progressed, many began to rebel, adopting some of Alfonso Vega's guidelines, the largest being the ownership of homes and property. This only added fuel to the fires, as more and more chaos and confusion shot up and down the corporations' lines of communication. Slowly but surely, local corporations were becoming somewhat independent entities as far as their executives were concerned.

Mid-level management was hard pressed to get their new regulations enforced on the breakaway local corporations because nearly all local corporations had one infantry division on their world, along with a small space fleet. If the mid-level executives wanted to launch a military strike on rebellious local worlds, their advisors pointed out that they'd probably lose half of their army and fleet, making this a very dicey situation. In turn, this forced the mid-level executives to seek more alliances to bring more infantry divisions and warships to bear on the rebellious worlds supposedly under their jurisdiction.

Those worlds began making alliances with other local worlds and even some that were not even in their own sectors. Anything to present a stronger military presence to the mid-level management became their operational byword. Thus, for the several months that Alis monitored the situations, a stalemate resulted. However, Alis knew that a stalemate was intolerable by those in power. Somehow, someway, the mid-level executives would attempt to break that stalemate in their favor. Genetic bio agent weapons could well be their answer, or so Alis greatly feared. At last, she decided that she simply had to know just what form these weapons might take.

Hence, after many of her friends gave birth early the following year and she personally saw the results, exactly as expected from the breeding chart that they'd uncovered, she decided it was time to take off and do some more investigating. Alfonso again wanted to send others along with her, but she vetoed it. "Look Alfonso, I'm just going visiting. There's no danger in that, just gathering intelligence." Reluctantly, he agreed, and in late March, Alis departed Scorpi-C for the mid-arm regions of the galaxy, diving into the chaotic zones to see for herself the exact situations there.

***

During these months, Alfonso worked tirelessly to get new homes and assistants setup so that the children and young adults could get a good education. Several corporations made a good deal of profit, as they geared up to meet the ever-increasing demand for the electrostatic hair machines and the extreme heels the victims truly needed. Even local hardware companies had a booming market for replacement doorknobs, that is, latches that the victims could use. Even automatically opening doors were in demand, to say nothing of laptop computers for the students, along with voice-activated software. The sudden influx of new students created a demand for more teachers, particularly at the high school and Academy levels. Thus, the addition of these forty thousand victims was met not with sarcasm, hostility, or disgust, but rather were welcomed as a boon to the local economy of Scorpi-C.

When Alicia finally gave birth to Roberto and Ernesta, Alfonso was extremely pleased. His son had arms! He would not suffer a life like his father. Ernesta, on the other hand, was obviously going to be a gorgeous raven-haired UFB woman. Two months later, Carmela gave him another daughter, Donica, who would also grow up to be a UFB woman with raven hair.

However, a wholly unexpected factor developed when Alicia gave birth to her twins. Alfonso's breasts swelled up with milk, and he found that he had no choice but to share nursing duties with Alicia and then two months later with Carmela. All the UFBMD men who were married and whose wives gave birth soon discovered this unexpected side effect. These men had no choice and took it in stride, though Alfonso firmly believed that in doing so, he felt far closer to his new son and two daughters.

As the snows melted and spring blossomed on Scorpi-C, Alfonso believed the worst was over. Perhaps now he could sit back and enjoy his family and especially his children.

Chapter 22—A Search Bears Fruit

Dr. Marcel Louvel smiled broadly. Finally, he, the greatest geneticist of the galaxy, had just done the impossible! Perfection at long last. For the last twenty years, he and his staff had been working to salvage the lost work of ancient geneticists. Archaeologists had recovered samples of incredible genetic modification agents that were over five hundred years old. Degradation of the samples was to be expected, but in this case, it had been severe. Count Edgard le Masters had given him and his staff the greatest challenge of the century: the restoration of lost genetic mutation agents.

He and his staff had some partial successes early on, and Count Edgard had taken those samples and put them to good use, or so he claimed. Here on the relatively isolated rim world of 9-Cetus-C, at the le Masters' Institute for Genetic Studies in the heart of Bordeaux, the world's capital city, Dr. Marcel and his staff of eleven continued the painstaking research and development, using hardened criminals given to them to experiment upon by the OEN, the Opérations d'Espionnage Noir.

In ancient times, this organization had been called the Intelligence Division. Later, it merged with another internal organization and became the Black Operations or BOPs. With the total takeover of the galaxy by the corporations centuries ago, it had been reformed as the enforcement arm of the Corporations, the OEN. Even the mention of that name struck fear in the minds of most ordinary men, for if the OEN was after you, that meant certain death. The main headquarters of the OEN was on Corporate Prime, as were so many top leadership headquarters, though their location was a total secret known only to a few top executives of the largest and most powerful corporations, who were wiped out by the Master and his genetic bio agent strikes months ago, thereby giving the OEN total independence of operation.

Dr. Marcel cared little for anything but his genetic research. That Count Edgard had backed him all the way, financially and concept-wise, put Dr. Marcel into a unique frame of mind. As long as Count Edgard used his results that in some way furthered the doctor's pet ideas was all the scientist desired. Initially, the driving force that lay behind Dr. Marcel's seemingly monomaniac drive of genetic research was a simple one, if vain and personal. Beauty. His wife, Tilde, had been horribly disfigured in an accident shortly after they were married. Mr. Marcel swore he would devote his life to creating a genetic modification that would somehow return Tilde's beauty back to her.

Thus, part of his initial success with the recovered ancient genetic bio agents lay in his use of the discoveries of those geneticists who worked on this project since its conception some hundred plus years ago. His predecessor some forty years ago created an accidental modification that resulted in a genetic mutation that left the women impressively beautiful. That is to say when Count Edgard initially setup the institute and placed Dr. Marcel in charge of the research, Count Edgard provided numerous samples, along with copies of all the documentation that he'd stolen from the research facilities on Rho-C, though Dr. Marcel did not know how Count Edgard had gotten all these samples and data.

Dr. Marcel spent half that first year studying all that had been done with the ancient bio agents and with the modifications and failed attempts that the Rho-C scientists had done thus far. With immense interest, he read about how the researchers had become emboldened by that initial but accidental success, which so enhanced a woman's beauty. Subsequently, they had gathered up all the known data of just what constituted the ultimate in feminine beauty and jelled it all down to the characteristics of the UFB woman, which subsequently required only some slight changes to this initial chance discovery. Dr. Marcel was truly impressed with just how thorough those researchers had been in getting the UFB modification developed just right. True, the genetic modification also caused three side effects that were part of this ancient bio agent, namely the altered hair, loss of arms, and distorted feet. A second strain produced gigantic breasts, favored by some CEOs. Still, the women guinea pigs were simply stunning. Thus the breeding program had begun nearly forty years ago.

Dr. Marcel studied the research papers, the photos of the results, and finally decided this was the answer he was searching for and six months after taking this new position for Count Edgard, he used a sample on his wife, Tilde.

Tilde didn't mind the side effect, for she had her beauty back, could finally look at herself in the mirror, and venture out in public once more. (She had been a hermit since the disfiguring accident.)

His initial study of the prior work showed that the original samples in their degraded form produced three different results. That testing was done on hardened criminals. In one batch, the men simply died, presumably from the degradation of the bio agent. In another batch, the men ended up looking like females, except they retained male reproductive organs. In a third batch, the men were unaffected for unknown reasons. At Count Edgard's request, Dr. Marcel and his staff worked up batches of these incorporating the small modifications. One batch yielded what were then called the UFB woman and the UFB man. A second batch resulted in dead men but UFB women. A third batch, similar to the second batch, had two components; one had a longer incubation period in a woman's blood stream before it took full effect. These, he supplied to Count Edgar, as promised, and after that, he was allowed to continue on with his research of the ancient bio agents for many years without further intervention.

Count Edgard was seldom around these last few years, but Dr. Marcel's standing orders were to continue to restore fully that ancient genetic bio agent. Who knows what other startling and useful knowledge could be gained by doing so? The doctor told his eleven researchers that nearly every day. "Knowledge has been lost, so it is up to us to restore it."

Dr. Marcel had a very special phone number to use when he finally was able to restore that ancient bio agent. And today, he smiled and dialed the number. He'd done the utterly impossible. Not his staff, but he himself. Sections of the DNA strands in each bio agent cylinder had degraded, but in different ways. By analyzing that portion of the genetic structure in ten million samples, he'd been able statistically to restore what the original pattern must have been. True, it had been a long, laborious process, tremendously tedious, one which none of his fellow geneticists wanted any part of doing. Yet it had produced the desired results. He, Dr. Marcel Louvel, had restored that ancient genetic bio agent to what it once had been! His fellow researchers had just completed testing it on six subjects, three of each sex, and fully documented the unexpected and quite startling results. Now it was time to alert his benefactor of this incredible breakthrough.

No answer, not even a "leave a message" option. He tried a dozen times during the next two days, but heard nothing but endless ringing. Something was very wrong. Always before, he had been able to reach Count Edgard within a day. Then, he remembered something that the Count had once told him, "If you can't reach me on my private line, I've left sealed orders for you to follow in your safe." Quickly, Dr. Marcel opened his office safe and found he sealed envelope with his name on it. He opened it and read.

Dr. Marcel Louvel,

If you are reading this, it means you are unable to reach me. I'm afraid something may have happened to me. It is possible I have been killed. Your work must continue. Your funding is still secure. You're to go to Corporate Prime and discuss everything with the Countessa Bianca le Masters. She can often be found at Symphony Hall performances.

Sincerely yours,

Count Edgard le Masters

Dr. Marcel sighed. *Dead?* His heart skipped a beat. *My invaluable research?* He reread it. "Ah, my work must continue!" He breathed a huge sigh of relief. Was this Countessa Bianca related to Edgard, he wondered? *Sister? Wife?* "I must take everything to her and hope she can understand the vital importance of our work."

"What's that doctor?" the alto voice of Dr. Michelle d'Mireio broke in. The twenty-five year old brunette geneticist was his second in command. She had been here for three years now, a brilliant, new geneticist, who had rapidly risen to her current position. She'd walked into his office to relay some of the lab's latest test results, rather alarming ones, and had overheard his last words.

"Oh, I'm to take our latest findings and some samples to Corporate Prime," he replied, hastily putting the note behind his back. Dr. Marcel and Dr. Michelle had become antagonists this past year. She had pointed out the striking similarities between their own genetic bio agents and those that had been used in the many terrorist attacks on corporate headquarters on several worlds, including Corporate Prime.

She'd argued, "Some beast has stolen our samples and is using them to terrorize innocent people, to kill and main our corporation leaders. We have to let our boss know, and we should conduct a thorough investigation of our research facilities and find out who has been giving our samples to these terrorists." Oh how she'd become so vocal on this point, so much so, that he'd had their facility's security guards conduct a thorough investigation. That had turned up nothing, of course. Still, that didn't appease Dr. Michelle.

In fact, with these latest test results proving he had recovered the actual genetic bio agent that was in use centuries ago, Dr. Michelle had become extremely critical of their continued research. "Look, I know these test subjects are hardened criminals, murderers even, but look what it's done to them. They are all hermaphrodites! You can't tell the men from the women any longer!"

Another researcher protested, "Yes, Dr. Michelle, but look, they are all very beautiful women now. Surely that should factor into our thinking and theirs too." That made no difference to Dr. Michelle. Worse, of late, she was threatening to take the matter up with the corporation leaders on Corporate Prime, but with their demise by the hands of the terrorists, she was stymied in her threat.

Dr. Michelle responded to Dr. Marcel's statement that he was to take them to Corporate Prime. "All right then. I insist on coming along with you. Someone has to stand up for what is right and just. We must tell them we have gone too far in this."

Dr. Marcel felt boxed in. There would be no living with her if he refused to let her come with him. His greatest fears were she'd somehow convince this Countessa Bianca to terminate this incredibly valuable genetic research project or that she would try to get some corporate executives to intervene and stop him. Still, he couldn't leave her behind, since she'd surely try to get a hold of some top executive somewhere. "Of course, Dr. Michelle, you should come with me. We will have to go to the Symphony Hall, so you will need to dress appropriately."

Mollified, Dr. Michelle agreed, "Okay then, that's better. I will explain to them just how awful and inhumane our research has become. Just so you know." She turned on her heels and headed back to her own office to jot down what she believed to be the salient points she'd need to make.

The next day, Dr. Marcel had a brief case filled with several cylinders of his newly created genetic bio agent, one that most closely matched the theoretical ancient agent. He packed a suit and essentials into an overnight bag, handcuffed the briefcase to his left hand, and headed off to find Dr. Michelle. She was also ready, wearing a black skirt, white blouse, black nylons, and low black pumps, a proper professional woman's outfit. She too had an overnight bag, but she also had a large bag containing the fanciest dress that she owned, hoping it was suitable for attending a concert at Symphony Hall on Corporate Prime. Together, the pair took a shuttle to the spaceport. Soon, they left Bordeaux and 9-Cetus-C behind.

Two days later, they landed on Corporate Prime. Both were appalled at the sheer number of shuttles darting about the giant capital city of Stella. They passed through customs, where security was overly tight. So many corporate headquarters had been attacked that everywhere, people took security to new heights. Many were more than willing to tell the two newcomers just how bad things had become. Both got quite an earful before they reached a fancy hotel downtown and reasonably close to Symphony Hall.

Dr. Marcel did some checking and found they were in

luck. The next concert was scheduled for tonight at seven. They had time to clean up and get dressed for the event. Arm in arm, the two doctors entered Symphony Hall, discovering that they were about the worst dressed pair there! She wore a red gown, but it looked very much out of style compared to the elegantly dressed women, who rather paid her no attention.

"Excuse me, sir," Dr. Marcel said to an usher. "This is our first visit to the Symphony Hall. I am Dr. Marcel Louvel, and I was told I was to see the Countessa Bianca le Masters here at the symphony. Pray sir, how can this be done? I've very important business to discuss with her." The usher directed him to the manager, who also wore a tuxedo. His eyes rolled when he saw the doctor wearing a simple business suit, but that was allowed here. Again, Dr. Marcel explained the situation to the manager.

"If you will give me your card, I will present it to the Countessa when she arrives."

"Here, let me jot a short note on the back," Dr. Marcel replied, greatly relieved. So far, so good he thought, handing the manager the card. He and Dr. Michelle then were ushered to their seats. Neither had been to such an elegant symphony concert before and was most impressed with the music and the one hundred fifty-member orchestra. All he could do now was wait and hope that this Countessa would see him.

"Ah Countessa le Masters, an ill-dressed man asked me to give you this card. He claims to have important business with you, but I would be hesitant in such a dealing," he said politely, allowing the card to "magically" float over before her eyes. He'd seen this bit of magic many times before.

Countessa Bianca le Masters was one of those incredibly beautiful women, a UFB woman if one wished to insult her with such a downgrade comment, with wavy, knee-length blonde hair. Her sky blue eyes matched the satin of her tight-fitting gown, one that displayed her fabulous figure, even though she was now thirty-six. One couldn't even guess that she'd had three children. Some claimed the jewelry that she wore was worth millions, and the manager didn't doubt that rumor in the slightest. A mink stole was draped over her shoulders with her thick hair draped over that and down her back. Her lower legs were encased in the finest black seamed nylons and her extreme pumps matched her dress.

However visually impacting this elegant woman was, it was her unique magic that often shocked others. Objects simply moved for her, as though being carried about by invisible arms and hands. She alone of all the UFB women known had no use for arms and hands. And her presence demanded and commanded the attention of everyone in the room. "Ah. Please tell him to meet us here when the performance is done. Thank you," she replied, floating the card on over to her three daughters.

Blanche was eighteen, Celestine, seventeen, Dianne, sixteen. Looking at them, one would say immediately they were all UFB women. That was their outward appearance. Each had their mother's knee-length, shiny, thick, wavy blonde hair and light blue eyes. Each was the epitome of feminine beauty, though they each preferred different colored gowns, light red, light purple, and light lavender. Each teen also had their mother's magical gifts and found the lack of arms and hands of no consequence at all.

Tonight, they were being escorted to the symphony by their boyfriends. Arnaud Armel, the same age as Blanche, kept a steadying arm around her, glancing at the card and its brief message. The twins, Beneoit and Edmond Berenger, eighteen, were doing the same with their girlfriends, Celestine and Dianne, respectively. "I do so wonder what this doctor wishes of mama," Blanche whispered to Arnaud.

"Hush. We'll meet him later," her mother whispered back, silencing her daughter's speculations. Regally, the four women entered the main floor and took their box seats near the center front, their permanent seats. They always had season tickets and always had the same prime seats, year after year. The Countessa Bianca had rarely failed to bring her daughters to the symphony concerts, ever since they were old enough to walk. These days, the teens preferred to spend the time embracing their boyfriends instead of listening to the music. Conveniently, the Countessa understood why and didn't chastise them for doing such. She knew she'd soon have to get them married.

An hour and a half later, the small group waited for the manager to bring this doctor to them. Soon, they spied them coming towards them, while hundreds made their way out of Symphony Hall. Blanche turned up her nose. "How can they come here wearing such rags?" she whispered to Arnaud, who merely grinned.

"Hello. I'm Dr. Marcel Louvel, head of genetics research at the le Masters' Institute for Genetic Studies in Bordeaux on 9-Cetus-C. For many years, I have been conducting genetics research for Count Edgard le Masters. I have made some incredible breakthroughs recently, but I have been unable to contact the Count. In such an event, he left orders for me to come here to Symphony Hall and speak with you, Countessa Bianca le Masters. I do so hope you'll see me and hear what I have to say. Oh, this is my second in command, Dr. Michelle d'Moreio."

"Ah yes, Dr. Marcel. My late husband has spoken often of you. I'm so very glad to meet you. Count Edgard recently passed away very suddenly, but this isn't the proper place to discuss things of importance. Where are you staying? I'll have Arnaud here bring you both to visit me, say, at ten tomorrow morning. Will that be acceptable?" Countessa Bianca replied demurely.

"I'm so sorry. I didn't know. Yes, perfectly," he answered, startled. He had no idea the count had such a fabulous looking wife and daughters. He told them their hotel and hastily left.

Arnaud was prompt. He had a private shuttle waiting for the pair at precisely ten the next morning. Dr. Marcel suggested they both wear the same clothes they'd worn to the symphony the night before. "We don't want to seem too poorly dressed for the Countessa. She'll probably be funding our further research. Good impression, Dr. Michelle, is everything." She frowned but agreed. Dr. Michelle hated dressing up. Besides her feet still ached a little from the three-inch pumps she'd worn the night before. Always, she wore comfortable lab clothes and soft-soled shoes.

Neither had been to Corporate Prime before and soon were completely lost, though Arnaud knew precisely where he was taking them, purposely taking a circuitous route to get to the mansion of the Countessa. He didn't want these doctors to be able quickly to find the mansion on their own. He set the shuttle down on the pad just before the six tall marble columns supporting the ornate porch protecting the giant double doors of the mansion.

Just inside, he led them to the right into a plush study where the others were already seated, awaiting the arrival of the two doctors. "Ah here you are, Dr. Marcel, Dr. Michelle. Please have a seat. I assure you this room is safe. No eavesdropping, completely secure," Countessa Bianca began. "Edgard has kept me fully briefed on your incredibly valuable research and development projects. In turn, my daughters and their boyfriends are also privy to this information. So please feel free to discuss anything with us that you would have with my late husband."

The doctors took the indicated chairs, probably very expensive antiques Dr. Marcel thought. "Okay then. As I hope you know, Count Edgard had me further working on that ancient genetic bio agent, in hopes somehow I could reconstruct that portion of it which had degraded during the long centuries. I have done just that, using Comparative Elimination, a process that allowed me to reconstruct that portion of the basic genetic strings that had degraded."

The Countessa smiled, "Please, spare me the scientific details. I'm sure I have no idea what they are. Results. That is solely what concerned my late husband and now me. Please, you have succeeded?"

"Ah yes. Yes, of course. As you know, long ago we were able to reactivate certain portions of that original agent, adding some most desirable extra features, which have given rise to the UFB women and UFBMD men. My further work has finally retrieved all that was lost. With Dr. Michelle's invaluable assistance, we have merged those missing pieces with our current formula. We've actually done it, Countessa Bianca. Here, allow Dr. Michelle to show you some photos of the results. I hope seeing naked bodies will not offend you, but it is very important you see the results."

Dr. Michelle took a stack of photos out of the briefcase

and started to hand them to Arnaud, uncertain how to show them to the Countessa, who appeared to be just another helpless UFB woman. To her amazement, she felt them being lifted from her hands by invisible hands, rather startling her. "Oh do show us, mother," Blanche broke in. Soon, the photos were floating around the room, though the men passed them on using their hands.

"All women? No, wait, I see. . ." the Countessa began and stopped.

"Precisely. Hermaphrodites," Dr. Marcel pointed out the rather obvious dual sexual organs. "From their positioning, we believe it's possible for one of these to impregnate themselves as well as others. Yes, half of those are actually men. The only way you can tell their sex is by either a DNA test or seeing them urinating. And yes, these modified subjects will breed true. Their offspring will be hermaphrodites as well, looking much like their parents, as much as a normal child will look like his or her parents. Isn't this just incredible?"

"Dr. Marcel, Dr. Michelle, yes, this is just fabulously incredible. It's all that my late husband was hoping you would be able to restore. Incredible work, doctors, incredible," Countessa Bianca exclaimed, almost at a loss for words.

Dr. Marcel beamed. "I've brought along three sample cylinders of our new product. Of course, I do hope to continue our research. There is so much more we can learn."

"Certainly, Dr. Marcel! I wouldn't dream of ending your funding! Yes, this is indeed a tremendous breakthrough," the Countessa replied.

"But there's another aspect I simply must bring up," Dr. Michelle decided now was the time to speak her mind. "You have no doubt heard of all these terrorist attacks." Everyone nodded. "Well, I'm nearly certain those terrorists somehow stole the genetic bio agents they used in these horrific attacks from our lab. Of course, Dr. Marcel conducted a thorough investigation, er well he had our security people do it, and nothing was found. Still, somehow these vicious terrorists have stolen our work. And with these new results, I'm terrified they'll attempt to steal these as well. If they do and unleash this new bio agent on a world, the results will be even more disastrous and inhumane. I would like to ask you if there was some way you could strengthen the security surrounding our laboratories. This new bio agent simply must not fall into the hands of the terrorists. I wanted to go to the corporate executives with my suspicions the terrorists stole their agents from our labs, but unfortunately, the terrorists struck here on Corporate Prime before I could do so. Surely, you can see what I mean by this. The publicized results on the men and women are precisely those that we obtained from our different genetic bio agents." She finished up. *There,* she thought, *I can't make it any clearer.*

"Yes, I see," Countessa Bianca replied. "We certainly don't want this new bio agent falling into the *wrong* hands! I'll see your security is strengthened appropriately. "How many others know about this new version, if may call it that?"

"Just our research staff. Twelve of us, including us," Dr. Marcel replied. "The test subjects are all hardened criminals. They don't count and are never allowed out of the research facilities. I'm sure Dr. Michelle is exaggerating. Surely, these terrorists, as wicked as they may be, did not get their hands on our bio agents."

"You can't ignore the results on the victims," Dr. Michelle protested, though refraining from being argumentative in front of these people; such was neither prudent nor professional. "Personally, I think our line of investigations should now focus on finding cures for the thousands of terrorist victims, not trying to work out more features that ancient bio agent once had. There are thousands of innocent people who desperately need genetic cures. That should be our focus now, don't you think?" She purposely tossed out her ultimate objective, changing the total direction of their research.

"I'm sure the terrorists got their bio agents elsewhere," the Countessa Bianca replied, again flashing them a disarming smile. "Still, I'll look into it. Your humanitarian efforts are noted, Dr. Michelle. I'll give them some thought and get back to you." They chatted at length about the actual physical results until it was nearly lunchtime. As Arnaud rose to escort them back to the shuttle, Dr. Marcel stayed behind, allowing

Dr. Michelle to go on out with Arnaud.

"May I have a private word with you, Countessa Bianca?" She nodded. "I've been having an awful lot of trouble with Dr. Michelle. She's determined to let the authorities know the terrorists have stolen our bio agents. She's carefully documented the known results on hundreds of terrorist victims, correlating them precisely to our own bio agents' results. While I agree they resemble each closely, until I could get DNA samples from many victims and study them, I cannot say conclusively the terrorists got theirs from us. Surely, that is impossible. Still, she continues to try to force this issue, and I've not been able to either stop her or convince her that this surely couldn't have happened. Then, as you have heard, she wants us to forsake our studies on the ancient bio agent and work on genetic cures for the terrorist victims. Honestly, we can't do both."

"I see. My good doctor, you certainly don't need such distractions on your plate. I need you to focus fully on your research. Leave such matters to me. I'll work out something for Dr. Michelle. Please, continue your research on the ancient bio agent."

"Thank you, Countessa, thank you for everything. I do so hope to have more results for you later on," he said quite propitiative, grateful to hear he could continue as before and not be sidetracked down Dr. Michelle's avenue. She smiled coyly, and he headed after the other two, confident she would convince Dr. Michelle for him.

Two days later, they were back on their rim world and their home. Dr. Marcel was fired up to do further research, while Dr. Michelle decided to wait and see if Countessa Bianca would be contacting the authorities and obtaining the needed victims' DNA samples, samples she felt would prove the terrorists were using the lab's genetic bio agents!

When the two doctors left, the seven had a long discussion. "Well, Edgard was always a bit foolish and careless. Still, his investment in the research facility has paid off. We now have just the weapon we have waited so patiently for and for so long!" Countessa Bianca declared.

"Yes, but this Dr. Michelle could well pose a very

serious problem, mom," Blanche interjected. "I sensed she is very serious about exposing everything connected to the research lab. She's gotten the sense of it all and isn't going to stop."

"Oh I very much agree with you, Blanche. Excellent observation. I thought so too. Like I told the good doctor, we will take care of Michelle for him. Now we have the perfect way to do it too. We will have to test this new bio agent for ourselves and what better test subject than Dr. Michelle. Once she's become a hermaphrodite, she will be handled quite nicely indeed."

What neither doctor knew or nearly anyone else for that matter was the fact that Countessa Bianca le Masters was the leader of the highly secret organization: the OEN, the Opérations d'Espionnage Noir. Long ago, her husband had put her in charge of the organization in his place, just before he took off to carry out his own grand plan. In fact, Blanche, Celestine, and Dianne oversaw the branch offices of the hub and two key mid-arm sectors. Their three boyfriends were each the captain of their own Strike Teams, which carried out surgical, secretive strikes. In the past, most of these had been undertaken for the Corporate Prime top executives, the only men who knew their actual identities in the OEN. Often, these strikes were assassinations disguised to appear to be an accident. Now those executives were dead. No one was effectively leading the corporations from Corporate Prime, just as Count Edgard had intended. Thus, the OEN now embarked on its own agenda, as ordered by Countessa Bianca, its top leader. Her official title was simply Supreme Commander. Her daughters had the title of Commander.

In the past, though the OEN seldom struck, even mentioning their name brought fear into men's minds, as though they were some kind of unseen gods, bringing death in their wake. In fact, the OEN was more of an intelligence gathering and analyzing network, though carefully planned strikes were sometimes called for. For the past twenty years, the OEN had very carefully avoided interfering in the works of Count Edgard, naturally, which was a major reason why the top executives on Corporate Prime never took the situation in the Abelard Sector seriously or the threat of the strange spiders.

Countessa Bianca bit her lip, and then said, "Okay. I agree. It is time someone looked into just how Edgard managed to get himself killed. The official story out of Kingston-B just isn't adding up. If I know Edgard, he was always wearing his PDS. Dianne, Kingston-B is closer to your mid-arm sector. Take Captain Edmon's team with you and do a proper investigation, will you dear?"

"Sure mom. As I said, we should have done this last month. So what are we going go do about Dr. Michelle? Isn't Dr. Marcel just as much a liability as she is? Certainly, anyone who knows about the research facility there could likely trace the bio agents to their labs. Do we really need him any longer?"

"Yes and no," the Countessa replied in a non-committal manner to her daughter's question. "He may prove useful. Don't forget, your father installed a self-destruct device in the facility way back when it was being built. I've the signal codes here. So if it looks like trouble is coming, I'll eliminate them. The device will remove the anti-matter containment field. Poof. Nothing but atomized dust will remain."

"Mom, what about us? I mean dad always promised us that we could make use of the bio agent again when it was finished. Now it is. You saw those pictures. Hermaphrodites. Just what we all wanted," Blanche spoke up. This was on her mind ever since she saw the photos. She added, "Then, we can finally have our perfect bodies, and not these screwed up ones." She was referring to her UFB woman's body.

Countessa Bianca smiled deviously. "Even I'm quite anxious to have mine redone properly too, daughters, but we're going to wait just a while longer. After all, you have waited eighteen years, Blanche, a few more weeks shouldn't matter. I want to see the results of it on that rather homely Dr. Michelle first. If she turns out as we anticipate, then yes, all four of us will finally get what should have been done to us in the first place. Just make sure your boyfriends are okay with this change." The three teens giggled. Either they would accept it or they wouldn't be their boyfriends any longer.

Mentioning this brought back a flurry of memories from eighteen years ago. She and Edgard had discovered each other the year before, shocked and amazed to find another person who had similar mental skills as they had, including telepathy. While telepaths were exceedingly rare all throughout the galaxy, their extra *magic* powers were unheard of. Hence, both had been very careful never to reveal them to others, fearing they'd be kidnaped and put into some kind of research facility. Back then, Edgard had just been appointed to head the OEN and had accepted that powerful position. The first few months of their marriage had been a most happy one for both of them.

However, just as she'd become pregnant with Blanche, the corporations struck, GD in this case. The top executive there had been responsible for appointing Edgard to his new position. "If you want to retain your position, Edgard, then you and your new wife *will* join our special breeding program." His words still rang in her ears after all these years. They had no choice. Bianca had to undergo the mutation process, awaking to find her body mutated into its current form. The lack of arms wasn't so much of a problem, though it forced her to begin to use her magical gifts in public. No, she didn't mind the fact that her body was most notably more physically attractive than before. Rather what so angered both of them was first that they'd been ordered to make this ultimate sacrifice against their desires and second that the mutation wasn't complete. She wasn't a hermaphrodite.

That is, both had studied ancient history and knew the proper form of the perfect human body was that of a hermaphrodite. There had been entire worlds of these perfect humans half a millennia ago, though for unknown reasons they'd all vanished long, long ago. While neither of the two could actually say why they believed this was so, nevertheless, this notion of the ultimate human form was precisely what both wanted to one day achieve.

Countessa Bianca believed that was what started Count Edgard on his grand plan. Well, she too wanted revenge on the unethical, vicious executives of the corporations on Corporation Prime. Hence, he'd formed up that secret research laboratory and kept it funded these past eighteen years, particularly after learning of the archaeology discovery on Zeta Scorpii-C and the recovery of the ancient bio agent cylinders. In secret, he sent a Strike Team there and acquired a number of sample cylinders, sending them to this new lab. He'd said back then, "Bianca, my love, one day down the line, we will be able to have our perfect bodies. I promise you. Until then, I aim to bring these corporations down some."

Well, the man had done that, she mused, reflecting on her memories. She had gone one step further. She'd investigated just how those ancient, perfect societies actually operated. Virtually all the documentation from that era, the Dark Ages, had been lost. Still, she managed to uncover some basics and began her own secret project.

Countessa Bianca wasn't stupid. After the corporation executives had their way with her, she and Edgard began to obtain a tiny portion of their revenge. Each year, they siphoned off billions of credits, both from the OEN budget as well as from the accounts of the many corporations on Corporation Prime. Then, when the corporations' headquarters were destroyed by the "terrorist attack," she acted, transferring all of those corporations' headquarters funds to her own account. Now, she was backed by close to fifty trillion credits!

Some fifteen years ago, she'd established her own private company on a backwater world near the outer edge of the mid-arm region on a world known as 2-Zeta Ursa Major-C. Her company began manufacturing electrostatic hair machines in quantity. Plus, the research staff were given ancient photos and sketches of other devices that would enable one of these hermaphrodites to survive on their own. A model home had been build, and five years ago, she'd gone there to inspect it. She found she could mostly accomplish what she needed to without resorting to her magical powers, though many of the labor assisting devices were crude. She ordered the automatic cooking machine redesigned, and to accept more and varied voice commands.

So yes, the Countessa fully anticipated this day would come—that the ancient bio agent would be restored, allowing hermaphrodites to be made, just as they once had been. Further, that the bureaucrats were finally beginning to depart the overpopulated world played right into her planning. Her agents began buying up choice housing, as the bureaucrats had to sell and get away fast. As each of these homes was vacated, she sent orders to Ace Remodeling Corporation to remodel them fully, using the many labor assisting devices that her company had developed and tested. Slowly, she would have proper homes here on Corporate Prime for these new and perfect hermaphrodites.

Countessa Bianca came out of her reverie. "Okay, Blanche, you and Arnaud will arrange the accident for Dr. Michelle d'Mierio. Also, see if she has a romantic partner and do them as well. If not, find someone compatible with her and do them. We all know how important having a satisfying sexual relationship actually is. It will be even more so once she has become a proper woman, a hermaphrodite. We can't have her impregnating herself, at least not this soon. We need a broad gene pool initially."

"We will see to it. Do we bring her back here?" Blanche asked.

"Yes, while she is in a coma. That would be best. She can then wake up in a proper home. Hell, we best get her some proper clothing to wear. She looked like some common worker when she was here. That will never do for a perfect woman, will it?" All three teens giggled, but the boys only smiled, greatly appreciating the incredible style their girlfriends always displayed.

As Countessa Bianca watched her daughters and their boyfriends depart, she again drifted into her past memories. Long hours, she and Edgard spend discussing just how they had come by their magical powers, which were so similar. In the end, neither had any idea how it had happened, only that they and they alone had them it seemed. When she became pregnant, both hoped and prayed their children would inherit them. In fact, daily for nine months, Bianca had focused on her growing child, as though willing it to have them.

Both were relieved when Blanche first began to use powers similar to theirs. Now that they were in their late teens,

Bianca knew that, while each had these powers, they were not as great as hers or their father's. She suspected her daughter's children might not have any such magical powers at all. Hence, she wanted to make sure they would have a perfectly designed home for her grandchildren to be able to live very well on their own as perfect humans.

Now finally alone, Countessa Bianca sighed. "My long patience has finally borne fruit! At last, I can begin remaking humans into truly glowing models of perfection and without the infernal interference of the greedy, unethical corporations!" She then placed a thought in Marion's mind, and soon saw her lover entering carrying a tray of tea and biscuits.

Marion d'Oriane was thirty-five, with lovely auburn hair and enchanting hazel eyes. Years ago, the two had met each other at a Chamber Music Festival and took an instant liking to each other. In less than six months, the two had become lovers and Marion had then moved in to the Countessa's mansion, acting as her assistant as far as outsiders were concerned.

"Well my dearest, I believe soon we will be able to satisfy each other fully. It appears the way has finally opened up. I'll let you know in a week or so. I can't tell you how excited I am about it. Ah, you spoil me. Earl Grey again," Bianca said, flashing her a big grin.

Chapter 23—Accidents

Dr. Michelle returned to her home in Bordeaux, 9-Cetus-C. It had been a long flight, and she was tired, though hopeful because this Countessa at least listened to her two proposals. Perhaps now a better investigation into the terrorist attacks would be done. More importantly, she'd listened to her suggestion on changing the research focus to far more humanitarian pursuits. She showered and texted her longtime boyfriend that she was back and wanted to see him tomorrow night.

Captain Ernst Fry headed up a company of security guards for the research facility, which is how the two had met. Chatting about the weather soon turned into chatting about their love of taking long walks along the picturesque hiking trails. Before long, they had become fast friends and since last year, lovers, though neither was quite ready to commit to marriage. He was a year older than Michelle was and had short black hair. Neither was particularly attractive, though one could not go so far as to say that they were homely. Perhaps average looking might be complimentary for the two.

Right on time, Captain Ernst dropped by her small apartment. After a hug and kiss, he asked, "So how did your trip go? Any headway?"

She beamed, "Well, yes. I do believe so. We met the person who actually funds the research center, a Countessa Bianca le Masters. What a knockout blonde. Really, though, I think she's a UFB woman herself. She has three teenaged daughters, also UFB women or I am a duck." Both chuckled.

"Anyway, she said we have our funding as long as we need it, and she'll look into this mess with the terrorists. I hope I've convinced her that further study is warranted," she explained.

"Well, I don't see how the terrorists got their hands on your stuff. You know we've done a thorough check. Nothing has ever gone missing, but if it'll make you happy and relieved, I too hope this Countessa conducts a thorough investigation," he replied diplomatically.

"I even told her I think we need a new direction of research."

"Oh yeh? What did she think about that?" he asked, rather interested in her answer.

"She's looking into that too. At least, she didn't shoot me down. I'm hopeful that soon we will get new orders to start working on cures for those poor terrorist victims. Honestly, Ernst, I don't know how they can even live like they are," Dr. Michelle said a bit dramatically.

"Hey, me either. I think they must be completely helpless and have to have someone around all the time to help them with everything. I do hope you can find some cures for them," he replied sincerely. After this exchange, they chatted about taking time off on Saturday to hike their favorite trail again.

***

Blanche giggled, enjoying teasing Captain Arnaud. She insisted on flying their deep space transport to 9-Cetus-C. They had left six hours after the two doctors departed and were thus not far behind them. Her body sitting in the pilot's seat, Blanche used her magical powers to control the stick and handle the many other controls, all of which appeared to be moving of their own accord, bringing that special smile to his face, one that she fell in love with. Of course, Captain Arnaud brought along his Strike Force Team 1 with him. Their charge: arrange the accident for Dr. Michelle d'Mierio.

First, however, they needed intelligence on her. Specifically, did she have a boyfriend or lover of some kind? The Countessa was explicit on that point. Part of their delay was spent in duplicating one of the samples of the new genetic bio agent cylinders that Dr. Marcel had brought along and left with the Countessa.

Upon arrival, Captain Arnaud sent two of his team members off to locate her place and set up some spying equipment in her home. Already, there were quite a number of them inside the research facility, all unknown to the doctors there. Edgard had them installed when the facility was originally built. So while Captain Arnaud's men were out carrying out their short mission, his Comm Officer began monitoring the chat within the facility. He had little to report other than the dozen doctors were pleased to hear that they still had proper funding.

Thus, the following night, Captain Arnaud and the others listened in on the private chat of Michelle and Ernst. "Well, looks like he is her boyfriend. We will take them both," Captain Arnaud announced. "Make the plans."

Blanche sat back and watched the seven men carefully laying out their ideas for the best way to pull this off and make it look like an accident. "Look, how about this. We plant a fake record on her desk saying she's checked out a small vial of the bio agent to study at home. Then, we take them both out there with our new supply."

"But that's not allowed, taking dangerous bio agents out of the safety and security of the lab," another pointed out.

"Right, so that will add to the believability of her having an accident," Captain Arnaud broke in. "She'll have been doing something slightly against all protocols. We should make it look as if she was following her pet project, trying to find cures."

"You can pose as a bio containment squad leader, captain, and inform Dr. Marcel about the *accident* and our handling of it," one added.

"The tricky part will be getting the incriminating document onto her desk in the lab. We don't know where her office is at," another pointed out.

"Okay, Bernard, tomorrow you get to play bio containment inspector. Visit the lab and pretend to be inspecting its safety features. Find her office and hide a teleport transponder there. We can then teleport the document onto her desk if the transponder is properly placed," Captain Arnaud ordered. "We will use the paperclip version. So it won't look out of place on her desk. Better yet, substitute it for another paperclip on her desk if you can."

"We will put a tiny charge onto the bio agent cylinder; sneak it into her home. Underneath her couch would be a likely place. We will use the IR scanner and monitor them. When they are sitting on it, we'll blow it remotely. Once they drop into comas, we'll give them a couple of hours to absorb enough of the fumes before the bio containment crew arrives to handle the situation. Accidents will happen." All seven chuckled.

Their demolitions man headed off to prepare the tiny charge, making sure that it could not accidentally cause a fire when it went off beneath the couch. That done, while Dr. Michelle was at work the next day, two donned their PIS belts. Invisible, they used their fancy door lock opener machine to gain entry to Dr. Michelle's home. Two minutes later, the charge and small cylinder were properly positioned, and the pair left quietly. Once outside, they were locked onto and teleported back up to their very well equipped deep space transport, currently hovering above the city and cloaked.

"Kiss me. I hate this waiting," Blanche insisted, and Arnaud was more than willing to obey.

Dr. Michelle came home around six, showered, and fixed a light supper. Soon, her heart raced. The unique knock on her door told her it was Captain Ernst. She rushed to the door and embraced him. "Come on in. I'm just finishing up in the kitchen. Want some coffee?"

Above the city, Captain Arnaud and his team listened in on their idle chatter, while watching the red forms on the IR scanner. "They are moving into the living room," Arnaud announced, though he need not have; that was obvious to all. "Come on; sit down on the couch," he added, as if his words would somehow make them obey. Blanche was about to suggest that she could intervene and plant such a thought into Michelle's mind, when the two finally did sit down on the couch, embracing each other passionately. "Now," Captain Arnaud whispered. His demolitions man pressed a button. On the IR scanner, they saw a tiny flash of red appear and then vanish. "Keep alert for an accidental fire." All eyes watched for additional red images appearing. After five minutes, he relaxed. A fire was now unlikely.

"Now we wait," he said.

"How long will it take?" Blanche asked, growing curious. *This is so much fun!*

"Don't know. We see if they appear to go into a coma.

That's the first step," he replied. They watched and waited. After some time, neither form seemed to be moving. "We'll hazard a peek," Arnaud ordered. One of his men was teleported down beside the apartment and peeked in their window, while via live streaming everyone else watched what he saw. Both appeared to be knocked out.

As the hour drew late, he decided to leave them for the night, since they were unlikely to get late night visitors. At dawn, they began their next phase of the operation. Wearing bio containment suits, two men headed down, entered the apartment, and found the pair in comas. Quickly, they opened the windows to air out the bio agent and carried the pair outside, where Arnaud got a teleport lock on them, bringing them onto the transport. They were carried to a back cabin and stripped of their clothes. They'd never be wearing them again, if this new bio agent actually worked.

Once their sensors indicated the apartment was safe, dressed as a bio containment squad leader, Bayard headed off to the research facility. "I need to see Dr. Marcel Louvel. This is an emergency. There has been some kind of bio agent accident at one of his research geneticist's home," he explained to the security guard, who recognized him from his previous day's inspection visit.

"What's going on?" asked a suddenly worried Dr. Marcel. He'd come running to the entrance when his guard called.

Bayard explained what they had found. "We were called in to check on a suspicious situation at Dr. Michelle d'Mireio's apartment. We found her and a Captain Ernst Fry in a coma on her couch. There was a small vial labeled bio agent hazard on the floor, apparently dropped or stepped on by accident. Can you verify that Dr. Michelle took such a vial home with her? If so, then we can log this as an unfortunate accident. If not, then we will have to contact the authorities and report this as a potential terrorist attack on some of you research geneticists."

"Oh my God! None of us would ever violate such protocols, but I best check her desk. Maybe she left an explanation," he said, leading him back to her office. The two men looked over the items on her desk, and Dr. Marcel found a short note.

"Oh dear me! She says that she's taking home a small sample so that she can carry on her research into cures for the thousands of terrorist victims. I'm so sorry. She's violated all our protocols! I won't stand for that. I'll see that this can't happen again, sir," Dr. Marcel blurted out, hoping this would satisfy the man. "Obviously a tragic accident. No need to report it to the authorities. What will happen to her and the captain?"

"We will take them to proper medical facilities and see that they get the best of care. Yes, unfortunate accident. You doctors be more careful in the future! Thank you," Bayard barked, turned, and left the building. A block away, he was teleported up to the ship. Since he wore a video camera, everyone had saw and heard the exchange.

"Mission complete," Captain Arnaud reported officially to Blanche, his boss.

"Take us home, captain. Top speed. We must get there before they come out of their comas," she replied. "Oh crap. I forgot to get myself into the pilot's seat."

Arnaud laughed. "Too bad. He's got it now, dear." She grinned and gave him a kiss, then headed back to look at the two victims.

"Kind of homely, aren't they? Well," she added, "this will change all that. Now they can both be simply gorgeous."

"If you say so. I'm going to wait and see," Arnaud replied.

***

"We're not going to wait and see," barked the sixteen-year-old Dianne. She, Captain Edmon, and his team officially called Strike Force 6, had landed on Kingston-B. One of his men had flashed his OEN id card and had been hastily taken up to see the spaceport's major, who was in charge of investigating the terrorist attack, at least that portion which had occurred here at the spaceport. He'd just said to the OEN man, that they'd just have to wait and see if the dead man's identity showed up.

Edmon spoke into the mike, and his voice was

382

transmitted into the earpiece of his man on the ground. "Have him tell you where the body is located. Have him show you the video recording they may have made of the aftermath, since there weren't any security cameras in the area of the fight."

After jotting down the name of the morgue where the Master's body was being held, the major began showing him the official crime scene photos. "Say, was this unknown terrorist's defense shield on when your men got to his body?"

"Well, yes it was," the major answered, growing nervous. Dianne read his surface thoughts from her seat in the transport. *That is the weird part. I hope he doesn't ask me how it was possible to get himself shot in the chest with it on.*

"So you are telling me this unknown terrorist was shot in the chest—must have been a large caliber shot, cause it looks like a three inch hole here in front—but his PDS was on and working?" he asked the major, who began to fidget with his bottom shirt button.

"Yes sir. I've no idea how that is possible. We are testing the PDS for defects, but the results haven't come back from the lab yet," the major tried to deflect him.

"Can you call the lab, and see if they had tested it yet?" he asked, following what Edmond whispered into his earpiece.

"Yes, sir. Right away!" The major slipped out of this room, entering his own private office, leaving the OEN man to continue to look at the pile of photos of the attack. So many things were simply not adding up. Not to the major and not to Edmond.

Two minutes later, the major returned a bit more flustered than before. "Tests show the PDS found on this unidentified victim is in perfect working order. I've no idea how he could have been shot, sir. Like I said, we're going to have to wait and see."

"Okay. Let's go over these photos here. You said that there were six explosions on the other side of the control tower?"

"Yes sir. That was the first hint we had that something was going on here at the spaceport. Loud explosions. My men raced there, but saw nothing out of the ordinary," the major answered.

"He's telling you the truth," Dianne whispered. Their man gave a barely perceptible nod that he understood her.

"So it would seem to me that this was in fact a decoy, designed to pull all of your men away from the other side where the battle took place."

"Well yes. That is my conclusion. As soon as we heard the gunfire coming from the other side, we all raced around the building and found the two groups firing at each other. We've identified all the dead men as having come from Taurus-C. We also arrested thirty-three other men and women who set off the terrorist bombs in the corporate headquarters. We got them when they tried to return to their ships—those marked in red in the photos."

"But you failed to apprehend some of those who were fighting?"

"Well yes. Another second and we would have had them. I'm certain I was able to blast a large hole in the second transport, just as it took off. It's probably dead in space. Certainly, all the air has left it. However, as yet, we haven't located it. Again, just give us more time, sir. I'm sure that hulk will show up, along with the wounded woman who jumped into the ship at the last second."

"A woman? Wounded?"

"Yes, there on page 6. One woman took a shot to her upper left arm. She was the one who took the second ship, the one that I blasted a hole into as it took off. The others, two men and two women, got into the first transport before we could reach them. That ship was cloaked as it sat on the tarmac. Kind of weird looking into its cargo bay, while the rest of the ship was invisible. That ship took off seconds before the other one did."

"So major, what is your current theory of what exactly happened here?"

"Well, mind you, it's still early in the investigation, but I'd say that this unknown man, a terrorist, probably got into an argument with his fellow terrorists. They fought it out and he lost."

"I see. Okay. Please keep the OEN informed on the results of your investigation. I'm off to inspect the dead unknown man." He turned and headed back to the official OEN transport, which was painted all black, except for the skull and crossbones on its side, identifying it unequivocally as belonging to the OEN.

Dianne said, "Well the major isn't too bright. His so-called theory is full of holes. For one thing, that doesn't explain six bombs going off on the other side of the control tower, drawing his men there first. It also doesn't explain why the bombs didn't actually damage anything, just a few potholes in the tarmac, but there were plenty of high value targets within mere feet of the explosions."

Edmond laughed. "No kidding. You spotted those anomalies too, dear. Way to go, hot shot."

Dianne giggled. "Guys, it looks more like an OEN hit than anything else."

"That's what I am leaning towards," Edmond replied. "A hit of some kind. Okay, we need to check on that unknown man. I'll send someone over there right now. While he's gone, would someone like to explain to me how that man who was wearing an operational PDS took a large round to his chest? Those two concepts are at odds with each other. Considering the man's wounds, he would have been unable to turn the device back on after he was shot. Hell, the man was dead at that point."

"Sorry captain," his ordinance man spoke up. "Can't happen. If the PDS was working, he couldn't have been shot, unless someone knocked him off his feet and then shot at him upwards from his feet. Either that or the man was foolish enough to allow his opponent to slowly move that large gun inside his protective shield and then fire it. But that couldn't have happened. The wound's appearance suggests the shell was fired some distance away, not close up. The only other rational explanation is that the man had it turned off when he was shot, and one of the major's men accidentally turned it on afterwards. Otherwise, it makes no logical sense."

The group discussed this improbability, while waiting for the morgue report. Finally, his man got to examine the remains of this unknown terrorist. As the group saw the images coming in from the live video stream, Dianne screamed, "Dad! That's dad. Count Edgard le Masters! Oh my God!"

"Shit!" Edmond cursed. "I'm sorry, Dianne. You don't have to be up here with us, if you don't want to be."

"No, I'm staying. We have to find out what happened to dad. We can't leave his body here either. Eventually, it's going to be identified. We can't let that happen," Dianne declared, fighting to control her swelling emotions. So dad was this mysterious Master terrorist, she thought. It figured. She had her suspicions, but this clinched it.

Captain Edmond told his man at the morgue, "Pull rank on this one. Bring that body back with you. It's Dianne's father, the Count." Via the video stream, he saw the slight head nod that indicated his man understood. "Dianne, I'm going to visit the major and pull rank with him, confiscating all their evidence. Stay here and let me know if anything else comes up." She nodded, thankful that she didn't have to say anything right now.

"Yes major, I'm afraid this has become an official OEN matter now. Your people can continue with the terrorist bombing investigation, but this spaceport matter is officially in the hands of the OEN at this time. We will let you know the outcome later on, if your security level is high enough, depending upon what we find out. I'll need to take custody of all the evidence you've gather here at the spaceport. Sorry, but I have my own orders to follow."

"Yes, yes of course!" He'd expected some resistance from the major, but instead the relief emanating from the man was noticeable to Edmond, who had not a telepathic molecule in his body. Two hours later, the official chain of custody documents were properly signed, and the pile of evidence loaded into sealed boxes, which were then carried out to their deep space transport. Shortly after that, his man arrived with a coffin holding the body of the count.

A few minutes later, they were in hyperspace, and Dianne placed a secure call to her mother to report their startling discovery. She was somewhat surprise to find that Bianca wasn't surprised by all this. "Good thinking, Dianne," Countessa Bianca replied. "We need to go over the evidence with a fine tooth comb. We need answers and need them fast, but I expect that's not going to happen or that major would have already found them. Over and out."

By the time they landed on Corporate Prime, his demolitions man confirmed the major's lab's findings. The Count's PDS was in perfect working condition, nearly fully charged even. At this point, Dianne and Edmond knew that they had a serious investigation ahead of them, one they might not actually be able to solve. No conceivable way should the Count be dead with a giant hole in his chest, and yet he was most certainly dead.

Biding their time on the long homeward trip, Edmond began theorizing with his men and Dianne. "Look, much of this looks like one of our own OEN hits—those six explosions were obviously meant to distract spaceport security, while the attackers took out the Count and the other men. They were terrorists, so a hit squad perhaps? We're going to have to check with every one of our OEN strike teams. Could one of them have done this?"

"I'm on it now," Dianne replied, glad this was something that she could do. As Commander, she had enormous pull, second only to that of her sisters and her mother. "I'm demanding all strike force records for a two week period around the time of this attack and from all our many teams. Mom will back me up on this if any others balk at disclosing them."

By the time they landed on Corporate Prime, the Countessa had received the many logs. There had been some field reconnaissance trips, but no actual strike force teams had been sent out from any OEN base anywhere, at least according to the records. Countessa Bianca didn't discount that perhaps one team had gone rogue on her and had the various Commanders questioned about such a possibility. A week later, even that notion was dispelled. It had not been an OEN strike, in spite of how closely it resembled one.

Their conclusion did hold though, that this had been a surgical strike by parties unknown, a hit on the Master most likely. But by whom? Finally, lacking any real data, Countessa Bianca ordered every Strike Team out into the field, searching for clues about anyone claiming to have *hit* the Master.

It was early spring on Scorpi-C when word finally reached Countessa Bianca that the GD Corporation executive there, a UFBMD man named Alfonso Vega, had ordered the strike that had killed her husband. Now she sent several Strike Teams to Scorpi-C to learn all they could about this man and what had been going on in the Abelard Sector the past year.

She didn't have long to wait. Alfonso had done many incredible things in that sector and was now its official leader. The stranglehold that the corporations once had on the sector had been abolished. The people now owned property or they were paying for it so that one day it would belong to them. He had been a terrorist attack victim himself, now a UFBMD man. He had been instrumental in accepting all terrorist attack victims from any world in the galaxy and had close to forty thousand of them now residing on his world. He had established scholarship for all students, and gotten them into high schools and their Academy there. This alone was shocking to the Countessa and her daughters. These were UFB women and UFBMD men, supposedly helpless men and women that were now going to schools.

"Clearly, this Alfonso Vega fellow is close to being on our side in this mess," Countessa Bianca explained to her three daughters. "It's amazing what he's done and for a whole damned sector, and so much of it while being a UFBMD man!"

"But mom, it's only one of those sparsely populated rim sectors. Not such a big deal. Besides, he ordered the hit on dad," Blanche declared testily. "We need to hit him."

"No dear, no we don't. This man is actually working for us, though he has no idea that he is. Right now, we need him and his ideas to spread across the galaxy. More importantly, we need to acquire one of those new assault guns that his other UFBMD man designed. That's what was used to kill Edgard. Your father knew that eventually someone would come gunning for him. You can't go around committing terrorist acts across the galaxy without making powerful enemies. I simply couldn't talk him out of it, the old fool. At least, he has been darn successful at bringing the major corporations to their knees. I doubt very much if they can even recover. I believe they'll be simply ghosts of what they once were. So your dad has laid the groundwork for us to follow to complete our vision of perfect worlds filled with perfect humans," Countessa Bianca explained.

Blanche grumbled, "But he killed dad."

"Yes, and most will feel that he was more than justified in doing that, dear. Now come on; we have a lot of planning to do, the four of us. Besides, it is time that we four get our promised perfect body forms." That bought smiles to her three daughter's faces, and Blanche forgot about her desire to get revenge for her dad's slaying.

Chapter 24—Trials and Testing

Dr. Michelle d'Mireio finally woke up. The last thing she remembered was kissing Ernst, while they were sitting on her living room couch in her home on Bordeaux, 9-Cetus-C. But this wasn't there. This wasn't even herself, but some horror-filled nightmare. *Perhaps I'll wake up soon.*

Countessa Bianca had both Michelle and Ernst sitting up on the same bed. She'd used a bit of her *magical* force to get them sitting there. Across from them, she had two full-length mirrors facing them. This way, they could both see what they now looked like. However, she first had to get them over their intense shock. They kept waking, gasping, muttering something not quite comprehensible, and passing out. After the third failed attempt, she resorted to using her powers on them, placing a command in each of their minds, "Stay alert."

"This isn't me; it can't be," wailed Michelle.

"This isn't me either. Not even my voice," wailed Ernst. His voice had risen into the alto range from his previous bass.

Now that they stopped passing out, Countessa Bianca explained, "Yes, this is both of you. You were the victim of a bad genetic bio agent accident at your former apartment, Michelle. The vial of bio agent you brought home with you to study broke while you were on the couch. Perhaps you accidentally sat on it? We don't know, except that a bio containment crew found you and handled the situation."

"I never ever took out of the lab! That goes against all our protocols," she wailed, protesting her heart out, while still imagining this was some terrible nightmare, but she couldn't pinch herself to wake up. No arms. In this dream, Ernst had none either.

"However it happened, it doesn't matter now, Michelle, Ernst. It's done. Just look at your stunningly beautiful new bodies! Gorgeous. Just fabulously gorgeous, both of you. Your shapes are perfect. Your hair, Michelle, is so lush, so long, so brown, so wavy. Soon you'll see how fantastically you can feel with it. It has neurons and axons in each strand, so you have a powerful new sense of touch with each strand. It's knee length just like mine. Your feet are just like mine as well, so now you can wear the same fabulous, exotic heels that my daughters and I do. And your breasts! Now I have to admit, yours are so much more perfect than mine are. I'm so envious of them. I thought mine were stellar, but yours are even bigger, firmer, perkier. Incredible, Michelle. You do look far, far better than the usual UFB woman does, and that's saying a *whole* lot. You should be very proud of your new form."

"But I have that thing," she fairly screamed.

"Of course, you do. Your body is a hermaphrodite now. Just be careful. I'm told you can impregnate yourself. Now you have the form that God intended for us humans to have, perfect in all ways. No longer must you always be on the receiving end when having intercourse. Now you can give as well. Just fabulous," Countessa Bianca explained.

"But what's happened to me? This can't be me. I'm not a woman!" wailed Ernst.

"No, you are a hermaphrodite as well, Ernst. Look in the mirror. Can't you see a bit of your old self in the reflection? You too have a stunning body. Your lush raven hair is incredible, don't you think? Now you not only can give Michelle your love, but also you can receive hers in return. You both are gorgeous, fabulously attractive, stunning, don't you think? Perfect in all ways."

"But we're completely helpless," Ernst protested.

"Well, perhaps a bit, but when I heard of your accident, I had you brought here to Corporate Prime. I've been working for years trying to design a proper living environment for us special women and now hermaphrodites. You are in one of my model homes. After we get you dressed up, I'll show you around. There are so many labor-assisting devices that I'm sure that you both can manage to live very nicely on your own. You will see, but it may take some time to get used to everything. My girls were born this way, so they didn't have to adjust suddenly, as you both are doing. But I'm sure you can manage just fine. This first time, I'll have my girls help you get dressed and then we'll show you around your new home and how to run things."

"But I can't live like this!" Michelle wailed.

"Me either. Can't you just kill us? Please," Ernst begged, still staring at his reflection in the mirror.

"Oh don't be silly, Ernst. You have a gorgeous body, a body that many women would die to have—a body that most men drool over, so don't be so silly. Besides, your Michelle needs you now, just as you need her. I will see that you are married yet today," Countessa Bianca advised the two. "And don't worry about credits. I'll take care of everything, as long as you both just try to learn and do your best. You are, after all, the first of the absolutely perfect humans now."

"But I can't do my work, not helpless like this. I wanted to find a cure for the victims," Michelle protested, "and Ernst is a guards captain."

"You don't need any cures now, my beautiful young women. You are just perfect. You are both a woman and a man, together in one body, just as God intended us all to be. In time, you both will see what I mean. Now let's get you dressed," Countessa Bianca replied softly, having already sent word for her daughters to join her and assist her just this once in helping to get them dressed up nicely, as fitting their new, exalted status. Besides, she knew how much the three teens wanted to see the pair for themselves.

Michelle and Ernst were still heavily enmeshed in grief and shock, nearly overwhelmed by feelings of helplessness. Like a pair of mindless zombies, they stood wiggling wildly to keep their balance or sat or this or that as the four proceeded to dress them properly. Neither notices they were wearing extremely expensive satin gowns, both a light blue as though they were twins, complete with matching extreme heels. Vague awareness that they could stand a little easier in the heels was only barely perceived, as both victims slipped on down into a solid apathy, allowing the four to do whatever they desired to these bodies, which were now no longer them or theirs.

Like two inanimate dolls, the wiggling pair stood while some strange man pronounced them married. Just as confused, the man said. "I now pronounce you wife and wife." The three teens, acting as witnesses, giggled at that, and the man departed, a little confused about all this as well. Still, he dared not say anything to the Countessa.

"Now then, perfect women," Countessa Bianca began speaking in her commanding tone once more, "it is time we showed you all these labor-saving machines and how you are to run them. Of course, each one has plainly written operating instructions on them, in case you forget. Now this is your automated kitchen."

How long the pair were talked at and moved about their rather spacious new home, neither could say—their eyes filled with blank, non-comprehension stares, their minds no longer accepting any input. "Mom, what's wrong with them?" Blanche whispered, having noticed this and becoming a little alarmed. "They look sort of dead. I'm not getting any real thoughts from them anymore."

Countessa Bianca finally stopped her near constant instruction of the two and gave both a stern look, touching their minds. "Hum," she said. "You're right. It's like they aren't there any longer. Perhaps the shock of all this was a bit much. Let's give them some time to realize what's happened to them. Maybe a few days are needed here."

"Maybe we should look at how the other new ones that dad made reacted?" suggested Dianne.

"Maybe we should leave them undressed, mom. I mean if they are left dressed up and then need to use the restroom, they won't know what to do," Celestine suggested, beginning to see that this wasn't working out quite as they had imagined.

"Perhaps you are right, dear," Countessa Bianca replied, biting her lip slightly between her sparkling white teeth. They undressed the couple and left them sitting on their living room couch for now. "We'll just hire a temporary assistant for them until they snap out of it," she declared in a positive manner. "Come; let's see about getting ourselves done." That brought the three teens out of their emotional slump. What had promised to be a gay, cheerful first meeting had turned out to be very depressing for all three of them.

Several hours later, a middle-aged woman named Riva arrived. "Land sakes, what have we here? Oh my! I've never seen anything like you two!" she stared hard at their dual sexual organs, but decided that they must be women, probably terrorist victims. She tried to cheer up the pair of zombies, but didn't get the slightest reaction from either of them. So she turned on the entertainment center, flipping to the Galactic News channel. She preferred to hear their constant banter as background noise while she worked.

"Oh my, such a strange kitchen. Well, the Countessa did say that there were instructions on everything. Let's see what I can whip up for the young women, something nourishing, I expect." Riva prepared a chicken-based meal and fed the pair. Try as she might, though, Michelle and Ernst remained unmoving zombies. Later on, she got them into bed and headed off to see about unpacking her bag in the spare bedroom. "Oh dearie me, this is going to be the most boring job I've ever had!" Riva spoke to herself as she undressed for the night.

***

Two days later, Countessa Bianca, Blanche, Celestine, and Dianne awoke from their relatively brief comas. The four had laid down on the Countessa's king sized bed and released a cylinder of the new genetic bio agent into the bedroom, which had been completely sealed off from the rest of the mansion. Arnaud, Beneoit, and Edmond stood guard at the mansion, watching over the four, along with the Countessa's companion for many years, Marion d'Oriane, who fixed the three teens their meals. While the three deeply cared for their three special teens and commanders, they were not so sure what the women were doing to their bodies now was right. After all, they were the men in the relationship. None of the three could fathom why the women would want a superfluous male organ. That was their domain, male pride and joy. Marion on the other hand knew why her lover, the Countessa, did, but she wouldn't dare mention such a thing to these young men!

When the four awoke from their comas, the first thing they did was to examine their anatomy. "All right!" Blanche declared, staring at her new appendage. So did the others.

"Now we are all perfect, the way we should've been in the first place!" declared Countessa Bianca. "Wait til Marion sees and feels this!" Her teens giggled, but as they looked at

394

each other, their new appendages activated. "Oh!" she added. Four slightly red faces glanced at each other.

"Mom, look at me. It's getting aroused by all of you," Dianne stated the obvious. "I guess it really does work," she added.

Hastily, the four used their *magic* powers to get dressed and headed out to find their boyfriends and Marion, eager to tell them they were just fine—perfect actually.

"Now I'm perfect for you," Blanche exclaimed, pushing her body into that of Arnaud, whose arms encircled her thin waist, sliding over her satin gown, but beneath her wavy blonde hair, just as he always did, and shared a passionate kiss with his fiancé. The other two young men did likewise, while Countessa Bianca took Marion into the next room before sharing a loving embrace with her.

Almost at once, Blanche sensed something wasn't quite right, not quite the same as before. Somehow, someway, Arnaud wasn't as attractive to her, an emotion that felt very strange to her. Nearby, Celestine and Dianne also felt the same strange feelings, though none said anything about it. Perhaps it was just an aftereffect of having been in a coma for two days.

"We should all go to the symphony tonight," Blanche suggested, finally pulling away slightly from Arnaud.

"Oh let's!" Dianne spoke up, delighted with the idea, though she didn't really like going there, except to make out with Edmond.

All four women found the evening outing drastically different from ever before. Of course, half of those attending this elegant affair were women. Suddenly, all four found their new male appendages reacting wildly. Even looking at an attractive woman walking into Symphony Hall aroused them, causing them no end of embarrassment, especially the three teens.

When they returned home and their boyfriends left for the night, Blanche broke down in tears. "Mom, something is very wrong with me. It's, it's reacting to all the attractive women I see around me. It's so embarrassing."

"Hey, mine too," added Celestine, very thankful that her older sister brought it up. She was too embarrassed by it to have said anything. "Somehow, I'm not as attracted to Beneoit as I used to be. Mom, what's going on with us?"

Dianne giggled girlishly. "Being around all of you makes mine go hard too. Isn't that the strangest thing?"

"Oh dear. You noticed that too!" Countessa Bianca spoke up. "Well, it's probably nothing. Remember, we only woke up from the comas this morning. Let's give our bodies a few days to adjust. After all, kids, we're now perfect women." Besides, she was dying to head to bed and the waiting Marion.

In the morning as the teens gathered around their mother for a light breakfast that Marion was preparing in the kitchen, they noticed a glow about their mother's face. She giggled as her girls had. "Wow. That's all I can say. Wow. Incredible experience. Marion loved it."

"Oh, tell us all about it? Does it really work? I mean like the men's do?" Blanche asked eagerly, though her eyes darted about to make sure Marion wasn't close enough to overhear her.

Lowering her voice, Countessa Bianca whispered, "Yes, yes it most certainly does! What a feeling. It's been denied to half of all humans, until now that is. This is absolutely what God had intended for us all to be!" She hastily became quiet and began talking about today's weather, because Marion came walking in with a tray and their breakfasts.

Later while Marion was cleaning up the dishes, the four met in Bianca's private study. "You know girls; I must admit I was only half-satisfied last night. Thinking about it over breakfast, I've figured it out. Marion needs to be like me as well. Then, together we share completely, both ways at the same time. That must be how it is supposed to be."

"Oh!" Blanche blushed in a sudden realization. She wasn't suddenly attracted to women instead of men, but rather she wanted desperately to be with another hermaphrodite, one who could, as her mother just said, share both ways at the same time. "But Arnaud, he's a guy and my captain in the OEN. I'd love to have him like me, mom, but dare we? What if he reacts as Michelle and Ernst have? Besides, he doesn't have our magic powers. He couldn't still be my captain, could he?"

Countessa Bianca bit her lip, seriously thinking over

this new revelation. "Well," she finally said, "let me see what I can do with Marion. If she can make the change properly, then we'll see about your boyfriends. I suppose if worse comes to worse, we could always find replacement captains for their teams and get you three married."

***

"But love, I'd be completely helpless. I couldn't do all the things that I do for you anymore. I don't have your magical powers," Marion protested. It was a half hour later. Countessa Bianca has shooed her daughters out, and Marion joined her, bringing the two of them their morning tea. The Countessa just told her what she wanted to do to Marion's body so they could be truly a perfect couple for all time. Obviously, Marion was frightened, bordering on terrified of becoming a helpless UFB woman or whatever this new version was called.

"I understand, Marion. I promise you we'll have all of those new automatic labor saving machines installed here. Then, you would be able to still do everything you're currently doing, just using these marvelous machines that have been invented for us. Don't you see, you would then also be perfect. We could even have our own children. We're both not too old yet."

The Countessa knew she was pushing a sensitive button in her lover. Marion had not married, but desperately wanted to have children of her own, and her biological clock was ticking away very rapidly now. "Just think of it, Marion. We could then have children of our own, you and I, as many as we can manage in the time our bodies have left," Bianca continued to push Marion's button.

Slowly, her lover began to give in. "But would you like it if I was that helpless?"

"Look, you have always been here for me, so it's high time I was there for you. Besides, with all those special machines in here, why, in no time you would be doing everything you are now doing, though in different ways. I'm sure it would work out perfect for you, just give it a little time, Marion. I do so love you and so want to have your children too."

Marion gave in. Motherhood was the one thing so far

397

denied to her in her life. Here was perhaps her one and only chance to have her own. "Well, all right then, but only after we get this place all fixed up."

After a very busy week, the workers finished up installing all manner of new devices in the mansion, from automatic sliding doors to voice-activated controls to the fancy kitchen machine, which would prepare their meals for them. Marion experimented a little with each one, becoming familiar with how it worked and then finally agreed to have it done.

Four days later, Marion came out of her coma. Now she had the same knee-length hair as her lover, though hers was a rich auburn. Her face looked like that of angel, and her body shape was quite stunning. So much so that Bianca couldn't keep from becoming passionate with Marion as soon as Marion woke up and had examined her new form in the full-length mirrors in their bedroom. Both women were quite surprised by the overwhelming new sensations flooding over their bodies as they lay on their sides facing each other and sharing their love simultaneously—so powerful that after a brief rest, they did it again.

All that day, Marion talked of nothing else but the incredible sensations that she was now experiencing. She stood in the electrostatic hair machine, activating it a dozen times before stepping out of it. "That is beyond description, Bianca! I can feel the air with every strand of my hair! It's so sensuous, an almost overwhelming one. I just can't stop doing it!"

Bianca kept saying, "I know. I know. Fabulous, isn't it?"

Her teens simply couldn't stand it and telepathically peeked in on the two from time to time. Now they too understood. They simply had to have lovers who were like themselves, perfect women, but could they do it to their boyfriends? That remained a huge obstacle.

Their boyfriends weren't stupid or unobservant. From the very day that their girlfriends changed, they knew somehow they weren't as close to them as before. They seemed a little distant. As the days progressed, they began to grasp what was going on, particularly so when they found out Countessa Bianca was changing her long-time assistant

Marion into one of them.

"Look, we all know our girlfriends are, well I don't know, more distant since they changed," Arnaud suggested. The three were meeting in Arnaud's room in the OEN base there on Corporate Prime.

"Yeh, but look, Bianca's just converted Marion. From what Dianne has been telling me, Bianca just loves the change. That's a bit scary, fellows," Edmond pointed out.

"What if they want to change us too?" asked a worried Beneoit. "We'd suddenly be one of those UFBMD men, and helpless too."

"And with female organs. Don't forget that!" Edmond added sarcastically.

"Guys, you are scaring the crap out of me! Surely, our girlfriends wouldn't do that to us. Right?" asked Arnaud, nervously.

"Haven't you noticed that what the Countessa wants, the Countessa gets?" Beneoit pointed out. "I think we're going to get screwed!"

Arnaud laughed nervously and added, "Literally, if they change us. Can't we find a way to stop them from doing that to us?"

"Hell, they can read our minds as easily as we can read our orders," Edmond pointed out the futility of their situation.

"We could just take off. Grab a transport and head out there somewhere," Beneoit suggested. "We could get our ID cards changed. We have funds. We could just disappear, maybe. Guys, I don't want to become a helpless sex toy of Celestine's. That's what we'd be, helpless sex toys, and women no less!"

"I agree. I'd rather die than become whatever they are now, beyond freaks. I mean they were great before, but not now, not with pricks," Edmond said crassly.

"Okay then, we best make our plans to disappear and damned quick," Arnaud decided. On the sly, they made themselves new ID cards and setup corresponding bank accounts. They agreed to depart the day after the girls' joint birthday party. Dianne was turning seventeen on Saturday, while Celestine would be eighteen two weeks later, and

Blanche would turn nineteen three weeks after Dianne's birthday. Hence, the Countessa always celebrated her girls' birthdays at the same time, since that was more convenient. The boys knew they had no choice but to be with their girlfriends at the party.

"Mom, Arnaud is planning to sneak away!" a worried Blanche told her mother. Countessa Bianca was in her private room sipping her tea and making plans.

"She looked up. "What?"

"I sort of peeked into his mind. He's been acting a bit funny around me, ever since I became perfect. So I peeked. Honestly, mom, he is terrified of becoming perfect too, like us. So are Edmond and Beneoit," she whispered.

"Do your sisters know about this?" the Countessa asked pointedly. She'd not thought the boys would react this way. After all, who wouldn't cherish the opportunity to become perfect in all ways? From glamorous, ravishing beauty to a stunning physical form, they were perfect humans, hermaphrodites actually. She could not imagine anyone not wanting to be the very best in perfection.

"No, I didn't want to scare them," she answered. "How could they do this to us? Men! I don't understand them. I've been giving all my love to Arnaud, and this is how he repays me—running away, like some petty thief in the night."

"I've sent for Dianne and Celestine. We should discuss this together, dear. Yes, I know what you mean about men. Remember, I couldn't talk any sense into your father and look where that got him—dead. Well, we can handle this easily. I'm sure in time they will just love being perfect like you three are."

"But mom, what if they don't? I mean, what if after we make them perfect, they detest us?" Blanche protested. "Marion, well she knew about it and even practiced some with the inventions before you changed her, but she agreed to it. Arnaud is terrified of it; I just know it. What if he hates me after we make him perfect?"

"Well, I can tell you that having sex this way is utterly fantastic, beyond description really," Countessa Bianca tried another angle. "I'm sure after you and Arnaud do it once, he'll come around. Of course, we'll have to get you three married before doing that. It's not proper to have sexual relations when you're not married. Such might be for common women, but not our family. We, the prefect women, must set high standards for those who will follow after us."

"But how can I marry him if he's going to hate me afterwards?" Blanche continued to whine.

"You're just going to have to use your female charms on him to get him to come around, dear," Countessa Bianca declared. "We will take care of them at your birthday party on Saturday evening. Don't worry, my child."

***

"Don't worry guys," Arnaud insisted. "This will work. Besides, I think Blanche already suspects something is up with us. Ten to one, if we don't try this, we'll never leave their birthday party whole. Trust me. This is going to work."

"Damn, Arnaud, it had better or our lives are kaput," Beneoit barked angrily. "I can't believe they want to wipe us out, after all we've done for them these past few years."

"Screwed up," Edmond added. "Those are four screwed up bitches, but they're our bosses, and they've got all the credits. Wouldn't be so bad if they didn't have those magic powers or could read minds."

Arnaud laughed, "Edmond, that's the brightest thing you've said all afternoon. You're damned right. If they didn't have magic powers and couldn't read minds, hell, they would have been ideal wives, but not now, not with them having our big guns." All three laughed at that, but twas a nervous laugh. The three felt very ill at ease around their once-girlfriends, ever since they'd become *perfect women*, like their mother and Marion.

"Well, just in case it doesn't work," Beneoit added, "I'm bringing along this." He waved a vial of cyanide. "No damn way am I going to be one of those freaks! I'd rather be dead."

"Me too," Edmond added.

"Bring it, Beneoit, but I hope we don't need it," Arnaud replied, giving the vial a long stare. *Women shouldn't be this damned powerful, certainly not over me and my friends. It goes against the laws of nature.*

As Saturday evening approached, the three teens put the finishing touches on their appearances, using the electrostatic hair machine to redo their long, flowing hair, allowing it to lie across the backs of their light blue, satin gowns, purchased especially for tonight's party. Looking into their full-length mirrors, the three teens admired their appearance, particularly their significantly larger bosoms, compliments of the new genetic bio agent modification. While their bosoms were not yet as large as their mother and Marion's, they were quite noticeably larger, forcing the three to discard their old dresses and purchase new ones that fit properly, accentuating their new curves rather sensationally. These new gowns had tiny ruffles at their shoulders and a modest neckline, since the Countessa still didn't allow them to wear the provocative, plunging necklines that she and Marion now wore.

Satisfied that she looked perfect, Blanche headed off to chat with her mother. "Is everything ready?" she asked. Countessa Bianca was just adjusting the fall of Marion's auburn hair, using a touch of her magic powers.

"Oh Blanche, you look positively stunning. The light blue so does match your eyes, dear. And yes. All is ready. I'll release it after we have your cake, so stop fretting, dear," Countessa Bianca chided her eldest daughter.

Promptly at seven, their doorbell rang, and Blanche rose from their plush living room couch to answer it, followed by Celestine and Dianne, eager to get their boyfriends finally converted into perfect women like themselves. Blanche had been counting the days, four for the coma, then minutes for the wedding ceremony, and finally she could take Arnaud to bed and satisfy this incredible craving that she had been enduring. Using her magic power, she opened the door wide, her sisters just behind her. However, what she saw took her and her sisters by surprise.

True, their boyfriends stood there, dress nicely in their grey tweed suits, but each had a stunning blonde young woman around their supporting arms. Arnaud said coyly, "Ladies, these arc the birthday girls. Blanche, Celestine, and Dianne. We've brought you a birthday treat, especially for you.

These are the Oda sisters. Monique and Neva are nineteen and Noelle is eighteen, your presents for the evening or longer. May we come in?"

The three sisters were extremely beautiful UFB women, who looked nearly identical, with knee-length, wavy, rich blonde hair and perfectly formed, round faces. They had a sparkle in their light blue eyes, radiating the excitement that they felt, having been invited to come to this particular party. Everyone knew that the le Masters were incredibly wealthy. Just driving up to their mansion suggested enormous wealth and power lay just inside.

"I'm so very pleased finally to get to meet you in person, Blanche," Monique gushed, unable to contain her enthusiasm at this incredible meeting. "I've seen you often at the symphony. You look just fabulous, and happy birthday to all of you," she chatted away as the six entered the spacious living room, where Countessa Bianca and Marion had just stepped in from the far end, staring at the three unexpected guests.

Arnaud didn't need telepathy to notice the instant arousal of Blanche the second that her eyes swept over the form of Monique! She said, "Oh! Wow, Monique, you look simply stunning. Welcome to our party. Please come in; sit with me. We must chat." Gently, Arnaud released his steadying arm, and Monique moved up to Blanche, pushing her body gently into Blanche's, their unique form of greeting. Of course, both women got a huge surge of tactile sensations from the touching of their very sensitive long hair, exciting both women. Arnaud glanced at the others and saw similar reactions from Celestine and Dianne.

Within a minute, all six were sitting beside each other chatting away, leaving the three men completely out of the conversation, which allowed Arnaud to walk over to the Countessa. "Might I have a private word with you?" he whispered.

Still rather shocked with the surprise guests, she swallowed, and said, "Of course. Marion, we'll need three more settings, please. This way, Arnaud." She led him into her private study and magically closed the door. "What is the meaning of this? These three UFB women?"

Arnaud knew this was it. Life or death hung on what he said next. "Look, Countessa Bianca, we three are sworn to protect the four of you. We are the best in the OEN or you wouldn't have given us our positions. We three were planning to marry your daughters, but that's changed now. Haven't you noticed since they became like you and Marion, after that last genetic modification, they haven't been the same? There's a cold distance between them and us now. We know they desperately need a proper mate, such as you have with Marion. We both know you could go ahead and genetically turn us into something like Marion, but we both also know we three guys don't have your *magic* powers, so if you did that, we three would be helpless, unable to fulfill our obligations to protect the four of you. Between you and me, Countessa, we're men, and we take this obligation to heart. We simply couldn't live if we let you down like this. So we brought them a present, one which will better fulfill their needs now."

He went on, "Have you noticed all three of your daughters are simply star-struck with these three sisters? They're ignoring us fellows ever since Blanche opened the door as saw them. I don't need to read her mind to know she and her sisters are very highly aroused by the Oda sisters. These three sisters would make ideal mates for Blanche, Celestine, and Dianne. I might add, three very willing mates."

Countessa Bianca smiled. She'd already sensed this quite strongly in her three daughters, which is why she'd not said anything when she saw the sisters entering her living room. "I see your point. Just who are these three sisters?"

"Their father used to be a GE Corp executive, but he was recently killed in the terrorist attack. Their mother was beside herself with grief, fell down some steps at their home, and died, leaving these three charming sisters orphaned. So you see, they would be perfect for mates of your daughters, leaving us three free to continue to be your protectors. Besides, since they've always been UFB women, they are very accustomed to life, whereas if you turned us into Marions, we wouldn't be. There are many advantages in this for all of us. What do you say, Countessa?" Arnaud finished. He couldn't think of anything more to say, and hoped and prayed this was

404

enough to save his life and that of his two friends. If not, well there was always Edmond's solution close at hand.

Countessa Bianca smiled, thinking fast. Michelle and Ernst were mostly zombies, a very unexpected result. Clearly, modifying normal people into perfect people had adaption problems associated with the change. Here, the sisters had always been UFB women, were completely happy with their lives, and the minor change to their bodies would be probably cause them little troubles. However, she wasn't known for acting hastily. "Let us see how the evening and party progresses, shall we? You have very valid points, but I have my darling daughters to think of."

"Of course," Arnaud replied diplomatically, and slipped a steadying arm around her, leading her back into the ongoing party in the living room. Already, Blanche had turned on their music system. The pair found all six women had paired up and were dancing with each other, totally engrossed in each other. Beneoit and Edmond were being completely ignored, sitting on a back couch and watching the women dance.

As the two stood at the doorway to the living room, Arnaud heard sobbing coming from the kitchen, Marion. He turned and headed to see what was wrong. Countessa Bianca followed behind him, much more slowly. Marion now had one of the new automated kitchens and had used the voice-activated system to prepare tea and their large chocolate birthday cake. However, she wasn't able to do much more. Arnaud found her sitting on a chair sobbing.

"What's wrong, Marion?" he asked gently, as Countessa Bianca finally joined him.

"I don't have Bianca's *magic*. I can't get the tea ready to serve, and I can't handle their cake. There it sits, but I can't serve it, not anymore. I'm so helpless like this," she wailed, nearly breaking the Countessa's heart.

"Dearest Marion. I'm so sorry. It does take some time and practice to learn how to do things. Come, Arnaud and I'll lend you some help. It will be just fine, you'll see," the Countessa said oozing sympathy. Hastily, Arnaud and the Countessa got everything moved over to the elegant table, complete with party favors, and gaily decorated.

Then, the Countessa said, "Marion, you have to give yourself time to learn. The UFB women have grown up as they are, so you can't expect to be as able as they are in just a few days. I think you're doing wonderfully well, my dear." Somehow, Marion stopped sobbing and attempted to smile. Arnaud carefully wiped her face with a party napkin, while giving the Countessa a glance that said, "Told you so." In his mind, he heard, *Perhaps, you are right on this.* Arnaud finally relaxed a little; maybe this was going to work out in his favor after all.

"Cake time," Countessa Bianca finally called out, ending the teens wild time of dancing. Breathless, the six came into the dining room where the party treats were nicely arranged, compliments of Arnaud and the Countessa.

"Oh, such a beautiful cake! And party hats even," exclaimed Monique. "Oh someone please help me get mine on." Blanche used her *magic* powers, showing off to Monique, lifting Monique's hat up and getting it securely on her head, very much impressing the three sisters, who had never seen such things. Further, Blanche, Celestine, and Dianne just had to feed their new friends. Six sets of forks and spoons rose and fell, much to the amazement and awe of the Oda sisters, who continued to chat between bites of cake. At least, Marion had straws in their punch glasses. Again, the three young men were completely ignored by the Countessa's daughters, for their entire attention was devoted to the Oda sisters, whom they found charming, delightful, and gorgeous.

Later on, the three sisters needed to use the bathroom. Blanche took this opportunity to speak privately to her mother. "Mom, these UFM teens are ideal for us, a hundred times better than Arnaud and the fellows."

Grinning, Countessa Bianca replied, "So I and the fellows have noticed. What say we change our plans and invite the Oda sisters to be your mates instead of the fellows, who truly do want to be our protectors?"

"Oh, can we? That is perfect, mom, perfect. Let's do it. I know Celestine and Dianne want this too," Blanche gushed merrily.

A bit later when everyone was back in the living room

once again, Countessa Bianca addressed the Oda sisters. "You three are just so wonderful. We'd love to have you three come here and live with us. My girls have never been so happy."

"Wow! Here? Live in this mansion?" Monique exclaimed, her eyes nearly popping out of her head. At least, they were wide open, as far as Arnaud saw.

That was settled. Arnaud promised to retrieve their belongings tomorrow. Quietly, the three young men took their leave, knowing that in all likelihood, the Countessa would be unleashing the genetic bio agent onto the three UFB teens. Well, he thought, they'd not notice any real changes, except the one thing that would endear them to the Countessa's daughters. He was right.

"My god, Arnaud, they fell for it! We're off the hook!" Beneoit exclaimed as they took their shuttle back to their apartment.

"No kidding, Arnaud, it worked. I can't believe it, but it worked," Edmond added, very much relieved. "We owe you a big one. Guess I don't need the cyanide anymore." The three chuckled.

Five days later, the three young men were invited to the weddings of the Countessa's daughters to the three Oda sisters. While they had been in their comas, the lads had cleaned out the Oda home, moving the sister's things over to the le Masters' mansion and even helped Blanche shop for new gowns for the three sisters to wear when they woke. When the men saw the Oda sisters at the wedding, they truly did relax. The six were extremely happy and very much wanting the ceremony to be concluded. In fact, the moment it was, Blanche took Monique off to their bedroom, while Celestine ushered Neva to hers, and Dianne led Noelle to her bedroom. The three men took this as their signal to depart, but the Countessa looked very pleased, even nodding to Arnaud.

Once outside the mansion, Arnaud exclaimed, "Well, we sure escaped that one! I need a drink!" The three headed back to his apartment and got rather wasted, celebrating their incredibly narrow escape.

Chapter 25—Plots, Counterplots, Escapes

Dr. Michelle d'Mireio finally woke up from her state of abject apathy. For weeks, she and Ernst had merely sat around like zombies, while Riva took care of them. Riva always kept the TV on during the hours she was awake, more so on this new caretaker job that she now had. The zombies never talked or responded much at all, so the background chat from the newscasters was her substitute for chat. Often, Riva would hear something on the TV and chat back at it, as though it were somehow alive and responsive.

After several weeks of this, the newscast featured a report from the rim, specifically a report on how the thousands of terrorist victims were doing. A reporter had done an interview with Mr. Alfonso Vega and had short video clips of various young adult victims who were attending either the Academy there or one of the local high schools. At first, both Michelle and Ernst simply stared at the giant monitor, but when Alfonso Vega appeared, both paid a wee bit more attention. They saw what at first glance appeared to be a professional woman. She wore the expected outfit, but her arms were missing. Soon, both realized that this was a man, not a woman. Both paid slightly more attention to what he was saying.

"So yes, we are making very sure these many victims are getting a good new start on their lives here on Scorpi-C. We have nearly fourteen thousand UFB women now attending our Academies and around sixteen thousand in local high schools. Plus, we have around five hundred of us UFBMD men attending the Academy and that many in high schools as well. At last report, most are doing well, though I will admit we do need personal assistants part of the time." Here, he chuckled a little, adding, "This past year, that's been the single largest growth industry, personal assistants."

The reporter asked, "And all these young people came from many worlds?"

"Ah yes. From the beginning, Scorpi-C always invites

408

any of these terrorist victims and other UFB women and UFBMD men to come to our world. In fact, GD Corporation has established full scholarships for these worthy Academy students. Several other corporations have also followed our lead. So yes, Scorpi-C willingly accepts these people, for they are truly people, just like the rest of us."

The reporter probed, "And Mr. Vega, you aren't ashamed of your mutated body that many find utterly freakish? You are content with it?"

Alfonso broke into a good laugh. "Sir, never in a million years would I wish what was done to me to be done to any other person! Those of us who have been horribly victimized have two choices: we can give up and sit around waiting for disease or old age to put us out of our misery or we can accept what's been done to us and get on with our lives, doing the best that we can. I'm amazed at just what we can actually accomplish, given the will to do it and time and patience, and with some assistance from others when needed. I'm not about to give up and sit around, waiting to die. If that was the terrorist's plan, he's very wrong on that count. But make no mistake, I'm not happy with what's been done to me and to forty thousand others. Nevertheless, I and thousands of others are getting on with our lives in spite of our handicaps."

Ernst finally spoke up, his alto voice still sounding foreign to himself. "He's a man, isn't he?"

Michelle turned her head to look at Ernst, also surprised with his mellow voice. "That's what the reporter said and what he is claiming, Ernst. Look, he's as helpless as we are."

"But he said others like us are going to their Academy. How can that be?" Ernst asked.

"I don't know."

"Lordy, you are speaking!" Riva exclaimed, having just walked into the room and overheard them speaking. "That's a miracle, if I say so."

"Where are we? This isn't my home or Ernst's," Michelle asked.

"Why child, you're on Corporate Prime. This is one of the Countessa Bianca le Masters many homes. She's had it all fixed up for you, hair machines, automatic kitchen, closets full of the finest clothes—everything your hearts could want, dearies," Riva explained.

"Hardly. I want my arms back," Michelle declared, slightly hostile.

"And I don't want this female body. I want my old one back," Ernst added, very hostile in spite of his alto voice.

"Sorry, I'm none of those doctors or anything, just a humble housekeeper, mind you, but that has to be your body, Ernst. People don't just go around getting into other people's bodies, now do they?" Riva retorted. "The Countessa Bianca has been mighty generous with you two, giving you all this stuff and this home."

"But she had this done to us, I know it. I never took any genetic samples from my lab to my home, not ever. Hell, I've never taken any out of the lab for any reason. Why did she want to wipe out our lives, Riva? Tell me that if you can," Michelle said angrily.

"She ruined our lives!" Ernst fairly yelled, his face reddish with anger. "We're nothing but two helpless freaks now!"

"Well calm down! You don't need to yell at me," Riva retorted. "You're certainly helpless; that's why she hired me to be your caretaker. That's true enough, only if you would just read the damned instructions on the stuff around here. You're supposed to be able to do some things for yourselves with them. Still you do look like freaks, but only when your clothes are off, mind you. Otherwise, you look like fashion models or something, so it can't be all that bad. Stop your griping, read the instructions, and stop making me do every damned thing for you."

"Hey, everything in here is foreign to us, strange. Hell, Riva, we have no idea where we are. We're lost here," Michelle pointed out.

"Well you can start in by getting yourselves familiar with your new home here and all the gadgets and machines. Your hair is a mess again, so start there with that electrostatic hair machine," Riva pointed out.

Both tried to get up from the couch on their own and

very nearly fell over, waving their non-existent arms about wildly. Only some extreme wobbling kept them from taking a tumble. "You should learn to walk better too," Riva added, rushing to catch them, hoping they wouldn't take a fall and get hurt. The Countessa would certainly not react well to her letting them get hurt.

A bit later, standing side by side, each using their own machine, Michelle gushed, "Wholly wow! This is an incredible feeling!"

"No kidding! I have more sensation coming from my hair than I have from my whole body, Michelle," Ernst exclaimed. "I could stand here all day." She giggled and agreed. Thus, the two finally began to examine the various gadgets and machines that the Countessa had installed in this home, theoretically so they could survive on their own. Soon, it was obvious to the pair they needed to practice getting up, sitting down, and walking. A day later, they took a huge step forward and walked outside of their home, where everything around them was totally strange and foreign to them. Nothing was familiar, giving the pair quite a shock.

"I've never felt so lost in my life," Ernst whispered, looking out at the metal and glass world around them. Shuttles danced about the tall spires, the skyscrapers that lined the horizon in all directions. Their home was only a single story building, but surrounded on three sides by fifty-story, shiny steel and glass spires, while several other smaller homes lay down the street from theirs. Their gaze lighted upon the huge mansion beyond which more of the taller skyscrapers rose. Hundreds of people were walking in various directions not far from the pair, but none took any notice of them.

"I feel really empty, Ernst, lost and so alone," Michelle whispered, "and so scared. I feel completely helpless too."

"I'm here Michelle. I feel the same way. All we have now is each other, for all the good I'm worth to you like this," Ernst whispered back. If asked why they were whispering, neither could say, except perhaps they didn't want anyone to see how lost they actually were and felt.

"Ernst, the sky—it's so different, like a glowing ball of lights. The sun is down but it's still daylight," Michelle finally noticed a bit more of her surroundings, glancing up at the star-filled skies. Here in the hub, the stars were so dense that nights were almost as bright as days, drastically different from their home world far out on the rim, where utter blackness covered most of the sky and the jeweled, misty ribbon of the entire galaxy lay spread in a thin slice across the sky.

"We are so far from home, Michelle, so very, very far," Ernst whispered back, a hitch in his new alto voice. A tear formed but he was powerless to wipe it. The two continued to stare at the sky for a while.

"I want to go home," she sighed.

"Maybe we could go to that Scorpi-C place," Ernst suggested, remembering the newscast. "They won't take us back on our world. We'd be freaks, but that Vega fellow said our kind is welcome there. We best go where we might be welcomed."

"True, we are so unwelcome here. No one is like us except that Countessa woman who did this to us," Michelle replied. "Say, how can she and those daughters of hers do all those strange things? You know, moving forks and spoons about, like invisible hands or something?"

"Dunno, but that's sort of what it looks like, invisible hands. What's even more scary, they read your thoughts," Ernst added. "Unnatural."

"Ernst, we simply have to get away from here, go to this Scorpi-C place, and talk to that Vega man. I can't stay here. My head feels like it's being crushed or something. There's nothing here but city and uncaring people. Total strangers."

"I agree. It's scary here, but how can we get away? If she reads our minds, there's no hope. We don't dare ask Riva for help. She'll just tell that Countessa woman right away," Ernst replied.

"We've got our new ID cards, Ernst. Maybe there are enough credits in our accounts for us to book passage there," Michelle suggested. "Only I don't know how we can manage to do any of that. It must take days to get there."

Ernst sighed, "We are so screwed. If we weren't so darn helpless." His voice dropped off to a barely audible sigh. The two continued to stare forlornly at the strange city around them. Neither had any idea that the "city" covered nearly all the available land of Corporate Prime!

"Travel agent! Ernst, that's what we need. A travel agent to book it for us and arrange for the help we're going to need," Michelle blurted out. "Oh, how are we going to do that? I know, we can try when Riva goes out on an errand."

"You think there is some way we could find one?" Ernst asked; she'd kindled a faint hope.

"Sure dear, the comm and entertainment center should have Net access. It's a touch screen, so maybe if we use our noses as our fingers, we can do it. When's Riva going to be gone for a while?"

Mid-afternoon, Michelle got her chance to attempt to arrange their passage. Riva headed off to do some of her own shopping, declaring that she needed some new shoes. Part of the booking process was voice-activated. "Yes, two UFB women, one way to Scorpi-C, visiting," Michelle confirmed what the system displayed on her comm entertainment monitor. She used her nose to push the Special Handling notice on the booking screen. Please wait appeared, followed by more automated responses. "Ten," Michelle said, growing annoyed with the automated system. Someone tried to identify all the special handling situations that might arise, and none fit her situation. Her last response finally connected her to a person.

"How may I assist you on this travel request?" a bored woman's voice said.

"We are two UFB women traveling alone on this trip. We will need someone to pick us up here at our home around nine on Saturday so we can make the flight. We will need someone to assist us with our personal needs during the two day flight, please," Michelle explained politely.

Now we're getting somewhere, Michelle thought, while waiting on the woman's reply. "Highly unusual Special Handling, Mrs. d'Mireio-Fry. Okay, I have you covered. Nine Saturday morning a shuttle will pick you both up. Thank you for choosing Galaxy Wide Transportation." She thanked the woman and disconnected. A few nose presses later, the newscast was back on, waiting for Riva to return.

413

"I can't believe you did it, Michelle!" Ernst exclaimed. For the first time, he felt a tiny spark of hope, temporarily pulling him out of his depression.

"We're going outside for some air, Riva," Michelle explained Saturday morning.

"Fine, just don't get lost. The Countessa would be furious with you," Tiva declared. "Still, it is good that you are getting some air, as polluted as it is on Corporate Prime." She continued her dusting, and the pair headed to the door, commanding it to open for them. They were a bit early, but Michelle didn't want anything to interfere with their catching this shuttle.

Around nine, a shuttle landed nearby. At least the man helped them inside and fastened their seatbelts for them, wondering why they had no baggage. Michelle decided to reply, "We can't manage bags, sir." He smiled, shook his head, and headed for the spaceport.

The dumping of—or to be polite, the mass migration of—UFB women and UFBMD men to Scorpi-C was long over. However, unknown to Alfonso and many others, certain individuals continued to monitor passenger traffic heading to Scorpi-C. When Michelle booked her travel arrangements, her unique situation caught the attention of one of those watchers, who quickly sent an electronic message to Alis. Thus, when Michelle explained her needs to the travel assistant, Alis jumped on the request, answering the travel assistant's request for a personal assistant for these two UFB women, who were traveling alone. Alis needed time to get to Corporate Prime, and hence got the travel assistant to re-book Michelle's travel request for Saturday, giving her a six-hour layover on Corporate Prime.

"Welcome, Mrs. Michelle d'Mireio-Fry?" Alis said. These two UFB women had to be her charges. She'd not seen any others arriving at the spaceport since she stepped off the Galaxy Wide Transportation air liner, which was a passenger ship built on a light cruiser's foundation.

"Yes. Are you our personal assistant for the trip?" Michelle asked politely, though Alis detected some nervousness in her voice. Her companion or mate was even

414

more nervous and hadn't said anything yet.

"Yes, Alis Anrhod, at your service on this two-day flight. Let's get your tickets. Have you any baggage?"

"Okay. No, we can't carry any bags. I—we hope that we can purchase what we may need when we get to Scorpi-C, Alis. Thank you so much for helping us," Michelle replied.

Alis helped them pick up their tickets at the counter, but she also noticed the attendant pressed a Red Flag button. That could only mean trouble, which Alis fully expected. She backed the pair away from the counter, allowing other customers to move up in the queue. Whispering, Alis said, "Trouble is coming. Are you two fleeing from here? Is anyone after you?"

Alis didn't need telepathy to sense the sudden surge of fear from the two women. "The Countessa Bianca le Masters— she is keeping us more or less prisoners here—something about us being the first of her perfect humans. We have to get away from here, please! We heard that many UFB women are going to Scorpi-C. Please, help us," Michelle pleaded.

"Of course I'll help you. Follow my orders explicitly. We have to board the ship before they discover that we've done so. This way," Alis said, leading them out of the ticket purchasing arena of the giant spaceport. Now to get us lost, she thought to herself. That was easy enough to do, for there were thousands of men, women, and even some children thronging the spaceport. These days, many bureaucrats and their families were departing for greener pastures, since the collapse of the headquarters on Corporate Prime. Of course, many of these were shipping their personal possessions along with them, at a steep cost, that is. Hence, Alis found it easy enough for the three to get lost in the sea of humanity flowing through the huge facility.

Cleverly, Alis led them to a back corridor that led to the crate shipping section, where the many crates were being stamped and loaded onto any number of waiting Galaxy Wide Transportation ships. While the nervous pair shuffled along supported by the steadying arms of Alis, Alis spotted the loading zone for their flight and moved them over to it. She spotted a number of crates about to be moved into the cargo hold of their ship. "Excuse me. We are here to verify that these crates get loaded properly. They contain fragile items."

The dockhand looked up at her and then eyed the two seemingly gorgeous young women with her. He smiled coyly. "Of course." His eyes swept over the pair for a bit, adding to the pair's nervousness. Then, he carried the next crate into the cargo hold, but Alis cleverly followed him, making sure the two kept their balance getting into the ship.

"Thank you sir. Which way to the passenger compartment?" Alis asked. The man pointed, and she ushered the shaking pair on past the mountain of crates and shortly entered the passenger section. Five minutes later, she had them safely in their small compartment. Here, there were two small beds, a tiny desk and chair, and a small bathroom. All three squeezed in. She sat the pair on the bed and took the chair.

"Okay, we are onboard. Someone will be by shortly before takeoff to collect our tickets. We should be safe enough until then. Relax, if you can. It shouldn't be more than about a half hour or so now," Alis explained. "Better yet, I'll take the tickets up front. That way, no one will see either of you. Stay here until I get back, all right?" The nervous pair nodded, and Alis left them sitting on the bed.

"Maybe this isn't such a good idea," Ernst whispered. "What if they search the ship and find us?"

Michelle bit her lip. "Well, if they do, they do. What can she do to us? We're already helpless. Right about now, I wouldn't mind it if she had us shot. Our lives are pure misery, Ernst, but this Alis seems to know what she's doing. So maybe we are going to get away from that Countessa woman."

"But then what? When we get there, then what do we do?" Ernst whispered, trying as hard as he could to keep from crying. *Never in my life have I felt so emotional as I have these past weeks after the horrible coma and mutation. I have to fight breaking down. I wonder if perhaps my acute emotions are due to my body being so altered, nearly into a woman's body. I've only have one male aspect left to me now. Michelle has been more aggressive than she used to be before the genetic mutation that is. Does that tie into the mutation as well? Hell, I dare not speak of that. I just know I'll break down and sob if I did. I welcome death, if it comes.*

After what seemed to be an eternity to the nervous pair, Alis finally returned, a smile on her face. "Liftoff is in one minute. We've managed to give them the slip. Definitely, someone didn't want you two on this flight. Well, too bad for them. Ah, here we go." Alis sat down on the chair just as the huge ship began vibrating slightly. Then, all three felt the acceleration, as the ship rose into the skies over Corporate Prime. Minutes later, they felt the sudden jerk as they dropped into hyperspace. Only now did Alis relax.

"Okay, I'm a close friend of Mr. Alfonso Vega, head of the GD Corporation, sole leader of Scorpi-C, and now of the entire Abelard Sector. He'll be meeting us when we land, personally welcoming you to our world. He's given sanctuary to nearly forty thousand UFB women and UFBMD men, so you won't feel so all alone there. Now then, what is your story? Who are you running away from? If you are honest with me, then I can relay such to Mr. Vega."

Michelle sighed. "I suppose we should tell you all of it. We're doomed anyway. He probably won't want us on Scorpi-C, not when he finds out what we really are now. Besides, we haven't had anyone to talk to about everything since the accident, if it even was an accident. You see, I used to be a geneticist working on a secret project at the le Masters' Institute for Genetic Studies in the heart of Bordeaux on 9-Cetus-C. You see it was founded by Count Edgard le Masters. There were twelve of us, and Dr. Marcel was in charge of our project: the restoration of lost genetic mutation agents. We were hoping to gain some valuable clues about how that ancient bio agent worked so we could use it to help revolutionize medical treatments. Anyway, Dr. Marcel had some partial successes early on."

"Then, we heard about all these terrorist attacks. The victims became UFB women and UFBMD men. I was shocked! You see, I believed back then and still do that somehow the terrorists got their samples from our lab! I had Dr. Marcel conduct a thorough investigation, but he claims none of our samples were missing and that our security wasn't compromised. Ernst here, my husband now, was a security guard captain and did some of that investigation work. I kept saying we should get some DNA samples from the victims. Then I could prove my theory that the terrorists got theirs from our labs, somehow. No one listened to me."

"Then, a few weeks back, he had a major breakthrough. Believe it or not, he found a way to restore those degraded samples, recreating that ancient genetic bio agent, the one used way back in the Dark Ages. I know some of our work wasn't so ethical. We needed human test subjects. Count Edgard le Masters provided those for us. He was head of the OEN, the Opérations d'Espionnage Noir, before he died. He supplied us with hardened criminals to experiment on. Anyway, Dr. Marcel and I headed to Corporate Prime to find out what happened to Count Edgar and we met his wife, Countessa Bianca le Masters, who told us that he had died, that she was now our new boss, and that our foundation should continue its work. I pleaded my case, that the terrorists stole samples from our lab and that we should now go to work finding genetic cures for all the thousands of victims, but she wouldn't hear of that, and ordered us back to work on those ancient samples."

Michelle sighed. "You're going to find out what we are soon anyway, so I guess I should explain what happened to us next." She explained somehow one of those vials had been broken open in her home and that they'd gone into comas, waking up on Corporate Prime. "We're officially hermaphrodites now, utterly beyond embarrassing, particularly for Ernst here." She told what the Countessa and her daughters had done for them, claiming that they were the first of the new perfect humans that she was making.

An hour after she began her lengthy explanation, Michelle finally finished up. "So there, that's all, but I swear I never, ever took any bio samples home from the lab. That violates every protocol we have. Someone must have planted it there, but I don't see how it could have even broken open to expose us. It's a big mystery to Ernst and me."

Alis kept calm, paying acute attention to Michelle's tale. "So you believe that Countessa Bianca is running the OEN?"

"Yes, we think so and her daughters, UFB women, Blanche, Celestine, and Dianne are also heavily involved with the spies too," Michelle added. "But what so scares us is they can read our minds, and they have all these magical powers."

"Oh my. Telepathy? Magical powers?" Alis suddenly came very alert. She listened to the pair describing all manner of magical powers, telekinesis and levitation perhaps, along with strong telepathic skills. Just then, a small light turned on, indicating lunch was being served.

"That's the lunch signal. If you don't mind, I'll go bring us some lunch back here so you don't have to sit out there among all the other passengers," Alis suggested.

"Oh please! We're so helpless and freakish," Ernst exclaimed, greatly relieved. He dreaded being out in public with everyone staring at him.

While she was off doing so, she sent a lengthy, encrypted electronic message prefaced with "Top Priority." That done, she carried a full tray back to their cabin, fed the pair, and helped them with their bathroom needs, obtaining visual proof of their mutations. Later, she paid an exorbitant fee to send Alfonso an encrypted text message via the ship's comm center.

"Dr. Michelle, I talked to Mr. Vega. He would like it very much if you would agree to help Dr. Gisa Wolfgang in her research into genetic cures for the terrorist victims. She was a partial victim herself, but her fast action prevented the secondary mutation from occurring in herself and several others," Alis explained to her.

"I would love to help, but I am so helpless," Michelle complained. "Still, I do know a lot about genetic research. I wonder if I will be allowed to test some victims' DNA and prove my suspicions that the terrorists somehow stole it from our lab," she added.

"That will be your first assignment, Dr. Michelle," Alis answered with a wry grin.

"And I'll just sit around like the vegetable that I am," Ernst lamented. "I'm useless now."

***

"You're men are worthless!" barked Countessa Bianca.

419

"A simple snatch at the spaceport—honestly, you're worthless! You call yourselves OEN men. Ha."

"They eluded those who were searching for them, Countessa," Arnaud explained. This part of his job he detested—having to report a mission failure to her. "We have confirmed the pair are onboard the ship and will be arriving on Scorpi-C late Monday. What are your orders now? We could get there sooner and assassinate them."

Countessa Bianca bit her lip. "No. It seems there are thousands of the nearly perfect humans on Scorpi-C. I supposed I should go there and see if we can't bring some back here to make into perfect humans. Supposedly, they are adapting well to being UFB women. We'll see."

Arnaud relaxed. He wasn't going to be sacked today. Still, he knew just how angry the Countessa could get and just where her anger sometimes went. Further, he was still terrified she could subject him to that nasty bio agent at any time. He'd gotten himself and his two pals off the hook with her daughters, but only just barely. No, Arnaud was paranoid of the Countessa, rightly so he believed. At least if she was reading his mind now, she would know he wasn't lying to her. She dismissed him, and he left her mansion as quickly as possible, not even pausing to say hello to his former girlfriend, Blanche, who was busy with her new mate, Monique.

Back at his OEN base, Arnaud met with Beneoit and Edmond, both of whom were greatly relieved to find their pal still in one piece. "So how did it go?" Beneoit asked the obvious.

"Nasty, but she didn't strike back like I thought she would. We don't have to kill any of our agents today," Arnaud replied, a sour tone in his voice. "This is getting out of hand. One false step and we'll be another Monique." That turned the other two men rather sour, and they left him. Alone at last, Arnaud mused. *If only they didn't have their telepathy and magic powers.*

He poured himself a dark stout and sat back sipping it. Suddenly, it came to him—something that Dr. Hershall once told him about these four. According to him, they each had a greatly enlarged pituitary gland, and the doctor believed that accounted for their "special" abilities. Further, the doctor had mentioned there was a medical cure for an enlarged pituitary gland, something about bombarding it with electronic signals or was it chemical signals? Arnaud couldn't remember. Still, this idea had potential.

He dropped by the med lab and looked at the scheduling charts. Once a year, each member of the OEN was required to get a full medical checkup and cures as needed. The Countessa and her daughters were due to have theirs again in a week. Slowly, an idea formed in Arnaud's mind. He knew all four women were pregnant, compliments of their new hermaphrodite partners. Grinning, Arnaud decided now was the time to plant his idea.

"Ah, Dr. Hershall, the Countessa Bianca, Blanche, Celestine, and Dianne are due for their yearly checkup soon, if I remember right," he began, having found the good doctor looking over some x-rays.

"Indeed, I believe I'm seeing them in a week," he replied absentmindedly.

"Good. You know they are all pregnant, right?"

"Oh? Well, no. They are, are they?"

"Yes, I've heard that from the Countessa herself. Of course, she will want the very best of care for herself and her daughters."

"Naturally, son, naturally. Nothing is too good for our Supreme Commander."

"No indeed. Say, you should program the medical machines to cure everything that is wrong with their bodies," Arnaud suggested.

"Quite true. We don't want anything to affect their new children. Good god, man, if something went wrong with her next child or those of her daughters, why, I'm as good as dead," Dr. Hershall replied, growing a tad worried. He too knew her violent temper. "I should make sure the machine applies all known cures."

"Indeed you should, doctor, *all* known cures," Arnaud re-enforced his idea.

Later, Arnaud took a gamble and paid a social call on the Countessa. "I've been checking the records and you and your daughters are due for your annual checkup next week. I told Dr. Hershall that you four were pregnant and that you demanded the very best of care."

"Oh how thoughtful of you. Why yes, I'm expecting again, though it will probably be a girl hermaphrodite. Heavens, there really isn't any difference between male and female hermaphrodites, unless you count where the pee comes out." She gave a sardonic laugh. "Oh, can you arrange for an exam for our mates as well? I know Marion is also pregnant."

"Consider it done. You'll want them to have the best care possible as well. I'll tell the doctor that. Every known cure, right?" Arnaud cleverly installed his idea in the Countessa's mind.

She chuckled, "Of course, Arnaud. Are you that stupid? Every known cure. I want my next perfect human and Marion's to be just that, absolutely perfect. I still think I erred in not making you, Beneiot, and Edmond into perfect humans as well. However, just now, I don't have any potential mates for you. After all, you can see how strong the sex drive is in them, so when I do it for you three, I'll simply have to have three perfect mates for you fellows. By the way, you haven't found other girlfriends yet, have you? Other UFB women?"

"Er no. So many have moved off-world, Countessa. We know how badly Michelle and Ernst reacted, so it would be wise to use already existing UFB women who have grown up that way, don't you think? After all, Monique and her sisters have taken to all this extremely well," Arnaud replied.

"Yes, they adapted without the slightest bit of trouble. That's why we're going to have to go to this Scorpi-C and recruit UFB women there, though I suppose we can recruit UFBMD men as well, though they are so rare," she explained. "Of course, when we do go there, keep your eyes open for three UFB women for you and your pals."

Arnaud kept himself from grimacing or flinching. "Of course. I best go let the doctor know to expect eight of you on Monday then—all known cures." He turned and left, punching home his idea once more.

He visited Dr. Hershall once more, explaining about the additional four women, their mates. "The Countessa was very explicit, doctor. She demands *all* known cures be given to them. She's counting on having eight, new perfect human babies."

"Well, I don't know that I'd say their new mutations make them perfect or not, but I will make darn sure the machines are programmed to deliver *all* known cures to them, son. I value my head." Both men chuckled.

Later that night, Arnaud snuck into the med lab and did a bit of checking of just what the "All Known Cures" implemented. Scrolling down the exhaustive list, he stopped and smiled, before turning the machine off and quietly exiting the lab.

On Monday, Arnaud, Beneoit, and Edmond helped Countessa Bianca, Blanche, Celestine, Dianne, Marion, Monique, Neva, and Noelle get to the OEN facilities and safely into the med lab, where Dr. Hershall was waiting for them. He had eight machines lined up in eight neighboring stalls, waiting for them. "Ah, good morning ladies," he greeted them, "one into each stall please."

"Doctor, I remind you that we're all pregnant with very special babies," the Countessa barked. "Make sure all of us are in perfect health, mind you."

"Of course, Countessa. All known cures will be applied. I assure you that you'll have eight perfect babies. Now then, let's get this started, shall we?" he replied, sweating a little, as he always did when he had to provide care for the Countessa or one of her daughters. As a safety precaution, he said, "Here, check the setting for yourself, Countessa."

She leaned over and magically touched the touch-screen, verifying it was indeed set to "All Known Cures." Satisfied, she used her powers to get herself undressed and then to undress Marion. Finally, she used her powers to help Marion into the medical machine, before getting her own body into the one in the next stall. She then relaxed. All the stupid doctor had to do was push the damned button, she thought, closing her eyes. She hated these yearly exams, but already, the machine had caught a small tumor in her left breast and cured her, but that was several years back. In another eight months, she thought, we'll have eight more perfect humans, but I best get to this Scorpi-C soon though. We need thousands of perfect humans. Must have a sufficiently large gene pool.

The machine began to hum as it scanned her body. Soon, the Countessa, Blanche, Celestine, and Dianne slipped into unconsciousness. The machines then began blasting their pituitary glands with high-energy beams, focused solely on that organ, though occasionally pausing to inspect the gland's shrinkage. Meanwhile, Marion, Monique, Neva, and Noelle were soon given a clean bill of health by their machines.

"Ah, eight months and it will be birthing time," the doctor explained. "I'll want to see each of you every month until we get to the ninth month. You're to receive the very best care that modern medicine has to offer, compliments of your mates." That brought smiled to the four women's faces.

Monique hesitated and then asked, "Will our babies be like us?" She flushed slightly.

"Yes, of course, in all ways, though I can't guarantee they will be gorgeous blondes like yourselves," he replied, bringing a grin to the charming young face.

An hour later, the Countessa and her daughters were still out. Meantime, Dr. Hershall had his nurses get the others dressed. Examining the four machines, he saw that two days more was the estimated completion time for the cures. Hence, he suggested that the fellows take the four home. "No, it's nothing to worry about. They are getting all known cures so that they and their babies will be as perfect as you four are," he assured the four women, who began to get worried about their powerful mates.

Four shrill screams echoed through the med lab. The four came out of their unconsciousness. For the first time in their lives, they didn't hear voices in their heads. Their telepathy was gone, as were all their *magical* powers, which was the reason for their screams of terror and shock. Dr. Hershall and his nurses came running.

"What's happened to me?" shrieked Countessa Bianca. "I can't move anything. My powers—they are gone! I'm completely helpless. What have you done to me? I'll have you shot for this!"

"Calm down. I have it on record. All known cures, Countessa. You are now in perfect health. All known cures have been done. Your abnormally large pituitary gland is now quite normal in size, as those of your daughters are as well. I don't understand what you mean about losing your *magical* powers, Countessa," Dr. Hershall countered. He had made a video recording of her specific orders as a safety precaution. Now he was very glad he'd been paranoid enough to have done that. She'd ordered her own destruction.

"Put it back the way it was! I'm utterly helpless," she shrieked.

"Medically, Countessa, that isn't possible. Now let my nurses get you dressed. Your mates are a bit anxious for you to return home."

"Mom!" Blanche screamed from a neighboring stall, "I'm helpless! I can't move anything or lift anything. I can't hear anyone's thoughts. Help me!"

A few minutes later, Arnaud, Beneoit, and Edmond assisted the four out of the med lab. All were sobbing. Blanche cried, "I am so helpless now. I can't hold on to the walls for support as I used to do. Arnaud! Don't let me fall, please. Mom, how could you do this to us?"

"But Blanche, dear, this is what you all did to Michelle and Ernst, making them into perfect humans, just the way the Countessa wanted them," Arnaud punched in, trying to keep a straight face. *Victory is so sweet!*

"But you can't just leave us here," the Countessa wailed. The three fellows dropped the four women off at their mansion, where their four mates were waiting anxiously for their arrival. "We're completely helpless now!"

"What's the matter?" Marion asked, growing worried in a big hurry.

"Our powers—they are gone! We're as helpless as you four are now. This is intolerable," the Countessa replied.

Monique chuckled. "Of course, we are, silly. Didn't you know that? We've been helpless since we were born, though now with some of these new inventions of yours, Countessa, we can do a few things for ourselves, but it's really hard."

"But I can't live this way, helpless!" Blanche wailed.

"But it's the only way we can live," Monique replied, wondering why Blanche was so darn upset. After all, she was this way since she was born. "Did you think we weren't helpless UFB women?" she asked, suddenly wondering what Blanche had thought about her.

"But I'm helpless now too!" Blanche continued to wail, joined by her sisters. The Countessa simply broke down and bawled long and hard. Her life was suddenly ruined utterly, and she was helpless to do anything about it. Worse, she knew it.

"I'll send Riva by soon," Arnaud called out, quickly making a hasty exit, joining Beneoit and Edmond. As soon as they got into their shuttle, all three roared with laughter and pent-up relief. No longer would they be under the constant threat of becoming genetically modified into these freaks or perfect humans of the Countessa. Her yoke was permanently off their necks.

Arnaud finally stopped his hysterical laughter. "Give them a few days of freak-out, and we'll get them to appoint us as the OEN Commanders."

"Best get the Countessa's bank account transferred over to the OEN," Beneoit added.

Once back at their base, Arnaud did just that, shocked at the incredible fortune the Countessa had in her account. He left her with a few million credits, dividing the huge sum among all the various OEN stations around the galaxy. Even so, each had a small fortune, more than enough to guarantee their long-term survival no matter what misfortune fell upon the civilized galaxy.

A week later, the Countessa begrudgingly appointed the each of the three men to the Commander position in their respective organizations. She insisted on remaining the Supreme Commander of the OEN, however, she had no idea then that no one would ever again follow any of the orders she would issue. As far as the various Commanders of the OEN, Countessa Bianca le Masters was simply a helpless non-entity, but one who yelled a lot. Her sting was gone, totally gone, and many felt quite significant relief.

To be on the safe side, Arnaud later visited them and

confiscated the remaining samples of the genetic bio agent, storing it in his secure headquarters, along with many other accumulated such samples, each one properly labeled.

Chapter 26—Unnatural Allies

"Dr. Michelle d'Mireio-Fry, this is Dr. Gisa Wolfgang, who is leading our current research into genetic cures for the many terrorist victims," Alfonso Vega, supported by Alicia, introduced the two women. Upon landing, Alis and her two rescued victims from Corporate Prime were met by Alfonso, who quickly got them through customs, bypassing most of the spaceport's security. He took them to his office in the GD Corporate headquarters building and listened to their lengthy story, having encouraged them to withhold nothing. Diego quietly entered and gave the pair some new ID cards, along with resident status. That done, he then took the trio down to the GD research labs and introduced Michelle to Gisa.

"So pleased to meet a fellow geneticist, Dr. Michelle. You look quite stunning indeed. Ernst, you have quite a catch with Dr. Michelle. Such lovely brown hair. I do hope you will come work here in the GD labs. I sure could use your assistance and knowledge. We've quite a mess to handle," the short brown haired geneticists chatted politely. Via Alfonso, via Alis, she had been informed of the previous work that Dr. Michelle had been involved with and really wanted Dr. Michelle's input.

"I'm totally helpless now, Dr. Gisa, but I want to help if I can. Most importantly, I want to examine some DNA samples from the victims to see if the genetic bio agent the terrorists used came from our laboratory. That's been bothering me since I first heard of the terrorist attacks," Dr. Michelle explained.

"Now that would be absolutely perfect, Dr. Michelle. Plus, we need to get a sample from you and Ernst as well, since your genetic modifications are even worse," Dr. Gisa added. "Alfonso, have you decided where they are going to be staying?

If not, I'd love to have them stay with me. That way, we can work all hours."

"That would be ideal, Dr. Gisa. I will have Diego deposit more funds in your account and into their new ones. Both will need new wardrobes, since they were not able to bring anything with them when they fled Corporate Prime," Alfonso agreed and explained. "Another thing, Michelle and Ernst had a specially designed home incorporating quite a few things that were supposed to allow them to live more independently, far more than we have here. Somehow, I'm going to have to check on that, probably have to go pay a visit to this Countessa Bianca le Masters and see if some arrangements can be made to purchase them or get a license to manufacture them here. I've now got quite a lot of things to handle, but please keep me informed of any new developments, doctors." They agreed, and Alis, Alfonso, and Alicia left the new arrivals in Dr. Gisa's care for now.

When they returned to his top floor office, Diego was waiting them. "Well, I take it Dr. Gisa agreed to look after them," he said, as Alfonso made his slow way across the office suite and tossed his head about, getting his long black hair to his front so he could sit down.

"Yes, but now we have to figure out what to do. This new mutation is worse than what I've had. I can't imagine how those two feel, hermaphrodites. Where will this genetic experimentation end?" Alfonso gushed angrily. Just then, Anka arrived, making her just as careful way into his office. Alis rose and helped her get seated, getting her equally long hair to her front so she didn't sit on it.

"Is it true? The new arrivals from Corporate Prime have been mutated into hermaphrodites?" Anka asked, both worried and very curious.

"Yes, verified so," Alis answered briefly. For Alis, what Alfonso intended to do in response was critical.

"Oh dear God! Here we go again. History repeats itself!" Anka gushed, unable to withhold her anger.

"Indeed, Anka," Alfonso replied. "Now then, I believe many things are becoming clearer, perhaps finally falling into place. I'm confident that soon we will have positive proof that the genetic bio agents that the Master used in his many attacks will have come from Dr. Michelle's secret lab, this le Masters' Institute for Genetic Studies in Bordeaux on 9-Cetus-C. We know this Countessa Bianca and her three daughters, all four once having been UFB women, possessed telepathy, and what Dr. Michelle calls magical powers to lift and move things, but that they no longer have those abilities. Further, we know that this Countessa Bianca was instrumental in making first use of this new genetic bio agent that mutates men and women into hermaphrodites. From Dr. Michelle, the Countessa Bianca and her mate Marion, along with her three daughters and their new UFB women mates have all voluntarily undergone this horrible mutation. According to the doctor, Countessa Bianca believes that these are the perfect humans and is working on a program to make all humans into her perfect human forms. To that end, she has established her own corporation that manufactures machines and devices, enabling those without arms to live more independently. So it seems to me she is well on her way towards her diabolical goal."

"Shit!" Diego exclaimed, interrupting Alfonso.

"There's another hitch. It seems the Countessa and her daughters are somehow closely connected to the OEN!" he added.

"Oh my God! Not those people!" exclaimed Anka.

"Double shit!" Diego barked. "Nothing like having the backing of the secret police and their assassins!"

Alis broke in, "So as far as we know right now, there are only ten of these new hermaphrodites, eight on Corporate Prime, two here with us."

Anka chose to speak up. "But they will breed like rabbits. I've been studying the ancient history of Zeta Scorpii-C. The hermaphrodites there bred more than twice as rapidly as normal humans. Soon, the ten will become twenty. My guess is that there will be fifty of them before four years have passed. In a generation, they will number closer to a thousand. It just mushrooms all out of control, at least that's what the books said happened a half millennia ago."

Diego groaned. "And if the OEN or others decide to start making more of them, the situation will rapidly escalate beyond any possible containment. Alfonso, somehow, someway we have to put an end to this terrible bio agent before it gets used as the Master did with the other agents. If we don't, extrapolating from Anka's predictions, in just a few generations, our entire galaxy will be filled with these helpless hermaphrodites. Already the resources of Scorpi-C are stretched to the limit supporting the forty thousand UFB women and UFBMD men. Civilization is going to come to a crashing halt if there is Anka's predicted population explosion of hermaphrodites."

Alis relaxed a little. Diego was precisely correct. She spoke up, "Diego is correct. Right now, we have only ten of them. It isn't too soon to nip this in the bud, before it explodes into our part of the galaxy."

"Another thing that bothers me. This deceased husband of the Countessa's, Count Edgar, what is his connection to all this?" Alfonso continued. "And there is the million credit question of why hasn't the OEN gotten involved in all these goings on this past year? I have been scared of the OEN stepping in long ago, and yet, they have been silent. I just have too many unanswered questions right now."

"Well, I don't see any other way around it, boss. We're going to have to go to Corporate Prime and find the answers we need," Diego concluded, rubbing his chin. "Though I hate like hell to pay a visit to the damned OEN. Still, they've been quiet in all this, and I'd sure as hell would like to know why, if they would even deign to tell us."

"Diego, dig out the secure email for corporate communications to the OEN on Corporate Prime. Let's see if they will even agree to meet with me," Alfonso requested.

"But boss, you can't go there yourself," Diego protested. After all, his boss was darn near as helpless as the two newcomers were. *Is it my place to tell him that?* Diego debated.

"No, and I can't take Alicia. She has to nurse our twins. I'll take our deep space transport. Jackie and Melissa can fly it for us and their fellows can tag along. They can protect us. Plus, it would wise for Juanita to act as our comm center operator. Diego, I will officially transfer control of my executive position to you while I'm gone."

Alis spoke up, "I'll tag along too, Alfonso. I know my way around Corporate Prime, at least a little. You've never been there. Besides, we're going to have a number of things to take care of beside just the OEN, assuming they will even see us."

"Thank you, Alis. I do appreciate all that you do for us. You are a godsend," Alfonso replied. "We'll leave the day after tomorrow. That'll give everyone time to prepare for the trip. Now to dictate that email and hope they will see us." Alfonso kept the email short and to the point.

Dear Commander,

I am Mr. Alfonso Vega, CEO of GD Corporation on Scorpi-C, Abelard Sector, and the sole ruler of our sector. I would like to meet with you to discuss the ramifications of this new and most terrible genetic bio agent that turns men and women into hermaphrodites. I expect to arrive on Corporate Prime in three days. I too have been a victim of a terrorist attack and am officially a UFBMD man now.

Sincerely,

Mr. Alfonso Vega

***

The fiery redhead Jackie exclaimed, "Holy shit! We're going to see the OEN!" She and the others sat around the main table in Alfonso's office, having answered his request to join him for a special assignment. Alfonso outlined what they knew or suspected and that he was going to pay a visit to the OEN on Corporate Prime. Her reaction was typical. Even mentioning the OEN usually brought fear into most people's minds. They were, right or wrong, usually believed to be the corporation's hired assassins.

"You're kidding, right boss?" D. J. added, running his hands over his chin in dismay.

"The OEN? My god, Alfonso, have you a death wish?" added Armando. "Those bastards kill first and seldom ask questions."

"They have agreed to see me," Alfonso replied. "Look, thanks to Dr. Michelle, we now know for a fact that the genetic bio agents the Master used in all his attacks came from the secret le Masters' Institute for Genetic Studies in Bordeaux on 9-Cetus-C. We know Count Edgar le Masters used to be the Supreme Commander of the entire OEN and that for quite some years now, his wife, this Countessa Bianca, was running it for him. I'm afraid I have some very serious questions to pose to their current Commander, questions which must be answered."

Alfonso paused and took a deep breath. "This is something that must be done. Either they are in on the Master's plans or they are not. Either they knew what was going on, choosing not to act, or they did not know. Then, there is this new bio agent that turns humans into hermaphrodites, just like some five hundred years ago. So far, there are ten such victims that we know of. As Anka has pointed out, if this isn't ended immediately and that bio agent destroyed, we're headed for the same calamity that nearly wiped out the galaxy back in the Dark Ages. So gang, I have no choice. I have to find out the role the OEN is playing and whether they will help stamp out this new bio agent before it is too late to stop it from spreading, if we aren't already too late. One more thing, according to Dr. Michelle, this Countessa Bianca has created a company that designs and builds many useful things, enabling those of us without arms to live a bit more independently. I owe it to the forty thousand here on Scorpi-C to investigate this fully."

"Don't fret so, boss. We're with you all the way," Melissa broke in. "Just be damned careful. Everyone knows you can't trust the OEN, except for dirty dealings. Besides, maybe this Countessa Bianca's company will have some things that all of us could really use. Hope so anyway, so it's worth checking out."

"Thanks, Melissa. Okay, now is your chance to back out of this dangerous mission," Alfonso added. "I won't think any less of anyone who doesn't want to risk their necks on this one. I agree. This one could well be extremely dangerous to us all."

"We're all in, boss," Armando spoke up, glancing at each of the others. "When do we leave?"

**

Three days later, Jackie and Melissa set the modified

GD Corporation deep space transport down on the landing pad, a textbook landing. The two had definitely become topnotch pilots. From the comm center, Captain Juanita called out, "Boss, we're receiving a message that you are to report to Customs Bay Nine. I think the OEN is there."

Alfonso replied, "Okay. Thanks for a perfect flight, everyone. Now here's how we're handling this. Alis and I will leave and see if we can meet with the OEN. Meanwhile, the rest of you stay alert. If there's any trouble, I order you to take off. Somehow, we'll get in touch with you if we need you. Meanwhile, see what you can find out about this company of the Countessa's and just where she lives. After I handle this OEN business, we should check them out as well. Questions?"

Armando cautioned, "Boss, are you sure you don't want us with you? This could be extremely dicey. They are the OEN after all."

"Yes, I'm willing to risk myself. Hell, it can't be any worse than I already am, but I have to have someone to assist me. Alis has been here before and knows her way around Corporate Prime. Alis, you can still back out. I hate risking you too."

"Oh shut up, silly man. Why else am I along if not to assist you and help sort this mess out before it becomes catastrophic to us all," she replied slightly testily. "Come on. Best not keep the OEN waiting."

Alis and Alfonso both wore a professional woman's outfit, white blouse, black skirt, hose, and pumps, though Alis wore low heeled ones so she could better assist Alfonso. Each had a PDS attached to their belts along with a PIS, just in case they needed to become invisible to perhaps escape the clutches of the OEN, if things went south. Together, they walked across the busy tarmac, the smell of oil, grease, exhaust fumes, and hot tar filled their noses. The day was warm, but the horizon in all directions was filled with towering pinnacles of steel and glass. Corporate Prime boasted more skyscrapers than any other world, though some suggested this was a factor of a hundred over the next most populace world.

Shortly, two black-clad men moved up to them. Their uniforms bore the insignia of the OEN. "Customs Bay Nine?"

Alfonso asked.

"You the UFBMD man called Alfonso Vega?" one asked.

"Yes, that's me. Rather wish I hadn't become a terrorist attack victim, but that's me. We were told to go to Customs Bay Nine," he replied politely. Best behavior, he reminded himself.

"This way." The men directed them into the sprawling control tower. Up floors and down halls they went. Alfonso soon lost all track of directions. No way could he figure out the path he'd come. *Ah well,* he thought. *I'm not likely to be escaping if they don't want me to.*

The two men opened a door. "Customs Bay Nine," he said dryly. The pair entered and saw three young men, probably in their late teens, sitting at a large table. A water pitcher and many glasses were the only items on the black granite tabletop. The chairs were the usual steel, modern variety, utilitarian in nature, sterile and lacking any comfort. Well, this is a business meeting, Alfonso reminded himself as Alis helped him get seated.

One teen had black hair; the others, brown. All three looked young, fresh, and gave off an aura of complete power. The black haired lad spoke first, "I am Supreme Commander Arnaud Armel. Fellow commanders, Beneoit Berenger, Edmond Berenger. And you must be Mr. Alfonso Vega. Sorry, I still find it hard to believe that such a gorgeous looking woman is actually a man." Alfonso detected a bit of a covert sneer in his tone, but let it pass.

"I find it hard to recognize myself too, so I rarely look in the mirror," Alfonso replied, lightening the mood. "Thank you for seeing me. As you probably know, I am the head of GD Corporation on Scorpi-C and have been given a position of substantial power out there in the rim. Abelard Sector. Basically, I was able to stand up against the Master and his reign of terror there, when everyone else abandoned the sector," he began.

"We have heard most all the CEOs fled. Why didn't you?" Arnaud interrupted.

"Scorpi-C is my home. They are my people. I felt as the CEO of one of the largest corporations that it was my responsibility to defend first my world and then the others in our sector, particularly so since we received no help from higher ups. Of course, had I fled, I wouldn't be this UFBMD man now, and I assure you that my life would be a whole lot simpler. This is my assistant for today, Miss Alis Anrhod. Anyway, we were able to eventually hold off the Master and safeguard most of the worlds in our sector."

Arnaud broke in, "Yes, that is a matter of record, though we find it hard to believe a helpless UFBMD man was able to do that."

"We aren't as helpless as most people think. Besides, I had a good deal of help. I've come here today to try to get some answers to some lingering questions and to request the OEN's help in preventing a galaxy-wide catastrophe. First, in case you didn't know, my force finally killed the Master. However, his identity still remains a mystery to us, though perhaps we've recently discovered his true identity."

"Please, do continue," Arnaud smirked.

"Indeed. Recently, Dr. Michelle d'Mireio-Fry came to Scorpi-C seeking sanctuary. She has quite a story. First, she is a geneticist and was working at the secret le Masters' Institute for Genetic Studies in Bordeaux on 9-Cetus-C. There, they were attempting to recover the ancient genetic bio agents that were discovered by some archaeologist on Zeta-Scorpii-C. It seems originally, the founder of the research institute and her boss was one Count Edgar le Masters. Anyway, he apparently left them alone for many years. During this time period, these geneticists were able to manufacture, if that's the right word, several variations of this ancient bio weapon, all the while trying to recover its original properties."

Since the three men were continuing to listen to him, Alfonso continued, "Thanks to Dr. Michelle, we now know one critical fact. The various genetic bio agents the Master used in his many terrorist attacks actually came from and were developed at this genetics research institute. Dr. Michelle has verified this from DNA samples from a number of victims now living on Scorpi-C. Something about a unique signature they stored in some unused portion of the genetic agent structure. Sorry, I'm not a geneticist, and that's the best way I can describe it. If you desire a more scientific analysis, I can have Dr. Michelle and Dr. Gisa send the results to you."

Arnaud replied, "That will not be necessary. Please continue." Alfonso found the three teens a bit hard to read. They seemed to be enjoying listening to him. They weren't shocked or appalled and weren't asking questions. So he did.

"Of course, Dr. Michelle thought this might be the case long ago and requested a full investigation, which her superior Dr. Marcel Louves did, but he found nothing. At this point, we know that somehow the Master obtained his genetic bio agents from this research institute. How and why remain unanswered questions until the arrival of Dr. Michelle."

"Now she and her husband have quite a unique tale. It seems that Dr. Marcel finally was able to recreate fully that ancient genetic bio agent. When he tried to contact Count Edgar le Masters, he discovered that the man had recently died, though apparently he was still a young man. He was directed to visit his widow, a Countessa Bianca le Masters. He gave her the samples, and she ordered him to continue his research, providing unlimited funds. Dr. Michelle tried to get this Countessa Bianca to alter the research direction onto finding cures for the many terrorist attack victims, but she would have none of that."

"Then literally within a day of their return to Bordeaux, Dr. Michelle and her fiancé Ernst Fry were subjected to a genetic bio agent attack. This time, this new bio agent was used, the very one that Dr. Marcel had restored from those ancient samples. However, they awoke from their comas here on Corporate Prime, far from their rim world and in the care of Countessa Bianca, who told them that Dr. Michelle had brought a sample to her home from the genetics lab and that the sample had broken open, exposing both of them. Dr. Michelle swears she never violated protocols and brought home samples. We've subjected her to Truth Drug A and verified her story. Someone deliberately did this to her and her fiancé, turning them into hermaphrodites!"

Alfonso watched the men's reactions but saw expressionless faces. Conclusion: they must already know about this and the hermaphrodites. He went on, "So my first question is do you know of this Count Edgar le Masters and perhaps have a photograph of what he looked like? I suspect we will be able to identify him as the Master, the one who caused all of this disaster."

Arnaud didn't answer the question. "And what is the second question about? This catastrophe you mentioned in your email?"

"All right. This Countessa Bianca called Dr. Michelle and Ernst perfect humans. Apparently, she wants to convert all humans into this new form, the armless hermaphrodites, who look much as I do, except they have both male and female reproductive organs. According to Dr. Michelle, the Countessa has also infected her own three UFB daughters and four others, who have become their mates, if that is the correct term, making eight of these new hermaphrodites here on Corporate Prime."

Arnaud simply said, "I see."

"Okay then. How are you on ancient history?" Alfonso asked, but didn't wait to get their answer. "In the Dark Ages, some five hundred years ago, this same genetic bio agent was used in massive terrorist attacks and later to cause planetary genocide. The near collapse of the entire galactic civilization was prevented by the intervention of some robots and a strange race of telepaths. Now my point is simply this."

"We are in a unique position here. We have this one and only chance to *prevent* a new Dark Age from falling upon us. You see, if this new genetic bio agent gets used broadly, there will be nothing that can prevent humanity from being wiped out. A colleague of mine explains it this way. The hermaphrodites breed more than twice as fast as normal humans do. Since each partner can bear children and do so, their birth rates are double ours. Plus, they apparently have enormous sex drives, which means that they tend to have far more babies than normal women do."

"It goes this way, gentlemen. Right now, there are ten known hermaphrodites. We can expect that they will likely bear five children each, so the next generation will consist of fifty of their kind. The following generation will see the fifty become two hundred fifty. The next generation will bring forth over a thousand of them. A hundred years from now, they will total at least thirty thousand. Worse, each of these will need a normal person to be their personal assistant, since frankly fellows, I can do very little for myself."

"Now suppose that this new genetic bio agent gets used like the Master used its earlier versions. Suppose that a hundred thousand here on Corporate Prime is infected. A century from now, the hermaphrodite population will be closer to three hundred million, each of which will have to have their own personal assistant in order to survive. On the other hand, suppose someone works out a way to infect an entire world at one time. Now we are talking genocide again."

"This is not farfetched, gentlemen. Look, the Master infected at least forty thousand before we took him out. There are many more that were infected, but they were taken to another world where we cannot obtain any accurate count. So perhaps he infected nearly a hundred thousand. If this falls into the wrong hands, think of what could happen to many of our key worlds. Pick any dozen of them, infect a hundred thousand with this new bio agent, wait a century, and that world's economy will be destroyed with vast manpower and resources devoted solely to keeping these hermaphrodites alive. A century after that, and there won't be anyone left to be personal assistants. I assure you, gentlemen, I can't survive without an awful lot of help with the things I can no longer do for myself. In short, gentlemen, my second question is simply, will the OEN help prevent the coming of a new Dark Age? We must destroy all this new genetic bio agent, destroy all such research labs that are making it. If we don't take action immediately, eventually another Master will rise and put this horrific bio agent to work to the doom of us all."

Alfonso sat back. He'd outlined it as clearly as he could. Now, it was in the laps of these young men. He rather wished he were dealing with older men. These three couldn't be even twenty years old. He waited patiently for their response.

"Quite interesting, Mr. Vega, quite. Beneoit, bring up a photo of the late Count Edgar le Masters, will you?" Arnaud asked calmly.

Beneoit had a wry grin on his face, as he got out a

laptop and brought up a photo of the man. Then, he turned the computer around so that Alfonso and Alis could see the man's face. "Well, I'll be, Alis. Put that crazy top hat on him, and you have the man we knew as the Master. How very interesting," Alfonso declared. "So this man caused all of this trouble."

Arnaud straightened himself up, and then said, "Okay. That's that. Now then, if you are willing to share some new technology with us, we are prepared more fully to explain the situation with you and perhaps work out some kind of strategy, Mr. Vega."

"What technology?" Alfonso asked, growing curious about these men. What did they want and why?

Grinning, Arnaud answered, "You see, we conducted a full investigation into this man's death. He was the Countessa's husband. We know somehow one of your people was able to shoot a hole through his heart while his PDS was working perfectly. Of course, that is an impossibility, until now. We happen to know your people have invented a way to shoot through an operating PDS. We would like you to share that technology with the OEN, with us. If you will do so as a sign of good faith, then we will openly discuss many more things with you, things which directly impact your situation."

Alfonso chuckled. "Do you realize this new MK50 was developed by a UFBMD man? Yes, GD Corporation is now manufacturing these new guns on Scorpi-C and other Abelard Sector worlds for our defense. I'm willing to give you, say, perhaps a dozen of these new MK50 guns. Will that be satisfactory?"

"Perfectly. Excellent. Now we are getting somewhere, Mr. Vega. As soon as we receive confirmation of that shipment, we'll continue our discussion," Arnaud stated dryly, not trusting the man-woman sitting across from him.

"Alis, bring up our order system and get a dozen shipped here immediately, please," Alfonso replied, unwilling to delay any longer than necessary. "Plus, contact our ship and have Armando give one of the MK50's we brought along to one of these OEN men."

"On it boss," she replied. "Will one of you go out and pick up the gun now? Ah, here, you can see the order confirmation. Shipping address please?"

Fifteen minutes later, the three teens drooled over the new MK50. Arnaud seemed satisfied with the arrangement and resumed their meeting. "Okay. A bit of history for you two. Count Edgar le Masters used to be the Supreme Commander of the entire OEN." He paused for dramatic effect. Alfonso gasped slightly. A million more questions flooded into his consciousness.

"Yes, he was, but something like nineteen years ago, he put his wife, Countessa Bianca, in charge of the OEN while he was away. I'm sorry, but none of us knew he was off being the Master, not until we launched an investigation into the man's death at the spaceport at the Countessa's request. As soon as we saw his body in the morgue, we made the connection between our former leader and the Master, the terrorist."

"On our behalf, during the Master's reign of terror, no one asked the OEN to do anything about it, so we stayed back on the sidelines," Arnaud continued. "However, our immediate commanders were the Countessa's daughters, the UFB women, Blanche, Celestine, and Dianne. At that time, they were our girlfriends and fiancés. They held the Commander's post."

"Something else you don't know. That whole family was strange. You see, the five had telepathy, the ability to read our minds. Worse, the Countessa and her three daughters also possessed *magical* powers. Spooky really. They could lift things and move things around. Imagine sitting here and your water glass rises up to your mouth as though unseen hands are moving it. Spooky indeed. Powerful. No one ever dared cross those four women."

Alfonso interrupted, "You speak of them having these strange powers in the past tense?"

"Yes, but that's getting ahead of the story," Arnaud replied, noticing that Mr. Vega was quick to notice subtleties. "The Countessa Bianca ordered us to fake that 'accident' that infected Dr. Michelle and Ernst. Why? Dr. Michelle was too close to unraveling the truth of the situation and wanted to redirect the scientists' research to curing the mutations, something the Countessa was violently against. You see, she is nuts. Crazy. Insane. She wants to turn the whole human race into her perfect humans, the armless UFB-like hermaphrodites."

He went on, "After she got Dr. Michelle and Ernst done, she insisted on converting herself, her daughters, and her own lover, Marion into this freakish form. Well, we had to assist her in getting that done. Hell, I can tell you that we were darn scared, because once they were mutated, our girlfriends were sex-crazed. We three just knew that the Countessa was planning to convert us into freaks like themselves and marry us to her daughters."

Beneoit broke in, "Hey, we were terrified and made secret plans to get the hell off this world! But Arnaud got a bright idea."

Arnaud continued, "Right. You see, after their conversion, the three didn't seem to be attracted to us anymore, hardly at all, but were going ape over other UFB women. So I found three orphan UFB teens about their own ages and brought them to their birthday party."

"That's when the Countessa was planning to mutate us," Edmond broke in.

"Only, the three daughters went nuts over the three orphans and wanted them. So the Countessa mutated them instead of us. We barely escaped that one!" Beneoit declared with passion.

Arnaud continued, "Not long after that, all eight of them got pregnant. It's just like you said; they are sex-crazy. Anyway, as long as those four had telepathy and their *magical* powers, we three weren't safe. So when they came into headquarters for their yearly physicals, I made sure they wanted the medical machines to deliver all known cures. You see, the doctors believed they had these magical powers because their pituitary glands were much larger than normal. The medical machines are programmed to shrink them down to size. Well, I had the doctor do just that. Presto, when they awoke, their telepathy and magical powers were gone, a thing of the past."

Edmond laughed. "You should have seen their reactions! Wild! Now they get to experience what life is like for all the UFB women. Serves that insane woman and her daughters right!"

Arnaud continued, "So yes, we are quite freaked out about this new genetic bio agent. We confiscated all that the Countessa had. Look, you are probably quite right about them propagating like rabbits. Blanche is nineteen. I bet anything that she'll have a baby a year! Hell, she might even have twenty before she gets too old to have them. I think your estimates of the population explosion are way low, way, way low, considering how nutty they are on having sex all the time."

"Well done," Alfonso decided to break in at this point, showing them that he backed what they'd done. "So as far as you know, this new strain of bio agent is only available at that secret research lab and what you've confiscated?"

"Yep," Arnaud replied. "But you are dead on. Eventually, it's going to fall into other hands, and we will have a real mess on our hands. Of course, the version that makes you UFB women and UFBMD men is readily available at most all corporation headquarters. Can't do anything about that. Still, let me assure you, you don't want to become one of the Countessa's perfect humans! God no!"

"All such samples and research should be destroyed as soon as possible," Alfonso suggested.

Arnaud looked at his two friends and agreed, "Precisely. Leave that to us and the OEN. We will see the eight freaks here are terminated. Can you see that the two on Scorpi-C are also taken care of? Then, they can't spread their abysmal genes any further. We'll stamp this nightmare out of existence in short order, Mr. Vega."

Alfonso had no intention of terminating Dr. Michelle or Ernst, but agreed to handle them. "Before you terminate the Countessa, we've heard she has a company somewhere that is manufacturing or inventing useful machines we UFB women and men can somehow use to do more things for ourselves. I have forty thousand of them on Scorpi-C who could make darn good use of these."

Arnaud didn't like to be interrupted. "Look, I'll take you to the home that the Countessa fixed up for Michelle and

Ernst. You can see them for yourselves. After we handle the freaks, I'll see the company is transferred to GD ownership on Scorpi-C. Then, you can deal with them directly. How's that?"

"Excellent, Supreme Commander, excellent," Alfonso replied, satisfied that he'd get a chance to see these items at least. Then, he decided to change the subject. "Say, might I ask you what the OEN's opinion of the chaos that is occurring around the galaxy? What is your opinion of what I have done in the Abelard Sector, that is, undoing the centuries of corporate control over people's lives and such?"

Arnaud scratched his head, buying time. *Damned if I know or care.* "Well, your methods are working fine in your sector. Can't fault that. Of course, the other sectors are in chaos right now. CEO fighting CEO. I assure you the OEN will stay out of that entire mess. None of our business. Intelligence gathering is our forte. So, have we an alliance between us?"

"I'd shake your hand on that, Supreme Commander, but I seem to have left them back home," Alfonso replied with a teasing smile. All three teens roared.

"Good one, Mr. Vega, good one," Arnaud declared when he stopped laughing. "Okay, then feel free to email us whenever you have need. We'll do the same. Edmond, why don't you take Mr. Vega over to Michelle's old place and show him around. I have a few plans to make quickly."

"Sure thing, but I want a piece of the action too, you know. Don't hog it all, Arnaud," Edmond replied, grinning. Alfonso couldn't tell if his grin was just a continuation from his jest or whether there was something else going on between these teens.

"Say, by any chance do either of you know where Count Edgar and Countessa Bianca came from? Their home world? Do they have relatives?" asked Alfonso, taking the next step in his investigation, satisfied of the results thus far.

Arnaud's grin disappeared. "Er. No, they just appeared one day, from all accounts. GE Corporation here on Corporate Prime appointed him to head up the OEN, but that was before we were born. I—I looked into that a while back. Scary. That whole family is darn spooky, reading minds, moving things by magic. Not good for anyone's security."

"No, that's an understatement, Arnaud. Thanks. I had to ask. I sure as hell don't want another Master to appear suddenly. One was more than enough," Alfonso replied.

"No kidding, more than enough," Edmond added. "Come on; let's get you to the special home where they had Michelle and Ernst staying."

Hours later, the pair headed back to the spaceport and their shuttle. There were quite a few amazing devices in the home, along with special setups that Alfonso thought could be made to work for his family and vowed to look into this new company as soon as he returned. Once onboard and airborne, Alfonso spent an hour outlining all he'd learned. So many details now made perfect sense to everyone.

Some eight hours later, he received an email from Arnaud outlining the steps he'd taken. The Countessa and her group had met with an unfortunate accident. Apparently, their mansion had caught fire, and the eight were trapped inside and perished. Further, Arnaud had discovered the secret self-destruct codes the Countessa had. The secret research facility was no longer in existence. "All recent samples have been destroyed here. Good luck on your end," Arnaud ended with.

Alfonso sighed as he read it. Murder. Those teens had simply murdered the eight hermaphrodites and blown up the research labs, probably murdering many others as well. Alis said softly, "Just like the OEN." He nodded. "I do hope you aren't going to kill Michelle and Ernst."

"No. I am hoping she will find a cure, but I can't let them have more of those hermaphrodite children either," he replied, knowing he was in a tough situation.

Chapter 27—The Decision

After seeing Alfonso and the others safely home and assisting with the spread of the news he brought back, Alis once more took off in her special GD deep space shuttle. This time, she headed far across the galaxy, leaving Galactic Federation space and crossing into the other spiral arm, belonging to the ancient Galactic Union, before reaching a distant rim sector there. She landed on a small uninhabited moon of 9-Lethos-E, a gas giant planet. The air was breathable but cold, neither of which bothered her as she stepped out onto the barren, crater-filled landscape devoid of all life forms. Shortly, another deep space transport landed and her true boss stepped out, stretching her legs.

"Good to see you again, Minta. I wish it was under better circumstances though," Alis greeted the shapely woman with short blonde hair, who wore a brown leather suit and work boots.

"Good to see you as well, Alis. Indeed, your reports have been most disconcerting. Of course, we all expected something like this nearly five hundred years ago when those worlds broke away from the Galactic Union and formed up their own Galactic Federation. Again, I must assume the responsibility for this new genetic bio agent mess. I thought for sure that all of those old bio agent cylinders had been rounded up and destroyed way back then, but obviously, we missed some," Minta said softly.

"History repeats itself, at least among humans," Alis replied.

"Indeed. Humans are so predictable. Now then, this bio agent, the strain that produces hermaphrodites—do you believe that it has been destroyed?" Minta inquired.

"Yes, the three Commanders of the OEN were terrified of the stuff and its effects on humans. I'm certain they destroyed the existing samples along with all traces of the research facility," she replied.

"Yes, I sent Ames there to verify the lab's destruction. It

was totally destroyed along with the eleven research geneticists and fifty others as well," Minta stated without emotion.

"Then with the deaths of the eight hermaphrodites on Corporate Prime," Alis continued, "we only have two left on Scorpi-C, Dr. Michelle and her husband Ernst. Alfonso Vega does not want to murder them just yet, though he well knows the danger that they represent should they have children. He's hoping for a cure."

"Indeed, I had not pegged him for a murderer, Alis."

"No, he's quite honorable as humans go. The question before us is what do we do with the nearly forty thousand UFB women and UFBMD men on Scorpi-C? Already, many have had children, who are genetically like their parents. And then there is that other world which is out of the Galactic Federation space," Alis asked.

"Key problem, Alis. Some of those UFBMD men used to be the unethical CEOs of many key corporations. If they are fully restored, then they could well upset all the gains that Mr. Vega has achieved in Abelard Sector. It's a ninety-five percent chance they would return to their former positions, likely by forceful means if necessary," Minta noted.

"Agreed. Yet, we can't ignore this situation, Minta. Already, Anka, a UFB woman victim, has already worked out the population grown predictions of this human mutation form. Her estimates, based on four children per family, will result in millions of them on Scorpi-C within just a few generations. So it isn't a secret. They are barely able to cope with forty thousand of them now. A million will certainly create enormous problems in the near future."

"Agreed. The question is what do we do about it? The genetic mutation agent that creates UFB women is widely spread out among all the major worlds of the Galactic Federation, correct?" Minta asked, looking for confirmation of what she already knew from previous reports from this portion of the galaxy.

"Yes, that is an accurate statement of fact. Most of the major corporations on each key world have that genetic bio agent, though perhaps only in small quantities, enough to sustain their UFB woman breeding programs. However, recently, many of these worlds in mostly rim sectors have abandoned the program, sending their existing UFB women and a few UFBMD men to Scorpi-C, effectively getting rid of them. Still, there are plenty of other mid-arm and hub worlds which have not and are likely continuing with this program."

"That assessment jives with the intelligence I've had from other field agents. So do we interfere or not?" Minta asked.

"If we don't, then the future problems will haunt us, and yet I hate to interfere in their affairs," Alis answered. "My calculations agree with yours. If we restore them fully, then the former CEOs will cause enormous trouble. That is a near certainty. Still, those second generation UFB women are adapting very well."

"Yes, I reviewed your report on the numbers who are now in the Academy or highschool. It was that way many hundreds of years ago as well. Humans adapt and move on, but only in subsequent generations. Those who were genetically modified against their will either never adapted or did poorly. What impact will the new inventions from the late Countessa's company have?" Minta asked.

"Extremely crude devices, wholly unlike what we had for them on Zeta Scorpii-C, I'm afraid. Still, my predictions are that given enough time and incentives, the humans will re-invent robots to assist them, just as they once did so long ago. History repeats itself," Alis answered.

"Yes, that's factored into my calculations as well," Minta declared. "So if we do nothing, we will be facing a similar situation that we once faced many hundreds of years ago."

"It would seem that way to me, by my calculations. That's why I requested this meeting, Minta. I believe that we must do something to prevent that future path from occurring," Alis said firmly. "However, the what is problematic. Interfering with the self-determinism of humans is always fraught with peril. I point out that already, they have a genetic cure for the hair and foot mutations. Only a handful of the victims have chosen to have those cures."

"Ideas why they haven't taken advantage of the cures?"

Minta inquired.

"They are using the feeling in their hair as a substitute sensory perception, I believe from my observations. As far as their feet are concerned, I believe that many haven't gotten that done out of fear of looking different from all others of their kind. Alfonso Vega is a good example of just that," Alis answered. "If they had arms, I believe that many would then get the rest of the cures, though that still leaves the UFBMD men, who would still look like UFB women. Does our database have a cure for the men?"

"No it doesn't, and I'm not about to instigate genetic research into that aspect. Too many questions would arise and that would be opening a can of worms again," Minta answered. "Now then, what about the actual results of their UFB woman breeding program? And the UFBMD male program? I've your observations and some from other agents, but what is your opinion? You have had the closest relationship with these particular humans."

"Well, for sure Vega's male children by his UFB wife turned out to be overly muscular and a tad aggressive, but nothing more. My calculations suggest they can be ignored safely, only a minor situation there. Rather what does concern me are the offspring from the UFBMD men and a normal human woman. Supposedly, these male children have abnormally high IQs. I've not met any personally, though one called Felix was temporarily the boss of Mr. Vega, but he was also killed by the Master before he could have any significant impact. So this aspect warrants further studies."

"High IQ does not mean high wisdom," Minta pointed out.

"Of course it doesn't, just superior problem solving ability. Whether that is put to use for the benefit of humans or not remains the choice of the individual," Alis said dryly.

Minta then spoke decisively, "It is my decision at this time to restore their arms. Allow them subsequently to make use of their existing foot and hair genetic cures. The how becomes our next question. I'm hesitant to just give these geneticists the known cure."

"Accepted. I know that some researchers are following a

different path, one of using 3-d printing in an effort to grow replacement arms," Alis pointed out, "but that as a successful cure is decades away and wouldn't impact their offspring. A genetic cure is needed. Do we simply spread it across the whole world at one time? I'm afraid that this is beyond my current programming skill set."

"We have that option. However, three things argue against that rapid cure. First, the spreading of the bio agent cure over the world would certainly trigger their many bio agent attack sensors. Second, we don't know what effects there might be on normal humans. Third, it again overrides the victims' self-determinism. No, we need to go victim by victim, getting their choice to have it done or not. We can hope that most all these victims will desire to have it done and not remain mostly dependent people. Which then raises the question of just how do we get this cure to the geneticists?"

Minta continued, "While we could just send along the cure with you, Alis, that would then cause too many questions to be raised, since at this point in time, no humans in the galaxy know of the cure. It remains in our hands only, just as it once was. If we just give a sample to them, then they will be able to reverse engineer it and make all sorts of other connections, which might be undesirable. If we show up with a cure and not share it with the powers that be, simply injecting it into each victim according to their wishes, then obviously the leaders are going to launch a full-scale investigation, trying to find the actual source of the cure, which we cannot allow either."

"The solution might be to tweak some geneticist's mind so that they come up with the formula on their own, assuming there is enough material supplies available for the rapid handling of all the victims," Minta concluded.

"Doesn't that open the very same door to discovery of other genetic modifications?" asked Alis.

"Yes, it does. Yet, if serendipity occurs and if we can control who makes the discovery, perhaps we can contain it sufficiently," Minta replied. "My calculations suggest this is our safest course of action. What is the ethical situation with Dr. Gisa and Dr. Michelle?"

"Both are to be trusted, particularly Dr. Gisa," Alis answered. "But won't they need to test the formula on a victim? Human experimentation is still highly illegal and unethical on most worlds."

"Quite true. That is the biggest barrier to this solution. So we need to arrange for an accident to occur. A victim needs to be exposed to the curing bio agent by accident so that this Dr. Gisa will have the proof that it works, which she and everyone else needs," Minta explained.

***

Four days later, Dr. Gisa and Dr. Michelle arrived for work at the GD Corporation's genetic research labs on the fifty-first floor of the GD building. "Well, let's see what the culture has done since last night," Dr. Michelle suggested, knowing that Dr. Gisa would have to do the work. All she could do was observe, think, and make suggestions. While she hated being so incredibly limited, already she had made a number of key suggestions. *Perhaps, we are on to something this time.*

"Wait! Look here a second. Bringing it up on Scope One," Dr. Gisa exclaimed, suddenly quite excited.

"What?" asked Dr. Michelle, her curiosity instantly roused. Seldom had Dr. Gisa sounded this animated.

"Look. This isn't what we setup last night! It's entirely different," Dr. Gisa declared.

Peering at the monitor that projected the greatly enlarged image from the microscope, Dr. Michelle agreed. "This isn't the test that we setup. At least, I don't think so. It's produced a very different result in the CATG sequences there and there. What's going on? That looks an awful lot like the before mutation sequences."

"You don't suppose this new sequence—no it can't be," Dr Gisa began but stopped short. She didn't want to give Dr. Michelle false hope. Still, this new sequence looked promising, but would it really work and regrow arms? "We need to study this miraculous find thoroughly."

"But it could be the answer, Dr. Gisa, it really could be," Dr. Michelle exclaimed, grasping the significance of the results. Arms. This sequence dictated arm growth in humans!

Several hours later, the two geneticists could scarcely

450

contain their excitement. They had stumbled upon a possible arm regrowth sequence! At last, they called Alfonso to relay their find. Naturally, he dropped everything and went down nearly fifty floors to see his two geneticists. Alis accompanied him. "Serendipity, boss, that's the only explanation we have," Dr. Gisa explained. "An accidental discovery. No other way to describe it, though I'd like to say that we painstakingly worked it all out, but we can't. It just happened by accident. Now what do we do? We need to test it and see if it works, but human experimentation is verboten."

Alfonso sighed. "True. Here we are with a potential lifesaving cure, and we have no ethical way to find out for sure. Well, let me think about how we could do that. Well done, both of you. Very well done indeed." While they chatted, Captain Juanita, Linda, and Ernst dropped by to hear the startling and promising news from the two geneticists.

"Yes, it does look like we've stumbled upon a possible cure," Dr. Michelle explained to the new arrivals. "It's not like we made a brilliant discovery or something. It was just an accidental discovery."

While they were all discussing this incredible breakthrough, one of the glass vials containing their sample agent simply shattered, releasing the bio agent into the room. At once, the bio hazard detectors triggered. Protocols activated. Doors shut automatically, sealing the group inside the lab. Calmly, Alis examined the vial. "Glass fatigue. Nothing more. Simple glass fatigue. Well, we're all exposed now."

"Well, I guess we have our test now," Dr. Gisa swallowed and put on a brave face. "Let's get ourselves arranged in here in case something happens to us all." Shortly, Diego and many others arrived just outside the sealed doors. Alfonso relayed what was happening inside and brought calm to the hundreds of extremely worried workers in his building. Soon the exhaust fans removed the contaminant bio agent, releasing it harmlessly into the air around the skyscraper. Two hours passed before the seals released, and the lab was now safe.

Diego rushed everyone to the med lab on the floor below and thus began the long wait. Dr. Gisa and Alis suffered no ill effects at all, but three hours after the exposure, Ernst, Dr. Michelle, Linda, and Captain Juanita slumped into a coma. Soon it was more than evident that their arms were regrowing, if that was the correct terminology. None of the doctors was quite sure of that detail, but Dr. Gisa kept insisting that their arms would be back when they came out of their comas. That happened on the third day and all patients were starving. Wisely, as soon as the doctors saw the appearance of new arms, they hooked up IVs and injected what they suspected would be nourishing compounds for the arm rebuilding process, including a substantial amount of calcium.

The four awoke from their comas to find they now had quite serviceable arms! Word of this miracle cure spread throughout Scorpi-C. Poor Diego was bombarded with calls requesting more information on the cure and when it would be delivered to others. He had no choice but to rely upon Dr. Gisa's best estimates.

***

Six months later, the two geneticists finished curing the last of the many UFB women and UFBMD men on Scorpi-C. Not one opted out. All greatly desired to have arms, even those who had never had them. Curiously enough, about half of them chose to not have the hair genetic cure, but all also had their feet repaired.

"It's like I have been reborn, Alfonso," Linda declared when she awoke to the incredible surprise. "This is the best miracle ever! Thank you doctors!"

Dr. Michelle and Ernst flushed, but didn't say what they appreciated even more! No longer were they hermaphrodites! Still, the UFBMD men looked like women, that aspect hadn't been altered, but having their arms back and normal feet made a tremendous difference in their lives.

After the last had been handled, Alis sent off another electronic data burst informing Minta of project completion. The doom of the genetic mutations had been eliminated on Scorpi-C. A return burst notified her that others had secretly spread the cure across Beltazar, ensuring that the many thousands of younger ones there were cured as well.

Alis smiled. The reappearance of the ancient bio agents

had been eliminated for the most part. While there were likely a few UFB women and the even rarer UFBMD men around on other worlds and a part of their breeding programs, their numbers were minuscule compared to those on Scorpi-C and Beltazar. At last, the lingering aftereffects of the Master's reign of terror were over. Alis finally relaxed and began to enjoy the cheerful company of her friends.

The End.

A Favor to Other Readers

How about helping other readers? Many readers rely on reviews to make the decision whether to buy a book. You can help them make their decision by leaving your opinions and viewpoint in a short review of the positive things of this book. Writing the review and expressing your opinion only takes a few minutes, and other readers will appreciate your efforts.

Click this link: Slow Comes the Dark Series Volume 1 Creeping Darkness
                http://www.amazon.com/dp/B00NLN2HZE
scroll down to Customer Reviews; click on Write a Review, and enter your review. Thank you.

Author Information

Visit My Amazon.com Author Page
Vic Broquard Author Page
http://amazon.com/author/vic-broquard

Follow My Blog:
http://www.broquard-ebooks.com/blog/
http://www.broquard-ebooks.com/blog/

Follow Me on Social Media

Facebook
http://www.facebook.com/vic.broquard/

Google+
http://plus.google.com/102242823668960002176/

LinkedIn
http://www.linkedin.com/profile/view?id=297732151

YouTube
http://www.youtube.com/channel/UCQWcs-WAX2YqViIiafUqJuw

Other Books by Vic Broquard

Without Warning (fantasy)

The Trident Series: (fantasy)
Volume 1 The Trident and the Book
Volume 2 The Trident and the Scepter
Volume 3 The Trident and the Resurrection

The Adventures of Elizabeth Stanton Series: (science fiction)
Volume 1 The Evolution of the Path
Volume 2 The Great Messiah
Volume 3 Of Kings and Queens and Troubadours
Volume 4 Chaos in the Aftermath
Volume 5 Power Plays
Volume 6 Age of Exploration
Volume 7 Abducted
Volume 8 The Emperor and Empress
Volume 9 A Job Worth Doing
Volume 10 Degradation
Volume 11 The Second Crusade
Volume 12 When Worlds Collide
Volume 13 Dark Ages

The Lindsey Barron Series: (fantasy)
Volume 1 The Rod of the Apocalypse
Volume 2 The Board of Governors
Volume 3 The Crown of Moses
Volume 4 Dominus for President
Volume 5 The National Health Care Program
Volume 6 States Justice
Volume 7 Cross and Double-cross

Zoran Chronicles Series: (fantasy)
Volume 1 A Dragon in Our Town
Volume 2 Dragons, Power, Courts, and War

Planet of the Orange-red Sun Series: (science fiction)
Volume 1 When Kingdoms Fall

Slow Comes the Dark Volume 1 Creeping Darkness

The Return of the Wizards: Twelve Companions – The Making of Wizards (fantasy)

Slow Comes the Dark Series: (science fiction)

www.ingramcontent.com/pod-product-compliance
Lightning Source LLC
Chambersburg PA
CBHW050914030726
47503CB00007BB/2285